Like she'd said, th[...] [...] [...]li-
cated. But she supp[...] [...]ed
him. He helped her. They were just partners in finding a
solution and nothing more. And one day soon they'd go
their separate ways, and she'd forget how it felt to kiss him
or how good his body had felt against hers when they'd
made love. It was something they hadn't discussed
much—kind of like an elephant in the room.

It made it a little easier to pretend it had never happened.

"Go to sleep, Eden," Darrak said, his voice as warm as
his presence. "Everything will be better tomorrow."

"Promises, promises." She closed her eyes. It took a
while, but just after midnight she finally drifted off.

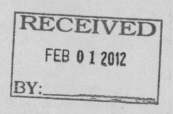

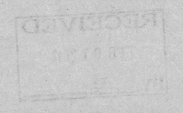

SOMETHING WICKED

 Michelle Rowen

B

BERKLEY SENSATION, NEW YORK

THE BERKLEY PUBLISHING GROUP
Published by the Penguin Group
Penguin Group (USA) Inc.
375 Hudson Street, New York, New York 10014, USA
Penguin Group (Canada), 90 Eglinton Avenue East, Suite 700, Toronto, Ontario M4P 2Y3, Canada
(a division of Pearson Penguin Canada Inc.)
Penguin Books Ltd., 80 Strand, London WC2R 0RL, England
Penguin Group Ireland, 25 St. Stephen's Green, Dublin 2, Ireland (a division of Penguin Books Ltd.)
Penguin Group (Australia), 250 Camberwell Road, Camberwell, Victoria 3124, Australia
(a division of Pearson Australia Group Pty. Ltd.)
Penguin Books India Pvt. Ltd., 11 Community Centre, Panchsheel Park, New Delhi—110 017, India
Penguin Group (NZ), 67 Apollo Drive, Rosedale, North Shore 0632, New Zealand
(a division of Pearson New Zealand Ltd.)
Penguin Books (South Africa) (Pty.) Ltd., 24 Sturdee Avenue, Rosebank, Johannesburg 2196,
South Africa

Penguin Books Ltd., Registered Offices: 80 Strand, London WC2R 0RL, England

This is a work of fiction. Names, characters, places, and incidents either are the product of the author's imagination or are used fictitiously, and any resemblance to actual persons, living or dead, business establishments, events, or locales is entirely coincidental. The publisher does not have any control over and does not assume any responsibility for author or third-party websites or their content.

SOMETHING WICKED

A Berkley Sensation Book / published by arrangement with the author

PRINTING HISTORY
Berkley Sensation mass-market edition / October 2010

Copyright © 2010 by Michelle Rouillard.
Excerpt from *That Old Black Magic* by Michelle Rowen copyright © by Michelle Rouillard.
Cover art by Craig White.
Cover design by Lesley Worrell.
Interior text design by Laura K. Corless.

ISBN: 978-0-425-23746-5

BERKLEY® SENSATION
Berkley Sensation Books are published by The Berkley Publishing Group,
a division of Penguin Group (USA) Inc.,
375 Hudson Street, New York, New York 10014.
BERKLEY® SENSATION and the "B" design are trademarks of Penguin Group (USA) Inc.

PRINTED IN THE UNITED STATES OF AMERICA

10 9 8 7 6 5 4 3 2 1

Acknowledgments

Thank you so much to . . .

Cindy Hwang, Leis Pederson, and the entire team at Berkley Sensation.

My wonderful agent, Jim McCarthy.

My friends, online and off, who support me and give me plenty of encouragement and pep talks when the demons who aren't as good-looking as Darrak show up at my doorstep uninvited. They're usually much smaller and uglier, and I call them the weasels of doubt.

My fabulous readers who have read my books, enjoyed them, and told me so, which never fails to make my day. I sincerely hope you enjoy this one as well.

My high school typing class and Mavis Beacon computer programs for teaching me to type properly back in the day. My handwriting has suffered greatly over the years, but I can do sixty words a minute on my MacBook, easy as pie.

Being a writer is a dream come true, and I'm thankful for the chance to continue to explore the strange, chaotic expanses of my imagination, where a year later they come out as pretty little rectangles with colorful covers and neat typography. It's truly amazing to get to do this for a living, and I'm still not convinced I'm not just imagining this reality. It's possible. I've seen *The Matrix* ten times.

⇥ ONE ⇤

"Would you look at this place? Equal parts lust and desperation. It's fantastic."

Eden grimaced. She'd been trying to pay as little attention to Darrak as possible, but it wasn't easy. The demon was very hard to ignore.

"It's a singles' club," she replied. "What did you expect?"

"This, of course. But it's even better than I thought it would be."

"You have a strange sense of what *better* is."

A tall man holding a bottle of Corona tapped Eden on her shoulder. When she turned to look at him, he leered approvingly at her. "Who are you talking to, sexy lady?"

She cleared her throat. "Nobody. Just talking to myself. I do that frequently now that I've stopped taking my medication."

"Uh . . . *okay*." He slowly backed away from her and went to hit on someone else. Someone *sane*.

Darrak snorted. "Busted."

She felt her face redden. She had to remember that no one but her could see or hear Darrak at the moment. He was her demon. Her *inner* demon. After all, Eden Riley was the current cover girl for demonic possession.

This time she spoke under her breath so no one would hear. "I thought you said you were going to keep quiet once we got in here?"

"I lied. Besides, you need me to coach you through this, don't you? I thought you said you're a bit out of your element."

He was right about that.

"Okay, so coach me. Now what should I do?"

"Walk over to the bar, order a drink, and scan the room. I know he's around here somewhere. I just have to spot him."

"You still haven't told me how you found this guy. How were you able to contact anyone in your, uh, current condition?"

"I have my ways."

Well, that was cryptic. But instead of grilling him about it, Eden walked across the floor of the dark nightclub, Luxuria. It was very upscale, with gleaming black floors and an indigo interior. A cascade of pretty sparkling light moved slowly across the hundreds of faces and bodies in attendance. But the lust and desperation Darrak mentioned seemed to permeate the entire building, giving it a distinctly unpleasant ambiance Eden was able to pick up with her subtle sixth sense.

As she walked, she tried not to twist her ankle in the four-inch stiletto heels Darrak strongly suggested she wear tonight. Her legs felt cold in her short skirt. She normally didn't like to show off so much skin, especially this late in October. However, a quick scan of the club made her feel that she was practically in casual wear compared to the other women on the prowl. They, however, didn't share her inner accessory.

No one could see the demon, but that didn't mean he

wasn't very much there, currently sharing her scantily clad body.

Why wasn't Eden freaking out over the fact that she was possessed by a demon? She had. Many times. She'd since realized that no matter how much freaking out she did, it didn't do much to change the situation.

Three hundred years ago, Darrak had barely survived a witch's death curse. It had destroyed his physical form, leaving only his essence behind. He'd existed for three centuries unseen and mostly unheard by the hosts he'd been forced to possess.

That is, until he'd possessed Eden.

For some reason—and it was probably because she was a little bit psychic and had been for as long as she could remember—he was able to feed off of her energy to communicate with her at night in her head and take physical form during daylight hours.

Until they found a way to break his curse and return him to full power so he could reform a permanent body, they were stuck like this. And screaming about it wasn't going to do anything except make her throat hurt.

There was someone in this club tonight who could help them. A specialist in the affairs of Others—aka the "otherworldly"—who would know where they'd need to go for curse removal. Whether this person was human or not was something the demon hadn't yet shared with her.

Demons, witches, fairies, and werewolves, Eden thought as she scanned the crowd of seemingly normal mingling singles. *Welcome to my new life. I definitely need a drink.*

The bartender eyed her when she slid onto a tall stool. "What's your pleasure?"

"Uh . . . I'll have a white wine. Thanks."

"That's so boring," Darrak commented internally. "A white wine? Could you order a more generic drink?"

She cleared her throat and tried to keep the smile fixed on her face.

"Sure thing," the bartender said, quickly uncapping a bottle of house white and pouring her a glass.

"Let me guess. You're not a fancy cocktail kind of girl," Darrak continued, even though she wished he'd just shut up for a moment. The demon hadn't had much conversation in three centuries so now he was a regular chat factory. It was a good thing he had such a nice voice—deep, warm, and usually filled with wry amusement at the human world he witnessed through Eden's eyes.

"Not particularly," she replied, dryly, when the bartender moved farther down the bar and out of earshot. "The little paper umbrellas can be so intimidating."

"It's all fun and games till someone pokes their eye out. So you've found something you like, and you stick with it."

"Makes things very simple."

"But how will you ever know if there's a drink out there that might be the best thing you've ever tasted?"

She shrugged a shoulder. "I'm perfectly content with my white wine."

"*Content*," he repeated, and the one word sounded like a pronouncement on Eden's boring life. At least, up until she got possessed. Things now were difficult, awkward, and frequently dangerous, but they couldn't exactly be described as *boring*.

There was a wall-length mirror behind the bar that allowed her to see both herself and the club behind her. Her gaze didn't go to her long, bone-straight auburn hair, green eyes lined with smoky liner, or plunging neckline that showed off too much cleavage to be considered remotely modest, but instead to the necklace she wore. The pendant was light gray with darker veins running through it. It looked like a two-inch oval piece of polished marble. She absently ran her fingertips over its cool surface.

"Don't worry." The previous amused and mocking edge to Darrak's voice was gone and replaced by a serious tone. "It's still practically white."

She tried to smile at her reflection. "You're a very good liar, you know that?"

"I have been told that once or twice before."

The amulet showed how damaged her soul was after having recently come into some . . . *powers. Dark* powers. She was now officially a "black witch"—a woman who had black magic at her fingertips to use whenever she wanted.

Using this kind of magic destroyed a soul piece by piece, little by little, eating away at one's ability to tell good from evil. The best solution—the *only* solution—was not to use the magic at all. Eden had used it just once and her soul was damaged from it. Just a shade darker, but it would never be completely pure again.

Eden could feel it now, only a short mental reach away—a bottomless ocean of power that itched to be used. It was like doing heroin. She'd heard that you became an immediate junkie the first time you did that drug.

Ditto black magic.

She hadn't told Darrak about this constant urge she now had to dip into the dark well of power. He was adamant that she never use it again, no matter what—it was too dangerous for her. He felt a great deal of guilt about her current gray-stoned predicament, which was understandable. After all, it was his fault she was now officially a black witch.

Having sex with the demon had—*hocus-pocus*—accidentally turned her into one.

She chewed her bottom lip and tasted her red lip-gloss as the memory slid through her mind of what had happened between them.

Well . . . Darrak *did* have solid form during the day. And that form was a *mighty fine* one.

What could she say? It had happened. Once.

But it could never happen again. *Ever.* Not unless she wanted to put more of her soul at risk. And she didn't. She was very fond of her soul, even in its current slightly dingy state.

"Do you see him yet?" she asked, taking her mind off other hazardous subjects. She turned away from her reflection to look at the faces in the crowd, slowly scanning the width of the room.

"Not yet. This place is packed. I think every desperate single person in the city is here tonight."

Eden took a shaky sip of her wine. It tasted bland and, to be honest, a bit boring. Not that she'd ever admit it.

"I don't believe it," a voice said to her left. "Eden Riley. Long time no see."

She turned, and her eyes widened with surprise. "You're kidding me. Graham . . . Graham Davis?"

The attractive dark-haired man grinned at her. "You remember me."

A matching smile blossomed on her face. "High school was only, oh, a dozen years ago."

"Seems like two dozen sometimes."

Darrak sighed internally. "Eden, you need to keep your attention on the room so I can spot my contact. Priorities, remember?"

Obviously the demon didn't realize how long it had been since she's seen Graham. It felt like forever. She had no idea why they hadn't stayed in touch. After high school, Graham had gone backpacking in Europe, she'd gone off to university, and time had simply passed. Too bad, really. Graham had been one of her very best friends.

Graham's gaze moved down the front of her. "You're looking fantastic. Just as gorgeous as you were back in grade twelve."

She grinned. "Right back at you. And that's a great suit."

Graham looked down at his gray Armani. "I dress to impress."

"Eden . . ." Darrak said tightly. "I know we're in a lustful, desperate singles' club, but that's no reason to let this guy hit on you."

Darrak thought Graham was hitting on her? She tried not

to smile at the thought. As attractive as Graham Davis was, and as good friends as they'd been back when they were teenagers, she and Graham had never hooked up and never would. It could have had a little something to do with Graham being gay.

But Darrak didn't know that, which would explain the jealous edge to his words.

The thought that another man's potential interest would make Darrak jealous, despite their mutually agreed to platonic partnership was . . . interesting.

But it only made things more complicated.

"You really shouldn't be here, Eden," Graham said.

That got her full attention. "I shouldn't?"

He shook his head, taking a moment to scan their surroundings. "If you're looking to meet someone new, there are better places than this to find someone. It's dangerous here."

"Doesn't look all that dangerous to me. Besides, what are *you* doing here?" She raised an eyebrow. "Doesn't seem like your kind of singles' club."

His mouth curled up on one side. "You don't think I can meet my future bride here?"

She smiled back at him. "Somehow, I doubt it."

Graham's grin widened. "I don't know. Maybe it's fate, us seeing each other again. Maybe I should leave my old life behind, and you should marry me, and we'll have lots of gorgeous babies together."

"I hate this guy," Darrak said. "Eden, letting this blast from your past drool on you is not productive to our goal tonight. Let's carry on, shall we?"

"Sounds like a perfect life," she said to Graham. "Shall we set a date?"

Graham held the smile a moment longer before it faded at the edges. "Seriously though, I think you should take off. This place . . . I don't know what's going on, but something's very wrong here."

She frowned. "Which means what?"

"I'm doing a story on this club for the *Toronto Star*."

"You're a journalist? That's so great. It's what you wanted to be back in the day."

He nodded. "Investigative journalist. And I've been investigating this club. There have been six women who've gone missing in the area, all of whom were regulars here since Luxuria opened for business last month. I feel like there might be a predator at work, and"—he shook his head—"I just have this strange hunch that it's directly related to the club itself."

The thought made a chill run down her spine. "Are the police investigating, too?"

"The disappearances, yes. The club itself, no. The missing women are only loosely connected to this place, and they don't see the connection as keenly as I do. There's nothing yet that ties it directly to the club except for a gut feeling on my part. If I find anything to substantiate my hunch, this place would be shut down in a heartbeat."

"So you're telling me to be careful."

"That's exactly what I'm telling you." Graham touched her arm. "Consider it a request from an old friend. Stay safe. Even though it's a big, lonely city and it's nice to find someone to be with, I figure it's way better to be alone and alive than alone and dead."

A chill went down Eden's spine. "You think the women are dead?"

"That's what I'm here to figure out, and I'm not leaving until I do." He cocked an eyebrow. "And, you know, if I win a journalism award along the way, then it's all the better. It's going to be a great story."

Eden reached into her purse and pulled out a business card. "Here. Take this."

He did and looked at it. "You're a private investigator?"

"I . . . well, I own half of Triple-A Investigations. It's just a small office on the outskirts of the city. I assist someone else, mostly, but what I'm saying is if you need some help, I'd be happy to pitch in any way I can."

Graham smiled and tucked the card into the pocket of his jacket. "I'll definitely keep that in mind. It was good seeing you again, Eden."

"You, too. Good luck with the story."

"I'll take all the luck I can get." He touched her face and shook his head. "Twelve years."

"I know. And yet we still have that youthful glow."

"I turned thirty last week. The glow is starting to fade." He laughed. "Let's not make it so long next time, okay? Good friends—people you can really trust—they're hard to find."

"You have my card. We'll do coffee and catch up?"

"Sounds like a plan."

Graham leaned over and gave Eden a quick kiss. She felt Darrak's presence tense inside of her, even though the kiss was only one of friendship.

However . . . something else happened with the contact. A sensation of dread, of fear, of darkness swept over her. As soon as it was there, before she could grab hold of it and analyze what she'd felt, it was gone. That was how her psychic abilities usually were. Totally useless.

"I'll give you a call tomorrow, Eden. Promise," Graham said before moving off into the crowd, which seemed to swallow him whole in a scattering of light and mingling bodies.

"I hate that guy," Darrak said. "Loathe him. And I can't believe you let him kiss you. I almost made you slap him, but luckily for him he didn't try to slip you the tongue. It's obvious to me that he's only after one thing from you and—"

"He's gay," Eden said simply.

"Oh." There was a pause. "I totally knew that."

"No, you didn't."

"No, actually I didn't. Huh."

"What do you think about the six missing women?" Eden asked quietly as she sipped on her glass of white wine and scanned the crowd looking for Darrak's contact. She felt disturbed by what Graham had told her and from her strange psychic flash.

"All I know is it has nothing to do with us. But he's right . . . sometimes people looking for love will find more than they bargain for. Places like this leave certain people exposed, willing victims driven by lust and desperation. Which, of course, is the vibe I feel here."

"Which you approve of."

"My incubus days are long behind me, but I still find it interesting how many people are so quick to mistake lust for love in a desperate attempt not to be alone."

She didn't particularly like the reminder that Darrak had once been an incubus, a demon who fed off the sexual energy of humans. However, he'd later been promoted to "archdemon," which, actually, was much scarier. Luckily for her, he'd changed a lot since being cursed.

"I liked being alone," she said. "I was perfectly content being alone before you arrived."

"Were you?" Darrak's tone turned amused again. "Or maybe I was the answer to your silent wish to have somebody in your bleak, lonely life. You're much too attractive to be a spinster."

"I think there's a big difference between having a live-in boyfriend and being possessed by a demon who will slowly but surely drain me of all of my energy until I'm dead."

She hadn't meant for it to sound quite so blunt, but the fact was, if they didn't find a solution to their problem, Darrak's demonic presence would eventually kill her. She knew in the three-hundred-plus years he'd been cursed, he'd been responsible for the deaths of hundreds of people he'd possessed. He'd tried his best to choose hosts that deserved death—murderers and other vile humans. But, still. Knowing she was possessed with someone who was essentially a metaphysical leech—even though he was a very attractive leech during daylight hours—didn't help her rest easy at night.

"We'll find a solution," Darrak said firmly. "I swear we will."

Eden downed the rest of her wine in one gulp, then dug into her purse to pay for it. "If you say so."

"I do." There was a pause. "And speaking of our solution, I just saw him."

Darrak's voice now held a thread of anxiety. This was important, after all. If they didn't find an answer to their mutual problem . . . well, she may as well invest in a nice gravesite with a view, and he'd be forced to find his next unwilling victim.

"Where?"

"Over by the dance floor. To the right. There's a table with three blonde women, and the bald man staring at their breasts is the one we're looking for."

"Charming," she said, keeping her voice low. "He's human?"

"I think so. He's the personal assistant to the local wizard master. The wizard master's the one we really need to get to."

"Wizard master?" she repeated skeptically. "What is this, Dungeons and Dragons?"

"That's a game, right?"

"Yes."

"This isn't a game."

No, it definitely wasn't. Wizard master it was, then. "So what do I do?"

"Go over and say I sent you. He'll know who I am and what you're here for. The dress you're wearing is just for him. He's very fond of the ladies, as you can see, but he has a special place in his libido for redheads just like you. We're golden. But if that little pervert touches you, I'll probably rip his head off. Just an FYI. We'll have to see how it goes."

"Try to restrain yourself."

"This is it, Eden. We're close. I feel like this is going to be the solution to our problem."

"I sure hope you're right." Because otherwise they were out of options.

She slid off the chair and adjusted her skirt, which had crept up higher on her thighs. Then she forced herself to be brave and cross the floor, keeping the average-looking human in sight just in case he tried to magically disappear. It could happen.

Only fifteen feet away now. Twelve. Ten.

"Wait a second," Darrak said suddenly. "Eden, stop walking."

She froze in place. "What is it?"

"I'm not sure. I thought I saw someone I recognized."

"Who?"

"Look over toward the left, just a quick glance so I can check."

She did what he asked, sweeping her eyes slowly across a sea of faces. "Who is it?"

The demon swore.

Eden waited, every muscle in her body now tense.

"We need to get out of here right now," Darrak said tightly.

"But I thought you said we need to talk to the wizard master's assistant." She looked over at him laughing with the three women, oblivious to her. Only ten feet away. They were so close.

"No. This isn't the right time. Leave, Eden. Now, before I make you."

"But why are you—?"

The next moment, she found herself forcibly turned around toward the exit. If motivated enough, the demon was able to control her body—or parts of it, anyhow. Since Eden didn't enjoy losing control of her bodily functions, so to speak, she'd set up rules that prohibited him from ever doing that. At the moment, though, instead of anger she felt panic well inside her at his unexpected reaction.

"Darrak—"

"I'm serious," Darrak said. "You need to get us the hell out of here right now."

There was something in his voice that made her decide not to argue any further. Eden began walking toward the door. She exited and put one foot in front of the other on her way to her car.

"Are you going to tell me what that was about?" she asked.

"I saw someone I used to know. Someone I haven't seen for over three hundred years, since before I was cursed."

"Who was it?" Her hand shook as she tried to get her key into the lock of her rusted Toyota.

"He's an archdemon like me."

Eden inhaled sharply. "Does he know you're here?"

"I don't know. But coincidences are usually fate giving us a kick in the ass. All I know is he's dangerous. He wouldn't know what happened to me with the curse. And he wouldn't understand that I'm . . . well, I'm different than I used to be."

This was shorthand for saying Darrak used to be demonically evil and now—thanks to being infused with humanity after possessing humans for hundreds of years—he wasn't.

Which meant this other demon would be everything Darrak once was—powerful, destructive, scary, without conscience or empathy. Someone she'd want to avoid in every way possible. "What would this demon do if he found out what happened to you?"

"I'm not sure."

She shivered as she got in the car and turned the key in the ignition. "So this demon . . . he's an old enemy of yours?"

"No," Darrak said wryly. "Actually, he was my best friend."

⇒ TWO ⇐

Four hundred years ago (give or take a decade)

Being promoted was a good thing. Even when it hurt like . . . *hell.*

Darrak braced himself as the fire scorched his body, burning away his former incubus self and replacing it with his new archdemon form. On the surface, he looked the same. Inside, it was a major upgrade.

Which was good. He'd always hated being an incubus.

Well, *almost* always. The job did have its perks, after all. Draining the sexual energy of humans was all kinds of fun—depending on the human, of course. But helping to stock Lucifer's personal harem with the human souls Darrak hadn't completely consumed, well, that just felt like work.

Ever since he'd been created from hellfire five centuries ago, he'd been made to feel like a lesser demon. Made-demons rarely were treated as well as fallen angels or humans who'd sold their souls in service to the pit. Demons like Darrak were treated as if they hadn't earned the right to any privileges and should feel, quote, "honored to exist in the first place."

No damned respect.

But that was all behind him now with this promotion to archdemon. Darrak wouldn't be used anymore to do anyone's dirty work—he was nobody's slave. New strength and power coursed through his improved form. From the corners of his eyes he could see his long curved horns. His skin was covered in amber fire. His upgrade came with fire as his element to call—appropriate, being that he was created from it in the first place. He looked at his hand, at the rippling flames that filled him with warmth and power. He could destroy a lot with this new perk. The thought pleased him.

"How do you feel, Darrakayiis?" Lucifer asked. He always observed promotions like this firsthand, although from an unseen vantage point.

The use of Darrak's true name made him stand up straighter and answer truthfully even if he'd been inclined to lie. "Never better."

"You're very lucky. Many do not survive what you have just been through. Their forms are destroyed and swept into the Void."

Sure, *now* they tell him. "It shows you that I'm worthy of being an archdemon."

"That remains to be seen, incubus."

Darrak's lips thinned. He wasn't an incubus anymore, but he didn't correct the prince. Lucifer had a nasty, destructive temper on him. Not that Darrak had ever met the boss face-to-face before. He'd only heard the rumors—and there were many of them.

"You now answer only to me," Lucifer said. "You are in my trusted circle. You will defend and protect me whenever I need you, without question or comment. Do you wholly agree to this?"

There really was only one acceptable answer to that question. Anything else would be asking for that one-way trip to the Void. "Yes, my prince."

Lucifer's archdemons were essentially his personal bodyguards—the only ones, outside of his vast harem, who ever saw Lucifer in person. But, except for his duties to Lucifer, the benefits of the job were endless.

"Go now," Lucifer said. "And I will summon you when you're needed."

Darrak lowered his head in an obligatory bow before turning and leaving the antechamber. He immediately shifted to his human form and raked a hand through his dark hair before grinning at his accomplishment. His demon form was necessary to wear when in Lucifer's presence—it was a show of respect, much like wearing a uniform—but his human form had always felt more natural to him. Plus, the horns ran the risk of scraping against archways. They were very impressive, but not terribly practical sometimes.

"So?" another voice asked him as he turned the corner of the mazelike halls of Lucifer's palace.

A smile twisted on Darrak's face as he turned to see his friend Theo. "So what?"

"How did it go?" Theo had long black hair he always wore tied back by a strip of leather. He had a slight exotic slant to his brown eyes that spoke of many different nationalities, which helped him fit in just about anywhere at any time in the human world.

"Don't forget the *arch* before demon when you're discussing my future triumphs. And you will be discussing them since I'll have many."

Theo's grin widened. "Told you so."

"You did indeed."

"Ask and ye shall receive. Seek and ye shall find. Knock and it shall be opened unto you."

Darrak laughed. "Reading the Bible again?"

"I love fairy tales. They make me feel all tingly inside."

"As you can see, I survived the conversion. Which I'm told is rare. Thanks for the warning on that."

Theo crossed his thickly muscled arms. "Warnings are for cowards. So now you're finally one of us. One of the chosen few that can do whatever we want and have power left over to spare."

"All thanks to you." Darrak's gratitude surprised even him. If it wasn't for Theo, he wouldn't have gotten this rare chance to move up the food chain.

Darrak and Theo had both been incubi created from hell-fire at the dawn of their existences. Both created to serve their masters. But Theo had a real drive to become something more, never satisfied with where he was. He made Darrak see it was possible to want more, to achieve more. All one had to do was put one's mind to it. He was very inspirational—for a demon.

"Follow me," Theo said. "I need to ask you something very important, but not here."

That was interesting. Darrak followed him until they were deeper in the palace, a place where they wouldn't be disturbed or overheard.

"So now what?" Darrak grinned. "Shall we go out and celebrate? Head up to the human world? I can go there now at will, can't I? I don't have to wait to be given permission."

"You can do anything you like now. *Anything*."

Darrak's smile faded and he tensed, feeling a strange sense of foreboding. "Is there something wrong?"

"No," Theo said, although he seemed preoccupied. "Do you trust me, Darrak?"

"Yes," he responded immediately. "Out of everyone I've ever known, I trust you above them all."

"That's good."

"Why?"

"Because I want to tell you something. Something important." Theo hesitated.

"You can trust me with anything you have to say," Darrak assured him.

"Can I?" A straight black eyebrow raised.

"Of course. You're like a brother to me."

Theo snorted. "Always so emotional, Darrak. You're just like a human."

Darrak knew an insult when he heard one. "Am not."

"I'm jesting, of course. I've seen you drain their energy and take their souls. No hesitation, no second thoughts. I've seen you tear apart the ones who cross you with your bare talons. Why do you think I'd recommend you for this promotion if I felt otherwise? You have the soul of a killer, don't you?"

It was an old joke. "Yes, and it was delicious."

Theo studied him a moment longer. "I don't know when it will happen, but I need you to be prepared when it does."

"When what happens?"

A smile snaked across Theo's face. "I'm not satisfied with being an archdemon. I want more."

"More? How can you get more? Arch is as far as we can go."

"Not exactly." He lowered his voice further so Darrak had to draw closer to hear him. "There are seven lords of Hell. I've recently discovered that if they were to be . . . *destroyed* . . . one by one, their power would shift to the one who ended their existence."

Darrak hadn't expected this. "You can't destroy the lords. They're omnipotent."

Theo shrugged. "Maybe that's only what they want us to believe. I've been secretly looking into things. There is a weapon that can kill them and send them to the Void just like any other lowly demon."

"What kind of weapon?"

"I'm still working on the details. It may take time. Patience is a virtue, you know."

Darrak snorted. "So is chastity. Luckily, demons aren't required to be virtuous. I have no desire to be either patient nor chaste."

"I want you to be a part of this. When I rise to power, you have the chance to take some as well. After all, I don't know if I can handle all seven rings myself." His grin widened. "Maybe four for me and three for you. We can rule Hell together."

Darrak's head felt heavy with this influx of information. "You'll be destroyed if they ever find out about this."

Theo's eyes narrowed. "And will you tell them?"

"Of course not."

"So you'll help me?"

"To kill Lucifer and the others and take their power for ourselves the moment we're given the opportunity?" Darrak said it very slowly so there would be no misunderstandings.

"Yes. So what do you say? Are we partners? Shall we take over Hell and leave those who oppose us in our bloody wake no matter how long it takes or how difficult it might get?"

Darrak gave his friend a slow grin and felt his newfound power rising inside of him, itching to be used as soon as possible. "I'm so in."

⇒ THREE ⇐

"I need to dampen you now," Eden told Darrak when she entered her bathroom, still disturbed by what had happened at the club.

"Thanks for the warning."

"Only for five minutes. Just need to do some stuff."

Darrak sighed. "I know. Your mysterious bathroom routine. But it's not necessary to dampen me. If you knew half the things I'd seen—"

She held up a hand. "And I don't want to."

"I have seen you naked before," he reminded her. "Trust me, you have nothing to be ashamed of. Your body is gorgeous. Right down to that little freckle on your—"

"You're not helping." She glared at her reflection in the bathroom mirror.

"Sorry." But there was a twist of amusement in his voice that made her think he wasn't all that sorry.

"Five minutes," she said again, and before he could protest, she flicked the metaphorical switch in her head that

shut the demon off from seeing or hearing anything for a
while. It wasn't without effort. This ability had more to do
with her meager psychic abilities than tapping into her
black magic. She could tell because it was hard to do. Using
magic was effortless and tempting. This was difficult and
gave her a headache if she tried to hold him back for too
long.

Eden finished in the bathroom as quickly as she could
and changed for bed. She used to wear a T-shirt or sleep
entirely in the nude, but ever since she'd acquired her new
roommate, she'd bought a few sets of full-length pajamas—
the least sexy ones she could find. One set even came with
feet attached. Tonight she chose the ones with a pattern of
small pink poodles all over the thick white flannel fabric.
Could not be less sexy if she tried.

Only after she'd gotten in bed, and pulled the covers up
to her chin, did she release the dampening. She immediately felt the demon's warm presence inside of her again.

"That felt like more than five minutes," he said.

"It was ten minutes. Maybe eleven."

"If you say so."

"I do. Now I'm exhausted. It's been a long night and it
wasn't even worthwhile."

"I know. But we'll try again," he told her. "The wizard's
assistant hangs out at that club every night, I've heard."

It still confused her. "And where exactly did you hear
this from? You're with me all the time."

"Don't sound so thrilled about that."

He was inside her head at night. And by day, even though
he could take form, he couldn't stray more than a hundred
feet from her side or he would be drawn back to her like a
magnet. A magnet in great pain.

"I was in Toronto for a week before we met, you know,"
he said. "Even though I didn't have much control, I did
manage to collect some information about potential ways
to break the curse."

Following his "only possess scumbags who deserve to die" philosophy, he'd been in the body of a serial killer who'd tried to kill Eden before he was shot dead, forcing Darrak to make the jump to a new host whether he wanted to or not.

She stared up at the ceiling. "I didn't like that nightclub. Something felt off about it."

"You found your old friend."

"So did you."

"Touché. However, you didn't scurry away in the opposite direction of yours."

"You didn't scurry. You were—"

"A cowardly fool afraid to face my past?" he finished.

"I was going to say you were being protective of me."

He groaned. "If you call me your guardian angel again, we're going to have a problem."

She smiled, but covered the expression with the edge of the bedsheet. "I'd never use a term you find so morally insulting."

"Good." He was quiet for a moment. "I honestly don't know why you sound so calm about all of this."

"About what in particular?"

"The curse. Me still harassing you internally. It must be completely frustrating for you."

"Well, yes it is. But why I'm calm is very simple, really."

"So why is it?"

"Because I trust you."

Darrak didn't respond to that for a moment. "You do?"

"Yes. I know we'll figure a way to break your curse before anything really bad happens. And until then I trust you to do the right thing."

"I . . . I appreciate that, Eden. I'd never do anything to hurt you."

"I know that." Despite all that they'd been through together, it was true. She trusted the demon. He'd done everything in his power to protect her, to keep her safe, and the fact that bad things had happened since they'd met wasn't really his fault. Even the things that seemed to be *entirely* his fault.

Like she'd said, their relationship was seriously complicated. But she supposed it didn't have to be. She helped him. He helped her. They were just partners in finding a solution and nothing more. And one day soon they'd go their separate ways, and she'd forget how it felt to kiss him or how good his body had felt against hers when they'd made love. It was something they hadn't discussed much—kind of like an elephant in the room.

It made it a little easier to pretend it had never happened.

"Go to sleep, Eden," Darrak said, his voice as warm as his presence. "Everything will be better tomorrow."

"Promises, promises." She closed her eyes. It took a while, but just after midnight she finally drifted off.

Darrak didn't sleep. He zoned out sometimes to restore his energy when needed, but actually being unconscious like a human didn't happen for him. All those awake hours gave him lots of time to think.

She trusts me, he thought.

He really wished he deserved her trust. However, if Eden found out what he could do at night, she'd strongly reconsider her position on the subject.

A half hour after she'd fallen asleep, Darrak sat up and swung Eden's legs out of bed. He'd never been able to do this before with past hosts, but when Eden was unconscious, he could possess her body completely if he wanted to.

And he *did* want to. He had things to do.

He walked to the bathroom and flicked on the light. Eden's beautiful face stared back at him in the mirror, and guilt twisted in his gut.

Demons really shouldn't feel guilt. It was so undemon-like.

He dressed quickly without sneaking a look at Eden's body. Okay, fine. He wasn't made of stone. He looked. But it was quick.

Several quick looks. That was all.

He'd never been this attracted to a human female before. He'd had his share of them during his time as an incubus, but Eden was the first woman who had been more than that to him. More than a meal, a snack, a soul to take back to Hell.

He'd rationalized that what he felt for her was only gratitude. She'd had the chance to have him exorcised several times, but she hadn't—instead choosing to believe he'd changed from his pre-curse days. She'd helped him, risking her own life to save his. Everything she did, even when she grumbled about it, was to help him.

He leaned forward to stare into her beautiful green eyes and felt a tug inside him that indicated what he felt toward her was more than simple gratitude.

Damn.

He shook his head. *You are so whipped, buddy. You know that?*

Well aware.

It was almost amusing, really.

Besides, it didn't much matter how Darrak felt about her. Once he'd broken the curse and had his own body back full-time, he'd have to high tail it out of the city. Out of the country. Off the continent. Hell had agents who'd be on his ass the moment he was at full power again and registering on their demon radar. Those demon agents would likely send him on a one-way trip to the Void, deeming him useless as an archdemon now that he was dealing with this pesky humanity issue of his.

Yeah. He'd like to avoid that, pretty please. The Void was an endless nothing where demons went when they were destroyed. Death for demons with no escape clause. He'd also like to avoid being the cause of Eden's inevitable death if he didn't find a way to break his curse.

Which was exactly why he was headed out again tonight in this borrowed body.

But before he could leave the apartment, first he had to get past the guard.

Forgoing Eden's heels for a more comfortable pair of flats, he left the bedroom wearing the same outfit she'd worn earlier. The skirt was a bit on the drafty side.

A small black cat jumped down from the sofa where she'd been curled in a ball. The next moment it shifted into an attractive woman with dark skin and long black hair who was wearing a blue tank top and shorts. She also wore a skeptical expression.

"Didn't you just get home, Eden?" Leena asked. "And now you're going back out?"

"Got a date," Darrak said. It felt very strange to hear Eden's voice as he spoke.

"A date?" Leena's eyebrows went up. "With who?"

"Just someone I met earlier." Darrak shrugged and tried to look coy. The less he said the better. The shapeshifter hated his guts. He wasn't particularly fond of her in return. If he gave her any reason to believe he was borrowing Eden's body when she was unconscious, that would *so* not go over well. To say the least.

In return for free rent in the apartment, Leena had appointed herself Eden's chaperone—keeping an eye on the dangerous demon in case he was up to no good.

"Okay, Ms. Mysterious. And what about tall, dark, and demonic?"

"I dampened him." Actually Darrak had dampened Eden so she wouldn't inadvertently wake up while he was out and about. More of that inconvenient and unfamiliar guilt coursed through him at the thought. "He'd just get in the way of me having a good time, anyhow."

"You're right about that." Leena studied her housemate for a moment before a smile spread across her face. She casually leaned against the laminate counter in the kitchen-ette. "You are so devious. I love it."

"A girl's got to do what a girl's got to do."

"Okay, have fun. I think it's good that you're seeing someone else, whoever this mystery man is."

"Really?"

"Yeah." Leena moved toward the refrigerator and opened it so she could grab a can of Coke. "But you should let Dar-rak know. Maybe it'll help extinguish that torch he carries for you when he sees once and for all you two can't be to-gether and you've fully accepted that."

Darrak struggled to keep his expression neutral. "He doesn't carry a torch for me."

"Come on. If you really think that, you're blind. He's in love with you and you know it."

"It's not like that. Trust me."

Leena held up her hand. "Fine. Stay blind. But that's why I'm here. Just in case you two want to go at it again, I'm here to make sure you don't risk your soul for that six-foot piece of chiseled brimstone. I don't care how good he is in the sack. Stick with humans. They're way less trouble."

"I'll keep that in mind." His jaw clenched. "I'll be back later."

Leena opened the can and took a sip. "I'll be here."

Oh, I know that, Darrak thought darkly, now in a foul mood. But the smile remained plastered on his borrowed face until he stepped outside the apartment and closed the door behind him.

In love with Eden. That particular emotion would be completely negligent and stupid of him. Not to mention entirely hopeless.

Stupid shapeshifters. Always so damn insightful, weren't they?

* * *

Ben Hanson watched Eden leave her apartment and glanced at the clock on his dashboard. It was after twelve thirty.

Instead of getting in her Toyota as she'd done earlier, she hailed a cab. He followed in his car at a discreet distance.

It had been a week and a half since he'd learned the truth—seen it with his own two eyes. After a lifetime of trying to do the right thing, trying to make the world a better place, a mind-set that guided him into a career as a cop, he'd seen that true evil really did exist in the world—and it was worse than any arsonist, murderer, or con man he'd ever faced before.

Demons existed. And one of them currently possessed Eden.

When he'd first met her on a case—Eden occasionally consulted for the police using her psychic abilities—he'd thought they had a connection. Possibly a romantic one. Even after his shaky history in that department—a murdered fiancée didn't exactly make him a catch without major emotional baggage—he'd thought it might be worth it.

Hadn't exactly worked out as smoothly as he'd hoped. Eden had chosen to protect the demon instead of allowing Ben to help her. It was clear to him she was in danger—that her *soul* was in danger.

His arm itched. The brand on his left forearm was of a fleur-de-lis enclosed in a circle. It had been given to him by the Malleus and was still healing. The Malleus was a centuries-old secret organization that fought against the darkness only a small percentage of humans were aware of. They'd seen his potential, so they'd inducted him into their numbers. And the ritual, culminating with the brand, had given Ben certain abilities—to see Others clearly and separate from humans, the extra strength required to fight against them, and the knowledge he needed to defeat them.

And to think, two weeks ago he'd scoffed at horoscopes as being ridiculous mumbo jumbo.

Virgos were naturally skeptical.

He'd done a little research on lots of things in the past week and a half. And most of it *still* sounded like bullshit to him.

At the moment his assignment for the Malleus was to keep an eye on Eden and report back any unusual activity. He'd do that. And when the moment presented itself to save Eden from the demon who'd taken over her body and her life, he'd do that as well. Without hesitation. Without fear.

Ben hadn't been able to save his fiancée, but he'd damn well save Eden. Even if she didn't want to be saved.

⇒ FOUR ⇐

If this doesn't go well, Darrak directed the thought toward the currently dormant Eden, *then I'm very, very sorry.*

Best to stay positive, though.

This might not suck.

Darrak slowly approached Theo, who sat on the other side of Luxuria, and didn't take his attention away from his target for a moment.

It had been a knee-jerk reaction to flee earlier. Not brave or proactive in any way. But he was back. He had to deal with this now before things got out of control.

Well, *more* out of control.

The other demon watched the last steps of Darrak's apprehensive approach before his dark-eyed gaze moved up and down Eden's body. Darrak kept a reserve of power in case of emergencies. He'd recently used up the last dregs of his healing power, but he still had some destructive power hidden away if Theo tried anything.

Whether or not it would work while he possessed Eden

was something he probably should have considered earlier. Hindsight was always 20/20.

There was a blonde sitting on Theo's lap. His hand was on her butt, under her skirt, and her enthusiastic tongue was exploring the demon's ear. Upon Darrak's approach, the woman turned and glared at him.

"Get lost," she snarled.

If Darrak hadn't been feeling quite so on edge, he might have laughed. Did it look as though he was approaching Theo to hit on him? Terrific. He never should have insisted Eden wear a skirt this short tonight. It definitely gave off the wrong impression.

"I've been lost for a long time," Darrak replied.

The blonde raked her hands through Theo's long black hair. "He's mine."

"Trust me, you're more than welcome to have him."

Theo just looked at him with mild interest, and Darrak realized his old friend had no idea who he was. Couldn't Theo sense Darrak's presence inside this body at all?

Darrak flicked a glance at several empty glasses lined up on the glass table in front of him. Theo had been drinking tonight. Heavily, by the looks of it. Alcohol and other drugs affected demons as much as they affected humans—at least when the demon was in human form.

It wasn't a huge surprise that Theo was drunk. He'd always enjoyed his vices.

"I grow weary of you," Theo finally said as he pushed the blonde away from him. "Go away."

She looked shocked. "What?"

"You heard me."

"But I thought we were going to—"

His lips curled. "Whatever you thought, you were mistaken. Now go, before I make you."

Her expression soured. "Asshole."

And with that proclamation, she took the hint and left.

A very wise choice, Darrak thought, half wishing he could do the same.

"Please, my dear, have a seat." Theo patted his thigh.

Darrak eyed him. That *so* wasn't going to happen.

"Thanks," he said, and instead tensely sat down on a chair across from the oblivious demon. Theo hadn't changed physically since Darrak had last seen him. Not one bit. But under the exotically handsome exterior, Darrak knew there was a fierce archdemon lying in wait, ready to pounce, talons out, at the first sign of trouble. He felt the power emanating from Theo, and it only reminded him how weakened his own powers had become. If he had a gas tank, it would be flashing a low fuel warning.

The knowledge that Theo was infinitely more powerful than Darrak at the moment didn't sit well with him—especially since his decision to come here had put Eden at risk as well. If he had a choice, he wouldn't be there at all. But he had no choice. Now he had to step very shallowly into these dangerous waters. He hoped very much the sharks kept their teeth to themselves, but he was prepared if they didn't.

"Why did you come here?" Darrak asked.

Then again, he'd never been one to step *too* shallowly.

Theo's dark brows rose. "Here? At this nightclub?"

"Sure. In this club. In this city. Why here and why tonight?"

"You're very direct. I like that in a woman."

So did Darrak, actually. "Are you going to answer my question or not?"

"Very well." Theo leaned back against the plush sofa. "I'm here for business reasons, but also because I'm looking for someone."

"Who?"

"An old friend who may be in trouble. I was given information he might be here tonight. I want to help him if I can."

Could it be that Theo was here looking for Darrak specifically? The thought didn't help him to relax. It could mean anything or it could be an outright lie. Theo could have been sent to destroy him.

Had he always been this paranoid, or was that thanks to Eden's influence?

Theo reached a hand over to squeeze Darrak's borrowed knee. "But don't worry. I also have plenty of time to get to know you as well, my dear. *Intimately.*"

Darrak pried Theo's hand off and deposited it back in the demon's lap. "Sorry. I'm not into guys."

Theo's eyes gleamed as a very nonhuman spark of fire lit inside their dark depths. "I do like a challenge. I think you'll find I'm very hard to resist. Your protests only make things more interesting for me."

Darrak's initial apprehension began to fade, and he restrained himself from rolling his eyes. "Theo, you've always been blinded by booze and babes, haven't you?"

The demon frowned. "How do you know my name?"

"Where did you get this information on your friend? And are you sure you're here to help him? Or were you sent here to destroy him?"

"Destroy him? But why would I—" Theo broke off, his expression turning wary. "Who are you?"

Darrak could leave now. Walk away and ensure Eden's safety. But he'd be ensuring it only for tonight. Tomorrow and beyond was another story.

"Look closer," Darrak said. "I'm sure you can figure it out despite the eight rum and Cokes you've choked back tonight. You're a smart boy."

Theo sat up straight and leaned a fraction toward Darrak, slowly taking in Eden's attractive exterior from head to toe with a blatant level of appreciation in his eyes.

"You're a very beautiful woman, despite your less than appealing footwear."

"Prevention of bunions is the new black. Keep looking. I'm sure you'll get it eventually."

Theo cocked his head as he concentrated harder. The loud music made it almost too difficult to speak, let alone to think. Men and women had to get very close to each other to be heard—part of the appeal of a club like this, Darrak figured. He took a moment to scan the room. Was Stanley, the wizard's assistant, still here? He couldn't see him anymore, at least not from this side of the crowded room.

That feeling he'd had earlier, of the lust and desperation—it felt like a solid thing now, touchable and real. All these humans after the same base need—sex. It worked to give the club an ambiance that was less than pleasant. As an ex-incubus, he was surprised he didn't appreciate it more. But he didn't. It felt . . . *threatening*.

He had no idea why.

"Well?" he prompted after another moment. Best not to get distracted from why he was really here.

Theo's gaze continued to move appreciatively over Darrak's borrowed body, lingering at Eden's chest for a moment before returning to her face.

Then, suddenly, his eyes widened with clarity. "Oh, shit." Finally. "Bingo."

The demon's mouth gaped open. "Darrak?"

"Yes."

"I've been staring at your tits for the last five minutes."

"They're not mine, of course. But they are lovely, aren't they? All natural, too." Darrak blinked. "You can stop looking at them now."

"Not sure I can." Finally Theo yanked his gaze away from Eden's body. "What is going on here?"

It was vaguely encouraging that Theo's first reaction was confusion rather than destruction.

"I was cursed," Darrak explained simply.

Theo raised an eyebrow. "Cursed."

"When I disappeared, I was summoned by a witch during the Salem trials. She trapped me and forced me to do her bidding before I managed to escape."

"You killed her, I hope?"

"Not exactly, although that was the original plan. She fought back and threw out a powerful death curse at me. If I'd been less than an archdemon, it would have decimated me completely. As it was, it turned my body to ash. Let's just say, it stung like a bitch. I've been forced to possess humans ever since."

Theo had covered his mouth with his hand, obviously shocked. But after a moment, Darrak realized he was concealing his laughter.

"Sorry," Theo managed after a moment. "It's really not funny, is it?"

"No, it's really not."

Theo snorted. "It's just . . . I mean, look at you. Just *look* at you."

Darrak stared at him. This was the fearsome demon he thought might destroy him on sight? The archdemon was practically giggling. "Maybe I'll laugh about it in the future. The distant future. At the moment, not so much."

"Oh, wow." Theo gasped for breath, then grabbed his freshest drink and took a quick swig. "I needed a good laugh. Things have been way too serious for me lately. Thanks."

"Glad my tortured existence can bring you some joy."

"Why didn't you summon me? I thought you'd gone to the Void."

"I haven't had any control over my previous hosts. Besides, even if I could, summoning an archdemon from inside a human never would have worked."

Theo eyed Eden's body again. "And you've taken this woman over completely? Burned out her soul so you can take up permanent residence?"

The thought made him inwardly cringe. There had been a few incorporeal demons who'd done just that, treating their hosts like nothing more important than taco shells. "No. She's just asleep right now."

Theo considered this. "So she knows about you?"

Darrak nodded. "We're looking for a way to break my curse and return my power. So far, no dice."

"Is your strength returning? I know witches' curses can be a bitch to deal with."

"A little, but not as much as I'd like. There's something different about Eden, though—"

"Eden?" Theo repeated. "That's her name?"

"It is." Darrak's lips curved despite himself. "Ironic, isn't it?"

"I'd say so." Theo laughed again. "At least you didn't pick a host named Heaven. That would have been hilarious."

"I'll take the potential for comedy gold into consideration next time I'm cursed."

Theo leaned forward and put his hand on Darrak's shoulder, his expression sobering. "Hell hasn't been the same without you. We used to have lots of fun painting the town red, didn't we?"

"Yes, we did," Darrak agreed. Although, their paint of choice at the time couldn't be found at Color Your World.

"I can help you find the witch, and together we'll tear the heart from her chest to break this curse. It's the least I can do."

Darrak tensed. "Sounds like a blast, but unfortunately the witch is already dead and not by my hand. The curse stands."

Theo laughed again. "So you're saying you're screwed."

"Essentially." If this was happening to someone else, he'd probably be able to see the humor a bit better. "I do have a perk with Eden, although we haven't figured out why it works. She's psychic, and I seem to be able to draw on that energy to take solid form during the day."

A waitress brought over another rum and Coke, placing it in front of Theo and indicating that it was bought by a brunette at the bar. He tipped it in the woman's direction and took a sip. Darrak glared at the woman, and she slunk back into the crowd.

How rude.

"Interesting." Theo rubbed his chin. "Never heard of that before—psychic energy assisting in possession."

"Me neither. But it's been helpful."

Theo templed his fingers and studied Darrak's current form, a frown creasing his brow. "The solution is simple. We kill this body you're stuck in to release you, temporarily trap your essence in a crystal for safe keeping, and return you to Hell where you might be able to be restored by hell-fire. It's just a theory, but it's worth a try."

The demon was dead serious as he said it.

"I'm not killing Eden," Darrak said evenly.

"But if you're looking for a simple solution—"

"I never said I was looking for a simple solution. I'm looking for a *solution*. One that won't result in her death."

"She won't survive a trip to Hell," Theo reasoned.

"Then there has to be another answer."

"Of course there is. You can come with me during the day when you have form. It won't take long."

Darrak shook his head. "I can't go far from her side. I'm bound to her."

"More reason to kill her, then."

"Not going to happen." Darrak glared at him.

Theo studied him, and Darrak grew uneasy. In the past he wouldn't have hesitated to take the simple way out. A human life for his continued existence? It was a no-brainer.

"You've changed," Theo stated. "Haven't you?"

Darrak clenched his fist, ready to will whatever power he could muster into it. "I don't know what you're talking about."

"You're all . . ." The demon's expression soured. "*Emotional*. And *human*. I can sense it now that I'm paying attention."

"Who told you I was here?" Darrak demanded, any attempt at friendliness disappearing.

Theo's eyes narrowed, and an unpleasant smile snaked across his face. "It was a rumor that I was sent to investigate. I confirmed it by talking to the local wizard master and convincing him to fill me in on the details. He knew more than I expected."

"And by convincing, you mean you tortured him."

"Of course. He's left town for a while to recover." Theo's knuckles whitened on his drink glass. "Do I see disapproval in your eyes, Darrak?"

Disapproval that Theo was acting as a demon should? That would be irrational, wouldn't it?

"I have to go." Darrak stood up and turned away, moving through the crowd. He now saw it had been a huge mistake to come back.

A hand closed over his arm. "Hey, you're back." It was the man who'd briefly hit on Eden earlier that night. His other hand closed on Eden's ass. "I knew you couldn't stay away, baby."

"Think again." It only took a modest shove to launch the loser across the room. He landed heavily on his back in the middle of the dance floor.

How do women put up with this kind of crap without resorting to violence?

Darrak turned, only to be faced with Theo now in front of him, blocking his way to the exit.

"I wouldn't try that with me," Theo said. "I'm a little harder to push around."

"Get out of my way or we may have to test that theory."

Theo's eyes went to Eden's amulet as if seeing it for the first time. "What's that?"

"What does it look like?"

"I thought you said Eden was a psychic."

"She is."

"And she's also a black witch?"

Darrak grimaced. "The original witch cast a spell on me so any psychically gifted woman I slept with would be imbued with black magic."

The grin returned to Theo's face. "I suppose I can fill in the blanks there."

Yeah, he could. Darrak had no further comment on the subject. Sex with the witch who'd cursed him had been business as usual. It was difficult for an ex-incubus to see such an act—especially one he was compelled to perform against his will—as anything more than a day at the office.

But with Eden . . . it had been different. He'd never felt true bliss before in his entire existence, but that moment came as close as he'd ever been to it.

However, that blissful moment had also ruined Eden's life forever.

Great. More guilt, right on schedule. He squeezed his eyes shut. *Bring it on.*

And if the wizard master had left town after being tortured by Theo, how was Darrak supposed to find him? They were out of answers, and he didn't know how much time they had left.

The next moment, Theo grabbed his arm and directed him over to a quieter corner of the nightclub.

"It's humanity," Theo said. "I smell it on you now. You're overflowing with it."

Darrak eyed him warily. He tried to will power into his hand to fight against his old friend, but there wasn't even a spark. "Three hundred years can change a guy. There's nothing I can do about it now."

Theo shook his head. "You're delusional."

"Excuse me?"

"You don't even realize it, do you? No wonder you're so screwed up. This, whatever it is you're feeling, is just an illusion. It's not real."

"What the hell do you mean?"

"I've seen it before. Not a lot, but it happens. You've been absorbing human emotion all these years without a body of your own as a shield. No wonder you're so concerned with this Eden babe."

Darrak's mouth felt dry. "It's not real?"

"Of course not. The moment we break this curse, you'll be back to normal. It'll be like shedding your skin and starting fresh. Quite literally, actually."

Darrak eyed him skeptically. "Yeah?"

"Yeah. And I can help you."

"Is this the killing Eden and putting me in a crystal plan again? Because real or not, I haven't changed my mind about that."

"No, something else. Something better."

"What is it?"

"It's all about knowing the right people," Theo said. "And I know the right people. As a matter of fact, I'm on an assignment at the moment for Asmodeus."

"Asmodeus?" Darrak was surprised to hear the name. The Lord of Lust was almost as powerful as Lucifer. "Since when are you working for Asmo? I thought you were with Lucifer."

"Things change. Opportunities present themselves. Anyhow, here's the deal—"

"Deal?"

Theo grinned. "Of course. It's all about deals. You know that."

True. Any demon who'd do something selflessly without any personal gain should be looked at with deep suspicion.

"What's the deal?" he asked cautiously.

"I'll help you break this curse—"

"How?"

"Not yet." Theo's smile widened. "First you need to do something for me. I want you to meet me the day after tomorrow at lunch so you can accompany me on an errand."

"What kind of errand?"

"I mentioned a weapon to you a long time ago. Do you remember?"

It only took a moment for him to locate that piece of information. Was Theo talking about the weapon he'd been searching for to destroy the lords of Hell?

Darrak nodded. "I remember."

"Good. It's nearly time, Darrak. I've been very patient. It's not my favorite virtue."

"So you found it in the human world?"

"Yes. And if you come with me to get it, I will move hell and earth to help break your curse and return you to your former glory. Do we have a deal?"

Was it true? If Darrak's curse was broken, would he shed this heavy suit of human emotion he had begun to wear on a daily basis? No more guilt, no more second-guessing himself, no more strange attraction and affection for Eden?

No more weaknesses.

It was almost a relief to think it could be possible. No, scratch that. It *was* a relief.

"Will it be dangerous?" Darrak asked. "Eden will have to come with us."

"It won't be dangerous."

Was he telling the truth? There was no way of telling. Was the risk worth the potential gain? Did he trust Theo even after all this time?

"She's never to know what you're after," Darrak said, working it out in his head. He couldn't turn down an offer like this. He had no choice but to agree to Theo's terms. "And you can't tell her we met here tonight. She wouldn't understand why I had to borrow her body. She's funny like that."

Theo held up a hand, grinning. "Say no more. Women are very particular about their bodies wandering around town without their knowledge, aren't they?"

"You have no idea."

"Then I promise not to say anything of your nocturnal omissions." Theo's grin widened. "Get it?"

"Your sense of humor has not improved in three hundred years."

"There's a restaurant next door. Meet me there at noon the day after tomorrow. Agreed?"

Darrak took a moment to turn it over in his head. Help Theo find the weapon to kill Lucifer and the other lords in return for the help he desperately needed to break his curse.

Sounded fair enough to him.

"Agreed."

Theo slapped his back. "Now, cheer up. It won't be long until you're back to normal. At which point, I strongly suggest you steer clear from witches."

Words to live by. He might even have it printed on a T-shirt.

Sunrise.

It was never a very pleasant time of the day.

Darrak gasped in pain as his essence was torn out of Eden's body. Bracing himself for what he knew was coming never helped. It was better just to give in to it as best he could.

Ten long seconds of agony later, he lay next to Eden on her bed as he instinctively changed from a formless cloud of black smoke to an exact replica of his former self. The pain dissipated. He lay still for a moment as he regained his strength.

As the pain receded, he was able to feel other things. Eden's bedsheets were soft. Her mattress was a bit lumpy, but the sensation of it—lumps and all—was sheer pleasure to him.

And, as she did every morning shortly after he became

corporeal, Eden reached for him in her sleep. She slid her hand over his bare chest, and he inhaled sharply at the feel of her warm skin against his.

"Darrak," she murmured. "Mmmm . . . yes . . ."

He had to agree with her.

Eden talked in her sleep. Frequently. It was one of the many reasons he'd decided to dampen her during his trip out to see Theo. Otherwise, he might have sounded like someone with Tourette syndrome.

She dreamed about him, and they were not always chaste and platonic dreams of friendship. Despite what had happened in the past, and the promise that it could never happen again, the thought that Eden dreamed about him pleased Darrak more than he'd like to admit, even to himself.

Her hand drifted over his now fully aroused body as he studied her beautiful face. Her lips moved as she whispered his name.

"Eden . . . this isn't real," he said quietly, remembering clearly what Theo had said, and stroked the long dark red hair off her face. His mouth was now only an inch from hers. She must have sensed this, since she closed the distance and brushed her lips against his.

Not real. None of what he felt was. It was just an illusion—one that would vanish the moment his curse was broken.

"I want you," she murmured. "Darrak . . . I want you so much . . ."

Her hand moved down his abdomen and slipped under the edge of the sheet covering him. He groaned and squeezed his eyes shut, but didn't try to stop her.

Then he had a vivid flashback to what had happened the last time she'd touched him like this—when she'd been awake and willing and about to make the decision that could ultimately cost her soul.

Guilt worked as well as an ice-cold shower.

He swiftly moved away from her and sat up on the edge

of the bed. With a focused thought he conjured clothes to cover his naked body—black T-shirt, black jeans. Same as usual. He watched Eden sleep for another five minutes, before forcing himself to stand up and leave the bedroom.

Real or not, he really wished he could dream as well.

⇶ Five ⇷

Eden's dreams lately hadn't been very helpful. Especially the ones she had about Darrak.

All of him. Every single inch.

After these dreams, she'd wake up all hot and bothered and still exhausted. It was like she'd been out all night gallivanting around town, rather than tucked safely away in bed.

At least Darrak was respecting her wishes. The first few days he'd possessed her, he'd stayed in bed after taking form, and she'd been dismayed to wake up wrapped around him like a flannel-clad anaconda.

Eden's unconscious self seemed compelled to grope the demon in her sleep. How embarrassing. During her waking hours she was totally in control of herself. To find that she couldn't do the same at night was embarrassing, to say the least.

This morning, he was gone. That was good, of course. What sane woman would want to wake up snuggled against a gorgeous, naked demon?

Not her. No way.

This morning, she awoke still feeling weary, but filled with purpose. They'd been close last night. *Really* close. She'd seen it with her own two eyes.

It had been a long, bumpy road, but the end was finally in sight.

Believing any differently wasn't going to help matters. Eden worked daily on staying positive. Not the easiest thing to do, but she really had no choice.

Things were going to work out perfectly.

Well, except for the black magic problem.

Her face tightened at the thought. *Put it out of your mind, Eden. One thing at a time.*

She could try to be positive about that, too. Honestly, she could.

Plus side: Even if she never used the magic that came with the designation of *black witch*, she was now immortal. She could live forever and not age. That was a definite perk.

Down side: she could still be killed. Witches were still human. Bullets, knives, a fall down a flight of stairs. A poorly chewed Chicken McNugget.

A slow but steady depletion of her life energy to keep Darrak in existence.

Yes, these were all dangerous and potentially deadly to her.

Oh, my God. I'm going to die.

No. Positive thoughts only, please.

She finally dragged herself out of bed and went into the bathroom, peering at her reflection in the mirror. She yawned so widely, she could see right down to her tonsils. Being possessed was a draining experience. Literally.

They had to get back to that club tonight and talk to the wizard's assistant. The rest, she assured herself, would run smoothly.

Darrak told her so. And she believed him.

She tried to unclench her jaw.

She showered and got dressed, then left the bathroom to find Darrak cooking scrambled eggs in her kitchenette. She wasn't sure why, but after dealing with him in her head every night, it was always a shock to see how attractive he was when he had a body. Tall, broad-shouldered, with dark hair he had tucked behind his ears since it was a bit too long and unruly. His eyes were pale blue and would seem cold if not for the glimmer of warm humor they almost always held.

Yes, Darrak was admittedly gorgeous and seemed utterly out of place in Eden's tiny, plain apartment. Let alone in her tiny, plain life.

"Hungry?" he asked, indicating the frying pan.

An explicit clip from her erotically charged dream flickered in her mind. "Not really."

"Breakfast is the most important meal of the day, you know."

"Followed closely by a steady stream of caffeine. Which I will grab at work."

"Fine. More for me." He scooped the contents of the frying pan onto a waiting plate. Demons didn't have to eat, but Darrak enjoyed the taste of food anyway. He could shovel it in and remain the same size, not jeopardizing those mouthwatering abs of his no matter how many calories he consumed.

Please think about something else, she instructed herself sternly.

She squeezed her amulet, focusing on the coolness of the stone. But that only helped remind her of why she had to wear it in the first place. Black magic stirred under her skin.

Ignore that, too.

Tonight. They'd go back to the club tonight. She wondered if Graham had ended up finding out any more about the missing women. She grabbed the newspaper Darrak had brought in earlier and flipped through the first few pages. Nothing stood out to her about the case. Of course, Graham was the only one who thought it was a case. To the police, it was a half-dozen adult women who'd wandered off without telling anyone.

She truly wished she could channel her psychic abilities into something more practical than an unhelpful and unreliable flash of information every now and then.

Leena sat quietly on the sofa in the living room reading a copy of *Cosmopolitan*.

"So?" Leena asked, glancing over at her.

"So what?"

"How did it go last night?" She waggled her eyebrows.

Why was she waggling her eyebrows?

Two weeks ago, Eden had allowed a small black cat to have some shelter one cold, rainy night. That black cat turned out to be a shapeshifter hiding from people she said wanted to kill her. After being possessed by Darrak, Eden gave off some otherworldly vibes that Others were able to sense. Because of this, Leena assumed Eden could protect her and wouldn't take no for an answer when she tried to get rid of her.

Whether or not Eden could protect her was one thing. However, they'd come to an agreement. In return for temporarily living there, Leena watched over Eden—she was extremely distrustful of Darrak and demons in general, and her presence helped ease Eden's mind a little bit when it came to him. Besides, there wasn't much of a chance for forbidden romance with a third party lurking about in the small apartment.

Not that she needed a chaperone for that. It wasn't as if she couldn't keep her hands off Darrak. Dreams were not indicative of reality.

"Well?" Leena prompted after a moment passed.

"Uh, it went okay last night," Eden said, still disappointed they hadn't talked to the wizard's assistant. But Darrak had been right to leave. She didn't want to meet any of his old demonic friends if she could help it. An unpleasant chill ran down her spine. "Could have been better, I suppose, but it was a start."

"And is there anything you want to tell . . . anyone?" Leena's head bobbed in Darrak's direction. He stood with his back braced against the fridge, eating his breakfast, watching their conversation carefully.

Eden glanced at the egg-loving demon. "Uh . . . like what?"

"You know," Leena said pointedly. "About where you were going late last night?"

"Late last night? What are you—?"

"Gosh, would you look at the time?" Darrak interrupted, dumping his empty plate into the sink. "Eden, we really should go. Andy said he wanted to talk to you first thing this morning, remember? He used the word *important*, so obviously it must be important."

"Right." Eden shook her head, trying to clear the early morning fog. Normally she was much more alert than this. "Hang on. I have to have my orange juice first."

Her morning rituals were important to her. She might not be in the mood for eggs, but she had to have her vitamin C. She quickly poured a glass and downed it in one gulp.

Darrak eyed her. "Beat the threat of scurvy for another day?"

"An ounce of prevention is worth a pound of cure." She glanced at the shapeshifter. "I'll talk to you later, Leena."

"Just remember that torch we talked about," Leena said meaningfully, with a sideways glare at Darrak. "It needs to be extinguished ASAP. Trust me, it'll make it easier on everyone involved."

What in the hell was she talking about? Had she been smoking some catnip this morning?

Best to play along or they'd never get out of there. "Right. Extinguish the torch. I'm totally on it."

Eden grabbed her purse and headed for the door, which Darrak now held open.

"Leena," he said dryly. "A pleasure as always."

"Bite me, demon."

"Is that an invitation?"

She morphed into her cat form, turned her back on him, and padded into Eden's bedroom.

Eden rolled her eyes. The two despised each other, but they hid it so well.

When Darrak closed the door behind them, she turned to him. "What torch was she talking about?"

"No idea. You seriously need to get rid of her." His expression soured. "I think she has fleas. And she's a trouble-maker."

"Takes one to know one."

"I don't have fleas."

A glance down the hall showed that her new neighbor was leaving his apartment at the same time. He fumbled and dropped a ring of keys on the floor as well as a bag of something. Were those marbles?

They scattered in all directions. He swore under his breath.

Adjusting her purse strap, Eden knelt down and gathered up the small, colorful glass spheres that rolled toward her.

"This is embarrassing," the neighbor said. He was tall and attractive with wire-frame glasses perched over light brown eyes. He wore a blue suit and tie that managed to look more casual than businessy. He raked a hand through his short, shaggy brown hair.

"What's embarrassing about marbles?" Eden asked, smiling. "I used to play with them when I was . . . well, I was ten at the time, but I'm not here to judge."

"They're actually not *my* marbles. I'm a teacher, and I've found simple rewards like these help to motivate students. Since I'm new here, I can use all the help I can get."

"So every student who answers a question . . ."

"Wins a shiny marble. You've got it." He grinned. "Welcome to the building. You just moved in, right?"

"Two days ago." He finished scooping the escaping marbles back into the little cloth bag he held, then extended his hand. "I'm Lucas Campbell."

She shook his hand. "Eden Riley. And this is . . . uh, Darrak."

"Charmed, I'm sure," Darrak said, sounding bored. "Eden? Shall we go now?"

"Nice meeting you, Lucas," she said.

"Yeah, you, too. I'm having a meet and greet in my apartment soon. Just a small thing. A couple bottles of wine and friendly neighborhood chat. Would the two of you be interested in coming?"

She shrugged. "Maybe. Just let me know when."

"I'll do that." He glanced at his watch. "Got to get going. I'm late."

"Us, too."

They rode down in the elevator together. Lucas was right, these days people kept to themselves, apart from awkward small talk. But Eden wasn't opposed to the idea of being more friendly with a neighbor. You never knew when you'd need to borrow a cup of sugar. Or ask them to ignore screaming and/or gunfire coming from within one's apartment walls.

One or the other.

They parted ways outside, and Eden and Darrak drove to Triple-A Investigations, a small, one-room private investigation office on the outskirts of Toronto. It was right next door to the Hot Stuff café.

Eden owned half the business because her mother had left it to her in her will. Caroline Riley hadn't been a fabulous and attentive mother, but she'd been a great gambler and had soundly beaten Andy McCoy—now Eden's partner—in a poker game to win part ownership in the agency. Eden had resisted working there because being a private investigator didn't appeal to her at all. She didn't have any experience in that line of work—after all, her last job had been as a telephone tarot card reader and occasional—*very* occasional—psychic consultant to the police.

Recently, however, she'd started taking this opportunity more seriously. She wanted to help others if she could. Helping others made her happy. It was a totally selfish motivation, really.

And if she could get paid for it, too, then all the better.

"You seem chipper this morning," Darrak commented as she pulled into her parking spot outside the office and shifted into park.

She pulled down her visor mirror to double-check her makeup. "I'm feeling strangely optimistic today. We came close last night."

"Closer than you even realize."

"Do you think it's safe to go back tonight, or will your friend still be there?"

Darrak hesitated. "I think it'll be fine."

He didn't sound completely certain about that. "Do we have to worry about him?"

That earned a smile. "We?"

"What *you're* worried about, *I'm* worried about."

"Then no. We don't have to worry."

She nodded and pulled her purse onto her lap so she could drop her car keys into it. "So we'll find this wizard's assistant . . . does he have a name?"

"Stanley. And he'll be there. He's there every night, apparently."

"Why does he hang out at a singles' club so much?"

"Because he's horny and alone. Does he need more of a reason?"

"I guess not."

"Were you planning on getting out of the car today?" he asked.

"It's a distinct possibility." She didn't move for another few moments, though. Andy had been very adamant that they talk this morning, but he wouldn't say what about. That worried her.

Worry seemed to be her default setting lately.

It was probably nothing.

"Eden," Andy greeted them as they entered the office. "We need to talk."

Maybe it wasn't nothing.

The brisk statement made Eden's back stiffen. She was hiding so much from Andy that it was about time he naturally clued in on something. In fact, he shouldn't have to clue in. She should just go ahead and tell him the truth.

Like Darrak, for instance. Andy was under the mistaken impression that he was Eden's brother. It might have something to do with the fact that Eden had introduced him that way. Andy was sharp, though. A former FBI-agent pushing fifty, with a fit, compact body, thinning blond hair, and keen eyes, he'd single-handedly run the agency by himself for years.

When Eden realized she was possessed by a demon, the shock of this gave her enough concentrated energy to eject Darrak from her body, forcing him to take form for the first time in this office. That much psychic power helped create a "hot spot," which helped to draw supernatural beings there like a magnet. Triple-A was now their private investigation agency of choice. Since even Others' problems skewed toward the normal—cheating spouses, insurance fraud, missing persons—Andy wasn't any the wiser about all the weird stuff going on there.

Andy stood up from his chair and flattened his hands on the top of his desk as he stared at her for a long moment.

"There's weird stuff going on here, Eden," he said.

She gulped. "Weird stuff?"

He nodded. "I don't think it's just my imagination. Look, I need to get this out and I need you to listen to me. Tell me if I'm crazy, okay?"

Eden and Darrak exchanged a glance. "Uh . . . okay," she said. "I really need some coffee, though. I'm desperate."

"Nancy's bringing over a tray shortly from next door." Andy also owned Hot Stuff, so one thing Triple-A never lacked was caffeine or high-caloric pastries.

"Is she bringing over some of those chocolate donuts I love?" Darrak asked.

Great, Eden thought. *Way to concentrate on the problem at hand.*

"I'd be surprised if she didn't," Andy replied. "That girl has a big old crush on you."

"On *me*?" Darrak looked pleased.

As if he didn't already know that. The Hot Stuff assistant manager, Nancy, drooled uncontrollably whenever she was in Darrak's presence. It was kind of pathetic.

Also, why were they discussing donuts when there were more important subjects on the table at the moment?

"I'd never normally be so crude as to say a lady's a sure thing." Andy walked to the glass door and peered outside at the parking lot before looking at Darrak again. "But, trust me, Nancy's a sure thing. So if you're interested, now's the time to get some." He glanced at Eden and grimaced. "I probably shouldn't say that in front of your sister, should I? Sorry Eden."

The day wasn't getting any better.

"We were talking about weird things?" Eden prompted, her arms crossed tightly over her chest. "What kind of weird things? Other than Nancy's dark desires, that is."

Andy rubbed the back of his hand over his mouth, his forehead furrowing. "I don't know exactly how to put this, but . . . our clients are *strange*."

Eden tensed. "Strange how?"

"I thought I saw one of them—" Andy shook his head. "It's just that I could have sworn I saw . . . uh . . ."

"What?" Her throat felt tight.

"Fur."

"Fur?"

"Just for a moment. A split second, really. I was doing some run-of-the-mill surveillance. A guy wanted me to keep an eye on his wife at home during the workday. And she"—he spread his hands—"had fur. And then the next moment she didn't. Like, *poof*."

Oh, boy.

"That does sound kind of crazy," Eden said cautiously. How would he react if he learned about shapeshifters and other supernatural species secretly milling about town? Would he freak out? Run away? Blame Eden for bringing this craziness into his life? Shut down the business? All of the above?

"Another client . . . I could have sworn her eyes turned white right in front of me when discussing a case. Like, no pupils or irises. Just stark white." He cleared his throat. "And they glowed a little, too. I'm crazy, aren't I?"

"Well . . ." Eden began. "Maybe you need to—"

"You're not crazy," Darrak interrupted. "The client's furry wife was likely a werewolf. They're the most common shapeshifter, after all. And glowy white eyeballs are a dead giveaway that you're talking to a fairy who's low on his or her power. Try not to get too close when their glamour starts to slip like that. It's this whole moth and flame thing they do. They'll suck some of your energy right out of you before you even know what's happening."

Andy's mouth gaped open. "What did you say?"

Eden's eyes were wide. What was Darrak doing? She was about to explain it away, and he'd just blurted out the truth like it was no big deal?

"Darrak . . ." she began.

"Andy's a part of this now," he reasoned. "I don't know why you insist on keeping this all a big fat secret . . . *sis*." He grinned. "Andy's trustworthy enough, isn't he?"

If looks could exorcise demons, Darrak would be bound for the Void right now.

"But—but . . . werewolves and fairies don't really exist," Andy protested weakly.

"Of course they do," Darrak assured him. "And that's only the tip of the iceberg. Just go with it. It's not a big deal."

Void bound. Decimation by eyeball, coming right up.

When did she lose control over this situation?

Andy sat down heavily behind his desk, his eyes shifting rapidly back and forth. "Oh, my God, you're right! She's a werewolf. Her husband is going to flip out!"

"He's probably a werewolf, too," Darrak said. "Shifters rarely crossbreed. They're very particular about that sort of thing. Something about keeping their family lines pure. It's very *Harry Potter*. Only werewolves instead of wizards. But wizards are real, too. FYI."

Andy continued to gape at him for a moment, then let out a long shaky breath as Eden looked on helplessly at this train wreck of a conversation. "I'm going to throw up."

"No, you won't." Then Darrak grimaced. "Or, you *probably* won't. I don't know."

"No . . . I'm—I'm fine." Andy swallowed hard. "This is going to sound nuts, but as bizarre as what you've just told me is, it's a huge weight off my mind. I thought I was going insane!"

"You're not. Well, *probably* not. I'm not an expert."

"My brain is one of my most prized assets." Andy leaned back and pressed his palms against his temples. His chair squeaked noisily. "Without it, I don't know what I'd do."

"The same could be said for most humans," Darrak agreed.

"Werewolves!" Andy exclaimed. "Here in Toronto!"

"And fairies, too," Darrak reminded him, finally noticing the death glare Eden was sending him. "What?"

She just shook her head.

"Fairies, too." Andy looked stunned. "How do you know these things?"

"That's easy. Because I'm a de—"

"Okay, that's enough." Eden clamped her hand over Darrak's mouth.

He grabbed her wrist and pried her hand away from his face before looking at Andy. "Because I'm very astute," he finished. "I've been aware of the supernatural world that surrounds us for a very long time."

"Unbelievable." Andy's face was pale. "And you, Eden? Did you know about this, too?"

"It's a recent revelation for me," she admitted, her voice hoarse. "Like, *really* recent."

Andy smiled shakily, but it quickly faded. "Werewolves sound dangerous. Do I need a . . . a gun with, um, silver bullets in it?"

"Fairies are more dangerous than werewolves, on the average." Darrak moved out of arm's reach of Eden. "But if they're your clients, they came to you for help. They wouldn't attack anyone they need."

"That's comforting."

Eden tried to relax. On second thought, this was good. Andy had learned the truth—part of it anyhow—and he wasn't running away screaming. Why had she been so worried? She couldn't control everything. After all, denying the supernatural world didn't make it go away.

"Are you done with the werewolf case?" she asked, feeling uncomfortable about saying the word out loud.

Andy shook his head. "I took off when I saw the fur. I have to go back and get some more pictures tomorrow. Werewolves might not be into interbreeding, but they don't seem to have a problem with infidelity."

The bell on the door jingled, and Nancy walked in with a tray of coffees in foam cups and a brown paper bag. She was medium height, with bleached blonde hair, bright red lipstick, and a permanent glow courtesy of her lifetime membership at the tanning salon down the street.

"Greetings, Triple-A!" she said cheerily.

"Nancy." Andy's voice was now weary. "Great. Wonderful. You're a peach."

"I have something here for you." Nancy's attention was on Darrak.

His eyebrows went up. "Oh, yeah?"

She nodded and reached into the bag. Eden strained to see what it was and then was sorry she did.

"Is that a . . . a gigantic donut in the shape of a heart?" she asked.

"It is," Nancy confirmed and bit her bottom lip. "I made it especially for Darrak. It has a creamy custard center."

"Sounds delicious," Darrak said. "Thank you."

"My pleasure. Really." She twisted her index finger into her crispy blonde hair and alluringly jutted out her chest after he took the donut from her. "Listen, I was thinking . . . if you don't have any plans tomorrow night, maybe you and I could—"

"He has plans," Eden cut her off. "With me. His sister. It's a family thing."

"Oh." Nancy's face fell. "Well, maybe another time."

"You know, there's a new club that opened up. Luxuria?" Eden forced a smile. "You should check it out some time."

"I've heard of it. Is it any good?"

"It's amazing. So much fun and so many great men there waiting to meet someone just like you." What in the hell was she doing? *Just shut up, Eden.* "Thanks for the coffee. See you later."

It only took a few more moments before Nancy took the hint and slunk out of the office, defeated.

Eden felt oddly victorious about that. It didn't make her proud.

She didn't dislike Nancy, but for some reason, the woman's obvious lust toward Darrak rubbed her the wrong way.

You're just jealous, her conscience scolded.

That was ridiculous.

Darrak bit into the donut. "This is really tasty. But it doesn't look much like a heart. More like two chocolate blobs stuck together. Two *delicious* chocolate blobs."

Eden felt a burning on the side of her face and realized Andy was openly staring at her.

She cleared her throat. "What?"

"That was kind of rude of you," Andy said. "You should have let Darrak answer for himself. He doesn't need you controlling his love life."

"Darrak doesn't have a love life."

Darrak stopped in midbite. "Meanie."

Andy pursed his lips. "Your brother should be allowed to date if he wants to without you interfering, you know."

Anger and frustration welled inside of her, quickly bubbling over the edge of her calm exterior. "He's not my brother. He's a demon."

Shit.

She glanced at Darrak to see he looked surprised at her unexpected admission.

Andy shook his head. "I'm sure every sister feels that way about her sibling now and then."

Okay. In for a penny, in for a pound . . .

"No, I'm actually being serious," she said. "He's a—"

The door jingled again, and Eden looked over her shoulder, certain that Nancy had returned for round two. But it wasn't Nancy.

Darrak threw his half-eaten donut down on Andy's desk, next to the coffees, and moved to stand closer to Eden as Ben Hanson entered the office.

Eden immediately tensed at the sight of the handsome cop. After all, the last time she'd seen him, he'd almost killed her.

"Good morning." Ben's dark blue eyes swept over the three of them, ending at Eden. "Long time no see."

* * *

A temporary infusion of humanity may have made Darrak lose his desire for death and destruction, but the exception to the rule would be Ben Hanson.

Detective Ben Hanson, that was.

Darrak hated the guy. *Hated*.

It wasn't that long ago that Eden had been crazy for Ben. Darrak wasn't stupid. He saw the appeal. Ben was tall, good-looking, square jawed, upstanding, and helpful.

Gag.

He was so perfect, Darrak's nickname for him was "golden boy."

To top it off, he had short blond hair and those dimples, when he smiled, that women swooned over. Luckily, Ben didn't smile very often.

Neither did Darrak when the cop was around. And it wasn't simply because he was jealous. Sure there was *that*. But there was also the fact that Ben had shot Eden—he'd been aiming for Darrak and she'd gotten in the way—and very nearly killed her.

Ben had been damn lucky Darrak kept a reserve of healing power, which he'd used on Eden. All of it. If she ever got hurt again he wouldn't be able to do a repeat performance.

Ben had begged Eden to come with him so he could protect her from the big bad demon, but Eden had stayed with Darrak.

A minor victory, but it still felt good that she'd chosen the demonic, cursed Darrak over the perfect, squeaky-clean cop.

"Why are you here?" Darrak asked unpleasantly. He could fake charm when he had to, but why waste it when it wouldn't do any good?

Ben turned to meet his stony gaze without flinching. "Several reasons."

Darrak imagined tearing the head off the cop's body with his bare hands. It was oddly satisfying.

Andy approached Ben and shook his hand. "Good to see you again. Ben, isn't it?"

"That's right."

Eden looked apprehensive as she and Darrak exchanged a glance. Andy hadn't been present when she'd been shot so he'd have no idea why they were acting so standoffish.

"Ben," she finally said. "Good to see you again."

Darrak had hoped for something along the lines of "Get out of here, you bastard!" Or "I hate the sight of you. Begone forever!" But, no such luck.

"You, too." Then Ben smiled a mouthful of straight white teeth, and that charming dimple sprang to life on his cheek.

Darrak glowered.

Hate him.

"What's going on?" she asked. "Why are you here?"

"I'm here on business."

"Business?"

He nodded.

"*Police* business?" she clarified.

"What other business is there?" His smile held.

Darrak stood so close to Eden that he was literally touching her, ready to protect her if he needed to. Ben made no overtly threatening moves. Smart guy. Darrak was ready, willing, and able to physically throw the cop out of the office if necessary. Or even if it wasn't necessary.

"What can I help you with?" Eden asked. She was smiling now, and leaning against her desk next to him, but there was a tightness to her mouth. Darrak retrieved his blob-heart donut again and took a bite in an attempt to look at ease. It didn't taste quite as delicious as it had before.

Ben had a manila envelope under his arm, and he pulled a picture out from inside. "Have you seen this woman recently? Her name's Selina Shaw and she's gone missing while on a book tour here. She hasn't been seen in well over a week."

Darrak stopped in midchew. The photo was of a very recognizable dark-haired beauty. Selina was the black witch who'd originally cursed him—although she'd chosen not to use her magic very often in favor of saving her soul.

Selina had grudgingly agreed to help Darrak and Eden, recognizing that Darrak had changed over the years as much as she had. She was to break the curse and help Eden deal with the black magic they both shared. But before anything could happen, a power-hungry member of the Malleus murdered her. A simple dagger through Selina's heart was all it took to part the witch from her immortality.

Darrak's hands clenched at his sides at the memory. He didn't mourn the witch. Their history hadn't been a pleasant one. But he mourned the chance to have his curse broken and save Eden.

When a black witch died, her body disintegrated—not unlike the wicked witch in the *Wizard of Oz*. So, no body, no evidence, no potential murder investigation.

Sorry, Ben.

Even Selina's clothes disappeared shortly after her body had. The only thing that remained of Selina was the amulet Eden now wore. Any witch who cared about the state of her soul would wear a similar one. Eden's, however, was thankfully covered by the green sweater she wore today.

"I know her," Eden said evenly. "I went to her book signing, and we met the next day for coffee."

Everywhere they would have been seen together. Ben couldn't accuse her of lying. Very good. Darrak's eyes narrowed on the cop to study his reaction.

"Did she say anything that would indicate if she was going anywhere? Or if she felt threatened in any way?" Ben asked.

Eden shook her head. "No. Sorry. I wish I could be more helpful."

"You've been helpful enough," Darrak said. "We're done here. Wonderful seeing you again, Ben. Bye, now."

Ben smiled thinly and his eyes flicked to Darrak. "You sound a bit defensive. But I'm just asking questions today, nothing more. I'm sure Ms. Shaw's disappearance has nothing to do with you, does it?"

Somehow he managed to make the sentence sound like a direct accusation.

"Of course not," Darrak replied. "She probably went on vacation and didn't tell her handlers. She's a famous author, after all. They're very flaky."

Ben's eyes narrowed. "Of course. And I take you at your word. I know you're very trustworthy."

"I appreciate it, Detective." Two could play the double-meaning game. It was big fun.

Ben's smile didn't cover up the overt hatred in his eyes. He'd seen Darrak's demonic visage, and it was obvious he hadn't forgotten a horn or talon. After a moment he tore his gaze away from Darrak and turned to Eden. "There's something else here I want you to look at. Do you know this man?"

He pulled out another photo. A headshot of the guy Eden had been talking to last night at Luxuria. The gay one.

It was important for Darrak to keep Eden's male acquaintances and their sexual orientations clear in his head. Not that he was being possessive—no pun intended. He was just cautious of her safety.

Eden nodded. "That's Graham Davis. I knew him back in high school. Haven't seen him in twelve years until last night. Is he in some sort of trouble?"

"Trouble?" Ben repeated. "I'd say so. He's dead."

⇉ SIX ⇇

Eden's breath left her in a rush as if someone had just punched her in the stomach.

"Graham's dead?" she managed.

Ben watched her carefully. "Yeah, he is."

"But—but I just saw him last night."

"It happened last night."

Her throat felt tight. It was impossible, the last thing she would have expected. Was Ben serious? Or was he just testing her, checking her reactions and applying it to whatever he thought she had to do with Selina's disappearance?

Eden caught a quick glimpse of other photos Ben held that he hadn't yet waved in her face. Pictures of Graham lying in an alley, his eyes open and glassy. It was just a brief look, but it told her everything she needed to know.

Ben wasn't lying. Graham really was dead.

"He was found out back of the Luxuria nightclub at four a.m., strangled," Ben told her. "Someone called in an anonymous tip. You were seen with him earlier in the evening."

Eden felt something wet on her cheek, and she pushed away a tear. "H-he was a good friend. I hadn't seen him in forever, but we were going to have coffee soon and catch up."

"A male friend of yours ends up dead. Interesting." Ben glanced at Darrak.

"Don't look at me," Darrak bit back. "I didn't strangle him."

"I never said you did. But the fact you'd jump to that conclusion is also interesting, isn't it?"

Eden gritted her teeth. Ben would look for any reason to accuse Darrak. All he saw was a demon—something to fear. He didn't know who Darrak really was. "Of course Darrak didn't do anything. He was with me last night."

"Yes, I'm sure he was." The intensity of Ben's searching gaze was uncomfortable. "You've very close, aren't you? *Unnaturally* close. Half the time, anyhow."

She'd been waiting for this confrontation since Ben stormed out of her apartment last week, after seeing the truth with his own eyes. He'd wanted to save her. Instead, he shot her. An accident, of course, but the pain was something she wouldn't be forgetting any time soon. Pain was one thing she now associated with Ben.

The crush she'd once harbored for the handsome cop had all but disappeared. A bullet to the chest did wonders in dousing any romantic aspirations.

Eden touched her throat, her heart aching at imagining Graham's sudden end. What had he found? Who had he pissed off enough last night to get himself killed?

Andy sat perched on the edge of his desk watching them. "Darrak's staying with his sister while he's in Toronto. Of course they're close."

"Right. His *sister*." Ben glared at her. "Forgot you two are supposed to be related. After all, there's not much of a family resemblance, is there?"

"They're *half* siblings," Andy replied defensively.

"Sure. That makes much more sense, doesn't it?"

Sarcasm, table for one. It was obvious that Ben could barely keep his disgust for the demon under control.

The whole thing was making her feel ill. A twinge of pain flittered through her stomach.

"What did you talk to Graham about?" Ben asked.

She glanced at Darrak. He was so tense that veins stood out on his neck and along his arms as he crossed them tightly over his chest. He looked ready to forcibly drag Ben out of there.

She licked her dry lips. "He was doing an investigation of the club, that's why he was there. He's a—he *was* a journalist. Several women have gone missing in the area, and he thought something strange was going on." She exhaled and it sounded shaky. "I guess he was right."

"Missing women?" Ben repeated. "Like Selina Shaw?"

The two cases weren't remotely connected, but letting Ben know that would only dig her in deeper. "I don't know. He said there were six women missing, all regulars at Luxuria. So he was investigating the club, trying to find some leads."

"Had he found anything?"

She shook her head. "Nothing when I talked to him. It was just a gut instinct on his part. But . . . there's something else . . ."

"What?"

"When I touched him, I had a flash. This overwhelming feeling of dread and fear came over me."

"Is that some sort of psychic thing?"

Even now that Ben was a believer in all things supernatural, there was still a hard edge of skepticism in his voice.

"Yeah," she said dryly. "A psychic thing. But I didn't know what it meant. I guess I do now."

"You think you sensed that he was going to get murdered?"

"I'm not sure. It felt like there was a dark aura around

him. I can't explain it." Grief constricted her throat for a moment. Damn it. Why couldn't it have been more clear? Maybe she could have helped him.

"A dark aura," Ben repeated, his expression turning sour. "Great. That's helpful." His eyes flicked to Darrak. "You were there, too?

"In spirit."

Ben snorted at that. "Yeah, I'm sure you were. And did you happen to see anything. . . .well, I hesitate to use the word *strange* since murder and mayhem would likely be your regular worldview—"

"What is your problem?" Andy interjected. "Sorry if things didn't work out between you and Eden, but that's no reason to come into my office this morning and be a dick to her and her brother."

"For Christ's sake," Ben said, disgusted. "You have no damn clue, do you?"

"About what?" Andy replied, and there was no more friendliness toward the cop in his voice.

"Ben, enough," Eden said. Her heart pounded hard. She didn't want him to say anything he'd regret. Because, by the look on Darrak's face, Ben was getting too close to the edge and had no idea how far the drop was. Darrak was good-humored and amiable up to a point—but he was nobody you wanted to mess with. He *was* a demon, after all.

"Darrak's evil," Ben stated.

Fabulous. This conversation wasn't looking up.

"Says who?" Andy challenged. "You?"

Ben clenched his fists at his sides. "Eden, I'm giving you one more chance. There's still time to fix this mess you've gotten yourself into before it gets totally out of control. You don't know what's happened to me . . ." He swallowed hard, his expression tense. "I've changed . . . and it's all so I can help you. I *want* to help you."

She really wanted to be completely and unforgivingly

pissed off at him. But why did he have to have that pleading tone to his voice? Ben was truly worried for her safety.

All he'd seen of Darrak's demon form was seven feet of hellfire and horns towering behind Eden at her apartment the day he'd nearly killed her by mistake. He had to be filled with guilt and rage and powerlessness about that.

Ben wore a small gold cross around his neck on a chain. He had strong beliefs about good versus evil. It wasn't his fault he had a hard time believing anything different.

And it wasn't Eden's fault, either.

"You need to go now," Darrak said darkly from behind him.

Ben's shoulders stiffened. "He's killing you, Eden. Little by little. You can't deny it."

It was true, she couldn't deny it. So she said nothing.

Darrak remained silent as well. After all, he *was* killing her slowly but surely. The fact someone, especially a cop, might take issue with that wasn't surprising.

Andy, who knew nothing of this, wasn't so quiet. "What the hell are you talking about?"

"Darrak's a demon," Ben said bluntly. "From Hell. Didn't you know that?"

For a moment, the only sound in the office was the quiet whir of the ceiling fan. Eden stared at Ben bleakly before her attention turned to Andy.

"Your brother is a demon?" Andy said, stunned. "You said that before, but I thought you were kidding."

"He's not her brother," Ben spat out. "He's a disgusting, evil minion of Satan who's seduced Eden into doing his bidding, and he's sucking her dry of every last ounce of her energy. He's killing her and she's letting him."

Well, put that way it didn't sound so great, did it?

Darrak laughed, but it wasn't a pleasant sound. "I haven't been Satan's minion for a long time, cop. And for what it's worth, he prefers to be called Lucifer most of the time."

"Darrak's not evil," Eden blurted out. She suddenly wasn't feeling so good. This whole conversation had only helped the pain still swirling distractingly through her stomach to increase.

Ben shook his head. "You're a fool if you believe that."

Eden turned to Andy, who looked pale with shock at the direction of this conversation. "It's not true. He's *not* making me do anything I don't want to."

"So it's all a lie? Darrak's not a demon who seduced you?" Andy managed.

"Uh . . ." She cleared her throat. "Well . . . no comment."

Ben groaned. "I was speaking figuratively. I hoped I was, anyhow."

"So let me get this straight." Andy paced to the far side of the room and then back to his desk. He pointed at Darrak. "He's a demon."

"I am," Darrak admitted. "And at this time I, uh, have no comment on the seduction issue, either."

Eden held her breath, waiting to see what would happen next. This had to be enough to put Andy right over the edge, wasn't it?

Andy went behind his desk, sat down heavily, and pulled a silver flask from his top drawer. He unscrewed the lid and drank deeply from the contents before wiping his mouth off with the back of his hand.

"Christ on a cracker!" he exclaimed. "This has been the craziest day ever!"

Okay. That was better than she'd expected, at least.

Ben's face was red. "Damn it, I didn't come here for this today. I'm not ready, I have more training to do before I can . . ." he trailed off and looked at Darrak. "Screw it. Eden's soul is at risk. And if you think I'm going to allow you to be near her, to touch her, to destroy her life, you filthy, evil, selfish, demon piece of shit, then you're—"

Darrak lashed out and grabbed Ben by his throat, digging his fingers in on either side of Ben's windpipe, slamming him up against the wall behind him. Eden gasped out loud at the suddenness of it. Darrak had been calm and contained all this time. His quick turn to violence had taken her by surprise.

"If you don't leave now, I'm going to lose my temper," Darrak growled, and his eyes changed from ice blue to fill with amber flames. "You don't want that to happen."

"And what would you do then?" Ben rasped. "Tear me apart? Devour my soul?"

"Thanks for the suggestion. That donut wasn't nearly as satisfying as it should have been."

Ben fought against him, grabbing Darrak's arms and managing to break the hold, before connecting his fist with Darrak's jaw in a quick punch that snapped Darrak's head to the side.

"Really?" Darrak glowered, recovering quickly. "You're stronger than I thought, but is that the best you've got?"

Darrak grabbed Ben by the front of his shirt, and for a moment, Eden feared for the cop's life.

"Are you going to kill me?" Ben snarled.

"Will you leave Eden alone?"

"And let you destroy her? Not a chance."

"Darrak!" Eden let out a frustrated breath. "Let him go. Ben, you need to leave right—"

The next moment, a scream tore from her throat as the shallow pain that had been in her stomach shot through her entire body. It managed to stop all coherent thought, quickly submerging her in white-hot agony.

What the hell was this? What was going on?

Every cell of her body was filled with pain. It felt as if something, both inside and outside of her, was attempting to tear her apart.

Darrak was at her side in an instant.

"Eden," his voice was panicked. "What's wrong?"

"I . . . I don't—" She screamed again as another wave of pain ripped through her. She clutched at Darrak's arm, digging her fingernails in, trying to use him as an anchor so she didn't get swept away by whatever this was.

"What the hell's going on?" Ben demanded, his voice breaking with stress. "Andy, call an ambulance. Now!"

Being shot had been the worst pain she'd ever felt until now. This . . . this was a thousand times worse.

Andy stumbled toward the phone on his desk and grabbed the receiver to hold it to his ear. "There's no dial tone."

"This is because of you, you selfish asshole." Ben jabbed a finger at Darrak. "You're killing her."

"This isn't my doing," Darrak snapped back. "Not this. Not now."

But as strongly delivered as the reply was, Eden could hear the doubt in his voice. Whatever this was, it had to do with Darrak. There was no other explanation.

Another bolt of pain tore through her, and she clung tighter to Darrak—tight enough that it would probably break the ribs of a regular human—and then it was over. The tearing sensation ceased and her body relaxed. It had weakened her so much she couldn't move, couldn't think clearly. Her eyes closed, and her head fell slackly against Darrak's chest.

She could hear Ben's erratic breathing. "Is she dead?"

Darrak pressed his fingers against her throat, feeling for a pulse.

"She's alive." He sounded deeply relieved.

"Let me take her with me. I can help her."

"Not going to happen."

"Damn it, demon, you want to destroy her, don't you? Is that your goal?"

Darrak's muscles tensed, and he drew Eden closer to him, cradling her in his arms. "If you really think that, then you don't know me."

"I don't want to know you."

"You're not wanted here, cop. Get that through your thick head. I'll handle this."

Ben laughed, but it didn't hold an ounce of humor. "You'll handle it. Yeah. Looks like you're doing a stellar job so far. Eden's too blind to see what you really are, but I can. She needs me."

"Yeah. She needs you to *leave*." Darrak gently stroked the hair off her forehead. "She's not your dead fiancée, you know. You can't fix your past mistakes by saving Eden from the big bad demon."

Ben went silent for a moment. "You son of a bitch."

"Bzzz. Wrong. I never had a mother. You'll have to find another insult."

Eden heard them as if they were miles away. Ben's words were harsh, but she could hear his concern.

"What happened with my fiancée is none of your damn business."

"Eden is my business," Darrak replied.

"Right." Ben's voice twisted unpleasantly. "Got to protect your host, don't you? Without her you'd have to find another body to highjack. One that might not be so willing to put her existence on the line to save yours. You may have Eden fooled, demon, but I'm not so naïve. I can see right through you."

"You can, can you?" Darrak's words were cold as ice.

"I've done some research on demonology, enough to know that there are no selfless or caring demons. You all think humans are food or playthings. Nothing more than that. It's impossible for you to feel otherwise. So whatever you're pretending to be, whatever Eden believes you are—it's all a lie. No demon in history, no matter what the circumstances have been, has changed their base nature. *Ever.* You protect her because you need her. The moment you find a way out of this hole you've dug yourself into, she's useless to you. The only question is, will she still be breathing when that day comes?"

Argue with him, Eden thought. *Tell him he's wrong. Please.*

"Leave" was all Darrak had to say in his defense. He was so tense his chest and arms felt like marble.

Ben snorted. "See? You don't even deny it. You know the truth even if she's too blind to see past your flashy exterior. I swear to God, demon, I'm keeping a close eye on you. If anything happens to her, you'll have me to answer to."

The bell above the door jingled as Ben left the office. After another moment Eden managed to pry her eyes open. She looked up at Darrak.

Why hadn't he argued and told Ben he was wrong? Maybe no other demon had ever changed before. But . . . but Darrak was different.

Wasn't he?

"I have a dial tone now," Andy announced shakily. "I'm calling an ambulance."

"No," she rasped. "No ambulances. I'm okay now."

Darrak slowly helped her stand, supporting her all the way. His brows were drawn together and he looked worried.

But was it only an act?

Shit. She hated that Ben had managed to plant a seed of doubt in her mind about him. She and Darrak were over this, weren't they?

So you trust the demon? she asked herself. *Completely and totally?*

Yes, of course she did. She had to. She had no other choice.

"What happened?" Darrak asked.

Eden braced herself on the edge of her desk and tried to breathe normally. "No idea. One moment I was okay, and the next . . . I felt like something was trying to rip me apart." She frowned. "Maybe Nancy poisoned my coffee so she could get to you without your bossy fake sister around."

"Sounds reasonable. But you hadn't drunk any coffee yet."

"Then that cancels out that theory." She placed a hand

over her abdomen and pressed. The pain was completely gone.

"Were you conscious?" Darrak asked. "Did you hear everything Ben said before he left?"

"Not really," she lied. "I was in and out. Didn't hear much. Why? What did he say?"

"I don't think him and me are going to be best friends."

"What a shock."

"He cares about you, Eden." Darrak's jaw clenched. "For real."

"Hooray?"

"Does somebody want to explain to me what in the holy hell is going on here?" Andy demanded.

Eden moved away from Darrak and went to sit behind her desk. Sitting was good. She gathered her hair, now tangled, and pulled it over her right shoulder.

"Where do you want us to start?" she asked.

Andy pointed at Darrak warily. "He's a demon."

"Yes."

"From Hell."

"Originally," she replied.

"But . . . is he evil?"

She looked at Darrak.

"Not at the moment," he said.

"Okay." Andy took another gulp from his flask. "But you have to possess Eden when it's dark out, I gather?"

"Uh-huh."

"And you lied about being her brother."

"Just playing along with what sis says."

Eden grimaced. "It seemed like a good idea at the time."

"And now?" Andy asked.

"Not so good."

Andy took another drink, draining the flask, and then exhaled shakily. "Okay, I think that pretty much covers it."

She was surprised. "Really?"

"Just so you know," Darrak said, "you don't have to be afraid of me."

Andy waved a hand. "Oh, I know that."

Darrak was surprised. "You do?"

"You do?" Eden echoed.

"Sure. I'm a good judge of character." He shook out his flask, confirming it was now empty, and placed it next to the untouched coffees on his desk. "I've never sensed anything evil in you. And even with the, uh, revelations of the day, I'm sticking by my original impression." He moved to hunt through his desk drawer, succeeding in pulling out another flask. "And I'm also going to get completely shit faced starting right now. Just wanted to let you know."

Darrak gave him a tense smile. "Sounds like a plan."

"Now if the drama of the day is over, I need you to pour through my recent files, Eden. Make sure everything's in order. There's enough here to keep you busy all day . . . that is, if you've recovered from . . . whatever that was."

Good old Andy. He'd never suggest she take the day off sick. It was strange, but she felt nothing now—not even a twinge. It was as if what had happened had all been in her imagination. But it wasn't.

"Don't you want to know any more about Darrak?" she asked, surprised that Andy was willing to take everything he'd learned so far at face value.

Andy pursed his lips. "Is he going to kill me and drag my soul through the gates of Hell?"

"No!" she yelped, but then frowned. "At least . . . I don't think so."

That earned her a look from the demon. "Your soul is safe around me, Andy. I don't drag souls back to Hell anymore."

Andy gulped. "*Anymore*?"

"Uh . . ." Darrak grimaced. "Time changes many things."

"Indeed it does," Andy agreed.

Time changes many things. Was it true? How could she

ever know for sure? Yesterday at this time she'd believed in Darrak 100 percent. They'd been through enough together for him to earn her trust. But what if she was wrong?

You're not wrong, she told herself. *Ben is overreacting.*

That was it. And now it would be best if she immersed herself in work for the rest of the day. Tonight they'd go back to Luxuria and find Stanley, the wizard's assistant. That was all she wanted to focus on.

"Are the phones working again?" she asked.

"They are." Andy frowned. "Strangest thing. It's like it was some kind of power surge."

"Let's hope it doesn't happen again," Darrak said, although he didn't seem certain about it. She could still see the worry in his blue eyes.

Eden forced a smile. "Fingers crossed."

His gaze met hers. "You know, golden boy's not going to give up on you."

"I know. But at the moment, Ben Hanson is the least of my worries."

At least, she really hoped so.

⇴ SEVEN ⇴

Three hundred years ago (give or take)

If there was one place that knew how to do torture right, it was Hell.

And if there was one being that could take it, it was an archdemon.

"That was fantastic," Darrak gritted out as he was dragged in front of Lucifer. "I feel so much more relaxed now. Thank you, my prince."

Coal black eyes stared back at him from the darkness. Darrak felt his wounds healing rapidly and tried to put the last three months out of his mind as much as he could.

"You liked it, did you?" Lucifer's voice was cold. "Perhaps you'd enjoy a few more months of the same treatment?"

Darrak swallowed. "That is entirely up to you, of course."

"Yes, it is, isn't it?" Lucifer rose from his throne. Darrak's eyesight was blurry, but he saw Lucifer's outline. It glowed a little. Remnants from his beginnings as an angel. A constant reminder of where the Prince of Hell, the Lord of Pride, had come from.

"Although," Darrak reasoned, "I would serve you much better at your side."

"Would you? I have to argue with that. Is there anything you want to tell me, Darrakayiis?"

"Like what?"

Lucifer smiled. "I know you want to destroy me."

Darrak went very still. He said nothing.

"I have to say I'm surprised. I've given you so much. I took you from your humble beginnings as an incubus and gave you the power of an archdemon. And you choose to repay me by plotting my demise. Do you really think it would be that easy?"

Panic ripped through him. This was all Theo's fault. Stupid plan. But he hadn't heard any more about it in a hundred years.

He opened his mouth to defend himself, but Lucifer waved a hand, sealing Darrak's mouth shut. It felt as if he was being choked. Demons couldn't die as humans do, but they could feel pain and they could be destroyed—some more easily than others. Since Lucifer was the one who'd originally created Darrak from hellfire, he had more power over him than any other being in the universe. A simple thought from him would be enough to end Darrak's existence.

Darrak hated being at another's mercy.

If nothing else, at least he was dealing with a coherent Lucifer. Sometimes he wasn't like this—he turned into more of a beast, one that couldn't be reasoned with. One that only wanted to destroy anything that came into his path. That was when Lucifer insisted on being called Satan.

Total split personality.

"I know you've been working with Asmodeus," Lucifer said evenly. "He hired you to destroy me so he could take my throne."

Huh? That was surprising. Darrak had seen Asmo briefly last year, but it hadn't been a meeting of conspiracy. Asmo, being the Lord of Lust, had needed some input from an ex-incubus about his own growing harem of human souls. Darrak happened to be an expert on the subject.

That was all it was.

Where had Lucifer gotten this information?

"The thing is," Lucifer said, "I will get to Asmodeus before he comes close to destroying me. But I won't destroy him completely. I'm going to make him suffer for his sins."

Terrific. The Prince of Hell lecturing a demon about sinning. Something seemed wrong about that.

"As for you—" Lucifer's eyes narrowed. "What shall I do with you?"

Let me go on my merry way, you crazy ex-angel? Darrak thought. Being that he had no mouth, presently, he couldn't speak this aloud.

"Shall I return you to your incubus self?" he mused. "Or should your punishment be a bit more severe than a slap on the wrist?"

Darrak waited to be decimated. It couldn't hurt any more than three months of torture had. He hoped. He'd been totally faking it when he said he'd enjoyed it.

Torture was not enjoyable, even for a demon.

Lucifer smiled. "I think I have it. There was a time that I went against the rules set forth for me and I was cast out of Heaven. Have you heard that story?"

Many times. Yawn.

"For my beliefs, for my so-called pride and untrustworthiness, I was evicted from the only home I'd ever known. The protection and love of Heaven was no longer mine." His voice twisted with pain, and Darrak could have sworn there was a shine of tears in his black eyes. "Being here, created by me, you have been under my protection for all these centuries. This is something that you've obviously taken for granted. You've attempted to use my trust in you against me. Believe me when I say this, Darrakayiis, it will not happen again." He was quiet for a thoughtful moment. "So that is how it shall be—my decision is made. I wish you luck. You will need it."

Darrak's mouth appeared again, and he gasped as a light breeze touched his leathery skin, the flames that coated him extinguishing for a moment before they lit again as bright and hot as before. He looked down at himself, expecting to see a change, but saw nothing different.

He looked up at the throne, but Lucifer had already disappeared.

"You have been under my protection for all these centuries. This is something that you've obviously taken for granted."

Whatever that meant.

Maybe this was a test to see how Darrak would react. To see if he'd sell out Theo at the first opportunity to divert attention from himself. Lucifer was wrong, after all. Asmodeus hadn't conspired with Darrak to destroy Lucifer.

Uh, that had been Theo.

Asmo was in big trouble. That demon lord wasn't the smartest one in Hell—usually he ignored Hell's politics in favor of being preoccupied by his dens of lust and building his harem to be bigger than Lucifer's. It was his hobby. Asmo would never see it coming.

Oh well, not Darrak's problem.

He stood from his position on his knees and stretched. He felt fine. Better than fine, really. There was nothing like three months of torture to give you a new lease on—

There was a sudden twinge in his chest. Then his left horn began to tingle. What was that?

He looked around the dark room. Could he hear . . . chanting?

Yes, chanting. A woman's voice. Latin words. Familiar, somehow.

It was a—he listened closely before his eyes widened in

recognition. It was a summoning ritual. And it wasn't originating from Hell itself.

But how could he—?

He gasped as he was suddenly pulled upward through Hell's core, through the gates, up through the vast expanse of nothingness, and into the human world. It felt as if he'd been crushed by a huge hand and then mashed down into the soft ground and grass and . . . he blinked . . . were those daisies?

He was crouched in the center of a circle of salt.

Looking up, he saw a beautiful dark-haired woman staring at him, her hand held to her mouth in surprise.

"But you are a . . ." She inhaled sharply. "An *archdemon*. I only meant to summon an incubus."

Summon. She'd summoned him?

Archdemons didn't get summoned. They *couldn't* be summoned. It was in the job description.

He really didn't have time for this.

He bared his razor-sharp teeth at her, and she cowered away from him.

"Let me out of this circle, woman," he snarled.

It took only a moment for the fear to leave her expression. He couldn't move, couldn't escape. And she knew it.

Her lips began to move again. Another spell, but he wasn't sure what it was. When she was finished, she took a deep breath.

"Tell me your true name, demon," she said with command in her voice.

"Darrakayiis," he replied without hesitation, but then fury rippled through him. How did she make him say it aloud? Giving her his true name gave her near-absolute power over him.

It had to be a spell.

"You're a witch," he said.

"Yes. But I want to be a much more powerful one," she told him. "Show me your human visage, Darrakayiis."

He tried to resist, but it was impossible. He shifted form as she requested. Her gaze swept appreciatively over him.

"Very good," she said. "You're going to make me a black witch. That's why I've summoned you. I've already cast a spell over you that will make this possible."

Ah, a woman with aspirations. Intriguing. Still annoying, but it was vaguely intriguing as well. "That's truly what you want?"

"Yes."

"What else do you want from me?" he asked.

She smiled and he could see the dark greed in her eyes. "Everything you've got to give."

Lucifer was responsible for this. Whatever happened now to Darrak was entirely Lucifer's fault. Lucifer had removed Hell's protection over Darrak, leaving him vulnerable to be summoned by this common witch.

One day soon he'd get his revenge. Right after he'd killed this witch for having the audacity to think she could use him as she pleased.

This wouldn't take too long, would it?

⇒ EIGHT ⇐

Andy proceeded to get so drunk thanks to his hidden supply of alcohol that he had to call a taxi to take him home at five o'clock. Darrak spent most of the day at Hot Stuff next door—no more than a hundred feet away—giving Eden the chance to concentrate on Andy's poorly written case files as she tried to make sense of them.

It was good to have something to focus on, even if it was trying to decipher really bad handwriting.

She forced herself not to think about anything that had happened earlier. But not thinking didn't change a damn thing.

The bell jingled at ten after six. Eden looked up to see Darrak had returned.

"It's time," he said.

Sunset.

Darrak held his hand over his stomach. Perspiration had broken out on the demon's forehead, his shoulders were hunched, and he looked like he was in severe pain. She knew why.

Her heart began to race, but she nodded. "Okay, I'm ready."

"You're sure?"

"Yes."

As the sun slipped fully behind the horizon, Eden watched as Darrak's six-foot-tall form grew darker and more transparent until he changed completely into a cloud of black smoke hanging in the air in front of her.

She shrank away from him. It was an unconscious reaction. Every time, every evening, the sight of him losing form filled her with fear. Seeing it made everything that was happening even more real and impossible to deny or rationalize. Especially when the black smoke began to edge closer to her.

She backed away from it until she hit the edge of her desk.

The smoke appeared to hesitate.

"Just do it," she said out loud. Her voice shook.

It swirled for a moment longer before launching itself at her. It only needed to touch her skin—that was enough to find entrance to her body.

Darrak thought this act caused her pain, but he was dead wrong. As much as being his official human host and being possessed by him every evening at sunset filled her with fear and apprehension, the actual act itself as he entered her—that was . . . *orgasmic*.

At the moment, though, it was her little secret.

After all, just because it *felt* good didn't mean it *was* good. She wasn't born yesterday. There was a reason demonic possession had screen time in horror movies, not erotica.

"You okay?" Darrak asked after a moment, his voice now in her head.

"Yeah," she managed. Her knees felt weak, but she remained standing.

"I guess I see why Ben has a problem with our relationship. If he got to see that, he'd probably have me exorcised on the spot."

"Forget him. I already have."

It was a lie. What Ben had said earlier still weighed heavily in her mind.

Two men who claimed to care about her. Despite their obvious differences, they did have a lot in common, actually.

Ben had short, light hair, and Darrak had longer, dark hair.

Ben had dark blue eyes. Darrak had light blue eyes.

Ben was a police detective from Toronto. Darrak was an archdemon from Hell.

Very similar.

She sighed. Okay, not similar at all. But they were both exactly the same height. That had to count for something, didn't it?

Luxuria looked exactly the same as it had last night when Eden arrived—a sea of singles looking for love.

And if Graham had been right, *dying* for love as well.

What did you find? Eden wondered. *And what got you killed?*

Maybe it had been completely unrelated to his investigation. An unfortunate coincidence.

No. This wasn't a coincidence. She sensed something here. Something she couldn't quite put her finger on, even past the strange feeling of desperation and lust. Something threatening. Her heart picked up its pace the moment she walked through the entrance and into the large, dimly lit club with music throbbing from one end of the indigo interior to the other.

She didn't enter Luxuria easily. Apprehension helped slow her down. This was where Graham had been killed. This was where Darrak spotted his demonic friend lurking in the shadows.

It was dangerous here.

The only thing that pushed her forward was the thought of talking to the wizard's assistant. Something good had to come of that and then this would all be worth it.

"There he is, same spot as last night," Darrak said. "Do you see him?"

She scanned the club until her gaze fell on her target. Pushing aside her apprehension and running her hands absently down the sides of her low-cut, form-fitting red dress, she walked directly toward him.

"Drink this." Stanley held out a glass of champagne toward a reluctant-looking brunette. "It's delicious."

"Ah, so that explains it," Darrak said.

Eden stopped just short of reaching the wizard's assistant. "Explains what?"

"I wondered why Stanley had women crawling all over him last night. It's obvious to me now that he's using a lust elixir."

"A what?"

"A potion that makes the victim lustful and unable to keep his or her hands off their object of desire."

"*Victim*?" she repeated, outrage quickly filling her and cancelling out all other worries at the moment.

"Uh . . ." Darrak began. "Maybe I shouldn't have said anything."

She closed the remaining distance between her and Stanley's table and snatched the glass away from the woman before she'd taken a sip.

"Hey!" Stanley swiveled around, and his eyes widened as he scanned the length of her. "Well, hello there, gorgeous. Yes . . . please feel free to drink the champagne if you like. There's definitely enough to go around."

The brunette just glared at Eden.

"Is there lust elixir in here?" Eden demanded, peering down at the clear bubbly liquid.

Stanley's eyes grew even wider. "I have no idea what you're talking about."

"Yeah, right." She tipped the glass and poured its contents onto the floor.

"Okay, I'm out of here. I'm not into three-ways," the brunette victim-in-waiting said unpleasantly.

"Wait, baby . . . I can change your mind." Stanley held up a hand to stop her, but it was too late. She stood and teetered away on five-inch heels. "Great. Thanks a lot. She was a total hottie, too."

"How dare you use a magical date-rape drug on an unsuspecting woman."

"Date-rape drug?" He grimaced. "Baby, you have me all wrong."

She put her hands on her hips. "Did you put a lust elixir in that glass without that woman's knowledge, or not?"

"Well . . ." He tugged at his shirt collar. "Yeah, I did. But it's not like it's a roofie or anything shady like that. My elixir only works if there is mutual desire from both parties involved." He grinned, but it faded as Eden continued to stare daggers into him. "It simply breaks down any potential barriers that would get in the way of a perfect sensual experience. It takes the attraction that's already there and multiplies it by . . . oh, about a million times. It doesn't make anyone do something they don't want to do down deep. If it worked on her, then it would mean she already wanted to, uh, rock my world. But her inhibitions just wouldn't get in the way to stop her."

"That's sick."

His expression turned wary. "You're not a cop, are you?"

"No, but I know one. And he's recently found out about the supernatural side of the city. He's dealing with some pent up anger right now that he might like to aim at a weaselly scumbag like you."

"Eden," Darrak cut in. "What's up with the badass routine tonight? I mean, don't get me wrong, I'm loving it. But don't you want this weaselly scumbag to help us? Or are you trying to scare him back into his hole in the ground?"

Damn. The demon was absolutely right. She just hated seeing women used and abused without their knowledge or consent. It was a major hot-button issue for her.

Better to pour on the sugar a little if she wanted Stanley's help. Just a smidge.

"I think we got off on the wrong foot," she said, extending her hand and pushing a smile onto her face. "I'm Eden."

He eyed her warily and then slowly and visibly relaxed. He shook her hand. "Great to meet you, Eden. I do appreciate a woman with an outgoing personality. Please have a seat. Champagne?" He raised another glass.

That wasn't going to happen.

"I'm with Darrak," she said.

He audibly gasped. "Oh."

"You know who that is?"

"Of course I do." He swallowed hard, then forced a shaky smile to his thin lips. "Why didn't you say so to begin with? Any friend of Darrak's is a friend of mine."

"He's not my friend," Darrak noted. "I've never met him before face-to-face. But it's good to know my reputation precedes me."

"Where is he?" Stanley's gaze shifted nervously around the room.

"Close. But he sent me to talk to you." Stanley didn't know she was possessed. It was best to keep that fact tucked away for the time being. "I need to talk to your boss. It's urgent."

Stanley cleared his throat and sipped on his own glass of bubbly. "That's going to be a problem, I'm afraid."

She frowned. "Why?"

"He's gone."

"Gone?"

He nodded. "He left town the other day for an extended vacation. He's recovering from some, uh . . . recent injuries . . . and needed the time alone to recuperate."

He was gone? How could he be gone? Her chest felt tight. She'd hoped this would go smoothly tonight.

"Where did he go?" she asked, her throat suddenly thick.

"He didn't say. He really wants to be alone right now. He's all Greta Garbo. Knowing him, though, it's somewhere with palm trees and drinks served in coconuts, but I don't know the exact location. My boss is super secretive about everything in his life. Maksim doesn't even want anyone to know his first name." Stanley paused. "Whoops."

"Maksim, huh?" Eden tried to remain calm. "I need to get in touch with him. How do I do that?"

"You don't. Sorry."

"Darrak is not going to be happy," Eden said, not liking that she felt the need to resort to veiled threats. Then again, this guy hadn't made a fabulous impression on her so far, so scaring him a little was okay with her. "You don't want an archdemon to get angry with you—all talons and sharp teeth and, um, *horns*. Big scary horns."

Darrak sighed. "I'll leave any horny jokes alone. Way too easy. And sadly accurate at the moment."

Stanley swallowed and wiped his sweaty forehead with the back of his hand. "Trust me, I don't want him to be angry. But there's nothing I can do. If Darrak wants to disembowel me because of this, it'll be a waste of his valuable time."

"You think he'd disembowel you?" Eden asked. Stanley seemed all too ready to jump to the conclusion that Darrak was just as dangerous as Ben thought he was.

"Of course." Stanley lowered his voice. "He's an *archdemon*. I try to avoid them whenever possible, but in my line of work . . . well, it's difficult. Can you . . . uh, tell him that I can create some elixirs for him for free? I work to order. It's my side business."

"I promise not to disembowel him," Darrak said. "The cleanup's a real bitch. We should just go now."

"Just relax," Eden said to Stanley. The guy looked ready to wet himself at the prospect of infuriating Darrak.

"I can't relax. Sex is the only way I can unwind, and you totally blew that for me tonight." He breathed deeply and downed the rest of his drink. "What's Darrak's problem anyhow? Must be something major. If he's looking for a wizard master to help him and his girlfriend—"

"I'm not Darrak's girlfriend," Eden said firmly.

"His bitch, then." He flippantly waved his hand. "Whatever you are."

Darrak snorted. "He called you my bitch."

"I heard him."

"What did you say?" Stanley asked.

"I'm not Darrak's bitch." She hissed out a frustrated sigh. "So what you're saying is talking to you is a big fat waste of time, is it?"

"If all you're looking for is my boss, then yeah. But if you're looking for something else"—he placed a hand on Eden's thigh—"then I might be able to help."

She looked down at his hand. "Do you have a death wish?"

Stanley removed his hand. "You're a difficult woman to love. No. No death wish. Although I have to say I'm probably in the minority around here. Anyone coming to this club who doesn't have any magical protection is asking for trouble."

That piqued Eden's interest. "Are you talking about the murder last night?"

"Among other things." He glanced nervously around the crowded club. "That's seven now, including the reporter."

She inhaled sharply. Stanley may not have been helpful in contacting the wizard master, but did he know something about Graham's murder?

"I thought the other women only went missing. Do you really think they're dead?"

"Once you disappear from here, you don't come back."

A shiver went down her spine. "So where do you go?"

"We really shouldn't talk about this." He scanned the room, his face paling. "The walls have ears."

She touched Stanley's leg to get his attention again. "You think it's someone who works here doing the killings?"

He licked his lips. "It's possible. It's connected to Luxuria, that's all I know right now. I wouldn't come here at all, but I can't seem to stay away. Wish I could."

"What does that mean?"

"Just what I said. I'd like to go to other clubs, but I keep coming back here. So does everyone else. Ninety percent of the people you see here return nearly every night like clockwork."

"Really?" She glanced around. She'd had friends who enjoyed going out on Friday and Saturday nights to let off a little steam after a long week at work, but to go to a singles' club more than that? Seemed excessive.

And expensive. The drinks here were way overpriced.

She needed to know more. Darrak didn't want her investigating anything to do with Graham's murder, but how could she resist a little prodding into things? She owed her old friend that much.

"Look, Stanley," she began, "I know you don't want to get involved, but if you're a regular here, maybe you saw something suspicious—" She stopped talking for a moment as something occurred to her.

The other demon had been here last night just before Graham's murder.

Of course. It made total sense. That demon had to have something to do with this. What other reason would a demon have for hanging out at a singles' club?

"What?" Stanley prompted.

Two people making out next to her jostled Eden's arm, and she moved out of their way, scooting down the couch to sit closer to Stanley. "Did you see a demon here last night?"

"Eden," Darrak breathed. "We need to leave. Come on."

Why was he trying to stop her from learning more? If she had a chance like this to find out more, shouldn't he encourage that? She could dampen him so he didn't get in the way, but she wasn't ready to do that yet.

"A demon." Stanley swallowed hard enough for it to officially be considered a gulp. "Yeah, I saw him. The demonic energy emanating off him was hard to miss."

Her heart drummed so hard against her rib cage that she felt it in her ears. "Do you think he has anything to do with what's going on here?"

"No."

Her eyebrows went up. "Really?"

A waitress emerged to retrieve the empty champagne glasses in front of Stanley before she was swallowed again by the crowd on the dance floor half a dozen feet away. The music shifted from dance to something slower.

Stanley rubbed his temples. "I mean, I don't think so. I don't know what happened to the women for sure, but I'm positive a demon didn't kill that reporter."

"Why do you think that?"

"Because he was strangled to death, right? A demon would never end anyone that humanely."

Eden repressed a shudder. "Being strangled is humane?"

"Demons enjoy digging in and seeing what makes a human tick before they snuff out the life completely. It's fun for them. And when they're done, it's not unusual for dental records to be necessary to ID the victim. That is, if there's even anything left over to ID."

Eden's stomach lurched. "I can't imagine all demons are like that."

Stanley snorted. "What fairy tale are you living in, sunshine? I haven't seen that much in my career as Maksim's assistant, but what I've seen has shown me demons aren't anything to mess with. And when they kill, they leave a hell of a mess in their wake. Oh—*a hell of a mess*. I made a pun. Listen to me. If my elixir business tanks, I should try stand-up."

"Happy now?" Darrak asked dryly. "He thinks he's witty."

Eden stood up on shaky legs. "Tell Maksim I need to talk to him the moment he gets back, okay? That Darrak and I both need to talk to him."

"You're going? You're sure you don't want some champagne?"

"Positive."

She turned and walked away from him, still queasy from the mental image of a demon's carnage. She'd seen Darrak's demonic form—all talons and fire and sharp teeth. And, yes, *horns*. If something like that, or *worse*, chose to end a human life . . . well, Stanley was right. They probably wouldn't use strangulation as their modus operandi.

Then who was the murderer?

And what was the other demon doing here? He'd been looking for Darrak, hadn't he? And Darrak had dismissed it so she wouldn't worry.

So what was this other demon's plan? To drag Darrak back down to home base or destroy him outright? Either option made her feel more ill.

"So, this was pretty much a wasted trip tonight," Darrak said, sounding weary. "I figured it would be."

"Who is this other demon?" she said under her breath, anxiety spreading through her. "He's after you, isn't he?"

"He's . . . uh . . ."

"You said he was your friend, but does he want to find you? Was he sent to hurt you?" She couldn't hide the growing panic in her voice.

"He doesn't want to hurt me."

"How do you know that? You haven't seen him in three hundred years, right?"

"Right. Yeah. About the demon . . ."

"What about him?" Her chest felt tight.

"We're meeting him for lunch tomorrow."

Her sharp focus on the exit to the nightclub blurred. She froze in place. "What?"

"Next door to here. It's a souvlaki place in case you're curious."

The music shifted back to a fast hip-hop song she'd heard on the radio during her drive to work that morning. She didn't speak for a full minute. *"What?"*

"Uh . . . the demon from last night. My old friend. Lunch tomorrow. Souvlaki. Yum?"

Was she hallucinating? Why was he saying things to her that made no sense? He'd made them leave last night, fearful of meeting his "old friend" face-to-face.

"When did you happen to make these plans with him?" she asked slowly.

"Last night."

"But . . . but *when* last night? We're together *all* the time."

"I know. Cozy, isn't it?" He was quiet for a moment. "It doesn't matter when. The fact is, the plans are made and I probably should have told you earlier, but I didn't."

It was like a puzzle she didn't have all the pieces for. "You're keeping things from me, aren't you?"

"Nothing major."

Oh, that was comforting. "So, at some time last night you talked to him? This old friend of yours?"

"Sort of."

"Sort of? What's that supposed to mean?"

A man walked past Eden on the way to the restrooms, and he looked at her strangely as she stood talking to herself like a crazy person. At the moment, she didn't really care.

There was silence from the demon for way too long. And then, "Just get us out of here, and we'll discuss this matter privately."

She searched her memory from last night. He'd possessed her at sunset like usual. They'd come to the club. They'd left the club in a hurry. She'd gone to bed. That was all that had happened.

Then she had a thought. "What are you doing? Stealing my body when I'm asleep?"

Darrak didn't reply to that. She'd hoped for laughter at how ludicrous that theory was, especially since she'd only been joking.

She struggled to breathe. "No way. That's impossible."

"I can't help that you're a good guesser."

She gasped. "Oh, my God! You're stealing my body at night!"

Two women on their way to the dance floor gave her a wide berth as they passed and exchanged a look.

"*Stealing* is such a harsh word," Darrak said. "*Borrowing* is much more pleasant, really."

Eden practically kicked the door open and emerged into the cold night air, ignoring the steady succession of strange looks she was now receiving from anyone she passed. She was livid. There hadn't been many moments in her life when she'd felt this level of rage before. She felt ready to burst wide open. A tingling electricity coursed down her arms and into her hands. It crackled against her skin.

"Eden, you have to calm down," Darrak said with concern. "Anger makes the black magic come to the surface. You know that."

"Shut the hell up."

However, she couldn't argue with him. Sharp fluctuations in mood caused the magic to begin to spark inside her, ready to be channeled into destroying something. She *wanted* to destroy something. And his name began with the letter *D*.

Darrak borrowed her body when she was sleeping.

She'd trusted him and this is how he repaid her?

"It had to be done," he explained.

"It had to be done, huh?"

He hissed out a sigh of frustration. "I had to find out what he wanted, and I didn't want you to get hurt."

"You didn't want me to get hurt."

"You're repeating everything I'm saying. You must be pissed."

"Just trying to wrap my head around this. You didn't want me to get hurt. But you borrowed my body. If your old buddy had been so inclined to rip out my throat, how would that not be hurting me?"

"I can handle Theo," he said simply.

"Theo? Great. Your demonic BFF is named for one of the Cosby kids."

She'd never felt so violated. And it wasn't just that. It was the trust issue, already shaky after what had happened with Ben. She'd been a fool to trust an archdemon. Damn it. She felt so stupid.

And she'd thought Stanley and his lust elixir had been bad. Still was. But this felt much, much worse.

"Theo can help us," Darrak said firmly. "He's willing to help us. I explained everything to him."

She took a deep breath and let it out slowly as his words managed to sink in. "Keep talking."

"All I know for sure right now is he promised to do everything in his power to help break my curse. And when Theo says he's going to do something, he gets it done. He's very resourceful."

Eden rolled her eyes. "I think Stanley just filled me in on how resourceful demons can be when they want something. All that's left is a red smudge to scrape up off the pavement. I'd prefer not to become a red smudge."

"You won't."

"Because you're looking out for me?" It didn't sound particularly sincere.

"I'm not claiming to be perfect, Eden. But I am trying to make solid decisions here."

"You're trying, all right." Her anger had come down from a boil to a steady simmer.

She stood at the edge of the parking lot now. Eden's car was a few rows in. She felt in her purse for her keys.

"Hey, Eden!" a familiar voice called out to her.

She turned and was shocked to see Ben approaching her. He was with a pretty woman with waist-length blonde hair. She wore a tight blue dress.

"We need to go," Darrak said warily. "We don't need any more confrontations with golden boy today."

So insightful, that demon. Really helpful internal monologue.

"What do you want?" she asked sharply. Perhaps that would be the first thing she always said to Ben from now on. Given their history it seemed appropriate.

"You're better," he said, looking relieved. "I'm glad. I was worried after . . . after this morning."

He took a step toward her, and she moved away from him.

"You didn't answer my question," she said firmly. "What do you want? Are you following me?"

He glanced at his companion, then back at Eden. "I said some things today that I regret. I wanted to apologize."

Her shoulders relaxed a little. "Apology cautiously accepted."

Ben smiled. He did look great when he smiled.

Residue of her earlier stress still tingled under her skin, but she tried to push it away. The evening had been a bust with Stanley. She'd learned some unpleasant things about what Darrak did when she was asleep. But at least Ben seemed to have himself together again. It was a strange relief.

"I don't feel good about this," Darrak said. "I sense something strange, but I'm not sure what it is."

Ben nodded at his date. "This is Sandy. Sandy, this is Eden."

Eden's eyes shifted to the woman.

"Nice to meet you, Sandy," she said.

"You, too," Sandy replied, smiling. She drew closer and extended her hand.

Eden reached out to shake it.

"No, Eden—" Darrak's voice turned panicked. "Don't touch her. She's a wi—"

But it was too late. Sandy's fingers wrapped around Eden's and an ice-cold wave rippled through her body. Darrak's presence disappeared like a lamp had been flicked off, leaving only a dark room behind.

Her eyes widened as she looked down at the blonde's hand. The red stone set into the ring on her index finger glowed.

"What—?" she managed before the woman let go of her hand. "Ben, what the hell's going on here?"

Ben cleared his throat. His arms were crossed firmly over his chest. "Sandy's a witch. And she just dampened your inner demon. Hope you don't mind. He'll just get in the way of what we need to do right now."

Eden could barely speak, she was so shocked. "But—but why are you—?"

Before she could say another word, Ben had moved toward her with something in his hand. A syringe. She felt a sharp pain as he jabbed the needle into her upper arm and injected her with the contents.

His expression was grim.

Immediately, the world began to darken at the edges.

"I'm sorry it has to be like this," he whispered. "But . . . I said I'd help you, and I meant it."

A moment later, the world disappeared completely.

⇉ NINE ⇇

"Hand me the smelling salts."

Eden heard the voice as if it was a long way away. The next moment, a sharp, pungent scent assaulted her nostrils, and she gasped, her eyes snapping wide open. She was in an unfamiliar living room seated on a leather sofa.

"Eden." She felt a warm hand on her arm, and she looked to her left, where Ben sat next to her. Sandy stood a few feet away with her arms crossed over her chest. "Please, don't panic."

Eden licked her dry lips, her thoughts cloudy and jumbled. "Give me one good reason why I shouldn't." Her voice croaked as if she'd been unconscious for a while.

"I want to help you."

"You have a funny way of showing it." Her throat hurt and anger and confusion flowed inside her. "Tranquilizers and kidnapping aren't exactly things that sound very helpful."

Eden tried to sense Darrak's presence, but there was nothing there. Was he okay? Had the witch hurt him? The thought filled her with fear. Only moments before she'd been wishing he was gone forever, and now she was desperately concerned that he'd been harmed.

"What were you doing at Luxuria tonight?" Ben asked.

"None of your damn business. Where the hell am I?" The longer she was conscious, the more the fog was lifting, and the more pissed off she was getting.

"My place," Ben said.

"As a cop, you should know kidnapping is a crime."

"I wish there was another way. But you're not thinking straight right now."

"I'm thinking fine."

"You're possessed by a demon," Sandy said.

Another worrying reminder that Darrak was currently AWOL.

"What did you do to him?" Eden snapped.

"Exactly what Ben told you I did. I dampened him."

Eden quickly scanned her surroundings. It was exactly the kind of house she would have expected Ben to own. Empty. The few pieces of furniture were practical. Hardwood flooring, cream-colored walls. There were no paintings or knickknacks to clutter things up or add some well-needed warmth. No framed pictures, either. However, he did have a wide-screen television with an Xbox hooked up to it. So Ben wasn't *all* business.

There was sweat on the witch's brow. The room was too cool to account for that. Eden guessed she was concentrating on keeping Darrak's presence dampened.

"Hard work?" Eden asked dryly.

Sandy gave her a tight smile. "For a good cause, hard work is worthwhile."

"And what cause would that be?" Eden glared at the both of them in turn. The black sofa was hard, with no give, and smelled new. The leather squeaked as she tried to move.

"Saving your life," Ben said.

"I didn't ask for your help."

"Which is exactly why we had to take extreme measures." Ben stood up and paced the length of the living room, his brow furrowed. "I saw that thing, Eden. It's horrible and it's destroying you."

"You don't know anything about this."

"And yet you defend it. And you *slept* with it, too?" His lips curled with disgust.

Eden repressed a grimace. "First of all, he's not an *it*, he's a *he*, and his name is Darrak. Second of all, what I do with my life or my body is none of your damn business."

"Did he force you?" he persisted. "Was it rape?"

"No," she said firmly. He gave her a sour look. "Would you prefer me to say it was?"

"I just don't understand how you could let a demon touch you."

"I think it's obvious that you don't understand."

His jaw set. "You know the way he looks in human form isn't who he really is, right? It's a trap. A way to get women like you to trust him, to defend him like this."

"Women like me?" Eden repeated. "What exactly is that supposed to mean?"

"Women who would risk their own lives to help him. Demons are deceitful and will do anything in their power to manipulate the free will of others."

She wasn't stupid. She understood why Ben was having trouble with this. Like he said, Darrak was a demon. And Ben had seen him in his demon form. Not exactly rainbows and happy faces there.

Did he think she'd simply been seduced by a good-looking man with a bit of a dark side?

She wasn't *that* easy. Her trust wasn't totally blind. There were still many questions she had about Darrak, and she was certain she wouldn't be happy with all the answers.

Despite her doubts and worries, Eden believed Darrak was good, and Ben believed him to be evil.

One of them was right.

"So the demon can take solid form during daylight hours?" Sandy mused aloud. "I've never heard of that kind of possession before."

"What kind of a witch are you?" Eden asked sharply, turning her attention from the frustrating cop to the blonde.

"A gray witch."

Eden had heard of black and white—evil and good—but she hadn't heard of gray before. "So that means you can do both black and white magic?"

"Yes. But I only delve into the darker arts when it's for a good cause."

"Doesn't using black magic damage your soul?"

Sandy wasn't wearing an amulet like Eden's. She was surprised the witch hadn't noticed it. Eden's dress was too low cut to hide anything tonight. Maybe it wasn't common knowledge that amulets like the one she wore helped pinpoint who's who in the world of black witches.

The witch shook her head. "My magic was born in me and developed over time, so my soul remains untouched. My black magic isn't as strong as my white, but for the *Malleus*, I'll be whatever they need me to be."

"The *Malleus*?" Eden recognized that name and it scared her. It was a group that had existed for centuries to combat the darkness that seeped into the human world. The slayers and executioners of the supernatural—of witches and demons and other things that went bump in the night. Eden could see how they could serve a purpose to fight against true evil. But she knew the Malleus had also been instrumental during the Salem witch trials. They'd tortured and put to death a great many innocent men and women all in the name of good versus evil.

There was a knock at the door.

"Who's here?" Eden asked, panic welling inside her again.

"Just relax," Ben told her. "It's somebody who can help you."

"I don't want your help." She fought to stand, but a wave of magic pressed her farther back into the sofa. Sandy was keeping her magically restrained.

Ben went to the door and returned with a short man who wore glasses. His hair was white. He looked like somebody's grandfather.

"Eden Riley," he said, sitting down on the edge of the coffee table in front of her. "It's a pleasure to meet you."

She regarded him tensely. "Who are you?"

"I'm Oliver Gale. I represent the Malleus organization, and I wanted to meet you personally."

Eden's gaze flicked to Ben, who stood next to Oliver. Ben had rolled up his sleeves and for the first time she noticed the raw-looking wound on his inner forearm. It was a brand of a fleur-de-lis enclosed in a circle.

She gasped in shock. "Ben! You're part of the Malleus now?"

Ben opened his mouth to answer, but Oliver spoke first. "He is. We're very happy to welcome Ben into our ranks."

She was stunned by this, and it made her feel sick to her stomach. She'd thought Ben was one of her lesser problems to deal with, but she'd been wrong.

Oliver studied her carefully. "I'm told you're infected with a demon, Eden."

She opened her mouth to deny it, but she knew it would be in vain. "You make it sound like I have a virus."

He continued to study her. "On a basic level, it's very similar. A parasitic entity that requires a host in order to survive. Something that will poison your body and make you very ill." He cocked his head to the side. "Tell me about your demon. *Darrak* is it?"

She pressed her lips together and shot a look at Ben.

"It's okay," Ben said confidently. "Oliver's here to help you."

She had a hard time believing that.

"Why would you join the Malleus, Ben?" she asked, not liking how weak her voice sounded.

He looked down at his brand and stroked his fingers over the healing wound. "I can help people, even more than I could being with the police."

"Even if they don't want your help. Like me."

His jaw tightened. "Sometimes the people who need help the most are the ones who resist the hardest. Like you."

Damn his sincerity.

She struggled to breathe and make sense of this. She'd been told the Malleus were bad. She'd also witnessed a power-hungry Malleus member try to take Darrak away from her and use his power for her own gain. But maybe it was a case of one rotten apple spoiling the bunch. Oliver seemed legitimately concerned. Ben was definitely worried about her safety. And Sandy was completely willing to dip into her natural-born darker magic in order to help out.

That didn't sound like a triad of evil to her.

"He was cursed," Eden said simply, deciding to be helpful instead of continuing to resist. It could make all the difference in the world.

"Your demon?" Oliver replied.

She nodded. "A long time ago a witch cast a death curse on him, but it only destroyed his body. We're searching for a way to break that curse so he'll be whole again and won't need to rely on me or anyone else for survival."

"How long has he been cursed?"

"Over three hundred years."

"Do you know his true name?"

"No," she said. But she did. It was *Darrakayiis*, but to give that information to anyone else would give them power over him, which is why Darrak went by the short form. Plus, it was much easier to pronounce properly.

"She's lying," Ben said. "I heard her use his true name before."

She sent a fierce look his way. He couldn't be less help-ful if he tried.

"And what is it?" Oliver asked.

Ben frowned. "I don't remember. At—at the time I didn't think it was important."

Eden noticed the clock on the wall for the first time and was surprised to see it was after three a.m. She'd been un-conscious for more than five hours. She had to get out of here. Even if their goal was to help her, they'd drugged and kidnapped her, and that wasn't right. She was at a distinct disadvantage. They had all the power, and she was feeling like a victim who didn't have any say in what was going to happen next.

She shivered.

"Tell me about the pain, Eden," Oliver said.

She looked at him with surprise. "What?"

"Ben told me what happened earlier today. Was it a tear-ing sensation? Did it feel as though you were being pulled in two different directions?"

She threw another fierce look at Ben, who'd obviously told his new boss everything he knew about her.

He didn't flinch. "You were in a bad way this morning. I thought you were dying."

Eden exhaled shakily. She never wanted to feel pain like that again if she could do anything to prevent it. "Yeah. It was a tearing pain. Really bad. How do you know how it felt?"

Oliver crossed his arms. "Tell me about your father, Eden."

That question seemed to come out of left field. She in-haled deeply and let it out slowly. "I never knew him. He was just some random guy my mother hooked up with."

"Your mother, Caroline Riley. She's recently deceased?"

Eden hesitated a moment before she answered. "She died two months ago. She fell down a flight of stairs at a casino in Las Vegas and broke her neck." Her throat thickened without warning. The grief at losing her mother came in patches, always unexpected and never appreciated.

"And she never told you about your father?"

"Nothing other than the fact that she met him when he was hitchhiking, they had a wild affair over one weekend, and that was that."

"Did she see him again?"

"No. But once when I was about five years old, he came by for a quick visit when I was playing in the backyard. That was the only time I ever saw him."

Why was she answering his questions so willingly? A glance at Sandy showed the witch's thin eyebrows were drawn together to show the strain of her fierce concentration.

Then it dawned on her. Eden was being forced magically to tell the truth. The thought only made her angrier, which helped to push away some of the fear that filled her.

"So you don't know who he really was," Oliver continued.

"No."

"Just tell her," Ben said tightly. "Eden needs to know the truth about her father."

"What about my father?" she demanded.

Oliver crossed his arms and leaned closer, looking into her eyes. "Your mother never knew who she met that night on the road. Daniel was finishing his stay here in the human world as a Cerberus. Do you know what a Cerberus is?"

"I'm not sure." The word sounded familiar. Maybe she'd heard it in one of her paranormal tutorials from Darrak.

"It's a guardian sent here from Heaven to watch over the gateways to the Netherworld," Oliver explained.

"Cerberus," she said. Like the three-headed dog of Greek mythology who guarded the entrance to Hades. "And my father was one of these guardians?"

"Yes." Oliver smiled. "Your father is an angel."

⇾ TEN ⇽

That was funny. Eden could have sworn that he'd just said her father was an angel.

Obviously she'd misheard him.

"I'm sorry," she said after a long moment of silence. "But could you repeat that?"

"Your father is an angel."

Maybe she hadn't misheard him.

She laughed nervously. "That's impossible."

"It's true," Ben said very seriously. "You're part angel. The proper term is *nephilim* . . . and it's very rare."

Eden gaped at him. She felt cold and pale as if all the blood had drained from her face. "How do you know all this?"

He shifted his feet, his hands clasped in front of him. "I've been studying up."

"I'm part angel," she repeated. It sounded completely and totally ludicrous.

"You're mostly human," Ben told her. "But there is a part of you that is . . . Other."

Her head was spinning out of control and she had the urge to throw up, but instead she pressed back farther into the hard leather and just tried to breathe.

Oliver reached for her hand and squeezed it reassuringly. "There is a ribbon of celestial energy inside of you. We think this is what the demon has been drawing energy from. And this, Eden, this is what is causing your complications."

She needed a time-out. A chance to get her head together. It was one thing to accept that Darrak had been dampened and Ben had drugged and kidnapped her. But it was another thing to be told her mother had a fling with a being from Heaven.

Her mother had been touched by an angel? Like, literally?

She finally had her answer. *This* was why she could hear Darrak when none of his other hosts could. *This* was why he could take form during the day. It was because she was human enough to be his host, just not *completely* human. She had a hidden bonus.

She finally heard what Oliver had said. "What do you mean by my complications?"

"The pain you've begun to feel—it's a war within your body, Eden. The darkness from the demon is fighting against the light from your nephilim side. Each is trying to claim dominion."

It was quiet then, enough for her to hear her rapid breathing. Her upper arm still ached from where Ben had stuck the needle earlier, and she tenderly rubbed the spot. She felt cold and stunned and confused and very afraid by all of this. "So you're saying that good and evil are playing tug-of-war, using my body as the rope?"

Oliver's gaze was serious. "Yes."

She already knew she was in deep trouble just by being possessed by Darrak. This definitely upped the ante. While everything she'd been told had come as a shock, it was as if these were pieces to the puzzle she'd been trying to put together for a very long time.

Ben stood a few feet away with his hands clasped behind his back like a guard. Sandy remained seated in a chair across from the sofa, watching Eden and Oliver's conversation carefully. Eden suddenly felt incredibly tired, and her head ached.

"I can help you," Oliver said. "But you need to let me. Will you do that?"

She looked at his kind face. Her first reaction had been mistrust, but now she wasn't so sure. Maybe the Malleus could help her. Maybe Oliver could help her right now.

"I . . .guess so," she agreed, tentatively.

"Very good. Now, I must concentrate." He closed his eyes, and a moment later Eden felt a strange sensation, as if something was searching her with cool, invisible fingers. She tried to sit very still.

Oliver's brow furrowed. "There's a shield over you." He looked over at Sandy. "Come here, please."

Sandy did as he asked. "Yes?"

"I'm having trouble sensing the demon. All you did was dampen him, right? You didn't exorcise him completely, did you?"

Panic shot through Eden at the thought. No, Darrak couldn't have been exorcised. She would have felt it. She would have known.

"No, it was just a dampening," Sandy confirmed.

Oliver peered at Eden's face. He stood up and pressed his hand against her forehead. "There's a strange energy coming from her. Please figure out what it is before I continue."

Eden's gaze flicked to Ben, and he nodded and gave her a small smile. "I told you everything would be okay."

That remained to be seen, but she was feeling cautiously— *very* cautiously—optimistic. This was much better than trusting Darrak's demonic friend to lend a hand. The Malleus was a strong organization of supernatural experts. This was the better solution.

Still, she felt nervous.

Sandy's cool hand replaced Oliver's against her forehead.

"Can you hear me?" Sandy's voice was suddenly in her head. Her lips didn't move.

Telepathy? Eden's gaze moved to her with surprise. *"I can hear you."*

"You're a black witch. I sensed it before and I shielded it from Oliver, but the shield is starting to slip."

This worried her. Eden's attention flicked to Oliver who was waiting with his arms crossed over his chest, then back to the witch. *"Why would you shield it from him?"*

"Because he'll kill you when he finds out."

Her eyes bugged. *"What?"*

"Malleus policy. Black witches are executed immediately upon their discovery."

Cold fear slid through her. *"He said he wanted to help me."*

"He lied. It's that demon inside you he's really after. He wants to see what possessing a nephilim does to a demon. You need to escape."

Eden struggled to breathe. *"And then what?"*

"Place wards around your home so you'll be protected from those who mean you harm."

"How do I put up wards?"

"You're a smart girl. You'll figure it out." Sandy smiled grimly. *"By the way, sorry about what I have to do right now."*

"What?"

"She's a black witch," Sandy said aloud. "She was trying to shield it from us."

Great. Eden's stomach dropped right down to the ground, and the fear she'd felt earlier returned in full force. So much for thinking she'd found an ally in the other witch.

A hand clamped down over her throat before she could move an inch. Oliver had moved in quickly. The warmth in his gaze had been replaced by ice. "I would have thought a nephilim filled with black magic was impossible. She's more dangerous than I thought, especially with that demon inside of her."

Eden grabbed his wrist, but the man was inhumanly strong. "Take your damn hands off me, you bastard. Ben, help me!"

Ben stood with his fists clenched at his sides. "Oliver, let her go. You said she wouldn't be harmed."

"That was before I learned she was a black witch." Oliver's head twisted to the side. "Come here and hold her still. Do it."

Ben grabbed Eden's arms and pulled her off the sofa to hold her firmly in place in front of him.

"What are you doing?" she managed, trying to look at him over her shoulder. His fingers dug painfully into her skin.

"I don't seem to have a choice," Ben said, his voice strained. "I have to do what he says."

Eden gasped when she felt the bite of cold, sharp steel against her throat. Oliver held a dagger there. Her gaze went to Sandy. The witch's gaze held fear for Eden, but she made no move to help.

"I'm sorry it had to come to this so quickly," Oliver said. Panic sliced through her as she felt a warm trickle of blood run down her throat. "I don't want to destroy a nephilim— such a rare, special creature. But you're a black witch, so I have no choice. Earlier I wasn't sure how to extract the demon without hurting you. With your death it won't be an issue."

He wasn't joking. He was going to kill her. She had seconds left. Her rapidly beating heart would soon stop forever.

"I'm so sorry, Eden." Ben's voice caught on the words, but his grip didn't lessen for a moment.

Ben had wanted to help her. Would he feel guilty for

holding her in place while another man slit her throat? Or would he be able to justify it to himself as another case of good triumphing over evil?

"You're making a huge mistake," she managed to say.

Oliver shook his head. "I don't make mistakes. I make decisions, and they are always the right ones."

He moved to slash her throat and a scream caught in her chest, but the knife froze in midair before it made contact. For a split second, Eden thought it was Sandy coming to her rescue. But it wasn't Sandy.

It was *her*.

Eden's skin tingled and something that felt like electricity moved down her arms and into her hands.

It was her black magic.

Oliver gripped the blade tighter and arched it toward her again. The rage that had been simmering inside Eden until now rose completely to the surface, and she gave in to it since she had no other choice. With a mere thought she was able to pull the dagger from Oliver's grasp and launch it across the room where it embedded itself into the wall.

Eden's mind cleared of all the fear and pain and panic she'd felt before as she opened herself to her magic. She didn't want to die. They'd left her with no choice but to tap into the very thing she'd promised never to use again.

Her soul was in jeopardy. But, at the moment, her life came first.

"Kill her *now*," Oliver snarled. He was instructing Ben.

Without hesitation, Ben's hands went around her throat from behind, and he began to squeeze. He was very strong, and it didn't take long before Eden began to see spots before her eyes as he choked her.

"I'm so sorry, Eden. I never meant for this to happen." His voice was hoarse with pain.

"I'm sorry, too." She grasped more of her magic and launched him backward. She spun on her heels just in time to see him hit the wall hard and slide down to the ground unconscious.

Her eyes widened at what she'd done so easily, but any guilt disappeared as quickly as it arrived. The more she used the black magic, the more her anger increased, like a huge, rolling wave ready to crash into the shore. She really wanted to destroy something—channel this energy that was growing inside of her with every passing moment. She knew she could level this entire house with a well-placed thought.

Hopefully Ben had a good insurance policy.

She turned to check where Oliver was, only to receive a backhanded slap across her face that sent pain skittering through her.

"Ow." She glared at him. "That's no way to win friends and influence people."

"Witch"—he'd retrieved the knife and had it in his grip again—"I will end you."

She cocked her head to the side. "And here I thought we were going to be buddies."

His teeth were clenched. "Black magic will destroy you."

"But not if you get me first, right?"

"I can help you," he said, raising the blade. "This is the only way."

"The only way you can help me is to kill me? Sure, that made heaps of sense, you sanctimonious prick."

When Oliver lunged at her, a ripple of magic exited her and wrapped him up in dark light. It raised him up off the floor, and he hovered in the air for a moment. The fear in his eyes made it clear that he thought she would kill him.

Why should she care about his life? He'd nearly ended hers. And he would have, if she hadn't tapped into her shiny black magic.

Her stomach twinged with pain from using her magic this time, but it wasn't anything she couldn't handle. A couple Midols would take care of these cramps.

"Come near me or Darrak again and I'll kill you. Understand me?" Her voice, just like her body at the moment, was filled with darkness.

Oliver nodded. "Yes."

Another focused magical thought from her and Oliver's eyes rolled back into his head. He dropped to the ground unconscious.

Eden cast a dark look at Sandy, who'd crawled away from them into the corner.

"Thanks for the head's-up," Eden said.

Sandy just nodded, her eyes filled with fear and apprehension.

Eden left the house, and the black magic continued to swirl around her. Her heart pounded hard, and the rage she felt earlier wasn't in any hurry to leave.

It scared her. And it also . . . excited her.

"Darrak. Are you there?" she asked quietly.

He didn't respond, but she could feel him under layer after layer of dampening.

Her head felt foggy, cloudy, dazed. She didn't remember how exactly she got home, but suddenly she was there. Her body trembled. The black magic continued to spark through her, but she felt drained, like an empty glass waiting to be filled.

She let out a shaky breath and looked up at her apartment building through the darkness. Sandy said she'd know how to put up wards. She did. With the magic flowing freely it was easier than she ever would have imagined.

She waved her hand through the air and turned slowly around in a circle.

North, south, east, west. No one shall enter this place who wishes deadly harm to me.

The area shimmered for a moment before going dark again to indicate that the wards were set.

Eden raised her eyebrows with surprise. *Well, that was easy.*

She barely remember traveling up in the elevator. The door to her apartment opened smoothly in front of her. No key required.

Home sweet home.

The black cat curled on her sofa stood up, stretched, and looked at her curiously.

"Hi, Leena," she said hollowly, and her throat felt tight.

The cat tilted its head, as if questioning her strange mood.

Despite everything, despite her worries about using her black magic and what it was doing to her soul, she felt . . . good. The more she used her power, the better she felt. The stronger she felt. She didn't want anyone to be able to harm her or Darrak again. Using her black magic had ensured that. She'd escaped. She'd lived.

Thanks to the magic she wasn't supposed to use.

The thought didn't make her feel the least bit guilty now, but she was weakened from using it. She needed more power and she needed it now.

Nosy chaperone shapeshifters would only get in the way.

"Go back to sleep, Leena." Eden flicked a finger in the cat's direction. The cat lay down and went back to sleep, no questions asked.

Good.

Eden walked into her bedroom and touched her chest. "Darrak, I need you. Right now."

She needed him. She wanted him. And she would have him.

Clarity was a wonderful thing.

Being dampened wasn't fun.

Especially not when Darrak desperately wanted to know what was happening. It was as if he was held prone and covered by a thousand heavy blankets. Suffocating and impossible to move no matter how hard he struggled.

Golden boy was up to no good. He could see that coming from a mile away. However, he hadn't seen this. So what had happened? Ben got a witch to dampen Darrak so he could talk some sense into Eden without Darrak being around?

Was Eden at risk? Would Ben hurt her?

He didn't think so, but he wasn't certain.

The thought was driving him insane.

Maybe he'd stepped over the line by borrowing her body. Maybe she'd finally see the light and want to get rid of him once and for all.

She had been pissed.

He ignored the twinge of guilt he felt. Seeing Theo had been vital. Not telling Eden about it had been . . . well, also vital. The woman could be stubborn.

What was happening? Damn it. He hated being power-less like this.

Hanging out down here in the dampening darkness, he couldn't do anything but wait and try to remain calm.

There was a time when it would have been much harder to keep him down. Back when he was a full-power arch-demon ready to lay waste to the human world as a fun Fri-day guys' night out with Theo.

The good old days. Weren't they? He wasn't sure any-more; the memories were a bit unclear. But back then at least he knew no one could have defeated him this easily.

Just a little, common witch—not even a full black magic practitioner—was able to bring him to his knees tonight. It was embarrassing.

Eden, he thought. *Please be okay.*

Worrying wasn't very demonic of him, but he really couldn't help it. Stupid humanity.

He didn't know how long it had been before he felt something—saw something. It was as if a hand had been held out to him. Not a literal hand, but . . . it was there.

He grabbed hold of it.

Then, before he could figure out what was happening, he was pulled at lightning speed up through the layers of dampening. He felt the cold air as he exited Eden's body, and then he concentrated on taking form. It was instinctual but it still required effort. He clothed himself as he became corporeal.

Eden stood in front of him.

He felt an immediate and almost overwhelming wave of relief at the sight of her.

"What the—?" He looked at his hands, his eyes wide. "Eden . . . what happened?"

"I did it," she said. "I wasn't sure I could."

He came toward her and took her face between his hands, his brow furrowed. "Are you okay?"

"Very much so."

"Ben . . . he was with a witch."

"Old news."

Her hair felt so soft and silky that he couldn't help but slide his fingers through it. "Where are they now?"

"They're gone. I took care of them."

"What time is it?" he asked.

"Quarter after four."

He frowned at that. "But . . . it's not even sunrise yet."

"No."

"Then how . . ." He blinked, then looked around to see that they were in Eden's apartment, in her bedroom. "How is this possible? What happened?"

"Ben's working for the Malleus now. He introduced me to his boss. His boss tried to kill me. I escaped. That's a quick overview."

Darrak shook his head, confused. "What?"

Eden took his hand in hers and brushed her lips against it. He drew in a sharp breath. She wasn't acting like someone who'd just survived a murder attempt. "Eden . . . what did you do to escape?"

She slid her hands up over his chest, her expression serene. "What I had to do."

It felt good when Eden touched him like this. Too good. She didn't do it very often—at least not when she was awake. What did this mean?

Oh, no.

He grasped hold of her amulet and looked at it closely, then swore under his breath.

It was a shade darker, just like he'd thought it would be.

"You used your magic," he said.

"I had no choice."

"You shouldn't have—"

But then he couldn't speak again because she kissed him.

⇀ eleven ↚

Darrak hadn't tasted her for much too long. A brush of her lips against his when she was asleep and dreaming wasn't nearly the same and not nearly as good. Eden managed to make him as weak as a human male with only a kiss. When her mouth was on his, he lost the ability to think.

"I want you, Darrak," she whispered, as their lips parted and her mouth moved over his jaw to his throat. Her hands slid up under his shirt, fingernails sensually scratching his skin as she pulled the material higher.

He was about to comment, but her tongue swirled over his left nipple and he had to struggle to remain standing.

Underrated, male nipples were—even the ones belonging to demons. Very underrated.

Eden pushed him backward until he hit the edge of the bed and sat down. Her hands went to the waistband of his pants, and she very effectively undid the top button and slid the black jeans over his hips, then kissed a hot line down his chest and abdomen. She didn't stop there.

He swore harshly. "Eden—"

This wasn't right. She wasn't thinking straight.

They couldn't do this.

Or . . . well, maybe they could.

No. No, they couldn't.

She'd used her magic to escape from Ben. The cop had threatened Eden, and she'd had to use black magic to get away. That powerful magic was still flowing freely through Eden's body. It allowed her to summon him before he was normally able to take form. Now it had condensed and changed into this . . . this *need*.

Black witches and sex magic went hand in hand, after all. It was how the other witch, Selina, had managed to take Darrak's power and force him to make her into a black witch three hundred years ago. Each time they'd been together she'd become more powerful.

And her soul had become more damaged.

It was the only thought keeping him from losing his mind and taking Eden right now.

Because he really, *really* wanted to.

Demons typically gave in to their carnal needs. It was kind of in their nature.

"Eden . . . please . . ." Darrak managed as she worked her way back up his body and kissed his mouth again—and yes, he kissed her back. He couldn't help it. There was such deep desire in her eyes. For him. This would normally please him very much, but at the moment he couldn't help but be scared by it. Scared for her.

This was a side effect of using her black magic. It instinctually drove her toward seeking more power. This was how she'd get it. If they were together again like this, it would take her deeper into the darkness; it would sacrifice more of her soul.

He just wished he was stronger right now. Not only physically, but mentally. But the more she touched him, kissed him, the weaker he got.

It was a single thought that stopped him from ripping off her dress and burying himself deep inside of her:

Leena was right.

He loved Eden.

Whether or not it was real or if it would last once his curse was broken was another thing. He loved her.

And he didn't want her soul to be damned.

Okay, it was more than a single thought. But it was all connected.

"Eden, uh . . . stop this right . . . right now." He really wished he could sound more convincing.

"Darrak, please, I want you." She pushed him back onto the bed and straddled his extremely aroused body.

Damn her mouth and her hands. They were not making this easy for him.

He caught her wrists in his grip, flipped her over, and pinned her down against the bed.

She smiled wickedly up at him. "That's more like it," she purred.

And he thought only Lucifer knew how to torture him? Wrong, so very wrong.

She wanted him. Would it really be so bad?

A few minutes of pure pleasure—

In return for her immortal soul bound for the pit for all eternity. He was a demon but he refused to be the one to damn her more than she already was.

Still. He couldn't honestly say he wasn't tempted. He wasn't that altruistic.

"Eden." He said her name harshly. "I know it's always been hard for you to keep your hands off me, but you need to snap out of this right now."

He forced himself to reconjure clothes that worked as a minor barrier between his body and hers. Didn't help much but it was something. She really didn't know how to take no for an answer and held tightly to him as he tried to push her away. Then he shakily got up from the bed, quickly moved to the bathroom, and poured a glass of water, which he brought back to her.

Eden crawled toward him on the bed, her eyes bright green and following his every move like a predator.

"Please, Darrak. I know you want me."

"You couldn't be more right about that."

Her hands moved up his legs to his chest again. She pressed her mouth against the fabric of his T-shirt. "Please make love to me."

Darrak gritted his teeth and forced himself to ignore her touch and the tempting invitation. "I brought this for you."

She looked at the glass of water. "But I'm not thirsty."

"It's not to drink."

He threw the cold water in her face.

Eden sputtered and wiped her eyes. "Darrak!"

"I didn't want to have to slap you. This is a little wetter but still effective. I hope."

Her eyes widened little by little as clarity came into her gaze. "Oh, shit."

"That's exactly what I was thinking."

She touched her lips as if remembering all the places they'd traveled in the last few minutes. "Oh, *shit*."

"Right. Well, don't worry, it's over."

"Took you long enough to stop me."

"Don't blame me that you can't keep your hands, or mouth, off me."

Eden fell back onto the bed and clamped a pillow over her face. "Oh, my God!" came the muffled pronouncement.

Embarrassment? Regret? Disgust? He wasn't exactly sure. But whatever she was feeling, she now seemed to be trying to smother the memory right out of herself.

He grabbed the pillow and pulled it away. She looked up at him with worry.

Darrak really hated himself for having these very inconvenient feelings for this woman before him. He wished they'd go away and never come back. He didn't like feeling so human around her, moving quickly between concern and desire. But he couldn't help the fact that he liked being with her, being close to her. He liked how she smelled, how she tasted, how she felt.

Was Theo right? Was what he felt for her only an illusion? Was this unfamiliar emotion that had burrowed deep into his chest a fleeting thing? Because of that emotion he'd single-handedly destroyed her life, and there wasn't a whole hell of a lot he could do about it now. All he could do was try to prevent further damage any way he could.

And he was not even slightly amused by the flush that had come into her cheeks as she realized that she'd very thoroughly molested him before getting a glass of water thrown in her face for her troubles. Well, maybe a *little* amused.

Something seemed wrong with this scenario when the water thrower was an ex-incubus.

In all his existence he'd never felt this way before. For anyone. To put it mildly, it was very inconvenient.

Luckily, if nothing else, she didn't feel the same for him. She might feel a strange affection for the demon who'd ruined her life, maybe a bit of lust—or *a lot* depending on the day—but Eden *didn't* love him.

It was a relief, actually. Her saving grace. It made things much easier.

"You need to rid yourself of any remaining black magic right now," Darrak said. "Try to concentrate. Can you do that?"

She nodded and closed her eyes.

The next moment all the magic that filled the room left in a rush. The glass he held fell to the carpeted floor as pain swept over him and he rapidly lost solid form again. It was only Eden's powerful magic that helped him attain that form during dark hours. Before he could say another word, his body turned to black smoke. He suddenly felt desperate to find shelter. In this form he was very susceptible, as close to true death as a demon could get, apart from being on the receiving end of an exorcism. He didn't even make a conscious choice; he simply moved toward Eden as if attracted magnetically.

As he possessed her, she cringed and clutched at the bedsheets.

He hated hurting her. If nothing else, at least it was fast.

"We'll fix this," he said when he was able to communicate with her again.

"Oh, yeah?" she replied after a moment. "I think I've heard that line before."

"Theo will help us."

She exhaled shakily. "You're sure you trust him?"

"With my very existence. Which seems to be rather appropriate right about now."

"What if he can't help?" she asked.

"He will."

"But if he can't?" she persisted.

"Then we'll find another way."

"The eternal optimist."

"Who knew?" He was quiet for a moment. "I know I shouldn't have borrowed your body . . ."

"No, you shouldn't have."

"But I've decided I'm not sorry."

She tensed. "Not even a little?"

"I'm sorry you were so upset about it, but it had to be done and I stand by my decision."

"Let's just forget it."

"Really?"

"For now. It's been a long night."

"What the hell did Ben want from you, anyhow? Did he really want to kill you?" Anger and hatred flared inside him as he thought about the cop who'd put Eden's life at risk that night.

She hesitated. "No. He wanted to save me."

He wanted to ask her to clarify. It felt as if she was holding something back, but he didn't push her. "Doesn't sound like it to me."

"He means well. He's made some . . . bad decisions, but he means well."

Why was she still defending him? That didn't sit well with him. "A lot of men have done evil all in the name of good."

"Kind of preachy for a demon, aren't you?"

"You're right." He hesitated. "It's disturbing, actually."

It only confirmed what Theo said. Demons didn't preach right from wrong. Demons weren't "nice." They were powerful and dangerous opportunists. They were loyal to their own kind when it served them. Their own existence was of first priority to them, bar none.

Darrak wasn't nice. Hell, he didn't even want to *be* nice.

If Eden had met the pre-curse him face-to-face . . .

Well, she wouldn't have been trying to make love to him. She wouldn't feel remotely safe with him. And he wouldn't feel this overwhelming need to protect her, even from himself.

Darrak trusted Theo as much as one demon could trust another. But Theo had no artificial humanity to deal with like he did. And Theo was not remotely *nice* by any definition of the word.

For the chance to break his curse, Darrak had no choice but to take a risk and meet with him at noon and take Eden along for the ride. He couldn't say he wasn't worried about this.

Even though demons didn't worry. Or, at least, they shouldn't.

On the bright side, he'd never had souvlaki before. It sounded delicious.

Eden slept in until after nine o'clock. The alarm clock didn't go off. She assumed Darrak turned it off so she could recover from what had happened last night.

Last night.

Oh, boy.

Darrak was nowhere to be seen. She dragged herself out of bed and went to the bathroom, staring at her bleary-eyed reflection. She splashed some water on her face, then stared some more. Her gaze then fixed on her amulet.

Just like the circles under her eyes, it was significantly darker this morning.

Her hand shook as she drew a brush through her tangled hair. Her throat felt thick and her eyes were shiny. She wasn't going to cry. That would be a really wimpy thing to do.

Everything was going to be okay.

Even though Eden's soul had darkened from using her black magic again.

Even though someone had tried to kill her the moment they found out she was a black witch.

And that someone had been helped by Ben, a man she used to have a major crush on.

Also, she'd been unable to stop herself from jumping Darrak's bones, and he'd soundly rejected her by throwing a glass of water in her face. The particular memory made her face flush with embarrassment.

Oh, and she couldn't forget the news that her father was an angel.

Yeah. That little fact was still hard to wrap her head around.

Because of him, she had some sort of celestial energy inside of her fighting with her black magic and threatening to tear her into two separate and very pissed off pieces.

Did that cover it?

Her stomach lurched. Not painful this time. Just sick.

Eden had always wished for an exciting life. She really should have been more specific.

She forced herself to get ready for the day. She showered, dressed, and makeupped. She still had a glimmer of hope, and to this she clung desperately.

Unfortunately, that glimmer of hope was Darrak's friend Theo.

The glimmer of hope flickered like a match in a strong wind, threatening to plunge her into darkness at any given moment.

Finally, she went out to the kitchenette to find Darrak and Leena both waiting for her.

"Morning!" Leena said cheerily. She obviously didn't remember a thing from last night after being put back to sleep.

"Morning," Eden replied, trying to force a smile to her face. She failed.

Darrak eyed her warily. "How are you?"

She couldn't look him in the eyes. "I've been better."

"Listen, about last night—" he began.

"I don't want to talk about it." She didn't want to talk about anything from last night. In fact, she'd decided against telling Darrak what Oliver said regarding her father. Besides, she didn't know for sure if it was true or not.

"But—"

"No, Darrak." She went to the fridge and poured her daily glass of orange juice. Her queasy stomach protested, but she downed it anyhow.

"What happened last night?" Leena asked.

"Nothing."

She felt Darrak staring at her, but she didn't look at him.

The phone rang and she picked it up on the third ring.

"Eden," Andy greeted her cheerily. Why was everyone so damned cheery this morning? "Running a little late today?"

"Yeah. Sorry. I'll be in the office soon."

"No worries. You got through a ton of files yesterday, so we're all caught up. Take your time. Listen, I want you to join me for my cheating werewolf spouse stakeout. It'll be good for you to see a master investigator like me at work."

If nothing else, she was glad Andy was accepting the

recent paranormal infestation in his life and business so easily. Although, it was likely he was in the land of denial. She really wished she could join him there. It was a happy place.

"When?" she asked.

"Noon. I can swing by the office and pick you up."

That was when they were supposed to meet Theo the demon for Greek food.

"Can't, I'm afraid. I have an appointment scheduled."

"Is it important?"

"Vital." She flicked a glance at Darrak, and memories of the prior night flooded back to her. "Can you handle it okay on your own?"

"Oh, sure. All I'm doing is snapping some pictures. It won't be a problem. Just thought I'd offer. I'll touch base with you later, okay?"

"Okay. Good luck."

She hung up. Andy wanted her to learn the ropes of being a private investigator, and she had to admit, she'd started taking more of an interest in the business. She was naturally curious. Her case of the moment, although it wasn't an official one, was figuring out who killed Graham. She wished she had more time to devote to it.

It wouldn't be today, however. Her only priority was figuring out if Darrak's friend was really going to help them or if he was just blowing smoke.

Since he was a demon, the smoke blowing might be quite literal.

"I feel like something's going on that you two aren't telling me," Leena said. "If you tell me, I might be able to help out a bit more."

"Yes, that would be nice," Darrak replied. "What exactly is it you do around here? Other than watch television all day, that is?"

She gave him a dirty look. "This isn't permanent."

"So you keep telling us."

"Us." Leena shot a glance in Eden's direction. "He makes it sound like the two of you are a couple."

Eden really didn't need any bickering today. She was seriously close to the edge.

"Currently we're a two for one deal," Eden admitted tightly. "But, no, we're *not* a couple."

"Let's leave, Eden," Darrak grumbled. "I need to get away from Catwoman or I might say something I'll regret."

"Feeling uncomfortable around me?" Leena asked. "Is it because I remind you you're as unwelcome here as I am?"

Eden hissed out a breath, wishing for the days when her apartment was empty except for her and a pile of magazines. Now she was constantly living an episode of *Three's Company*. From Hell.

She rubbed her temples. "You're not unwelcome. I promised you could stay until you sorted out your issues—"

"Which could take forever," Darrak said.

"Right back at you," Leena snapped.

"Come on." Eden grabbed Darrak's tense arm and directed him toward the front door. If they fought another minute, she was seriously going to lose her patience.

The wards she'd instinctively set last night wouldn't protect her after she left the building. She'd have to keep an eye out for Ben and Oliver. However, they knew what she was capable of, and they wouldn't know she didn't use that black magic every day of the week. She'd be surprised if they approached her today, figuring they'd take a little while to lick their wounds.

Just the thought of a threat made magic begin to crackle down her arm.

Bad black magic. Go away.

Just like yesterday, her new neighbor Lucas was leaving at the same time as they were. Eden glanced at her watch. Maybe his alarm clock hadn't gone off, either.

He looked over at her. "Hey, there. *Eden*, isn't it?"

"That's right." Small talk in the hallway felt like a chore

this morning, but she'd give it a shot. "How's that house-warming party coming along, Lucas?"

"Slowly."

Leena peered out the front door to see whom Eden spoke to, and her eyes widened as she took in the attractive man next door. "I don't think we've been introduced. I'm Kathleen Harris. But you can call me Leena."

He approached and firmly shook her hand. "Lucas Campbell."

"So we're neighbors, huh?" she grinned. "Feel free to borrow some of my sugar anytime you like."

"And by that," Darrak said, "she means she'd be happy to have sex with you."

Eden almost laughed. If a snort could manage to sound hysterical, she'd nailed it.

Leena glared at the demon. "Just ignore him. Darrak talks out of his ass most of the time."

Lucas's eyebrows were high, but there was a smile on his face. "So, *sugar*, you say. I'll definitely remember you're the go-to gal for borrowing the sweet stuff around here."

Her mortified look turned to one of amusement. "I am. Stop by any time. I'm always here."

"She's not kidding about that," Darrak said. "She never leaves. Sad, really."

Leena shot another death ray at the demon before her gaze returned to Lucas and she noticed the small bag he held.

"What are those?" she asked.

"Marbles," Eden interjected. "For his students. Lucas is a teacher. You know, I could use a shiny, lucky marble myself."

"That could be arranged." Lucas smiled. "But first, please answer this question to the best of your ability. Where's the best place for coffee around here?"

"There's a Starbucks just north of here on Yonge Street. Five minute walk. Lots of parking if you take your car."

"Excellent answer." He handed her a marble he pulled from the bag. It had a green twisty center set into the clear glass ball. "See? Positive reinforcement for quality results. I have no idea why some of my students hate me so much."

"Kids hate everyone." It was so nice to talk to someone totally normal. It helped ease her tension a little. He wouldn't be able to tell her many problems at a glance. It was encouraging.

He closed her hand over the marble. "Keep that safe. Maybe it'll bring you some good luck."

"I could use some of that today."

With a last appreciative look in their new neighbor's direction, Leena went back into the apartment and Lucas, Eden, and Darrak took the elevator downstairs.

"So . . . what do you do, Darrak?" Lucas asked.

"I leech off the charity of others," he replied smoothly.

Eden slapped his arm. She really wanted to appear completely normal to Lucas if she could. "Darrak is an . . . entrepreneur of sorts. And an aspiring comedian, obviously."

"I see." Lucas nodded. "And how did you luck out enough to live with two beautiful women?"

"It's my cologne. I have to beat the ladies off with a stick."

How long was this elevator ride? Darrak was in a strange mood, and she really wanted to get him away from anyone he might scare off.

"You're a funny guy," Lucas observed.

"Humor helps to mask the pain. It's my thing."

"Are you two married?" Lucas asked.

Eden managed to choke on a gulp of air. Darrak slapped her lightly on her back.

"No," he replied for her. "But we're together. So feel free to hit on Leena, but Eden's off the market, if that's what you're wondering."

Lucas's smile widened. "I think I understand."

Eden waited until she reached her car, got in, and started

driving before she turned to the demon. She scanned the area to make sure no Malleus members were around but saw nothing out of the ordinary.

"What was that?" she demanded.

"What?"

"'Eden's off the market'?" Her hands tightened on the steering wheel as she pulled onto the road. "We're *not* together that way, Darrak."

"I just didn't like the way he was looking at you."

"Oh, boy. You're delusional, you know that?"

"He gave you a marble."

"So what?"

He shrugged and fiddled with the radio. "In some cultures, the giving of a marble might mean you're engaged."

"Lucas is right. You are funny." But she wasn't smiling. "Listen . . . what happened last night—"

"Oh, so now you want to talk about it."

"I don't want it to be awkward between us."

He reached for her, and she froze, not knowing what to expect. He drew his index finger over the surface of her medium gray amulet before his ice blue eyes flicked to hers.

"It can't happen again," he said.

"I know."

"Then you're going to have to help me a little bit. Because last night . . . well, let's just say it was really close. This curse of mine is dangerous. I have to be close to you to survive, but the closer I get, the more I . . ." He swallowed. "Things just aren't as simple as I'd like them to be."

That was true for both of them. Eden tried to concentrate on the road, but then Darrak took her hand in his and kissed it. His lips felt so warm against her skin, and desire swirled inside of her.

"And that's helping?" she asked.

"Probably not." Then he grinned. "What can I say? I'm a demon."

He was. Sometimes it was a bit too easy to forget that.

⇒ TWELVE ⇐

Theo was waiting for them at Opa's, the Greek restaurant next to Luxuria.

The demon had ordered a flatbread and hummus appetizer.

Eden eyed him warily as they approached. His hair was black, even darker than Darrak's. Darrak's hair was usually an unruly mess in need of a comb, but the other demon's hair was sleek and shiny and pulled back at the nape of his neck. He had hooded eyes and an easy smile and skin that looked naturally tanned. He made Eden think of someone who lived in Hawaii and might consider surfing a way of life.

He was handsome. Then again, she hadn't expected him to be ugly. Whatever his demon form might look like, it was practically a guarantee that his human form would be appealing. Made him all the more dangerous to unsuspecting prey.

Therefore, the prospect of having lunch with two attractive demons didn't exactly ease her mind.

Theo smiled and stood up as Darrak and Eden reached the table.

"Darrak," he said. "Good to see you in one piece again."

Eden waited to see a tightness in his expression, something to betray the fact Theo was waiting to shift form and attack both of them. But there was nothing.

Maybe she shouldn't have had three coffees at Triple-A that morning as they waited for their appointment with destiny. She was seriously jittery and more on edge than normal.

Darrak grinned at his friend. "Good to see you, too. This . . . this is Eden."

Theo's black-eyed gaze swept over her. "A pleasure. Please, have a seat. Take a menu."

Her arm brushed against a faux Greek pillar. The entire restaurant had a Greek pantheon feel to it. A painting of Zeus on top of Mount Olympus stared down at them from the ceiling.

Zeus's eyes were a bit buggy. It only helped to make her feel more paranoid.

She sat down cautiously next to Darrak, every muscle tense. She didn't even glance at the menu.

"I know Darrak met you the other night," she said. "In my body. So let's not pretend the reason we're here is to partake in the chicken souvlaki special, okay?"

Theo took a sip from the glass of wine in front of him. "She's direct."

"She is," Darrak confirmed.

"But very ungrateful."

Eden bristled. "I wouldn't say that."

"No? Storming in here unpleasantly, not even giving me a smile. And yet, if you're here, you obviously expect me to help you."

He maintained his slightly amused expression. She didn't appreciate it very much.

"You're helping Darrak, not me."

"By helping Darrak I am helping you. So try to behave."

Wow, that was condescending. A wave of dislike moved through her, bringing with it an edge of magic that she felt at the surface of her skin. Instinctively, she felt threatened by this demon and wanted to protect herself. He wasn't infused with humanity like Darrak was. He was a threat.

But . . . he *was* right. She hated to admit it, but he was. If this demon helped Darrak, it would be helping her as well, wouldn't it?

What would Theo think of the fact she was a nephilim?

She still wasn't convinced of that. Mild psychic skills were not conclusive enough to make her blindly believe everything Oliver had told her last night.

One problem at a time, she thought.

She clasped her hands in front of her on the white table-cloth. "All I'm saying is that Darrak's your friend, right? So obviously you want to help him. Anything you do for me will be a side effect only."

Theo glanced at Darrak. "Does she win many friends this way?"

Darrak shrugged. "It's been a difficult couple of weeks for her. For both of us. She's normally quite adorable."

"I'm sure." Theo's lips stretched into a fresh smile. "This doesn't have to be unpleasant, Eden. I'm the same as Darrak, after all. And you feel comfortable enough with him, don't you? You can feel the same about me."

That was unlikely. She tried to push away any ill feelings or fear or distrust. "If you say so."

She took a sip of the water in front of her, hoping Theo hadn't poisoned it.

"So . . ." Theo began. "Darrak tells me you're a black witch."

She choked and the water almost came through her nose. "He did?"

Darrak cleared his throat. "It was relevant at the time."

The waitress, dressed in a knee-length toga and a gold laurel in her hair, came to their table. "I should let you know we have lamb gyros on special today. And for dessert, the baklava is extra specially delicious and a dollar off, now until one o'clock. Get it while it's hot! Have I tantalized your taste buds with Opa's food—fit for the gods themselves?"

Darrak had told Theo she was a black witch. She'd seen firsthand what happened when Oliver found out that little fact about her—she'd nearly been killed. And now Darrak was announcing it to every old buddy he came across?

There would be words.

"Where's your restroom?" she asked the waitress, feeling the desperate need to escape and gain control of herself before she allowed her black magic to fry Darrak where he sat.

The waitress pointed to her left. "Just along that hallway."

"Is it less than a hundred feet from here?"

That earned a frown. "Uh . . . I think so. Why?"

"Just because." Eden stood up, shot Darrak a dirty look for broadcasting her secrets, and left the table.

"I think she might need a little extra Tsatsiki," Darrak told the waitress tensely from behind her.

That put it mildly.

"So she seems like fun," Theo said dryly.

"Like I said, it's been a difficult couple of weeks."

"I understand that. But she's kind of high maintenance, huh?" Theo stared off in the direction Eden had escaped. "I mean, great body, cute face. Long hair I'd love to wrap around my di—"

Darrak glared at him. "Watch it."

"—digits." Theo held up his right hand and wiggled his fingers. He grinned. "So what is this? Are you gone on her, or something?"

"Define *gone*."

"Emotionally attached."

Darrak shifted uncomfortably in his seat. "I don't know."

Theo laughed and downed his glass of wine. "You're reminding me of what happened with me and Kristina. Also high maintenance. And you remember how that turned out, right?"

Darrak cringed. "All too well."

Kristina had been a human Theo had become involved with in the seventeenth century. He'd been sent to take the young virgin's soul just as she'd been about to become a nun. Along the way, he'd been trapped by a wizard, and Kristina had rescued him thinking he was an angel sent from God to watch over her.

Theo was no angel.

However, he'd fallen in love with her and refused to take her soul. Darrak had thought it humorous and rather pathetic at the time. Theo had changed into a puddle of very humanlike emotion, if only for a brief time. When news reached Lucifer of Theo refusing to follow through with a direct order, he'd sent another demon to finish the job.

Theo had had a choice—fight the demon and Lucifer's orders and risk being destroyed, or let Kristina's soul perish.

It hadn't been pretty.

Theo ultimately chose self-protection. Kristina was destroyed, and her soul was consumed by hellfire. And Theo had become very focused when it came to getting ahead in his career as a demon. He never mentioned Kristina again. Not until now, anyway.

He might hate Lucifer even more than Darrak did.

"Feeling anything toward a human is a bad idea," Theo said. "It's a risk we take in this business, but one that must be controlled."

Darrak's jaw was tight. "All I feel is pathetically dependent on her in my time of neediness. If I feel anything else, it is because of my curse, and as you said before, it will disappear once we take care of it."

"You really think so?"

"Of course." It was the truth.

"Good." Theo indicated to the waitress that he wanted another drink. "You know, she doesn't seem like a black witch to me. She's so . . . uptight. Witches I've dealt with are always ready for a party."

"Eden's different."

"So I'm gathering." The waitress returned with two glasses of wine, which she placed in front of either demon.

Darrak tried not to worry, but he couldn't help but feel a bit uneasy. He wanted to trust Theo, but he had some questions that needed answers.

"I want to know what the plan is today," he said. "Where are we going to get this weapon you told me about?"

"It's not far from here."

Still vague. Deliberately, it seemed. "And you promise this will bring no harm to Eden."

"Wouldn't dream of hurting your delicate little witchy-poo." Theo leaned closer. "What I want to know is if you're still interested in being a part of my master plan and taking over Hell, starting with Lucifer's throne?" When Darrak didn't jump up and down with glee right away, he continued. "Come on. Netherworld dominion. Seven lords. Seven thrones. Two demons with ambition. Sound good?"

He wouldn't speak so freely if Lucifer had any chance of hearing. Luckily for everyone involved, the Prince of Hell didn't come to the human world since he had no power here. His power had been blocked here after his fall from Heaven because of his timeless hatred of humans.

That was why he needed demons like Darrak and Theo to do his dirty work. The dirtier the better.

In Hell, Lucifer was all-powerful. But here? Not so much.

It was the only thing that helped relax Darrak when it came to the subject of his former boss's demise.

"Is there a problem?" Theo asked. "You seem . . . distracted."

Darrak shook his head. "Something happened last night that I'm having a hard time getting out of my mind. A problem with the Malleus."

"The Malleus," Theo replied distastefully. "What is that human scum up to now?"

"Eden knows someone . . . he's a new recruit, apparently. He almost got her killed last night."

"And that would be so bad?" At Darrak's sharp look, Theo laughed. "What's this do-gooder's name?"

"Ben Hanson. He's a cop, too. Thinks he's Mr. Perfect."

"Somebody sounds jealous."

"Oh, I am. Insanely. I could never have hair that perfect and blond. He's like a Ken doll."

Theo blinked and ran his finger over the edge of his wineglass. "Huh?"

"Barbie's boyfriend," Darrak clarified.

"Still not understanding."

"Teenage model."

Another blink.

Darrak sighed. "In any case, I can't compete."

"Why would you even want to?"

Darrak pushed the menu away from him, feeling anger toward the cop welling up inside of him again. "That son of a bitch is going to make the wrong decision in his quest to fight evil, and it's going to hurt Eden." Realizing how that sounded after his claims of disinterest, he clarified, "Which would affect me, of course."

Theo leaned back in his chair. "Sounds like an angel to me."

"It does, doesn't it? All self-righteous, squeaky clean, and self-centered."

Theo's expression turned thoughtful. "The best way to deal with an angel is to rip his wings off and enjoy his screams of agony. Remember that time in Paris during the plague?"

It had seemed like a fun afternoon at the time when they'd cornered an unsuspecting angel minding his own business. Now, the memory made Darrak cringe. Damn humanity bringing with it an unhealthy dose of guilt. "Good times."

"Totally." Theo downed his second glass of wine. "This Ben guy is only human, right?"

"He is. But now that he's with the Malleus, he's probably all supercharged and ready for a good fight."

Theo waved a hand. "An insect waiting to be squashed."

"The guy's a serious pain in my ass. If I was half the demon I used to be, I'd hunt him down and gut him like a fish. That would keep him away, wouldn't it?"

"It would indeed."

Darrak shook his head to clear it of thoughts of the cop. "Enough about him, let's get back to your plan. Destruction to Lucifer?"

"Can I get a hallelujah?"

Darrak snorted. "Hallelujah."

The plan sounded good centuries ago. Even worth risking his very existence for. Power, endless power. The chance to have anything he wanted, whenever he wanted it.

Lucifer was a bastard. Not literally, of course—much like Darrak, he didn't have a mother and a father as a human would. He was the original angel cast out of Heaven because his pride refused to allow him to bow at the feet of humans. He'd become the ruler of Hell. The head honcho. The numero uno. The six other lords had nothing on him, power-wise.

Lucifer was no angel anymore. He was a sadistic, selfish demon who could torture another—demon, human, or angel—with a mere thought.

He owned Darrak. He'd created him and could destroy him at will. Darrak had worked for him for centuries as an incubus, helping to stock Lucifer's harem. As the Lord of Pride, he didn't have a particularly lustful nature. It only occurred to Darrak later that the human souls probably weren't all meant for sex. Human souls also made for a tasty, high-protein snack for a hungry demon. And the Lords of Hell had very big appetites.

Beings like Lucifer made archdemons like Darrak in his prime look like big, friendly, fluffy bunnies.

Despite Darrak's loyal—if occasionally conspiratorial— service to the Prince of Hell, Lucifer had removed his protection over him at the first sign of disloyalty with Asmodeus. And it hadn't even been true. Had he not done this, Darrak never would have been summoned by Selina. He wouldn't have been cursed by her, and he wouldn't have needed to possess humans for the past three hundred years.

It had been sheer torture—a jail sentence with no end.

And it was the reason he was now conflicted about every damn thing in his existence, including Eden. Lucifer was to blame for this unwanted, and hopefully temporary, infusion of humanity.

Darrak hated Lucifer.

And now Theo was ready to step forward and destroy the prince. He'd apparently found the means to do it. Going with him today to get that weapon would ensure Theo's help in finding a way to break Darrak's curse and save Eden from certain death.

And when the curse was broken, Darrak wouldn't feel conflicted or guilty or overly emotional about anything anymore. He'd be restored to his former self, more than ready and willing to do whatever it took to gain more power and prestige. The lowly incubus had the chance to become a lord, and Eden would only be a distant, fleeting memory, much as Kristina was for Theo.

"So are you ready for the ride?" Theo asked, eyeing his friend cautiously.

Darrak grinned. "Giddy up."

* * *

Eden gripped the sides of the sink and tried to calm down.
It wasn't easy.

She hadn't made a stellar impression on Theo so far.
And did she care? Not really.

She had to pull it together, though. Sad but true, he was
their only hope at the moment.

She was a little surprised Ben hadn't shown his face
today. Where was he? Was the Malleus planning another
little intervention? She really didn't want to use her magic
again, but she would if she had to. She tried not to look at
her amulet, but the color had darkened enough to be noticeable. Was there a way to recover—like a washing machine
for graying souls—or was this only a one-way street?

Lots of fun questions. And mixed metaphors.

She frowned at her reflection and parted her hair, peering closer at it. Her bright red roots were showing again.
She was overdue for a trip to the salon to get them back to
the dark auburn color she preferred.

The bright color helped remind her of the man who'd
come to visit her as a child when she'd been playing out
back of the townhome in Reno her mother rented at the
time.

She remembered a bright smile. Green eyes. Red hair.

"Hello, Eden," he'd said warmly.

"Who're you?" She'd been wary, even as a little girl.
Some things never changed.

He crouched down beside her. "I'm your father. I'm very
happy to get the chance to meet you."

It was a hazy memory since she'd been so young. They
chatted for a bit longer, but she couldn't remember about
what. She'd liked him. He'd seemed . . . nice.

It had been the only time she'd ever seen him.

When he left, she went inside and told her mother about
the man with the same color hair and eyes as her.

"Don't talk to strangers" was all Caroline Riley had said about it. She'd seemed disturbed by this alleged visit. "They'll hurt you."

Words to live by. And Eden had tried very hard to stick close to that philosophy in the years that passed, but sometimes it was easy to forget. Trusting strangers or boyfriends or friends or mothers had inevitably led to Eden getting hurt—either emotionally or physically.

She didn't trust easily anymore. Which was one of the reasons Darrak stealing her body had bothered her so much. She *had* trusted him.

Did she still?

Not completely.

But did he mean her harm? Was he using her?

No. She didn't believe that.

So she didn't trust him. But she didn't *not* trust him.

Complicated.

She waited a bit longer until she felt calm and courageous enough to return to the table. Just as she took a step toward the door, she felt a pain in her gut. The next moment she doubled over, gasping in pain, as the tearing sensation increased. Perspiration broke out on her forehead, and she clutched at the wall to try to remain standing.

No, not again. Tears welled in her eyes. She couldn't handle pain like yesterday again. It was too much.

But the next moment the pain disappeared completely. She braced herself for its return, but it didn't.

She reached into the pocket of her jeans and pulled out the marble Lucas gave her earlier with trembling fingers. She squeezed it. She didn't believe it would really bring her any luck, but it was a pleasant thought. She needed some pleasant thoughts.

The marble warmed in her palm. When she looked at it, she realized it had started to glow.

Why was it glowing?

She frowned. "What the hell?"

Snap.

A bright white light, as if someone had just taken her photo, emanated from the marble and blinded her. She blinked and rubbed her eyes. When she opened them again, she realized she wasn't in Opa's ladies' room anymore.

⇉ THIRTEEN ⇇

Eden stood alone on the shore of an ocean, barefoot in the sand. It was warm out and the sun shone above her. There were palm trees and large pink and purple flowers she could see as she turned around in a circle.

She gawked at the nearest palm tree.

What the hell just happened?

Had she passed out because of the pain? Maybe she couldn't deal with it anymore.

Another thought occurred to her: Was she dead?

No. Her heart was still beating. She was breathing—more rapidly with each passing moment. She could feel the tropical breeze on her skin. This had to be a dream.

It felt too real to be a dream.

From the corner of her eye she noticed a man approaching her. He wore white pants and a white shirt and walked steadily down the beach toward her. As he drew closer, she realized that she recognized him.

"Lucas," she managed, her voice breathless.

"Glad you could make it, Eden."

"Am I dreaming right now?"

"No." He glanced at their surroundings. "This is real. I wanted to talk to you privately. I thought you might like this."

Her head hurt. She looked down at the marble sitting innocently in the palm of her hand. "And this is—"

"Not a marble."

"It looks like a marble."

"It does, doesn't it? But it's not. It's a summoning crystal created especially for you."

She flexed her right fist, ready to will black magic into it, but nothing happened.

"You can't use your magic here," Lucas said. "This is a neutral zone."

"Who the hell are you?" she demanded.

He smiled. "I'm your new neighbor. The substitute teacher."

"Yeah, right."

"You don't believe me?"

"Strangely, no. Take this. I don't want it anymore." She held the marble out to him.

He shook his head. "That's how we'll communicate."

"And why would we want to do that?"

"Because you're going to help me solve a problem I have at the moment. Someone wants to destroy me. And you're going to help stop him."

She looked around. "How do I leave? I need to get back."

"Darrak will be fine without you for a few minutes. Don't worry. This isn't far enough to strain your bond. It's a metaphysical location rather than a physical one."

She looked at him sharply. "How do you know anything about that? Tell me who you are, or we're going to have a problem here."

His smile didn't falter. "You're still welcome to call me Lucas. I like it."

"But . . ."

"But my full name is"—he raised his gaze to hers—
"*Lucifer.*"

That knocked the breath right out of her. "You're joking."

"Nope. No joke."

Her mouth went as dry as the sand she stood on. "Lucifer.
As in *the* Lucifer. Or were your parents just majorly Goth?"

"*The* Lucifer."

She didn't speak for a moment. She *couldn't* speak.

Just as she was about to freak out as fear and panic
spread through her, she forced herself to remain calm. This
couldn't be the real Lucifer. It was impossible. Wouldn't
Darrak have clued in when they'd met him in the hallway?

Of course he would have.

And wouldn't the Prince of Hell give off some sort of
important vibe? He felt 100 percent human to her. Not even
a wisp of magic.

"How do I know you're telling the truth?" she asked,
forcing herself to sound as skeptical as she felt.

"Seriously?" He stared at her for a moment. "You need
proof?"

"Well, yeah. Of course." She nervously poked her big
toe into the warm sand. What she really wanted to do was
turn and run away, but since she had no idea where she was,
she knew that wouldn't help.

"You need to take my word for it."

She crossed her arms. "Why would the real Lucifer be
concerned about anyone trying to destroy him? Wouldn't
you be all powerful and all evil?"

He raked a hand through his short brown hair. "This
meeting is not going nearly as well as I'd anticipated."

She was losing her fear the more she spoke. "Lucifer
wouldn't need my help."

"Oh, really?"

"That's right. And if I refused to help, he would have
already killed me. I've seen the movies, you know. I know
demons."

"You think so, do you?"

She glanced at the beach around her again. "Maybe you're that wizard master Stanley was talking about. Maksim. And you're trying to mess with me. He said you were at a resort right now on vacation. Is this it?"

Lucas rolled his eyes. "And to think you own a private investigation agency. You're no Nancy Drew, are you?"

She drew close enough to poke him in the chest. Even that felt completely human to her. More proof that's exactly what he was. "Okay, Maksim. Enough. You have no damn idea how close I am to the edge this week. You do not want to piss off a black witch who doesn't come with an instruction manual. You think PMS is bad? Guess again."

"I'm not Maksim," he said patiently.

"Then who are you?"

"Lucifer." He gritted his teeth. "Like I already said."

"Sure you are." Still, her voice shook a little.

"You want proof?" he asked. "Take my hand."

She looked down at his outstretched hand for a moment and then grabbed it. "Fine."

Snap.

The next moment the beach and ocean were gone. Eden now stood on a rocky precipice that jutted out from a cliff side. She looked down into bleak horror below. Flames undulated like a terrifying ocean hundreds of feet below. It was fire for as far as her eye could see. She felt the heat reach up and wrap itself around her, oppressive, making it hard to breathe. She couldn't see anyone else, but screams of terror and pain pierced her eardrums.

A rock shifted and fell to the canyon below, and she shrieked as she almost lost her balance. Lucas grabbed her arm before she fell.

"Welcome to my home," he said. "As a living human, you normally wouldn't be able to visit here, but much like the beach, this is only a representation."

"What is this place?" she managed.

"I'll give you three guesses, but the first two don't count. Let's just say it's a nice place to visit, but you probably wouldn't want to live here."

"Hell."

"Part of it. There are many other areas, but this is the place that looks the best on the postcards. Do you believe me now?"

She couldn't think straight. "I . . . I'm not sure . . ."

"Fine," he replied. "Have it your way."

He pushed her off the side of the cliff and she fell, head-first and screaming, into the ocean of fire.

Snap.

Back to the beach. Lucas sat beside her, dragging his fingers through the sand. A warm breeze wafted through her hair. Her heart jackhammered in her chest.

"Theo will require your help to find a weapon here in the human world," he said evenly. "He believes it has the power to destroy me. For now I only want you to observe, but eventually I'll need you to bring it to me."

She stared at him. He was Lucifer, wasn't he? No matter how much she tried to deny it, it didn't change anything.

"Why me?" She fought the urge to scramble away from him. He looked so harmless, but he wasn't. Looks could be so deceiving.

"Because you're close to the action. Also because we have a few things in common."

Her eyebrows went up. "I find that hard to believe."

He absently made patterns in the sand. "You've recently been dealing with a curse. I've been dealing with one for an eternity. You have a powerful darkness inside you that you shouldn't use. So do I."

She let that sink in. "Hold on. *You're* concerned that you have a darkness inside you that you shouldn't use."

"That's what I said."

She just stared at him blankly. "I find that hard to wrap my head around."

"I don't doubt it." He met her gaze, and he looked so incredibly human. "Many people confuse me with Satan. I don't doubt that you would, too."

A shiver coursed down her spine at the other recognizable horror movie name. "Are you trying to say he's the real prince of darkness and you've just gotten a bad reputation because of him?"

"Not exactly." He was silent so long she wasn't sure he'd say anything else. And then, "Satan is who I become when I use my dark powers. He's who you should really be afraid of. Satan is my curse, part of my punishment—the one I received when I was cast out of Heaven. And with your help I can destroy him once and for all."

Eden just gaped at him. It was a look she figured she'd perfected today.

Lucas stood up and paced to the waterline before turning and coming back. "And you're the one who gets to know the truth. Don't you feel lucky?" He grinned, but it was strained. "All of this time, thousands of years, I've been cursed to remain in Hell. Cursed with an inner darkness that keeps me from redemption."

More gaping on Eden's part. "You want to be redeemed?"

"More than anything. I was cast out of Heaven because I refused to kneel before humans." His face shadowed with disgust. "Insects. Powerless, ungrateful, and dirty, destroying the gift of this world from the moment they were created. And I'm supposed to love them unconditionally?" His lips thinned. "I tried to accept my punishment and make the best of it, but I never have. I want to go back to my home. But the curse works like an anchor, trapping me in Hell."

"But you're here." She looked around the beach, trying to make sense of what he was telling her. It wasn't easy. "I touched you in the hallway of my apartment. You're real."

"I've found a way to enter the human world, but . . ." He trailed off.

"But what?"

"But when I'm there, I'm not exactly the same as I am in Hell."

She studied him carefully and warily, trying to sense something in him, but there was still nothing. That alone helped clue her in to what was really going on here. After a moment, she gasped. "Wait a minute. Are you . . . *human* here? I don't sense anything more from you because there's nothing more to sense, is there?"

It was as if the answer came to her head directly from Alex Trebek himself.

He raised pale brown eyes to hers, and she could see the shock and immediate distrust. She'd figured out his little secret too quickly. "You sensed that, did you?"

Eden just nodded, waiting for him to deny it.

He didn't. "It's why I try to stay here as little as possible. It would be very embarrassing if I got hit by a bus while crossing the street."

"What would happen then?" she asked, trying to reconcile everything she was learning from him and failing miserably.

"Straight back to Hell on a one-way ticket. Unable to summon the energy to leave again for decades. It's an imperfect science, but it's the only way. In the human world I have to be human."

"Why?"

"My strong distaste for them might lead me to lay waste to everyone I see."

"You'd do that?"

"If I used enough of my power and Satan came out to play, it's very possible."

"You make it sound like Dr. Jekyll and Mr. Hyde."

"Because that's very much what it's like for me."

"So . . . Lucifer . . . or *Lucas*," she began, "is your nice side—"

"*Nice* might be a bit of an exaggeration."

"And Satan is the truly evil one."

"With my curse in place, I represent the darkness in either of my guises. But you wouldn't want to meet Satan. I'm not quite as good of a conversationalist when he's in control." He cocked his head to the side. "You're the first I've chosen to have this conversation with in a very, very long time. You should feel very honored."

Honored was one thing she didn't feel at the moment. Eden crossed her arms tightly in front of her. "I need to get back. Darrak will wonder where I've gone."

"Time isn't an issue here, but there's no reason to draw this out. I've told you what I want from you. The weapon Theo will acquire today may have the power to kill me. But I want to use it to kill Satan instead. If I can destroy my darkness, maybe my light can finally be restored."

She considered this for an uneasy moment. "You really think Heaven's going to welcome you back with open arms after all this time?"

His jaw clenched. "I've learned my lesson. There's no reason for them to continue to torture me by ignoring my existence. So will you do this for me? Watch Theo and bring me the weapon when I ask?"

"I don't know." She took a deep breath and let it out slowly. "Look, if what you're saying is true, you're Lucifer. *And* Satan. And that's just way too much for me to absorb during one day at the beach."

"You're saying you don't trust me."

"That pretty much sums it up."

"But you trust Darrak?" he challenged. "He's an archdemon. At his essence, he's nothing but hellfire. I created him to be a servant to me."

She swallowed hard. "A lot of people come from humble beginnings."

His expression was tense. "Say you'll agree to help me. To work for me."

"Work for *Lucifer*."

"Yes."

She chewed her bottom lip. "You need an answer right now?"

"Yes, I do."

"Then my answer is no. I . . . I can't do it. I can't work for you. My soul is in enough jeopardy as it is." She touched her amulet. "I'm sorry, but that's just the way it is."

"I see."

She expected him to get angry with her, but he didn't. Was he really going to take no for an answer? She really hoped so. "You'll find someone else to help you."

"There is no one else." He went quiet for a moment, his expression shadowed. "I have your mother's soul, you know."

A breath caught in Eden's throat. "What did you say?"

"Your mother, Caroline Riley. She died recently. She was a borderline case—her eternal fate was undecided but recently tipped in my favor when I chose to claim her as . . . insurance."

"She's in Hell." Her mouth was dry.

"Her soul is mine," Lucas said. "She was a horrible mother to you. She had terrible taste in men. Even your father, an angel."

She inhaled sharply. "You know about him?"

"Of course I do. I also know that he turned his back the moment the human world was out of sight, and he put you and your mother out of his mind. There aren't many angels who will give up Heaven for a mortal life."

"Don't hurt her," Eden said, her voice barely audible. He was right. Her mother had been a crappy one. Negligent and emotionally distant. But she didn't deserve an eternity in Hell for her sins.

"As soon as I let her out of my protective custody, there's no saying what torment she'll face. But, like I said, she's a

borderline case. And there is a grace period for me to decide what to do with her. If I reject her from Hell, then
there's a chance she'll be accepted into Heaven."

"A chance?"

He shrugged. "Also a chance she won't be."

"And what happens then?" Eden's throat felt thick.

"If neither Heaven nor Hell wants her, she'll wander the
human world as a disembodied spirit—a *drifter*."

This was too much. She'd said no, and he'd decided to
blackmail her. Well, he'd be happy to know it was working
perfectly.

"Fine. I'll help you," she said not wanting to give it any
more thought. "Darrak will help me with Theo."

"You're too late. Darrak's already agreed to help Theo
destroy me."

Her eyes widened. "What?"

"Darrak's not fond of me, so I can't exactly say I'm surprised by his decision, but he's making a grave error siding
with Theo." Lucas smiled. "Demons forged from hellfire can
be pretty but are ultimately very stupid. Since both started
off their existences as incubi, they weren't prized for their
keen intellects."

Panic rose up inside her. "Don't hurt him."

"Hurt Darrak? For wanting to end my existence?" He
grinned. "Thanks for the suggestion."

She swallowed hard. "No, look, there has to be another
way."

His grin disappeared. "Yes, there is. You bring me that
weapon when I ask for it. And you promise to say nothing
to Darrak about this. Otherwise, your mother will be
damned for all eternity. Human souls and hellfire are not
friends. The screams are very disturbing. I believe you got
a little sample of that earlier."

She couldn't forget it even if she wanted to. "Fine.
Whatever you say."

"If you need to speak to me, hold the marble and say my name."

"Lucifer," she said.

"Yes."

"But if that's your true name, why aren't you bound by whomever says it?"

"Because I'm the Prince of Hell. That does come with a few special privileges." He turned away and began walking down the beach. "Bye, Eden. Nice talking to you."

Snap.

The next moment Eden was back in the restroom of the restaurant, shaking, staring at her pale expression in the mirror.

FOURTEEN

"That was fast," Darrak said as Eden sat down next to him at the table.

"Really?" She looked surprised.

"I ordered you the daily special," he said, as the waitress brought plates of food to the table a few moments later.

"I . . . I'm not very hungry."

She looked distressed. He really wanted to touch her hand and assure her it was okay, but didn't want Theo to sense any weakness on his part. Not toward Eden.

No, it would be best if Theo felt Darrak was simply using Eden's body and any other emotions would disappear the moment he found a solution to his curse.

And Eden couldn't find out Theo's plan or the fact that Darrak had readily agreed to help him out. Keeping it from her might be tricky, but he knew she'd never approve in a million years.

Then again, the plan was to destroy Lucifer, not to go gallivanting all over town clubbing baby seals.

Still. The less said the better.

"So now that you have had some time to refresh yourself," Theo said, keeping his trademark charming smile on his handsome face, "I want to ask for your assistance today."

Darrak braced himself. While he'd told Eden Theo would help them, he didn't tell her the demon wanted something in return for his troubles.

"With what?" she asked.

"I'd like you to accompany me as I speak to someone."

"Who?"

Theo cocked his head to the side. "An angel."

Eden blinked. "An *angel*."

"That's right. He's going to help me get something I need."

"Why do you want me to come along?"

"I just do. Consider it a favor."

Eden blinked slowly, then took a sip from her glass of water. "Okay. Where will we find him?"

Well, that was easy. Too easy, actually. Darrak was surprised she hadn't flat out refused to have anything to do with this. Even he didn't understand why Theo needed to talk to an angel. It was a rare thing for demons and angels to even come face-to-face. They usually repelled each other like magnets.

"He hangs out at a pub just down the street from here every day at about this time."

"An angel goes to a pub?" she asked.

"He's an alcoholic."

Eden's eyebrows rose. "How is that even possible?"

Theo grinned. "Demons and angels are susceptible to human alcohol and drugs when in human form. Even more than humans are."

"Well, that's unfortunate."

"Just a taste is sometimes enough to create an addiction."

Darrak snorted. "Just like Eden and her morning OJ."

"Better than your chocolate donut addiction," she mumbled under her breath.

Okay. Somebody was still a bit cranky, weren't they?

Darrak expected her to ask more questions and demand answers, but Eden simply nodded as she pushed her untouched plate of food away from her.

"Okay, let's go."

He raised his eyebrows. "You're sure?"

She nodded. "Positive."

The pub was called the Pig and Thistle, and it was small, dark, and musty. There weren't many customers inside. One bartender. A waitress. A couple of people sitting in a booth. And one man at the bar, hunched over the nearly empty glass of dark ale in front of him.

"That's him," Theo said.

That was an angel? She had to say, she was disappointed. With thinning blond hair and gaunt cheekbones, the angel looked like an average man in his midthirties who drank more than he should while the wife and kids waited patiently at home.

After what she'd just experienced with Lucas, she knew looks could be deceiving. She assumed Theo would question this angel about the whereabouts of the weapon.

Just observe. That was all she was instructed to do.

She could do that.

After all, her mother's soul currently hung in the balance.

Why would Eden go out of her way to save her mother's soul? Caroline Riley had basically left her on her own from the time she was a kid to fend for herself, sometimes for up to a week at a time while she went off with whoever her latest boyfriend was.

She'd never physically abused Eden, but the emotional abandonment was enough to do damage. Eden always felt that her mother just didn't care. And when she was around, she always treated Eden more like a buddy than a daughter.

Would she be happy Eden had stepped up, without question, to do this? It wasn't as if Eden had agreed to help Lucas so she'd gain something. The last time she'd done a favor for her mother—paid off a credit card so the collection agency would stop calling—she'd been yelled at, not thanked.

Her mother hated it when other people—even her own daughter—interfered in her business.

But this wasn't a collection agency looking for a few thousand dollars. This was the fate of her mother's soul. And she didn't expect a thank-you card in return.

The fact that her mother had left her anything in her will when she died—half of Triple-A and a pair of earrings— still surprised Eden. The fact that her mother had a *will* surprised her. The woman basically lived out of a suitcase for most of her adult life.

It was hard to believe she'd been knocked up by an angel.

Eden still wasn't entirely convinced what she'd been told was true. And if it was—that her father was an angel— then it didn't exactly endear her to the heavenly species. Her father knew about her, had visited her once very briefly, and then that was it?

So as they approached the drunken angel, she didn't feel any particular emotion for him other than the desire to get this over with as soon as possible. And maybe there was some mild curiosity as well.

As she drew closer, a light brush of energy touched her skin. It felt pleasant, like warm sunshine. Was that an angel thing? That warmth and light? The feeling of acceptance and love just being near him made all her troubles seem to drift away.

She suddenly couldn't help but smile at the oddly disheveled man before her.

"Hey sugar tits," the angel said, sweeping his gaze down the length of her. "Wanna buy me a drink?"

Her smile disappeared.

Theo sat on the stool next to the angel. "You're Alistair, right?"

The angel blinked. "That's my name, don't wear it out."

"I want to talk to you about a business proposition."

"Oh, yeah? What kind of business proposition?"

"You help me, I help you kind of thing."

"And who are you?"

"Name's Theo. That's Darrak. And sugar tits there is Eden."

Eden looked at Darrak, who shrugged. She expected him to look amused by the angel's reaction to her, but he didn't. His expression was surprisingly serious.

"Is there a problem?" she asked under her breath.

"No problem," he replied tightly.

She touched his arm to find that his muscles were tense. He shook his head. "It's fine. I'm just edgy, I guess."

That made two of them. She really wanted to tell him about Lucas and what he wanted her to do, but she said nothing. This was a secret that had to remain that way.

She'd keep an eye on Theo as he acquired whatever this weapon was. She'd keep an eye on Darrak and make sure he didn't do anything that would get him into more trouble than he was already in. And when she was instructed by Lucas, she would grab the weapon and hand it over to him.

Simple.

Well, not simple at all, but she didn't exactly have a whole lot of choice in this scenario.

Theo nodded at a nearby booth. "Come on over here, Alistair. We'll buy you another beer."

"Okay," the angel agreed. "You know, I love meeting new people. Good conversation, good drink. I'm all over that."

"Then why would you hang out somewhere like this?"

Eden asked tensely as they moved toward the more private booth. "It seems kind of dead in here."

"They let me run a tab."

"Why would an angel need a tab?"

Alistair frowned. "How do you know what I am?"

She opened her mouth to answer, but Theo touched her back. "Eden's a bit psychic. She can sense the otherworldly. It's her gift."

"Ah," Alistair nodded. "That makes sense. Yes, sweetheart, I'm an angel. In human form at the moment. Impressed?"

"Very," she agreed, sliding into the booth next to Darrak. He sat close enough that she felt the warmth from his body. It made her think about last night. Even though she'd been in a black magic fog, she still remembered how good he'd felt.

Dangerous thoughts.

She scooted over to put a few inches of space between them.

Her phone vibrated and she glanced at the call display. It was Andy, probably calling to let her know how the werewolf case was going. That could wait. She pressed the end button to ignore the call.

Theo got another beer from the bartender and slid it in front of the angel, who accepted it eagerly, bringing the dark liquid to his lips and taking a long gulp.

"Delicious," he proclaimed.

"Is it right for an angel to drink so much?" Eden asked, then bit her lip. It sounded ruder than she'd meant it to. Stress made her lose her tact.

Alistair smiled. "Whatever gets me through the day. My time here is almost up. I'm ready to go back to my home. Can't wait."

"You don't like it here?"

"It's nice for a visit, but that's all. I won't be back for another tour of duty for a century, so I'll have lots of time to recoup."

"You're a Cerberus, right?" Theo asked.

Alistair's eyebrows rose. "You've done your research, my beer-buying friend. I am indeed. Then again, there isn't much place for an angel in the human world unless he's fallen or a Cerberus, is there?"

"No, I don't suppose there is."

Darrak remained silent, carefully watching their conversation.

"So you're a guard?" Eden asked. "You look after a gateway?"

He nodded. "To the Netherworld. Nobody's gotten through my gateway without my permission. Not once in seven years." He hiccupped and his grin began to fade at the edges. "Is that what this is about? You want to visit the Netherworld? Not a good idea for humans, you know. Get too close to the gates of Hell and your mortal bodies will be incinerated on the spot."

Humans? Eden frowned. Why couldn't the angel sense that Darrak and Theo were demons?

"No, that's not what we want," Theo said. "I'd actually like you to take a look at something for me. Something I recently acquired after a long search."

"Sure," Alistair slurred. "What is it?"

Theo reached into his pocket and pulled out a black crystal. It was three inches long, flat, and sharp on one end.

"It's very beautiful," Alistair said. "May I?"

"Of course." Theo handed the crystal shard to him.

Eden's phone buzzed again. *ANDY.* She ignored it.

"What is it?" Alistair asked.

"It's a black diamond."

"Precious."

"Very. Hard to find, let me tell you. It's taken me a long time to find one large enough. But time plus determination inevitably equals success."

Was that the weapon? Eden wondered. If so, why would he show it to an angel?

"I'm not a collector of rare gems, if that's what you're looking for." Alistair gave the diamond back to Theo and took a swig of his drink. "Us angels tend to hold no material possessions. Makes it easier to return to the heavenly realm."

"I don't want you to buy it."

Alistair placed the mug down on the table and turned to him warily. "Then what exactly do you want from me?"

Theo touched the angel's wrist, wrapping his fingers around it. "Your heart."

"My heart?" Alistair's brows drew together. "But angels don't have—"

Then his eyes went very wide, and Eden felt a tidal wave of energy crash through the pub. Her breath caught in her throat. "What are you doing?"

A sparkling white light exited Alistair's body and channeled into the diamond sitting in Theo's palm. It began to glow.

"Darrak," Eden managed, clutching his arm. "What the hell is going on?"

Darrak's brows drew together. He felt tense, every muscle flexed. "What are you doing, Theo?"

"Channeling our pal Alistair's angelic energy into this black diamond to create my angelheart, of course. What does it look like?" Flames filled Theo's eyes. "Now if you don't mind, I really have to concentrate. Almost there."

Eden reached across the table and grabbed Theo wrist, attempting to pry him off the angel, but she couldn't budge him an inch.

Instead, she began to feel a draining sensation.

"Perfect," Theo said, and winked at her. "That helps a lot. Thanks."

Alistair raised his gaze to Eden's. "You're a black witch."

It wasn't a question.

"Are you okay?" she demanded. "Is he hurting you?"

"Hurting me?" Alistair gasped for breath. "He's ripping my angelic energy right out of me. Yes, it kind of stings."

"Theo, stop it!" she snapped.

"And . . . he's a demon?" Alistair managed. "I didn't sense it. I couldn't sense it."

"Why didn't you?" she asked, her voice hoarse and panicky. It felt like electricity sparked through the pub, but it wasn't caused by her magic this time.

His face was strained. "A black witch's aura can dampen an angel's senses. The alcohol doesn't help, either. Should have stopped after my third one. But it's been a hard day at the office."

"One of the reasons you were chosen was your tendency to drink too much," Theo informed him. "Now, please shhh."

This was why Theo wanted her to come with him. He knew she was a black witch, and he could use that to do . . . whatever it was he was doing to Alistair. An angelheart. Is that what he called it? That was the weapon.

"Darrak," Eden looked at him. "Do something! Theo's killing him!"

Darrak didn't move for a moment, but then his hand shot out and he caught Theo's wrist. Flames had appeared in Darrak's eyes as well. "That's enough. You don't need to destroy him completely, do you?"

Theo grinned. "I guess not. But thanks for ruining the party."

"This is no party."

"If you say so. Doesn't matter. I got what I came here for."

The next moment, the flames left Theo's eyes. Alistair slumped forward on the table, his eyes closed.

Theo fisted the diamond and slid it back into his pocket. He slapped the angel on his back and threw a roll of bills on the table before he got up from the booth. "For your troubles. Thanks a bunch."

Eden scooted around to the other side of the table to check Alistair.

"Don't worry. He's alive," Theo said. "Darrak was right. There's no need to exert the energy to kill him."

"You took all of his angelic energy," Darrak said. "You put it into that diamond."

He sounded flat and emotionless about it.

"Yes, that's exactly what I did," Theo confirmed.

"What does that mean?" Eden demanded. "Is Alistair going to be okay?"

"He's human now," Darrak said. "All of his angelic power is trapped in the black diamond now."

"I need another drink!" Alistair slurred without raising his face from the table. "Maybe eight!"

"Give it back to him right now," Eden said. She was shaking. She was supposed to observe Theo getting his hands on the weapon. Well, she'd observed. She'd expected a dagger or something stolen from the vaults of a museum, but a diamond filled with angelic energy?

She knew crystals—most commonly, pieces of rock salt—were used to help imprison demons. Once the demon found himself trapped, the crystal was smashed to finish the exorcism and destroy the demon. The weaker the crystal the easier it would be for a demon to escape. If one was so inclined, clear diamonds could be used to indefinitely trap a demon and channel its power.

She didn't need a gemology course to conclude that a black diamond was meant to trap an angel's power, making it into a weapon to destroy someone like Lucifer.

"Can't give it back," Theo said simply, tapping his pocket. "This baby has one shot. One use. And I'm going to make sure it hits the target."

"You *used* me." Eden's eyes narrowed. "You knew having me here would be enough to render him clueless about who and what you are."

"I'm so clueless," Alistair murmured into the tabletop.

"Yes, that's right," Theo agreed. "And thank you. You were very helpful. But don't worry, I'm not going to go back on our bargain. You helped me and now I'll help you. Right Darrak?"

"Get out of here," Darrak said darkly.

Theo looked surprised. "What?"

"I would have liked to know exactly what was going to happen here today ahead of time."

"What do you care? He was just an angel." Theo shrugged. "And it's not like I killed him."

"He can't go back to Heaven now," Eden said. "Can he?"

Theo rolled his eyes. "He'll have more fun as a human than an angel."

"You need to go now." Darrak didn't sound as if he wanted any further argument. Eden found small comfort in the fact he wasn't celebrating alongside Theo at the moment.

Theo looked confused. "You are so harshing my victory buzz right now. Do you know how long I've been planning this? And now I'm going to help you out. *Both* of you."

Darrak didn't answer. His jaw was tight.

"I also have another surprise planned to show my gratitude," Theo said, then raised his hands when that received a glare. "Don't worry. It's something you're going to *love*." He cast a dark look at Eden as if he blamed her for Darrak's current treatment of him.

"I think Darrak said something about you leaving?" Eden said grimly.

He turned to face her. "Oh, Eden, what would Darrak do without you?"

She glared at the sarcasm but didn't reply.

"You're lucky he's sweet on you, you know that? Because, just between you and me?" Theo's eyes narrowed. "It's the only reason you're still breathing."

"Just try something," Eden said, feeling magic channel into her hand. "I dare you."

"Enough," Darrak growled. "Both of you. Theo, leave now."

"Hope she's worth it, Darrak," Theo replied. "Oh, and Eden? Darrak and me go way back. We're almost exactly the same and always have been. If you think he's any different, then you're fooling yourself." He grinned and patted his pocket. "Thanks again for the help. I owe you one!"

He left the pub without another word.

"Is he gone?" Alistair asked, facedown.

"He is."

Alistair pushed back from the table and looked at her wearily. "Well, I don't think that could have sucked any worse."

She shook her head. "I am so, so sorry. I had no idea what he planned to do."

"I feel drained." He raised his hand to catch the bartender's attention. "Smirnoff. And keep 'em coming."

"I'll do everything I can to get your angelic energy back."

Alistair laughed humorlessly. "Don't bother. It's too late."

"No, it can't be. I can fix this."

"What are you, stupid or something? Not everything can be fixed. This is one of those things." He drained his glass of beer and slammed it down on the table, before raking a hand through his thin head of hair. "My decisions have led me to this fate. If I'd been a perfect angel, I wouldn't be here, would I?"

"How can you just accept this?"

"Eden, leave him be," Darrak said.

"Theo stole his soul," Eden said.

"Angels don't have souls. Neither do demons," Alistair said. "He stole my energy, my power. My ticket back to Heaven. So, yeah, I'm pissed. But I only blame myself."

Eden looked at Darrak.

"Angels are very even tempered," he said. "Except for

the archangels. Don't want to mess with them. All flaming swords and fury. Not pleasant, or so I've heard."

Eden draped an arm around Alistair. "This is my fault, too. And I swear I'll try to make it up to you."

"Really?" Alistair said.

She nodded. "Really."

He clamped his hand over her left breast and squeezed. "I think I know how you can start making it up to me, pretty lady."

She pushed him away, her compassion and guilt turning quickly to disgust. This was an angel? "Not exactly what I had in mind."

"Oh, come on. I thought you were feeling guilty? Black witches are disgusting evildoers, but they're still soft and warm and human enough. You look like you might be good for a roll in the hay." He reached for her again, and she slapped his hands away.

"Darrak?" she said.

"Charity time over?" he asked.

"Afraid so." She stood up and looked at the former angel, who now just looked like a drunk man. "I am sorry. Really."

"If you were that sorry, you'd be giving me a lap dance right now." He patted his lap. "Come on. Make it up to me."

"You're disgusting."

Her cell phone rang again, and she dragged it out of her pocket. Andy again. She finally answered it.

"Andy, I'm a bit busy right now."

"Eden . . ." was the hoarse, weak reply. "Please . . . help me . . ."

Her back stiffened. "What's wrong?"

"I . . . I'm hurt. I need . . . help . . . please . . ."

"Where are you?"

The line went dead.

⇒ FIFTEEN ⇐

With shaking hands, Eden hit the speed dial for Andy's number. It rang but no one picked up.

"What's wrong?" Darrak asked.

That was a good question. What was wrong? She didn't know. But something was.

"It's Andy. He's hurt and I . . . I don't know where he is."

"Does everyone who knows you end up hurt, sugar tits?" Alistair asked, knocking back the first shot of vodka the bartender brought to the table.

Yeah. It looked like maybe he was right.

She had to find Andy. Darrak followed her out to the parking lot.

"I have to concentrate," she said, trying to tap into her psychic energy. She had been able to locate things in the past, but it had never been with much accuracy or when she'd wanted to. Images came to her mind without her asking for them and at unexpected times. She wished she could channel it to help her whenever she needed it.

However, she did have another power she could now channel whenever she wanted.

As if reading her mind, Darrak grabbed her arm. "Eden, no. You can't use your magic for this."

She shrugged away from him. "He's hurt, and I don't know where he is. I won't let him die."

"Eden, no—"

But it was too late. She flexed her mind and dipped shallowly into the surface of her magic that had been there lying in wait the whole time they were with Theo. She cringed as the force of it hit her and her stomach cramped with pain.

She had just one thought: *Where is Andy?*

Her magic reached out over the city as if it was a spiderweb, pulsing and moving, searching and reaching. The spiderweb turned thicker, like oil spreading out. A rancid black icing spread over the top of a rotting cake.

Gross.

But it did the trick. She saw it as clear as day.

"I know where he is." She opened her eyes to look at Darrak, who held by her shoulders and stared down at her, concern creasing his brow.

"Eden, why do you keep doing that?" He sounded furious with her, and his eyes blazed fire. "You *can't* use your black magic, no matter what. What about this don't you understand?"

Magic continued to crackle around her like static. "You're so cute when you worry about my immortal soul."

"Eden, I—"

She grabbed the front of his shirt and pulled him closer to her. Then she kissed him hard on his mouth.

When they parted and he looked at a loss for words, she slapped him.

"Ow." He pressed his hand against the side of his face. "What was that for?"

"For introducing me to your asshole buddy Theo."

"And the kiss?"

"Because using my magic makes me want to kiss a demon, and you were the closest." She took his hand and pulled him toward the car. "There's no time to talk about kissing or slapping. Get in. Hurry."

He did as she asked without further argument.

It took ten excruciatingly long minutes for her to drive to the location she saw in her mind's eye. It was an alleyway filled with Dumpsters and strewn garbage between two graffiti-covered buildings. She didn't wait for Darrak to follow her. She got out and started walking toward the spot she'd seen in her head.

"Andy," she called out. The magic that had been there for her a minute ago had finally faded, leaving her feeling cold and scared.

There was no reply.

"Eden, be careful," Darrak said.

She felt on the verge of hysterical tears. "He was trying to call me but I ignored him. He wanted my help on this case, but I was too busy dealing with everything going on with us."

"And Andy understood that."

"It doesn't matter. If something bad has happened to him, it's my—"

"Watch out!" Darrak yelled and grabbed her, pulling her out of the way as something launched itself at her. She hit the ground hard.

"What the hell was that?" she asked.

She heard a growling sound and looked up. A huge animal stood eight feet away from her, baring its teeth and growling. Saliva dripped from its jowls. It had gray fur and a dark streak down its back.

It looked like a . . . wolf.

"Werewolf," she managed.

"Don't move," Darrak warned.

Andy had been on the case—the werewolf case. The

cheating spouse. All he'd had to do was to take some pictures, but . . . but something had gone wrong.

Her stomach clenched as she saw the blood on the wolf's muzzle. It snarled and moved closer.

"Don't even think about it, puppy dog," Darrak rose to his feet. The wolf didn't back down; in fact, it drew closer.

"Darrak!" What did he think he was doing? "Don't get near it."

"Werewolves don't scare me," he said. "Should be the other way around, right puppy? What? Don't you sense what I am? I can understand that. I'm a bit different recently. But, trust me, not where it counts."

He held his right hand out. Eden's eyes widened as flames began to ripple across his skin from the elbow down until his hand could no longer be seen behind the fire.

The wolf whimpered and stepped back.

"That's right. I suggest you run away before I decide that well-done werewolf steaks are on the dinner menu tonight."

The wolf bared its sharp teeth again as if deciding whether or not it wanted to fight with a demon, but then it thought better of it, tucked its tail between its legs, and ran away.

Eden finally let out the breath she'd been holding.

Darrak glared at her. "That was way too close."

She scrambled to her feet. "Where is he?" She scanned the alley until she saw it. A boot attached to a leg, sticking out from behind a green Dumpster. Without hesitating, she ran to it.

Sure enough, it was Andy. He lay on the ground, half covered in garbage. His white shirt was dirty and ripped and covered with blood.

Three deep, red slash marks streaked across his face.

She clamped a hand over her mouth at the horrific sight, a sob catching in her throat.

Darrak pushed past her, knelt at Andy's side, and checked his pulse.

"Is he . . ." she began, not wanting to ask the question. If Andy had been killed because she'd ignored him, she didn't know what she'd do.

"He's alive," Darrak confirmed. "But barely."

She dialed 911 on her cell phone. Why would Andy call her and not an ambulance? She could yell at him for that later. Right now, they needed help.

The ambulance arrived five minutes later, and Andy was taken away to the hospital.

Eden and Darrak followed in her car.

It was funny how something like this, a friend who'd been hurt and almost killed, cancelled out all of her other worries. She'd endured blackmail from Lucifer himself, as well as helping a greedy demon strip an angel of his power, but Andy's well-being was the only thing that mattered to her at the moment.

Her fingers went to her gray amulet, and she twisted the chain nervously as she waited.

Darrak stayed by her side but didn't try to make her talk . She knew he was angry she'd used black magic to find Andy, but she'd had no other choice. In fact, it was one time that she was actually thankful she had some extra power. If she'd been a regular, everyday woman, then she wouldn't have been able to find him in time. She felt certain the were-wolf would have finished Andy off if they hadn't been there to stop it.

Over an hour later a doctor came out to speak with them.

"He's going to be fine," she said.

Eden exhaled shakily. "Thank God."

"Looks like a wild animal attack," the doctor said. "Something large. Unusual for the downtown core but not unheard of. He's lucky to be alive."

"Can we see him?"

"Are you family?"

"Yes," Eden said. "I'm his niece and this is my husband."

Darrak raised an eyebrow.

She lied very easily. Almost *too* easily. But she didn't want to wait.

Lies sometimes got you what you wanted.

In Andy's room, she slowly approached him in the hospital bed. He was covered in white bandages.

"Hey," Andy said weakly, raising a hand to her. She took it gently.

"What did I tell you about getting yourself hurt like this?" she said.

"I don't think you told me anything, did you?"

"No, I didn't. But that's only because I didn't think you would. Otherwise, I would have given you a very stern warning not to."

He grinned a little but then grimaced. "I'll have to keep that in mind for next time."

"There's not going to be a next time."

He touched the bandage that covered half his face. "You're right. I think I've learned my lesson about werewolves. They don't like being spied on, do they? Who knew? The wife's boyfriend is responsible for this. Smashed my camera and chased me, then beat the shit out of me, as you can see. He turned to his wolf form—which, by the way? *Freaky as hell*—and I thought he was going to tear my throat out. Feels like he did."

"Did he give you these wounds when he was in wolf form?" Darrak asked.

"Yeah. I guess women are going to have to love me for my personality now instead of my male-model good looks." Andy attempted to grin but failed.

Eden sat on the edge of Andy's bed, still holding his hand, and studied Darrak. "What's wrong?"

His light blue eyes met hers. "He was attacked by a werewolf. You saw it yourself."

"I know. But I don't know what we should say on the police report."

"There's not going to be a police report. The police won't know what to do with this," Darrak said. "It's just . . ."

"Just what?" Andy asked.

A sensation of dread crawled up Eden's spine. "What is it?"

"May I?" Darrak indicated Andy's facial bandage.

"You want to look?" he asked. "Kind of morbid, don't you think?"

"I just need to check something."

"Then go ahead." Andy eyed the door. "But Nurse Ratched will have a fit if she sees you. The women here . . . not charmed by me bleeding all over the place."

That sounded like a good opening for a snappy comeback from Darrak, but he didn't crack a smile at Andy's attempt to lighten the mood. Instead he gently peeled back the corner of the bandage.

His lips thinned. "That's what I thought."

"That bad, huh?" Andy said.

Eden had forgotten to breathe again. She'd braced herself to see horrible wounds, but instead, the only thing under the bandage were three faint red scratches. The wounds had almost completely healed.

"Oh, my God." Her voice was hoarse.

Andy cringed. "Hey, no reason to rub it in. I used to be very vain, you know."

Eden's hands trembled as she reached into her purse and pulled out a hand mirror, flipped it open, and held it in front of Andy. It took him a moment before he forced himself to look at the damage, his face tense as if bracing himself for the worst.

He blinked in disbelief. "That's not half as bad as I thought it would be."

"It *was* as bad as you thought," Darrak said. "You're healing."

"This fast? How's that even possible?"

"It's possible because the wounds came from a were-wolf."

"So what? That means they heal up faster than if it was a regular wolf? Like they're magic wounds?"

"No, it means your healing ability has now improved since you've become infected."

Andy frowned. "Darrak, I don't know what you're talking about. Infected with what?"

"*Lycanthropy* is the proper term," Darrak said. "Shifters can change whenever they like, with effort and practice. It's only on the night of the full moon that they lose any ability to maintain human form. Luckily, the next full moon isn't for a couple of weeks. You'll have time to do some research. You should meet some other shifters and ask for their as-sistance, although I'd probably suggest you stay away from the one who infected you, at least temporarily."

Andy stared at him.

Eden was still in too much shock to say anything for a moment. When she found her voice, she said, "Andy, it's going to be okay."

"Are you . . . trying to tell me . . . I'm a—a werewolf now?" he choked out.

Darrak nodded. "I'm afraid so."

Andy's cheek twitched. "I'm not even a dog person."

"It'll be okay." Eden touched his arm. She'd already said it, but she didn't know what else to say. She'd never dealt with something like this before. Andy wasn't the only one going into shock.

He struggled to sit up. "I'm—I'm a werewolf. A man who can turn into a wolf. With fur. And fangs. And the abil-ity to howl at the moon. Paws and claws. And flea baths. And . . . oh, my God." He was breathing so quickly now Eden worried he'd hyperventilate.

She searched her brain for something to say to help make this a little better but came up blank. She wanted to cry. "It doesn't change anything. You're still my partner at Triple-A. This doesn't give you the right to flake out on me."

He gasped for breath. "It . . . it doesn't?"

"No. You're the main investigator. I'm the girl Friday."

"Like Rosalind Russell."

"Exactly like that." She nodded. "And if you flake out, you won't be able to take on any new cases and . . . and you won't be able to make the lease payments on your Porsche."

"I love my Porsche." He nodded. "I have to keep her."

"Of course you do." This was working. She squeezed his hand harder. "Your Porsche loves you, too. So you see? It's going to be okay. Darrak and I are here for you, no matter what."

"I'm going to shed," he said. "Did you see the werewolf that did this to me? He was very hairy. And . . . and he drooled."

She managed to grin at that. "You're already really hairy, and I'm sure you drool more than your share. Really, the only difference is your love of cigars. You'll be a cigar-smoking werewolf."

He laughed, despite still looking panic-stricken by this life-altering news. "That's helpful. Thanks."

"And there are plenty of cases that I need your help on."

"Oh? Like what?"

"Well," she chewed her bottom lip and scanned her mind for something to tell him. Something he could latch onto as a reason to get back to normal life as quickly as possible. Darrak stood by with his hands clasped behind his back. "There's something strange going on at Luxuria. You know, that new singles' club that opened up recently? A friend of mine was murdered outside there the other night. You must have heard Ben asking me about him yesterday. And six other women have gone missing. My friend Graham was a reporter investigating their disappearances. We've been there a couple of times, and I sensed something strange about the place."

"You sensed it?"

"Yeah, I can do that. Sense things."

"That's because you're sort of psychic."

"Right." She didn't think this was a good time to discuss the potential of her having angel in her background. Or the black-witch thing.

One paranormal species at a time. Today would be Official Werewolf Day.

"Sounds intriguing and definitely worth investigating even though it seems like pro bono work." He swallowed and touched his rapidly healing face. "I'm so sorry for the loss of your friend. Were you close?"

"No. I hadn't seen him in years, but it still hurts to lose him." She grabbed Andy's arm and squeezed so hard he flinched. She loosened her grip a little. "That's why I can't lose you, too, you hear me?"

"I'm still here."

Darrak went to the door and glanced at the hall outside. "We'll have to get you checked out. If the doctor checks your wounds again, she's going to wonder what's up."

"I'm a werewolf," he said.

"You are," Eden confirmed.

"Well, *shit*."

That pretty much summed it up.

Together that made the three of them a werewolf, a part-angel witch, and a demon. Sounded like the beginning to a really scary joke.

Ben paced back and forth in his living room. He wanted the phone to ring. He wanted Eden to call and ask him about last night. Hell, it was okay if she *demanded* to know about last night.

He just wanted to know she was okay.

Oliver had told him not to leave the house. It felt as if

he'd been out drinking the night before. Apparently that's what black magic did. It knocked you out and left you with some lasting pain. Oliver had originally been wary of the demon, which is why they'd had Sandy dampen him, but he'd had no idea they had to be wary of Eden as well.

It would be amusing if it didn't scare the hell out of him.

There was a knock at the door, and he went directly to it, swinging it open, half expecting to see Eden. Instead it was Sandy.

He was strangely pleased to see her instead.

That pleased feeling departed when he noticed the fresh bruise on her cheekbone.

"Can I come in?" she asked.

"Sure." Ben stood aside, and she swept past him smelling pleasantly of vanilla. He'd met her shortly after being inducted as a member of the Malleus. She'd applied ointment to his brand. He'd called her Florence Nightingale at the time.

"I probably shouldn't be here, but I wanted to see you," she said, wringing her hands.

"What happened to you?"

She looked confused for a moment.

"Your face," he clarified.

Sandy touched her bruise and flinched. "Somebody's not too happy with my job performance."

A line of fury ripped through Ben. "Oliver did this?"

"It's nothing."

"Damn it, Sandy." He closed the distance between them and moved the long blonde hair off her face and tucked it behind her ear. Then he gently touched the light purple patch of skin. "He had no right to hit you."

"I tend to agree, but what's done is done."

"What is his damn problem?"

"He thinks I was keeping things from him. Like I should have known Eden was a black witch."

"Should you have?"

"Yes." She swallowed. "Actually, I did figure it out before I said anything."

"Why didn't you say anything?"

"Because . . . because Eden isn't evil. And the way they deal with black witches, well, it's not always a good thing."

"It's the demon inside her forcing her to do these things."

"No. I think Eden's going through a lot right now, but the Malleus . . . and you . . . are looking at things from the wrong angle. I honestly don't think the demon means her any harm."

"Why would you say that?"

"Because she's convinced he isn't."

Ben sighed with frustration. "Deception only."

"I think Eden needs help, but as far as your single-handed mission to save her . . . well, I think it's extreme, and as you can see, it doesn't go over that well with her."

"You think she'll continue to kick our collective asses if we get close to her?"

She managed to grin a little at that. "Yes. Without a doubt."

It was nice that one of them could see the humor in this. "So what do we do?"

"Quite honestly, I think we should leave her be. The Malleus has enough things to worry about other than her."

"I can't just forget about this." He clenched his fists and turned away.

"She doesn't want your help, Ben." Sandy frowned and looked closer at him. "Hey, did you hit your head last night when you fell?"

He touched his forehead at the hairline. "I got a bit of a bump, but it's no big deal."

"Let me see."

"Sandy, it's really not necessary."

"Are you going to argue with me or be a good boy?"

He smiled despite himself. "If I'm a good boy do I get a lollipop?"

"We'll see. Sit down."

He sat on the edge of his leather sofa. It was the same spot where Eden had been magically restrained twelve hours earlier. Sandy pushed his hair back so she could see the small cut better.

"Am I going to live, doctor?" he asked.

"Luckily, you seem to have a mutantly hard head to take any blows."

"Thanks. So what's required? A Band-Aid?"

Sandy's fingers slid farther into his hair. "No, but I think I can help a little."

He was about to protest. He didn't want her to use any magic on him, even if it was just to heal a cut. It felt wrong to him. But then he felt her lips brush against his forehead and a breath caught in his throat.

"Sandy . . ."

"See?" She smiled. "All better."

"Strangely it does feel much better."

"I'm very good at my job."

"And how about this." He touched her bruise.

"The same treatment might help," she said.

He nodded, then took her face in his hands and brushed his mouth softly over her cheek.

"Much better," she managed.

"First aid is a good thing."

"It is."

He'd noticed her mouth before—couldn't help it, really. Full lips. Lush, in fact. And she never wore any bright lipstick, just a touch of gloss to bring out the naturally pink color. He couldn't help himself. He pressed his lips against hers and kissed her. A small moan escaped her throat as her mouth opened to his.

A moment later she pushed him away, her cheeks reddening.

"Whoa, we can't do that," she said, scrambling back from him.

He touched his mouth, surprised by what had happened
as much as she was.

"Why not?" He stood up from the sofa feeling a bit un-
steady on his feet all of a sudden.

"Malleus members are not allowed to . . . well, not with
other members. It's unprofessional and distracting. That's
why it's against the rules."

"That's ridiculous."

"Ridiculous or not they're very strict about it."

"You're not even a member. You're a consultant."

"Still. If Oliver found out, he'd . . ." She swallowed hard.

"He'd what?" Anger returned to Ben right on schedule.

"He'd be mad. Besides, you're in love with . . . with Eden.
Right?" Sandy looked away. "I get that. It's why you want to
save her so badly. It's okay, really. It's easier that way for
me." She grabbed her purse, which had fallen to the floor.
"Look, I need to go. Let's just forget this ever happened."

"Sandy . . ."

But she wasn't sticking around to discuss their kiss, or
the fact Ben suddenly wanted to kiss her again.

"I'll see you later," she said.

Sandy went out the door and shut it behind her. A second
later he opened it, but he didn't chase after her. She was in
a hurry to go, and he wasn't going to stop her from doing
what she needed to do.

He wiped a hand over his forehead, which had suddenly
started to ache again. And his forearm itched. He wished
the brand would just heal up, already. He'd refused any and
all magical remedies. Just because he'd chosen to become
a member of the Malleus, didn't mean he necessarily believed in some of their practices.

Especially when some of those practices including strik-
ing women like Sandy for not living up to expectations. As
a cop, Ben had witnessed his share of abused women, and
it never got easier. Abusers, to Ben, were as bad as demons.
Unfortunately, the most you could do with a wife beater

was to throw him in jail. Couldn't exorcise him, even though that would solve a whole lot of problems.

Damn it. He couldn't just stay here and do nothing, waiting for Oliver to get in touch and give him permission to leave his house. It was his life, after all. And he would do whatever he wanted, whenever he wanted. And he wanted to make sure Eden was okay.

He scratched his brand again. It allegedly gave him extra strength, the ability to sense the otherworldly, and the power to exterminate them easier than the average Joe.

Ben wasn't sure what he'd do the next time he was face-to-face with Eden's demon, but he was damn sure he'd do the right thing. Whatever the hell that was.

After staring down his share of murderers, rapists, and arsonists, Ben knew he could tell the difference between good and evil. Darrak was evil. Ben had no doubt about it.

He grabbed his keys and left through the front door, locking it behind him. His old black Chrysler LeBaron was parked in the driveway. He slid a key into the lock.

"Excuse me," a voice said from behind him. "Are you Ben Hanson?"

"I am." He turned to see a tall man who looked to be in his late twenties standing there. The man had tanned skin and sleek black hair tied back from his face. "Who're you?"

"I'm a friend of Darrak's," the man said with a grin.

Ben frowned. "You're a—"

Pain suddenly washed over him, and a moment later he felt nothing.

⇉ SIXTEEN ⇇

Eden was concerned they wouldn't be able to get Andy released without a lot of questions. Darrak had a funny feeling
she might try to use some of her magic again to "persuade"
the doctor.

He wouldn't let that happen. She'd used enough black
magic for one day. More than enough.

He had his own way of persuading the doctor.

It did help that she was a woman—and one that was remarkably susceptible to his charms.

He still had it. Good to know.

Eden just shook her head as Darrak wheeled Andy out
of the room after a five minute chat with the doctor.

"Ex-incubus," he said simply.

"And that explains everything?"

He shrugged, and grinned a little wickedly at her. "It's a
miracle you can keep your clothes on around me. I'm usually impossible to resist. As was just proven with Dr. Anderson. *Monica* Anderson. She gave me her number."

"Congrats. You know, I did introduce you as my husband. It's so wonderful to see she didn't have a problem with that."

"I guess humans and werewolves are similar when it comes to their views of infidelity."

"Not all humans."

He couldn't really read her expression at the moment. Sure, he had a way with women, but it wasn't as if he'd proved it time and time again. Since he'd possessed Eden, he'd barely looked at anyone else.

Some ex-incubus he was.

Andy had nothing to add to the conversation, although Darrak couldn't blame him. He'd just discovered he was the latest werewolf citizen of the greater Toronto Area.

Andy would deal. After all, he had Eden helping him.

Darrak had been mildly surprised by the depth of her concern over the guy. Sure, they worked together and seemed friendly enough, but her reaction to his phone call and then the pain in her eyes earlier as he learned of his condition—well, she cared about him a lot. It was obvious.

Eden's compassion and distress had stirred something inside Darrak. It had made his feelings for her grow even deeper.

And that could not be more annoying to him. He was messed up enough as it was, without falling any harder for her.

So damn inconvenient.

Especially when he knew she probably hated him now after what happened with Theo. How was he supposed to know Theo planned on sucking the celestial goodness out of that angel right in front of her? Darrak had to say, he was torn. Theo now had the weapon he would use to destroy Lucifer. *Hooray.* But the whole thing felt kind of . . . *wrong* to Darrak, and he wasn't really sure why.

Boo.

He attempted to summon some enthusiasm, but he felt

drained. Using his power in the alley to scare off the were-wolf had taken it out of him. There were two ways he could recover this energy. He could just give himself time, and he would eventually recover naturally. Or he could absorb some of Eden's energy. This had two downsides to it—it would exhaust Eden for hours at a time, and the act also ran the risk of Darrak taking too much and accidentally killing her because she tasted so good he couldn't stop himself.

Probably not such a good idea.

Demons were energy mosquitoes when they had to be. Vampires from hell, only his drink of choice wasn't blood—it was life itself.

Something was bothering Eden, above and beyond what had happened with Andy. And it wasn't only to do with Theo since she'd had this cloud over her since earlier. Darrak watched her carefully, trying to figure out what she wasn't telling him. It would really help if he could read her mind. But, unfortunately, he couldn't.

They dropped Andy off at his house. Eden volunteered to stay with him, but he waved her off.

"I'm fine," he said and began to peel his bandages off to reveal the almost fully healed skin beneath. He touched it gingerly as if he couldn't believe it was for real after how much that werewolf had torn him apart.

Darrak supported him as they walked to the brown cor-duroy couch. An old *TV Guide* and an empty bottle of Coors Light sat on the coffee table.

"You're sure?" Eden asked, skeptically.

"Yeah, I'm sure."

She still looked concerned. "What about that werewolf who attacked you? Do you think he'll come after you again?"

Andy grimaced. "The last thing he said before he shifted was for me to leave him and his girlfriend the hell alone. If I don't go near him again, he won't have a reason to finish the job, will he?"

But Eden still looked worried. "Not if he knows what's good for him."

"I'm fine," he assured her. "Really."

She touched his face. "Really?"

He swallowed and then grinned a little. "Well, maybe I'm a bit traumatized. I'll admit it. But I'll survive."

Eden hugged him, and Darrak watched her emotional outpouring with a tight feeling in his chest. Andy wasn't really a father figure to her, or even an uncle. He supposed she thought of him as a good friend. He knew she didn't have very many friends in the city since she kept to herself a lot. It would make her cherish the ones she did have.

"Hey." Andy leaned back so he could see her. "What's this?"

"What?"

"Tears? Don't cry over me, Eden. It'll make your eyes all puffy and unattractive."

She laughed. "Wouldn't want that."

"Definitely not."

Her expression sobered. "This is all my fault, you know. If it wasn't for me, you wouldn't have werewolf clients in the first place. And you wouldn't have gotten hurt."

"And Triple-A wouldn't be thriving at the moment, allowing me to start paying off my monumental debt. Our new supernatural clients seem to have plenty of money, and that's more than okay with me." He looked at Darrak. "Take her home. She's exhausted. And growing puffier all the time. I can't handle anyone crying around me. It's going to make me start crying, too."

"I'm not crying. Demons don't get emotional like humans." Darrak didn't even know if he *could* cry. It had never been an issue before.

"Demons are manly creatures, aren't they?"

"Except for the demonesses. They're even manlier."

Andy finished removing his bandages and threw them on the coffee table in a white gauzy pile. "I've decided to

look into Luxuria later today and find out if something
funny's going on there."

"The hell you will." Eden had her arms crossed. "What
you're going to do is recover and deal with your own problems. The last thing I'm going to let you do is investigate
something else that might put you in danger again."

Andy rolled his eyes. "Yes, mom."

She huffed. "I'm just trying to think logically."

"You're very logical for a possessed redhead. Fine, I'll
take today off and watch some soap operas and talk shows."

"Good. Just heal."

His forehead wrinkled. "Is that a dog-trick command?
Because I might have to start taking offense to that."

"Not heel. *Heal.* With an *A*. And don't just take today
off. Take tomorrow off as well. Nothing at the office is urgent enough that it can't wait until Friday. Got it? That's a
direct order from your equal partner in the business."

"You only own 49 percent," he reminded her.

"Whatever." She leaned over and kissed his cheek. "And,
just so you know, if you get hurt like this again, I'm going
to kill you."

Andy laughed. "Such an angel our Eden is, isn't she,
Darrak?"

Yes, Darrak thought. *She sort of is.*

And he didn't even mean it as an insult.

Eden wasn't in a happy place when she and Darrak got
back to the apartment. Her neck strained from keeping an
eye out for Ben and Oliver. She wasn't complaining, but it
was a little, uh, *eerie*, that they hadn't even attempted to
make contact since she'd knocked them out last night. She
knew she hadn't killed them.

What were they planning next?

She had too much on her mind and thoughts were beginning to overlap, threatening to drive her totally batty. Too

much to do, too much to think about, her life had begun to spin completely out of control.

"I'm so bored," Leena announced. She was sprawled on the sofa. "Seriously. Bored. To death."

"You can leave the apartment, you know," Darrak said dryly.

"Leave? Are you kidding? I told you, people want to kill me if I step foot outside, especially if I'm in human form. D-E-A-D. I can't leave. Not yet. I've been making some calls."

"Long distance?" Eden asked weakly.

"Well, yeah. Of course. My issues are not local." She twisted a finger into her hair, and her eyes flicked to Darrak. "Speaking of local issues, somebody called for you, gruesome."

"Is that your new nickname for me?" he asked.

"Seems fitting enough."

"I have a few nicknames for you, too," he replied. "But I'll keep them to myself for the time being. They're not family-friendly."

"Someone called for Darrak?" Eden asked, frowning. Then she cringed. "Was it Theo?"

Leena shrugged. "No idea. I hung up on him before he could say."

She didn't sound particularly sorry about this.

Who else would be calling for Darrak? Who else would know he was even here?

Theo.

Just the name alone was now enough to fill her with rage. She'd been trying—sort of—to give him the benefit of the doubt since he'd been willing to help out her and Darrak. But Theo had proven himself to be an opportunist, a devious manipulator, and a scumbag without any conscience.

So, basically your average, everyday demon.

Your average, everyday demon she'd helped to completely drain an angel's energy. Funny, but that didn't sit so well with her.

She couldn't believe Darrak had actually been friends with this guy. And he was willing to conspire with him to destroy Lucifer?

It just proved that she didn't know Darrak half as well as she thought she did.

"What's up with you?" Darrak directed the question at Leena. "For someone bored, you look remarkably happy. Did you get a new cat toy to play with? A little catnip mouse to merrily bat around?"

Leena glared at him, but then a grin appeared on her lips. "I think I'm going to ask him out."

"Who?" Eden asked.

"Lucas from next door. Could he be any more adorable? And he's a teacher. Not normally my type, but I'm willing to make an exception. I don't usually get the attraction vibe right away, but I felt it between us this morning, you know?"

Darrak snorted. "Go for it. He looked pretty hard up for a date. You're perfect for him."

Leena ignored that. "Do you think he has a girlfriend already?" she asked Eden.

"Uh . . . I really don't know." Good question. Did Lucifer, the Prince of Hell, have a girlfriend, or would he be willing to take her shapeshifting roommate out to dinner and a movie?

The phone rang and Leena answered it, holding her index finger up to them and turning her back. The call must have been for her.

Eden's head began to throb. Oh, wait, it already did. The pressure had simply ramped up. She rubbed her temples and went to sit down heavily on her sofa, pushing aside an issue of *Cosmo* that was in her way.

"How are you holding up?" Darrak asked. "I know it's been . . . a bit of a difficult day."

"Difficult? Today? You really think so?" Sarcasm dripped.

"Can't say it's been boring, though."

"I'm fine."

"I find that hard to believe."

She snorted. "Oh, really?"

"I mean . . ." He sat down next to her, a bit tentatively, and took her hand in his, rubbing his thumb over her knuckles. She didn't pull away. "I know what happened with Andy was rough on you."

"Yeah, it was." His concern was oddly touching. She looked up and met his blue eyes. Even after everything that had happened, she still desperately wanted to trust him.

His gaze moved to her mouth. It helped a memory of him kissing her to vividly return.

Even after a day like today, the demon was still able to turn her on with just the direction of his eyes?

So not fair.

Did he feel it, too? This undeniable attraction between them?

Sometimes she couldn't give a smaller crap about the black-witch-imbuing spell Selina had cast on him hundreds of years ago. All Eden wanted was to touch Darrak and for him to touch her and to hell with the consequences. To feel his hands on her body again. His mouth on hers.

It was overwhelming.

I want you, she thought. *Badly*.

But then she cleared her throat and yanked her hand away from his, before standing up from the sofa without another word.

When Leena hung up the phone, Eden walked toward her in the kitchenette, behind the counter.

"What do you know about werewolves?" she asked.

Leena made a face. "Hate them."

"Why?"

"They're territorial, mean, and the mortal enemy of werepanthers like me."

"Werepanthers?" Darrak said. He remained seated on the sofa a dozen feet away, and he leaned forward to absently flip through the copy of *Cosmo*. "I thought you were a werehousecat."

"I'm more dangerous than I look. Size really doesn't matter." She eyed him. "I'm sure you'll be happy to know that."

"Size has never been one of my problems, kitty cat."

"Sure. That's what they all say."

Eden's headache was getting worse just listening to them.

Darrak stood up and came toward Leena with an unpleasant smile on his face. "I know it's difficult for you."

She frowned. "What is?"

"Not only having to use a litter box, but also being responsible for cleaning it out. Kind of disgusting, actually."

Why did they have to squabble like this all the time? It was getting old. And it was starting to piss Eden off. She was already way too edgy today as it was, and this wasn't helping one little bit.

"Is that the best you can do, you impotent incubus?"

He laughed. "I'm not impotent."

"May as well be."

"Oh, really?"

"Yeah, really." The shapeshifter's eyes narrowed. "I know you're holding out hope you and Eden can be together, but that's a stupid and pointless thing to do."

Darrak's smile disappeared. "What the hell are you talking about?"

"She doesn't love you, gruesome. Trust me. Despite how good you might look in that body, nobody loves you. She tolerates you because she has to, that's all. You need to get that through your pin-sized demonic brain."

Fire ignited in his gaze, and his lips twisted humorlessly. "Oh, Leena. Are you trying to tell me you think I'm hot? That's kind of sweet."

She sneered at him. "No."

He shrugged. "Sorry, though. Shifters repel me. In more ways than one. Alas, I won't be able to make your many lust-filled dreams about me come true."

"I'm going to throw up."

"Come on. You don't really mean that."

She grimaced. "I wouldn't touch you with a ten-foot scratching pole, you disgusting piece of—"

"Enough!" Eden smashed her fist down on the kitchen counter. "Could you two stop squabbling for one god-damned minute? Seriously, it's annoying as hell."

Leena and Darrak both looked at her with surprise.

Anger simmered under her skin, bringing with it her very-hard-to-resist black magic. Trying to keep an even mood at the moment was hard enough, but dealing with the bickering between these two was going to put her right over the edge.

Destroying something sounded pretty good right about now. The world was at risk of becoming her own personal stress ball.

"Look, Leena, listen to me," she continued, willing herself to remain as calm as possible. Her heart thrummed in her chest. "I get that you and Darrak have a hard time communicating, okay? I understand it. But you both live with me at the moment. And if you can't get along, then one of you has to leave."

"But—"

She held up a hand. "And since Darrak is kind of attached to me at the moment, it won't be him who's doing the leaving. Do you understand?"

Leena's cheek twitched. "I was trying to help."

"It didn't sound like it to me." Eden let out a long, shaky exhale.

"Why are you defending him? In case you didn't hear everything, he was giving as good as he was getting."

"I'm not defending Darrak."

"Jesus, Eden, you're not actually in love with this jerk, are you?" Leena's dark brows drew together with confusion.

Eden didn't need this. Not now. Not ever.

"Of course not," she said as firmly as she could. Her throat felt thick, and her eyes began to sting. The events of the day—Theo, Lucifer, the angel, Andy—washed over her like a tidal wave, and she thought for sure she'd burst into tears any second.

"Eden—" Darrak began.

She turned away and went to her bedroom. "I need to be alone for a minute. Don't follow me. This is a no demon or werekitty zone for at least a half an hour. Capiche?"

"I'm a were*panther*," Leena corrected her. And then, "This is all your fault, demon."

"I hope you get fleas," he snapped back.

Eden shut the door and pressed her back against it. She could still hear them, but at least it was muffled now.

Being alone was a good thing, but it didn't help her relax much. She had things to do.

She embraced the silence for all of five seconds, then reached into her pocket and pulled out the marble Lucas gave her this morning.

Had it only been this morning?

She really didn't want to do this. Too bad she didn't have much of a choice.

Clenching the marble in her right hand, she whispered, "Lucifer."

Snap.

Bright light blinded her and she blinked. The next moment her bedroom—including her unmade bed and the movie posters that adorned her walls—were gone and she stood on the now-familiar beach again. It was sunset this time, and the skyline was ablaze with red, purple, and pink light.

Lucas stood at the waterline skipping stones across the

calm surface. He glanced over his shoulder. "Hello again, Eden."

"What is this place?" she asked.

"My little piece of heaven. I come here a lot. Too bad it's not real." He brushed his hands off on his loose white pants. "Does Theo have the weapon?"

Business first. Sunsets and palm trees second.

She nodded, feeling tense despite the beautiful surroundings. Could have something to do with the company she kept lately.

His expression didn't change. "What is it?"

She hesitated before she spoke. "A black diamond with angelic energy trapped inside. All the energy of one angel, actually. Theo called it a . . . an angelheart."

Lucas took her chin between his fingers and looked down into her eyes. "You're telling the truth, aren't you?"

"Of course I am." Why would she lie about something like this? There was a bit too much at stake for her at the moment.

A flicker of surprise went through Lucas's gaze. "Theo's more resourceful than I gave him credit for."

"Are you afraid?" She bit her bottom lip. Probably shouldn't have asked something like that of the Prince of Hell.

"No. But I am concerned." He studied her for a moment. "I never thought he'd be able to get that close to an angel, but I didn't account for the fact that you'd be there. Yes, black witches have a certain affect on our angelic friends, don't they?"

"So I'm learning."

"I don't think there's any reason to wait. Bring the diamond to me as soon as possible."

A breath caught in her throat. "That might be difficult. Theo can't stand me and, uh, the feeling's mutual. It's doubtful he'll let me get close enough to grab it."

"Then have Darrak get it for you."

She almost laughed. "And how am I supposed to do that?"

"Ask him."

"What should I say?"

"Oh, I don't know. Maybe something along the lines of 'Darrak, I want that weapon. Get it away from Theo, will you?' "

"And you think he'll do it?"

"I think it's worth a shot. And if you're denied, well . . . then we'll both know where you really stand with your resident demon, won't we? But you can't tell him why you want it. You must say nothing about me or our deal is off. Do you understand?"

"I understand." Only too well.

"Good."

She paced back and forth, wringing her hands. "And if I manage to get the angelheart, and I give it to you, you'll let my mother's soul go?" Her chest tightened with anxiety as she said it.

"I will."

"How do I know you're telling me the truth?"

"Because I am," he replied simply. "Once I get what I want, there's no reason for me to renege on our deal. It's a very fair trade, I think. Your mother's soul for the angelheart."

Was that enough? Lucas was playing this game of give-and-take really well—everything had gone his way so far. He'd managed to intimidate Eden, and she'd given him no argument.

But how often would she get a chance like this? The Prince of Hell himself needed something from her. He hadn't gone to anyone else. Just her. He'd even moved in next door at her crappy apartment building with faulty plumbing and the occasional infestation of fruit flies in order to get closer to her.

She exhaled slowly, willing some well-needed courage to arrive ASAP. "I want something else."

Lucas's eyebrow rose. "Oh really?"

She nodded. "When I give you the angelheart, I want you to fix things between me and Darrak."

"Fix things in what way?"

She licked her dry lips. "Make it so that he no longer has to possess me."

"Are you changing the rules, Eden?" Lucas asked, smiling thinly. "That's not very wise, is it?"

She held his gaze steadily. She wasn't backing down. If he knew her mother as well as he said he did, he couldn't possibly believe, 100 percent, that Eden would help her unconditionally. She would, of course, but he couldn't know that for certain. But her mother was a well-known opportunist. Why wouldn't her daughter be one as well?

"Is that a yes or a no?" she asked. "How badly do you want that diamond?"

He turned and looked at the sunset.

"Well?" she prompted after a few uncomfortable minutes had gone by. The beach had suddenly grown colder, the wind picking up—more arctic than tropical now. It blew Eden's hair back from her face and she shivered.

Without turning to face her, Lucas said, "Fine. It's a deal. If you give me that black diamond, I will release your mother's soul and also ensure that Darrak no longer has to possess you. Agreed?"

She nodded even though he couldn't see it at the moment. "Agreed."

"Now, leave me alone."

Snap.

After the flash of light, she was back in her bedroom again. Hope and dread clawed for dominance in her chest.

She'd just made a deal with Lucifer, and he was going to help her.

Something about that sentence just didn't sit well with her.

⇀ SEVENTEEN ↽

Well, that pretty much confirmed it for Darrak, didn't it?

"You're not in love with this jerk, are you?" Leena asked, point blank.

"Hell no," Eden replied. *"Are you crazy? What a ridiculous question! How could I be in love with the demon single-handedly responsible for ruining my entire life? I couldn't, that's how! Never, never ever! Multiplied by a million!"*

Cue laugh track.

Darrak was paraphrasing, of course, but that was the message received, loud and clear.

Couldn't exactly blame her.

The funny thing, really—in an entirely unfunny way—was the fact that only a few moments earlier he could have sworn he saw something in her eyes as she looked at him. Something like . . . desire.

But, hell. Lust wasn't love. He knew that better than most. He'd just never put it to the test before.

Darrak was very comfortable with lust. It made things simple. *Love* on the other hand. Well, there was nothing simple about that, was there?

Lesson of the century.

The phone rang and Leena grabbed it immediately.

"Yeah?" she said before her eyes flicked to him. "Maybe."

Darrak held out his hand. "Give it to me." When she didn't budge, his eyes narrowed, and he tried not to let his exasperation with the shifter turn into outright anger. *"Now."*

That cocky look of hers vanished for a moment, replaced with what looked a whole lot like fear. Had she caught a glimpse of hellfire in his eyes?

Served her right. The shifter really didn't know who she was messing with.

Or maybe the bitchy, argumentative act was just that. An act.

It would be much smarter for her to fear him.

"Fine." She placed the receiver on the counter. Then she shifted to her small cat form—*werepanther* his ass—and skulked over to the sofa.

The shifter was an annoying intrusion. But, he supposed, that was the point of having her there in the first place. He'd realized last night, when Eden nearly succeeded in seducing him, how very seducible he was.

Would it really have made that much difference? a part of himself asked. *She's already a black witch. The damage is done. Just because Selina warned that every time you and Eden were together it would take her into darker territory, doesn't mean it's the truth.*

The voice was tempting. Almost as tempting as Eden's warm and very willing body had been last night.

Lust only.

So give into that lust, the voice said. *Have fun with it!*

Shut up, he replied internally, and held the phone to his ear. "What?"

"It's me," Theo responded.

Darrak couldn't help but be slightly amused. "Why are you using the telephone? Seems a bit too human for you, or have things changed that much over the years?"

"The telephone wasn't even invented the last time I saw you. No e-mail either."

"Why didn't you just phase here?" Darrak asked, referring to the ability demons had to teleport from place to place at will. He couldn't do it anymore. His hundred foot tether to Eden stopped him.

"I figured if I just popped by in a flash of fire and showmanship, your girlfriend would freak out and decimate me."

"You might be right. But she's not my girlfriend."

"Saddest excuse for a black witch I've ever seen, really. Does she sell cookies?"

Darrak frowned. "What?"

"I figured she might have some available, since she's such a Girl Scout. They're so delicious, aren't they? And the cookies aren't bad, either."

"Never tried them. The scouts or the cookies. Although, I am recently very fond of chocolate donuts."

Darrak felt the curious gaze of the shapeshifter. He walked to the balcony door and stepped outside so he could have some privacy from the spy in residence. He sensed the cold, but it didn't bother him. No phasing abilities, or unlimited destructive power, but he could stand outside in the chilly air for as long as he wanted.

Yippy.

Eden had recently bought him a black leather trench coat that hung to his knees. It would be November soon, and she thought short sleeves marked him as something different when they went out. Seemed a bit bulky and unnecessary, but he wore it to please her.

He rubbed his forehead at the thought.

To please her.

What the hell had happened to him?

"What do you want, Theo?" he asked as he watched the sun getting low on the horizon. They weren't in the heart of the downtown core of the city here. More like the outskirts. There wasn't much to see other than trees and roads and sky. Below him, in the parking lot, the streetlights flickered on.

Already, he felt a small twinge of pain in his very core that worked as a warning signal that his time to lose form was not that far off.

"I know you're pissed I didn't tell you about the angel before it happened," Theo said.

"I'm not pissed. It had to happen, of course, to acquire the weapon. But I would have liked a head's-up about it, yeah."

"I have something for you that might make up for it. A gift."

Darrak watched two people get into a car below and drive out of the parking lot. To the far left he could see Eden's little Toyota.

"A gift? But it's not even my birthday. Which, since I was never birthed, is understandable."

"This is more of a gift of friendship."

Darrak snorted. What was up with Theo tonight? Maybe he wasn't the only demon who felt guilt lately. If it brought him gifts, then Darrak was okay with that. "Oh, yeah? Do you even know my favorite color?"

"I think so." There was a smile in Theo's words. It was oddly intriguing.

"What is it?"

"Can't spoil the surprise."

"Is it the means to end my curse?" he asked hopefully.

"Nope. Still working on that."

Well, that was disappointing. "If it's another gift like our visit with that angel today, I'm going to have to take a pass."

"Why do you sound so morose about that?" Theo asked. "The plan is going perfectly."

Darrak kept his gaze fixed on the setting sun. Now that Theo mentioned it, he really didn't know why he was so morose about it. He never would have had a problem with taking the necessary steps to achieve something big before.

"Darrak," Theo said after a moment. "You're still into this, right?"

"Of course."

"Sorry, but I'm not hearing the enthusiasm I'd like to from you. It's her, isn't it?"

"Her who?"

"You know who. Your hostess with the mostest. She has you wrapped around her little finger."

His jaw tensed. "No she doesn't."

"Dude, I understand. Really. It's like . . . like what happened with Kristina and me. I can see it."

"It's nothing like that."

"It's all a test, Darrak. A big one. I was tested with Kristina and I passed. Now it's your turn. If you don't pass this test, then you're going to be eternally screwed."

"A test, huh? I think I'm failing at the moment. Badly." Darrak didn't want to have this conversation. He gripped the railing of the balcony so tightly it made a metallic groaning sound.

"You're stronger than this," Theo assured him. "You might think you have some sort of strange attachment to that witch right now, but trust me, it doesn't mean anything. The moment your curse is broken you won't feel this way any longer."

Darrak's tense shoulders relaxed a little. "You think?"

"You've been possessing humans for three hundred years, no wonder you're all messed up. I would have come here and helped you earlier if I'd known what was going on. But it's not too late to change things. Once you get away from this Eden chick, you'll start thinking clearly again."

Darrak could clearly see the protective wards Eden had put up around the circumference of the apartment building.

They shimmered. Humans wouldn't be able to spot them, though. They didn't see things quite as clearly as he did.

"Will I?" he asked.

"Yes, you will. She's just one woman in how many years since we were created? A thousand? How many women have you had in that much time? How many souls have you taken?"

Darrak swallowed. The sunset now looked like fire sinking into the ground. "Countless."

"And do you remember any of them?"

"Not many," he admitted.

"You're in the middle of an existential crisis. You think the witch is helping you, but she's not. She's only helping herself. She doesn't really care about you, does she?"

Darrak remembered what Eden had said to Leena. She didn't care about him. Lust wasn't love. "No. She doesn't. Not really."

Theo's pep talk was working. He was feeling stronger the more they spoke. This was exactly what he needed, and it began to fill him with strength and resolve.

But his pain increased with every second that passed as the sun sank lower. His body wanted to turn to smoke. He had a few minutes left at most.

"Meet me tonight without what's-her-name in tow," Theo said.

"You do realize she's my host, right? And I'm about to lose form any second."

There was a short pause. "Then you know what you have to do. Meet me at Luxuria at one o'clock to get your gift. Girl Scout should be sawing logs by then, right?"

It was impossible. Darrak couldn't borrow Eden's body again without her permission.

Hold on. Why the hell couldn't he? She never had to know. The only reason she'd found out the first time is because he'd stupidly confessed to her. And that had been met with one long, annoying reprimand.

Well, you did *steal her body*, his conscience reminded him.

Since when did he have a damn conscience?

Demons didn't have consciences!

"Okay." A smile curled up the corner of his mouth at the thought of doing something wicked without remorse. "I'll see you then."

Darrak hung up before he could change his mind. Then he heard a knock on the balcony door behind him and he turned. Eden stood there.

He tensed. Had she heard him talking to Theo?

She pointed at the sunset and slid open the door.

"Standing on the balcony when you lose form might get you picked up by the breeze," she said. "It's a bit windy tonight."

"Good point."

She looked at the phone in his hand. "Theo called again?"

"You guessed it." He didn't have to lie about everything.

"What did he have to say?" she asked tightly.

"He wanted to know if you hated him for sucking out some angel juice today."

She grimaced at the reminder. "And you told him I do?"

"Of course."

"Good." She stepped out onto the balcony and closed the door. Inside, Leena cocked her furry head to the side, a curious expression on her whiskered face.

"What's wrong?" Darrak asked. There was a definite searching look in Eden's expression.

"Lots of things." She leaned against the railing next to him.

"Tell me." His knuckles whitened. He would hang on to his form for as long as there was still a sliver of light in the sky. He hated losing it. It was like giving up in a fight.

"Do you think there are ever easy answers?" she asked. "Like the hard things in life . . . do you ever think, yes, absolutely, that's what I have to do? Or is it shades of gray for everyone?"

What the hell was this all about? His pep talk from Theo had helped remind him of a few important things, but Eden's unexpected mood after she'd stormed off earlier had managed to throw him a bit.

"I think it depends on the person," he said. "Some, like the Malleus, see the world in black-and-white terms only. All good or all bad. All easy or all hard. But it's not like that. There are no easy answers."

"Not for anything?"

"Again, I suppose your mileage may vary." His brows drew together, and he reached forward to squeeze her amulet in his fist. It was much too gray at the moment. It disturbed him more than he'd like to admit.

"It doesn't change color when it touches you," she said, looking down when he released it.

"You expect it to go completely black?"

She shook her head. "I honestly don't know."

"I'm not human. I don't have a soul for it to gauge. Therefore, there's no change."

"So demons definitely don't have souls?" Her expression was open, curious, and a bit sad.

"Not demons like me. Previously human demons do, although they keep their souls in jars for safe keeping. Angels don't have souls, except the angels that used to be human."

"And werewolves?" she asked, her voice catching on the word.

He touched her chin and raised it so her eyes met his. "Andy's going to be fine."

"Promise?"

"Yes."

"And his soul?"

"Is safe. Shifters and witches are still essentially human. Humans have souls whether you want them or not. It's your gift with purchase."

"My supernatural lesson of the day."

"There will be a quiz at the end of class. So is there anything else you'd like to get off your very delectable chest at the moment?" His jaw tightened. He couldn't keep fighting this pain much longer. "Because we're close to showtime."

"Oh, right." A flicker of fear went through her eyes that only made things worse for him.

"I . . . really don't look forward to hurting you like this every day," he said, not liking how hoarse his voice suddenly sounded.

She pressed her lips together and rubbed them, blinking rapidly. "There's something I need to tell you."

Was this the secret she'd been keeping from him? The one that seemed to trouble her so deeply? He could hold it together a bit longer if he had to.

"What?" he asked.

"When you . . . when you possess me"—her green eyes met his—"it doesn't hurt me like you think it does."

He hadn't expected this revelation. "It doesn't?"

She shook her head.

"What does it feel like, then? I mean, I hear you when I . . ." He swallowed. "Well, you sound like you're in pain. You gasp and moan and . . ." He trailed off and his eyes widened. "And you . . . you . . ."

"Uh, yeah." Color came to her cheeks. "Whenever you possess me, it feels like we're, well . . . you know."

"Like we're having sex."

Eden's lips twitched into a nervous smile. "Maybe."

If he wasn't feeling so much pain at the moment, he'd be very amused. "Why didn't you tell me this before?"

She shrugged. "I guess I didn't want you to get cocky."

"No pun intended."

"So what I'm saying is out of all the things you should feel guilty about—" Her smile widened. "The act of possessing me isn't one of them. Even though you and I can't, well, can't be together like that physically, every day I do get just a taste."

"Just a taste." He drew close enough to back her up against the railing. He stroked her hair to the side and whispered into her ear, "And is that all you need?"

She inhaled sharply. "It's going to have to be, isn't it?"

The hot line of her body pressed against his was almost enough to take his pain away. Or, possibly, make it worse.

This news was just too delicious. He could feel her warm breath against his lips. She didn't pull away as he edged even closer to her.

Just a taste . . . he needed it so badly . . .

Leena cleared her throat loudly from behind him. Darrak hadn't even noticed that she'd opened the door.

"Okay, gruesome," Leena snapped. "Get away from her. Eden, you are so damn lucky I'm here, but really. A little self-control goes a long way."

Eden bit her bottom lip. "Right. Uh, thanks Leena. I don't know what I was . . . um, what I was thinking." She shook her head, averting her gaze from Darrak's as she brushed past him and went back into the apartment.

Darrak followed, glowering at the shifter, who smiled sweetly back at him as she closed the door.

"You're welcome," she said.

With amusement, Darrak watched the horror return to her eyes as he changed to black smoke in front of her a little quicker than he normally would. She shifted to her cat form again, hissed, and scurried away from his noncorporeal form.

It was important to enjoy the small things in life.

Eden had sat down on the sofa. Even with her admission, she still eyed him warily as he approached.

"It doesn't change anything between us, you know," she warned.

No, she was right about that. No matter what the act of

possession felt like for her, it didn't change the fact that he was draining her of her life's energy every time he did this.

However, this time he did notice the slight arch to her back as he possessed her, her breasts straining against the thin material of her blouse. The soft gasp from her lips as she squeezed her eyes shut.

It made him strangely happy.

But the happy feeling didn't last long. His next thought managed to destroy it.

Selina's spell. The one that would imbue Eden with more powerful and soul-damaging black magic every time they were together sexually.

Shit, he thought with a dark, sinking feeling.

They didn't have to actually have sex to trigger the spell, did they?

The spell was triggered every single day at sunset when he possessed her.

⇉ EIGHTEEN ⇇

Darrak had been unusually quiet since sunset. But chatty or not, Eden had to take the next step.

"I want to ask you something," she said. She hadn't left the apartment all evening. She didn't know where to go at the moment, so she stayed in and tried to watch TV as she waited for the right time to broach this subject with Darrak.

Leena had disappeared into the bedroom and was currently sleeping under her bed. Eden wasn't sure why the shapeshifter was being so unsocial that evening.

"What?" he asked.

"What do you think Theo has planned for that black diamond of his?" she asked, trying to sound casual. Theo hadn't come out and admitted in front of her that he planned to destroy Lucifer with it. But that was what he was going to do. And she'd been recruited as a double agent to help stop him.

It was like the rerun of *Alias* currently flickering on her television. Only Eden didn't have cool multicolored wigs like Jennifer Garner.

Darrak hesitated. "I'm not sure."

"You don't sound sure about not being sure. Are you sure you're not sure?"

"Sure. Theo does his own thing. He always has."

She curled her legs up under her on the sofa and pulled a cushion onto her lap, hugging it to her chest. "So you don't even question him?"

"I guess not."

He was keeping things from her. Then again, she was keeping things from him, too, but that was for his own good.

She could call Darrak by his full demon name, *Darrakayiis*. Then she would be able to command him. The first time she'd used it, she'd forced him to show her his demon form. When Darrak was under her control, he couldn't lie to her, either. At the very least, he'd have a hell of a time trying.

As much power as that gave her, it felt incredibly wrong to take his free will away like that.

Eden used to think money made the world go around. After a lifetime of scraping by and a mother who either won big or lost big at the casinos, Eden was used to slim times. But now she knew it wasn't really money that made the difference. It was *power*.

And, hell, money still helped. Even a black witch had to feed herself.

Darrak broke the silence after a minute. "You need to forget about that diamond."

"I can't."

"Trust me, it would be better if you did."

"I want it," she said as calmly as she could.

"Pardon me?"

She grabbed the remote control and flicked off the television. "I want the angelheart."

A long moment of silence hung between them. "It's a bit

too big to make a fetching necklace for you. And, really, what would you wear it with?"

"I don't want it as jewelry."

"Then why do you want it?"

She stood up and paced back and forth anxiously. "Because I don't trust Theo, and I know he's going to do something stupid with it. If he doesn't have it anymore, no stupid can occur."

"Theo's not stupid."

"I guess we have differing opinions on the subject."

"Seems like. If you want the angelheart, maybe you should ask Theo for it the next time you see him."

She hissed out a breath. "He'll say no to me."

"Wear that blue dress of yours and he might change his mind."

"I don't think it's going to be that easy."

"I don't know about that," Darrak said slowly. "Theo did fall for a human once before."

That was surprising. Theo had been in love? "What happened to her?"

Darrak paused. "She died a horrific death and her soul was consumed by hellfire."

Her stomach lurched. "Why am I not surprised?"

"That's typically what happens when humans get involved with demons," he said pointedly.

She snorted. "Is that a promise or a threat?"

"Just an observation. But back to the angelheart . . . you need to forget it."

"Can you get it for me?" She held her breath as she waited for his answer.

"And why would I want to do that?" he said evenly.

"You need a reason other than 'pretty please'?"

"Afraid so."

His flippant attitude was quickly frustrating her. "An angel already suffered and gave up his immortality so Theo could take his power away."

"That angel didn't deserve to be an angel. You saw him. His returning to Heaven with wings intact was already uncertain without Jack Daniels pushing him in the right direction. Heavenly and hellish entities really need to be careful with human drugs and alcohol. Dangerous stuff."

"Theo didn't have the right to steal from him. It was wrong."

"I think you're forgetting something, Eden. Demons don't do things for the greater good of mankind. Humans are play-things, mostly. Meaningless diversions."

She stared at her reflection in the glass on the balcony door. Her arms were crossed tightly over her chest. "Is that how you feel?"

"How I *feel*?" There was an unpleasant twist to his words. "I shouldn't be *feeling* anything. I'm a demon, and I keep managing to forget that little tidbit. Maybe it's good that Theo's around to remind me of what I truly am. After all, what I really should be feeling is: 'Hooray, Theo drained an angel today. Point for us.'"

At her reflected look of shock, he actually chuckled.

"Sorry, I'm not quite as valiant as Detective Hanson. I'm sure he'd be scandalized and disgusted by what happened and willing to march off to war to retrieve that angelheart for you."

"You're right. He would." Ben had made some stupid decisions lately, but Eden knew he had made them for all the right reasons.

"Glad to hear you're still a fan." But Darrak didn't sound glad. He sounded pissed off.

This discussion wasn't going half as well as she'd hoped. But what had she thought would happen? That he'd choose to help her—some random woman he'd met by accident a couple of weeks ago—over his centuries-old friendship with another demon just like him?

Was Darrak exactly like Theo?

She would have said no before, but the way Darrak was answering her questions now—there was no revulsion for the other demon, no judgment. Theo was just Theo. And Darrak seemed to trust him implicitly, no matter what he did or said.

Eden had desperately wanted to tell Darrak the truth. While she couldn't say anything about the deal she'd made with Lucifer, for fear of repercussions if he found out, she could share what she'd learned about her father possibly being an angel. And about the Malleus being very interested in how that might affect the demon that possessed her.

But now she didn't want to tell Darrak anything at all.

"I'm going to bed," she finally said.

"Maybe you'll dream about golden boy tonight swinging in and rescuing you from the evil demon."

"I hope I do," she agreed.

"Sweet dreams." Darrak's tone was decidedly sour.

Eden could pretty much guarantee her dreams that night wouldn't be sweet.

She sincerely hoped tomorrow would be better than today.

It couldn't possibly get any worse.

Nothing used to get to Darrak. *Nothing*.

Ah, the good old days.

Back then, when he'd felt defeated or powerless or even afraid—although that had happened very rarely—he'd covered it up with a joke or a sarcastic comment. He still did that. His mask? Maybe a little. But a snide comment or witty comeback made things easier.

He wasn't feeling all that witty at the moment.

He felt angry mostly. And frustrated.

And . . . uncomfortable.

He refused to wear the fuchsia underwire bra. It pinched.

Leena watched him suspiciously as he got ready to leave the apartment in Eden's stolen body at half past midnight to meet up with Theo at Luxuria.

"What?" he asked with Eden's voice.

"Going to meet your mystery man again?" she asked.

"Good guess."

"Who is this guy, anyhow?"

"Love to tell you all about it," he said, "but I just don't want to."

A flicker of confusion went through Leena's gaze at the flippant reply. Darrak honestly didn't care if the shifter figured out what he was doing or not. He was a demon, and he could do whatever he wanted without worrying about any repercussions. In fact, he should revel merrily in it.

He'd revel merrily later. He mentally put it on his to-do list.

Darrak waited for Leena's accusation that was sure to go something along the lines of, "You nasty piece of demon shit. How dare you steal Eden's body to meet your nasty evil piece of shit friend just so you can feel whole again and not like a washed-up and worthless excuse for a once-powerful archdemon."

As he'd said before, the shapeshifter was very insightful.

In fact, he challenged her to say something. He stood there, one stolen hand on one stolen hip, and he arched a stolen eyebrow. "Got a problem with me, cat?"

She had to know, didn't she? Weren't shifters all intuitive like that?

Leena glared at him for five full seconds before her bottom lip wobbled. "I'm so sorry, Eden."

He frowned. "What?"

Leena inhaled shakily. "I know I'm difficult to live with. I know I always say the wrong thing and I can't get along with anybody. But I'll . . . I'll try to get along with the demon. It's not going to be easy, but I'm willing to try. I have the kind of personality that needs to fight with others.

Darrak's not the first. I just like to protect the people I care about from those I think are dangerous."

"You think Darrak's dangerous?"

"Well, duh. Of course he is."

He considered this for a moment. "You're right, of course."

She wiped her moist eyes. "I am?"

"Yes. I think he's probably going to get me killed if I can't find a way to get rid of him." Well, it was the truth, after all.

"You need to exorcise him," she said firmly.

He snorted. "I appreciate that being so top of mind that you didn't even hesitate before suggesting it."

Leena sat down at the tiny dinette table. "I know people, Eden. They can take care of a demon infestation in twenty minutes or less. They're independents, not associated with the Malleus."

"Really? You're associated with these people?"

She bit her bottom lip. "My ex is one of the leaders."

Interesting. "And he's your ex, because?"

"Because I . . . *may* have stolen something from him," she said tentatively.

"Stolen something like what?"

"Just something small and valuable and worth a fortune. They're like modern-day Robin Hoods. They steal from the supernaturals they slay and give to the poor victims. And, well, *themselves*, of course." She wiped a tear away and actually grinned a little wickedly. "It's in a safe spot right now waiting for my first opportunity to fence it."

Fence it? Darrak's suspicions were confirmed. Little Miss Kathleen Harris was a thief and a con artist who'd brought trouble upon herself and now relied on Eden's benevolent nature to protect her from harm.

And this little confession was because Leena trusted Eden and wanted to strengthen their burgeoning friendship.

She really had no idea who she was actually speaking to.

Poor, clueless kitty cat.

"I want you out of here in a week," Darrak said.

Leena's face fell. "A week?"

"I think that's more than generous. Now that I know who you're hiding from, it doesn't exactly make me feel comfortable having you around anymore."

She stood up so quickly the chair fell to the floor behind her. "But—but what about you and Darrak? If you're together—"

He laughed. "You know the saying about shutting the fence after the horses have escaped? That's how it is between me and Darrak, so don't worry your furry little head about the fact I can't keep my hands off the demon's amazing body." He added the last part to make himself feel better. It helped a little.

"But—but you just agreed that he's dangerous."

"Of course he's dangerous. He's a demon." Darrak said. That was the whole point of this display, wasn't it? He'd accepted that about himself. He *was* dangerous. And Leena got to be victim number one of his renewed outlook on life.

"But . . ." Leena looked at a loss for words. She wrung her hands nervously.

"Seriously, Leena. I know you say you hate him, but don't you think he's kind of hot?"

"Hot?" Leena repeated. "Well . . . uh . . . of course he is."

He grinned inwardly. Made her admit it.

This was getting to be fun.

"Eden, you need me—" Leena continued.

"No, actually I don't. Neither of us needs you." The crueler he was to her the more powerful he felt. He waited to feel guilt, but there was nothing. "Frankly, you're a waste of my valuable time. One week and then you figure out how to save yourself because I'm not going to help anymore. I have my own problems to deal with. Got it?"

Leena's lips trembled.

"Well?" Darrak prompted. He waited for her to freak out and start yelling and throwing insults.

Instead, two tears streaked down Leena's cheeks. "Got it," she said softly.

Well, that wasn't as much fun as he'd hoped. He watched her warily for a moment, waiting for her to gather herself together, but she didn't. He'd hurt her deeply. Or, rather, *Eden* had.

He didn't feel bad about that one little bit.

Did he?

Darrak forced himself to turn away and walk to the door. "Don't wait up for me."

Once he'd left the apartment, his head began to clear again. This was the way it had to be. Demons weren't concerned with hurting someone else's feelings. They were straightforward, blunt, and completely selfish. He had to look after number one—himself. That was the way it should be.

He'd only changed because of the humanity he'd been forced to absorb, but that didn't mean who he was underneath it all was any different. He liked being a demon, without all this inconvenient guilt or emotion to deal with. He'd enjoyed his work and had only grown more powerful until that fateful day with Lucifer that made him vulnerable to a witch's summoning.

But Darrak was close to putting the last three hundred years behind him once and for all. He would be cured, he would be powerful again, and all would be well with the world.

He was an archdemon. And any human or shapeshifter unfortunate enough to cross his path should fear him deeply.

Hell, yeah.

⇒ NINETEEN ⇐

There was something really strange about this place. But . . . what was it?

The other night, Darrak had sensed something unusual about the Luxuria nightclub, but he hadn't been able to put his finger on what it was. It was still too vague for him to figure it out, but it was decidedly not normal or completely human. There was a darkness here.

And darkness was good for a demon, right?

Right.

"Party on," Darrak said under his breath, refusing to let the sound of Eden's voice speaking his thoughts bother him. He took what he wanted when he wanted it. Period. And if his lovely host didn't like it, well, then that was just too bad.

He was in control at the moment and until such time as he decided to release it. Eden dampened him whenever she wanted to, so it shouldn't be a surprise that he could do the same.

The only difference is I gave her permission to dampen me, he thought.

Who cares? his other side chimed in. *Permission is for wimps. Take what you want when you want it. Be a demon!*

Great. He was a demon with a proverbial devil and an angel on either shoulder. That was going to prove to be very inconvenient.

He mentally flicked the angel off his shoulder. It crashed and burned to the floor.

Much better.

He scanned the nightclub for Theo but didn't see him. His gaze fixed instead on a familiar face who'd already spotted him. Nancy, the barista from Hot Stuff, made a beeline directly toward him.

Oh, great, he thought tightly.

"Eden," she said. "This place is fabulous! Thank you so much for suggesting it to me the other day."

"It's not bad." Darrak's attention moved across the hundreds of blank faces in attendance. No one there seemed to be enjoying themselves, despite the freely flowing alcohol and loud music and readily available cleavage. A lot of men and women weren't even mingling. They sat or stood and stared, as if transfixed, sipping on their drinks.

Strange.

So what did it all mean? He had a feeling he should be able to figure it out, to get to the bottom of this mystery.

Darrak smiled inwardly at the thought. Just because he'd spent some time at a private investigation agency lately didn't mean he wanted to become a PI, himself.

How ridiculous.

"This is my second night here in a row," Nancy said. "I can't seem to get enough of this place."

"Really?" It seemed to be a common refrain. Those who'd come here looking for love couldn't stay away.

Nancy nodded and her eyes darted around. "Where's Darrak?"

Right here. Present and accounted for. "I have no idea." Nancy pouted. "That's too bad."

Well, it was nice to see that somebody liked having him around.

"Listen, Eden, this might sound kind of blunt."

"I like blunt," he said.

"Do you think your brother would go out with me?"

Eden's brother. Nancy still thought they were siblings. If only she knew the sordid truth, she might run away screaming. It was an amusing thought. "Go out with you where?"

"On a date. I really like him." She twisted a nervous finger through her bleached blonde hair.

She liked him. That warmed his ego a little. "What exactly do you like about him?"

"You really want a list?"

"Yes, please." He should be hunting for Theo, but yes, he could use a list right about now. Pathetic, but true.

The hair-twisting became more thoughtful. "Well, he's charming and good-looking and really nice—"

Well, two out of three ain't bad.

"—and . . . and his eyes . . ." She bit her bottom lip. "They're so intense. Sometimes I feel like they're literally burning right into my soul as though he could devour me whole if he wanted to."

She was an excellent judge of character.

"So cool and blue, but hot at the same time," Nancy continued, "like an iceberg on fire. And his hair—well, I just want to run my fingers through it . . ." She shivered and then had the grace to look a bit guilty. "Sorry. I know it's probably gross having someone think that way about your brother."

"Oh, no. Not at all. Darrak is incredibly and sinfully attractive," he said. "It's not wrong for you to notice this. At all. More people should, in fact. Regularly."

"Wow, that's so awesome of you to say that."

"It's just the truth." He shrugged. "Unfortunately, Darrak's not available."

"Oh." Disappointment flickered over her face. A moment later she sniffed. "Well, that's not a huge surprise, I guess. I wish I'd known, though. I would have stopped making a fool of myself. All those donuts."

Darrak didn't want to lose his donut supplier. He wasn't ready for that ultimate sacrifice yet. "You know, Darrak really enjoys those. He mentioned it to me several times what a great donut maker you are and how you have a knack for putting in just the right amount of custard. It's an art, really."

She brightened. "He said that?"

Darrak nodded. "He definitely did. And don't worry about him. There's somebody out there for you. I know there is." Darrak's eyes flicked to their right. "Oh great. *This* guy again."

Nancy turned to see Stanley approaching them with two glasses of champagne in hand. "This guy's right for me?"

"No, that's not exactly what I—"

"Good evening, ladies," Stanley said. "Can I offer you a drink?"

Nancy's gaze moved appreciatively down the length of the wizard assistant's body. "Well, hello there."

Darrak rolled his eyes. "Stanley, this is Nancy. Nancy, Stanley."

Stanley's eyes widened. "Wow, Nancy. It's a pleasure to meet you. I think I saw you here last night, too, didn't I?"

"Guilty as charged. I noticed you, too. Couldn't help it."

Terrific. Love blossoms. Darrak's work here was done. That is, if he'd decided to turn in his horns for a shiny Cupid's bow and arrow. And he hadn't.

Nancy took the glass from Stanley. Darrak eyed it suspiciously.

Well, maybe his work wasn't *completely* done.

"I wouldn't drink that if I was you," Darrak said.

Her eyes went wide. "Why not?"

Why beat around the bush? He didn't have the time to

hint. He wanted to find Theo. "Because there's some lust elixir in there."

"Really?"

Stanley glared at him. "Thanks a lot."

"It's wrong, you know." *Great. Just listen to me*, he thought. *Who am I to say what's wrong and what isn't?* "Oh, forget it. Do what you want. Just don't . . . damn it. Just forget it, okay? Drink whatever you want, whenever you want."

"Seriously?" Nancy said. "Lust elixir? That's like a magic potion, right?"

Darrak looked at her with surprise. "What do you know about magic potions?"

She shrugged and gave both him and Stanley a wicked little conspiratorial grin. "A little. Doesn't everyone?"

"No," Darrak replied. "Not everyone knows about magic potions. Trust me on that."

"That's what I love about this club. I can feel the magic in the air." She shivered. "It's so exciting."

Now that she mentioned it, there was definitely a hum of magic here. Very low and quiet, but it was there surrounding them. Damn it, he really wished he could figure out the secret of this place. Even if it was just for bragging rights.

"That's probably me, baby. My magic is so powerful, you know." Stanley reached behind Nancy's ear and produced a red rose out of thin air.

Cheap parlor magic tricks? How sad.

However, Nancy seemed impressed. She took the rose from him happily. "And you gave me lust elixir because . . ."

"Because I think you're freaking hot," Stanley admitted. "But if you don't feel the same about me, it won't work. The elixir only works on the potential carnal desires that are lying dormant between us. You're totally in control of whether you drink it or not."

Nancy raised a mischievous eyebrow. "Well, let's put it

to the test, shall we?" She tipped the glass back and drank the champagne down. "Yummy!"

Stanley looked very pleased. "Maybe you and me should grab a seat in the corner and get to know each other a little better. What do you do for a living?"

"I'm a barista and assistant manager of the Hot Stuff Café. You?"

"Personal assistant."

She smiled brightly. "That sounds super interesting!"

Darrak stared blankly at the two of them. Nancy sure had gotten over him quickly.

"I have a message for you." Stanley tore his gaze from Nancy to look at Darrak.

Darrak grimaced. "Yeah, I bet. Trust me, my friend, you don't want to suggest that the three of us should get to know each other better. You think I was a ballbuster the other night? You have no idea."

Stanley looked at Nancy. "Will you wait a minute for me, doll?"

"I'll wait as long as it takes, lover." She blew him a kiss.

Stanley looked at Darrak. "This is seriously the best night ever."

"Hooray for you."

Stanley cleared his throat and looked shiftily from side to side. He lowered his voice. "Theo wants me to take you to him."

Darrak hadn't expected that. He actually felt a bit startled by it. "You know who I am?"

They began to walk away from Nancy, who sat on a stool next to the bar.

"Waiting right here!" she called after them. "For my fabulous new boyfriend!"

"I really hope that wasn't a mistake," Stanley said. "She's kind of hot, but is she clingy?"

"Looks like."

"I can deal with clingy. Anyhow, yeah, I know who you are. You're"—he swallowed and glanced at Eden's body sideways—"the demon. Darrak."

"And Theo told you that?" He was surprised.

"He did."

"And why would he do something like that?"

"Because I work for him. I'm his assistant."

Darrak frowned with confusion. "I thought you were the wizard's assistant."

"I can work for both of them. Theo made me an offer I couldn't refuse last night. Since I didn't want to bleed to death, I accepted enthusiastically. Theo's even interested in some of my elixirs. He's fascinated by non-demon magic."

Darrak considered this. "And you don't have a problem working for a demon?"

"Everybody works for somebody. Even Theo does."

Right. He worked for Lucifer. The same boss Theo wanted to destroy and steal his throne. Talk about the ultimate letter of resignation.

"Listen, Stanley, this club. This *Luxuria*." Darrak glanced around, now unable to shake the sense that there was some strange magic at work here that made him increasingly uncomfortable. "What's the deal with this place? I feel something . . . *unusual* . . . here."

Stanley grimaced. "You don't know?"

"Know what?"

"I can't believe you seriously don't know. It's obvious to me. Well, *now* it is, anyhow."

Darrak was beginning to feel frustrated with this human. Maybe he'd kill him. He hadn't had a problem killing humans in the past. Admittedly, it had been some time, but Stanley might make a good test project to see if his talons needed any sharpening.

Then again, in Eden's body he didn't exactly have access to his talons or any other demon appendage, including the ability to call his element of fire. He glanced down at her hands. She had fingernails scarcely long enough to do any damage at all.

He suddenly remembered those fingernails scratching down his back when they'd made love.

Okay. *So* not helpful.

Darrak hissed out a breath. "Tell me what you're talking about, or I'm going to pluck out your eyeballs and use them to play Ping-Pong."

Stanley gulped. "I can't tell you but you can guess. Just look around at this place. You'll figure it out."

Since the eyeball Ping-Pong threat had been mostly a bluff, Darrak sighed and glanced around the interior of the club. They were near the hallway to the side exit, but not away from the crowd enough that they didn't get jostled by drink-carrying patrons who passed them on the way to the dance floor.

Humans of varying colors and sizes and levels of attractiveness shuffled back and forth across the dark, shiny floor, barely making eye contact with each other. Some looked strangely sallow, but he wasn't sure if that was just from the flickering lights. Drinks rose to bloodless lips. Half-hearted dancing on the dance floor. That ever-present scent of lust and desperation in the air he'd noticed the first night he'd been here.

Darrak knew he should know the answer to this. If he was at full power, he *would* know. It was on the tip of his tongue, and it was driving him crazy that he couldn't figure it out.

"Is it a spell?" he asked. "One that compels people to come to this place?"

"Kind of. But not really."

Darrak shot Stanley a withering look. "A curse? Is this place cursed?"

"You're getting warmer. Seriously, though, if Theo was going to tell you, he would have."

Darrak frowned and pushed Stanley back into a hallway. Here the music from the club was muted. "Does Theo have something to do with this?"

Stanley wiped a hand over his mouth, his eyes now filled with worry. "I can't say anything. Theo's going to—"

"Theo's going to what?" A voice asked. A door had opened, and Theo stood there now with fire blazing in his eyes. He grinned. "Darrak, nice of you to join us. See? It wasn't that hard to borrow her body again, was it?"

"Surprisingly easy, actually." Darrak still felt unpleasantly confused. "Why does everyone walk around like the living dead here? Why are they compelled to come back night after night? And what does it all have to do with you, Theo?"

Theo glanced at Stanley, who shrank away from him. He laughed.

"Darrak, you scared him, you big meanie. Don't worry Stanley, I'm not mad. You do have a bit of a big mouth though. It might get you in trouble someday." His tone was light, but his meaning was not.

"I'm waiting," Darrak said, crossing Eden's arms and tapping her foot.

"All part of the plan."

"Speak plainer."

Theo's grin widened. "Ooh, so stern. Like an old-time schoolteacher. Must have something to do with being cramped up inside that uptight little body you have there." Theo reached around and pinched Eden's ass. Darrak barely restrained himself from hitting him.

Then, suddenly, he saw the humor in the situation and how much he was overreacting. He laughed and shook his head.

"Shit, look at me. I *am* acting uptight. You're absolutely right."

Theo nodded and slapped his back. "You just have to chill. Enjoy the view. Enjoy the ride."

"Believe me, I'm trying."

"It's been a rough few centuries. I get that. But it's all easy street from now on. I have the angelheart and soon we'll get rid of Lucifer forever." At Darrak's wary look toward Stanley, Theo chuckled. "Don't worry. My loyal new assistant knows everything."

"That's very trusting of you."

"Not really. I think Stanley knows what I'll do to him if he breathes a word to anyone, even his other employer. Right Stanley?"

"Yes, sir," Stanley replied. He looked terrified.

"So what's going on here?" Darrak asked. "And does it have anything to do with you?"

"A little." Theo leaned casually against the wall. "I'm still moonlighting for Asmodeus."

The Lord of Lust. Darrak hadn't heard Asmo's name since Lucifer accused Darrak of conspiring with the demon lord and sent him packing.

Darrak remembered a conversation they'd had a long, long time ago. "Let me guess: Your game plan is to take his throne after you take Lucifer's."

Theo laughed, a bit nervously this time. "Dude, say no more. I already told you the walls here have ears."

The walls have ears. It was a common human saying, but for some reason it seemed to carry more weight at the moment.

"How's Asmo doing?" Darrak asked.

"Not so good." Theo casually brushed off the sleeve of his black shirt. "Him and you have a lot in common, actually."

"Oh, yeah?"

"You weren't there for the big fight. He and Lucifer went at it pretty hardcore just after you disappeared. Lucifer accused him of trying to usurp his reign, or whatever, and they fought."

Damn. He missed all the excitement. "Who won?"

"Lucifer, of course. He brought Satan out to play and nearly decimated Asmo in front of everyone. It was kind of awesome, actually." He cleared his throat and looked around nervously. "No offense, Asmo."

Darrak looked around as well, but no one else was in the hallway with them except for Stanley, who'd chosen to stay as quiet as a magic potion-making mouse at the moment. "Lucifer . . . or, rather, *Satan* destroyed Asmo's solid form?"

"Yep."

"But he's still around?"

"He is, indeed. And he's finally figured out how to fix his problem after all these years." Theo grinned. "That's what I'm helping him with."

Hell had to have seven thrones to represent the seven deadly sins so there was never one true leader. It was a rule. If only one entity controlled everything, the Netherworld might actually rival the heavens in power instead of being the garbage dump for everything Heaven didn't want. The seven lords of Hell bickered endlessly and had civil wars playing out using lesser demons as soldiers. And they all hated—and *feared*—Lucifer since he had more power than the rest of them.

"Where is Asmo right now?" Darrak asked.

"Here."

If Asmo had no corporeal form, how could he be here? "Is he possessing someone in this club?"

Theo chuckled. "Oh, Darrak, you really have lost your edge, haven't you? You're so damn lucky I'm here to help you out. No, Asmo's not possessing someone. But he is possessing some*thing*."

It didn't work for Darrak, but it was true that bodiless entities could sometimes possess things. Furniture, electronic gadgets, mirrors, books . . . or even . . .

. . . entire locations.

The walls have ears.

Darrak's eyes widened as things began to click into place for him. Better late than never.

The magic he'd felt here—it was demon magic. He'd barely sensed anything at all to begin with. Just a little lust permeating the nightclub.

Asmo was the Lord of Lust.

"He didn't," Darrak said quietly. "He couldn't have."

Theo looked very amused. "Don't know. What are you talking about?"

Darrak's gaze shot to his friend's. "He's possessing this place right now, isn't he? Asmo . . . he *is* Luxuria."

There was silence for a moment as his attention moved between the amused-looking Theo and the scared Stanley.

Then Theo laughed loudly. "Dude, you've still got it. Don't let anyone tell you that you don't."

"I'm right?"

"You are. He's been very weakened for all of these years, but he's finally regaining his strength. I'm not surprised that you couldn't sense him until now."

The entire nightclub is possessed by a demon. Darrak blinked. *That is so cool.*

Then he had another thought.

"He's draining the humans here, isn't he? That's what's helping him to regain his strength. That's why they all look so . . . *drained.*"

Theo nodded and put an arm around his friend's shoulders. "They're dripping lust anyhow. It's the boss's favorite snack. It's not *all* bad for them, though. They love it. Keeps 'em coming back for more even if they're not sure what they're coming back for."

Darrak moved away from Theo and walked up and down the narrow hallway. He could still clearly hear the music from the next room, the incessant throb from some generic but popular dance song. He closed his eyes and opened his senses as much as possible. He could sense Asmo now. Everywhere.

Another thought occurred to him. "Six women have disappeared recently. Regulars at this club. Do you know anything about that?"

Theo crossed his arms. "Asmo got a bit too hungry. Took a little too much. He wasn't able to stop until there was nothing left." He shrugged. "It happens. No big loss."

No big loss. Just six lonely, lust-filled human women who frequented a nightclub hoping to find a man. Who cared about them? They'd become food for a demon lord. It was actually an honor.

This is what he told himself. Down deep he didn't entirely believe it.

Darrak had come close to draining Eden once before, but he'd stopped himself in time. Would she have simply disappeared as well?

The thought was extremely disturbing to him.

"What about the reporter? Did Asmo kill him, too?" Darrak rubbed his forehead and found his hands caught in Eden's long red hair. It was another reminder that he'd stolen her body. He kept his arms to his sides. It was safer that way.

"Nope," Theo answered.

"I didn't think so. He was strangled, not drained."

"Yeah, Asmo wanted me to make it look like human-on-human violence. Had to control my strength, though. It was really tempting. That guy was really rude."

Darrak's mouth went dry. "*You* did it?"

"Of course. He was snooping around, and Asmo got uncomfortable. I took care of it for him. Wouldn't have wanted the reporter to go get a couple of exorcists. That wouldn't have been pretty."

No, it wouldn't have.

Darrak tried to calm himself. It was just his hated humanity that was rising up right now trying to tell him that all of this was wrong. It wasn't wrong. It was the way it should be. It was perfect, actually. This was his chance to decide on which side he wanted to hang his hat and whether that hat would be black or white.

White had always made him look a bit pasty.

When Darrak's curse was broken, none of this would hold the same weight as it did now. He'd be back to normal, and he'd welcome the chance to drain some humans. Hell, he'd done it countless times in the past. Why was this any damn different?

It wasn't.

Darrak forced a smile to his borrowed face. "I really should have figured it out. I'm kind of embarrassed."

Theo laughed. "You should be. But you can make it up to Asmo tomorrow. Be present for his awakening."

"His awakening?"

Theo touched the wall and looked up at the ceiling. "He's gained enough strength to move to the next step of his plan. Tomorrow at noon he's going take form again." His smile was wide when he turned to Darrak this time. "Asmo's agreed to help you with your curse."

"He has?"

Theo nodded. "But he wants you present tomorrow. Once he heals himself, he'll heal you as well."

His answer, finally, and it was currently lurking in the walls and floor tiles of Luxuria.

Darrak's head swam from this information, but he forced any weakness away and instead focused on the most important bits—the ones that involved him again becoming the demon he once was. There'd be no more weakness then. It would be a nice change after all these years.

He and Asmodeus were both in the same boat. Both looking for a way out of a sticky situation Lucifer was responsible for.

The enemy of my enemy is my friend, Darrak reminded himself. It seemed to apply in this case.

"Thank you," Darrak nodded. "This is a great gift. I appreciate it more than you know."

"Oh, *this* isn't your gift. Actually, that's waiting outside. Unfortunately, I couldn't figure out how to put a ribbon on it." Theo moved toward the exit and touched the metal door. "Are you ready to see it?"

More gifts? Darrak was a lucky boy tonight. He pushed aside all the doubts he'd had and only a cool resolve was left behind. This clarity of what he wanted and what he had to do to get it was refreshing.

No guilt need apply.

"As ready as I'll ever be," Darrak confirmed, finally allowing himself to relax a fraction after being tense since he'd entered the club.

Hey . . . a familiar little voice in the back of his head said groggily the next moment. It was Eden. *What's going on—?*

With a quick flex of his mind he dampened Eden's presence again. She'd woken too easily. Damn, she was stronger than he'd thought.

If he tried really hard, it would be possible to permanently dampen her. He'd heard of other bodiless demons who'd done that, found a suitable replacement host and taken it over completely. If things fell through, he supposed that was an option . . .

Darrak ignored the twinge of guilt he felt at even entertaining that thought. Because demons didn't feel guilt. Eden was his present. But his future was undetermined.

It would be determined tonight.

"If you don't mind," Stanley said, and his voice shook a little, "I have a prior commitment."

Darrak had forgotten he was even still there, witnessing their very unusual conversation.

"Blonde, brunette, or redhead?" Theo asked.

"Blonde."

"Go for it. But I'll need your services again later so don't go far."

"Yes, sir." Stanley scurried off.

Theo pushed his shoulder against the door and opened it wide enough for Darrak to walk through.

This was a night to remember. The night that would shape things to come.

Darrak pushed aside the niggling feeling of dread he got. It was probably just indigestion.

He couldn't wait to see what this gift was. He'd always loved presents.

⇶ TWENTY ⇇

Darrak had to admit, he was hoping for a pony.

"I've cloaked the area for sound," Theo said as they exited the nightclub into the cold night air. "And anyone who wanders back here won't see anything."

"That's ominous."

"Just want to give you a chance to enjoy your gift. Here, give me your hand."

Darrak eyed his friend warily, then held out Eden's right hand. Theo placed the hilt of a knife into it.

"You shouldn't have. Does the serrated edge go with my eyes?" Darrak continued to follow Theo curiously as they approached the back of the building.

"The knife's not the gift." Theo stopped walking and nodded his head. "That is."

They'd entered a nicely deserted alley lit by only one small light set into the side of the building. The wind blew, making a hollow whistling sound and scattering garbage and dry leaves along the dirty pavement.

Standing in the dead center of the alley was Ben Hanson.

Theo approached Ben and thumped him on his back. "I restrained him for you. He can't move. But believe me, he'll be able to feel everything. Have fun."

Wow. This was a surprise.

So . . . does this mean I'm not getting a pony? he thought.

Ben's eyes were closed. His normally perfect face showed some damage—cuts and scrapes. Some looked deep. His blond hair was streaked with red. His right cheek was bruised and a thick line of blood trickled from the corner of his mouth and dripped to the ground. His shirt, once white, was also torn and bloody.

The guy was a mess.

"So, *this* is my gift?" Darrak asked evenly.

Theo looked very pleased with himself as he nodded. "He is. You said yesterday this guy was a pain in your ass and you'd gut him if you had the chance."

He did say that. At the time he'd meant it. This cop had been nothing but a problem since the day he'd met Eden, and now that Ben was with the Malleus he was even worse.

Ben had almost killed Eden last night thanks to his consuming drive to fight evil. Eden might be ready to make excuses for his actions and forgive and forget, but Darrak couldn't.

He was funny like that.

Ben's eyes suddenly opened as if he was just coming to. "Eden . . . what are you doing here? It's not safe. You need to leave right now!" He looked at Theo. "Get away from her, you asshole!"

It was almost amusing to Darrak. The cop thought he was Eden. Which, since he was currently occupying her body, wasn't that hard to believe.

His gift from Theo was Ben's head on a platter. It was very thoughtful of him.

Darrak approached Ben slowly, keeping the knife hidden behind his back.

"Can you move?" At the moment Darrak sounded so much like Eden that the cop's gaze didn't even seem to register anything different.

"No. Damn it. This . . . this demon grabbed me outside my house. Next thing I know I'm standing here and can't budge an inch. He's evil, Eden."

Ben was in bad shape. Darrak wondered what Theo had done to him in preparation for this moment. It didn't look like anything pleasant. Stitches would definitely be required.

Golden boy thought he knew evil? Darrak supposed he hadn't looked in the mirror lately. The Malleus weren't exactly squeaky clean.

"Well, of course he's evil, silly," he said dryly. "All demons are evil. It gives balance to the universe, don't you know, like a massive chess game. Black against white."

Shades of gray. Don't forget about the shades of gray.

Shut up, he told the nonexistent angel that had slowly and wearily mountain climbed back onto his shoulder.

"Aren't you afraid?" Ben asked hoarsely.

"Afraid? Why should I be afraid? Was I afraid last night when you tried to kill me?"

Ben's expression shadowed. "I didn't mean for that to happen. I wanted to help you. I—I still do. Just because you're a black witch . . . it doesn't mean anything. But you have to get out of here, Eden. It's dangerous."

Wasn't that sweet? He was willing to see past Eden being a black witch, despite the murder attempt by his associate. How generous of him. Darrak cocked his head to the side. "Actually, I'm not Eden, pal. But I'll be sure to give her your regards in the morning."

Ben frowned. "You . . . you're not . . . ?" Then clarity entered his expression. "You son of a bitch."

"Didn't we already go over this once before? No mother. You really have to find another insult."

"You stole her body."

"*Borrowed*," Darrak corrected, refusing to flinch at the reminder that he was being very naughty again.

He wanted to be naughty. That was the whole point of being a demon.

"You don't deserve to be ten feet away from her, let alone be able to do this." Ben looked disgusted enough to spit.

"Are you saying you don't want to kiss these lips again? Because I'm fine with that."

Theo walked a slow circle around the two of them. By the expression on his face, he seemed to be enjoying the show.

"Just an FYI, cop," Darrak continued, "but Eden doesn't need your opinion. Never has, never will. And this white hat routine doesn't work on me."

"White hat routine?"

"Yeah, you might be all high and mighty, busting criminals and drug rings or whatever you do during the workday." Darrak had a former host who'd enjoyed watching nothing but retro cop shows and movies, so his education on that particular job was a bit skewed toward *Lethal Weapon* and *Die Hard*. "But joining the Malleus? You have no idea how corrupt they are."

Ben glared at him. "There is corruption in every company. If you look close enough, you'll find it. But it's individuals, not the entire association. I believe in what the Malleus stands for. Even after what happened last night, I still do. My eyes are just a bit more open about the problems, that's all."

He sure looked sincere. Indignant, even.

"You're one of the bad guys," Darrak told him.

"No," Ben said. "That would be you."

Oh, yeah. Right. Why did Darrak keep forgetting that?

"Are you going to talk to him or gut him?" Theo asked. "I'm getting kind of bored here."

"How can you do this to Eden?" Ben demanded with

disgust. "Use her like this when you know damn well she's foolish enough to care about you."

Ouch. And Darrak had thought *he'd* get the first slice.

Darrak pulled the knife out from its hiding spot behind his back. "So tell me, Ben. You want a slow or quick death? I'm leaning toward a slow one right now. You've been that much of a pain in my ass."

Ben didn't flinch. "She has no idea what a monster you are, does she?"

"I've given her plenty of chances to figure it out. It's not my fault she thinks I'm delicious and nutritious." He smirked.

"She'll never forgive you for this." There was determination in Ben's eyes. He knew death was coming, and he'd accepted it. Embraced it, even. It was more than a little disappointing. Darrak had fantasized about the cop begging for his life.

There was still time for that.

"You really think she gives a damn about you either way anymore?" Darrak shook his head. "Dream on."

"You know she does" was Ben's reply. And he didn't even sound smug about it. Just matter-of-fact.

Darrak really hated this guy.

He clenched his jaw. This wasn't going very well. Theo had been so thoughtful, too, picking out a gift Darrak was sure to enjoy.

He wished he was enjoying it.

Ben's gaze moved to the sharp knife in Darrak's—or rather *Eden's*—hand and there was a short flash of fear in his expression before it disappeared.

So the valiant knight wasn't made of impenetrable shining armor after all.

"You shouldn't have kidnapped Eden last night. That was a bad move, cop."

"Eden's a special case."

"I'll agree with you there."

Ben swallowed. "As far as we know, she's the first nephilim ever possessed by a demon. The Malleus leaders wanted to know more about her and how what she is affects you as a demon. I didn't know she was a black witch, too. I didn't know that would put her in danger."

There was a long moment of silence as this new information settled in.

"*Nephilim*?" Darrak repeated softly. "Did you say Eden's a nephilim?"

Ben's expression tightened. "Didn't she tell you?"

"Hasn't come up."

Ben nodded, a look of resolve coming into his gaze. "I'm glad to see she's smart enough not to trust you. That's a start. Maybe there's still hope for her yet."

Theo started to laugh from behind him. "You have got to be shitting me. Red's a nephilim? I'm surprised you can even stand to be in that body."

"She's *human*," Darrak said. "I know she is. I never sensed anything else."

"Well," Theo interjected, "you didn't sense Asmo, either, did you?"

That was very true. But . . . a nephilim? Eden's father—she'd never known him. This meant he was an angel?

Holy shit.

"You're destroying her, you know that?" Ben said.

Ben gasped as Darrak pressed the knife against his throat.

"I know," Darrak snapped.

"You're poison to her," Ben growled. "Like a disease."

"I'd shut up now, cop. I strongly suggest it."

"Just kill me. Get it over with. Wouldn't want to keep you from destroying Eden's life any further."

"Yeah, kill him," Theo said. He sounded bored. "Let's move this along, shall we?"

Darrak didn't want to talk anymore. It was making his head hurt.

"Okay," he said. "Here it goes. Prepare to meet your maker. Or whatever."

"I'm not afraid," Ben said through clenched teeth.

"You should be."

"But I'm not."

Darrak sighed with exasperation. "Don't argue with me. I'm going to kill you. Seriously."

"Then do it already."

Darrak pressed the knife hard enough to make a thin line of red ooze up against it, and Ben actually flinched. Finally, a quantifiable reaction.

He expected to feel relief or a giddy sense of pleasure at inflicting pain on the asshole who'd been an inconvenient obstacle since the first moment they met. But there was no pleasure or giddiness.

Ben didn't deserve to die.

He never had. He really was a golden boy—making self-less decisions and trying his best to do the right thing, especially when it came to Eden.

How could Darrak possibly fault him for something like that?

Darrak swore under his breath. Why couldn't Theo have gotten him a pony? Now *that* would have been fun.

He eased up on the pressure before he did any more damage.

"Release him," Darrak said stiffly, his borrowed voice barely audible.

"What?" Theo replied. "I don't think I heard you right."

"You heard me right. Let the cop go. Let him go back to the life he's made for himself, being the Malleus's newest lapdog. I'm not going to kill anyone tonight, especially not while I'm in Eden's body. She wouldn't appreciate that very much."

Theo sighed with frustration. "Who cares what Eden wants?"

"I do," Darrak said firmly.

Ben looked at him with surprise and apprehension. As though this was just a ruse for him to let down his guard before Darrak sliced that knife right through him.

I should kill him, Darrak told himself. *I should be loving every minute of this.*

But he wasn't.

It was very disappointing.

"This is too difficult for you?" Theo asked, confused.

"I'm afraid so."

Theo held out his hand. "Can I have my knife back?"

Darrak returned the weapon to him.

"I'd be happy to help you out." Theo arched the knife toward Ben's chest.

Darrak caught his wrist only an inch from the target. While he was in Eden's body at the moment, his presence brought with it a demon-sized strength. Still, Eden's arm shook as he tried to hold Theo back.

"Drop it." Darrak squeezed until Theo dropped the knife that clattered to the pavement. "Now release him."

Theo glared at him. "Maybe I don't want to."

Darrak gritted his teeth. "*Theodraagaris*, I command you to release him."

Theo's eyes went wide as Darrak used his full name. It was a huge no-no for one demon to exert this type of power over another.

At the moment, Darrak didn't really give a crap about proper etiquette.

"Fine." Theo waved a hand. The next moment, Ben slumped forward. Darrak caught him before he hit the ground. He coughed and wheezed as if the crushing hand that had held him in place had finally let him go.

Theo stood prone at the moment, waiting for his next command.

"Get out of here," Darrak said to the cop.

"Why didn't you kill me?" Ben asked, his gaze more filled with anger than anything close to gratitude.

"Eden would never forgive me if I did."

"This isn't over, demon," Ben said, darkly.

"You're welcome."

His eyes narrowed. "I'll destroy you. I swear it."

"No, really. I'm blushing now. You don't have to get me a thank-you card. Just your endless and heartfelt appreciation is enough."

Still with that look of bewilderment at the fact he'd just been spared by the demon he blamed for destroying everything good in the world, including puppies and goldfish, Ben staggered out of the alleyway without another word.

"Are you going to release me?" Theo asked through clenched teeth.

"Of course." Darrak braced himself for the demon's fury. "Consider yourself released."

Theo crossed his arms and shook his head, glaring at him. No fury yet.

Darrak blinked. "So . . . thanks a bunch for the gift. I really appreciate the thought."

"This is Eden's fault."

So he wasn't going to blame Darrak for what just happened? "That is entirely possible."

Theo looked toward the route Ben had taken out of the alley. "We should be stomping on that nobody's entrails right now."

"Which does sound like tons of fun."

Theo shook his head, disbelievingly. "You even stopped me from finishing the job. You used my true name to make me let him go. That's not cool, Darrak."

"I remember. I was standing right here. Very happy I chose not to try the heels tonight. How do women walk in those things?" He looked at Eden's bare wrist. "Gosh, look at the time. I really need to get going."

"Asmodeus will help you," Theo said. "When he's regained his power, he'll help you regain yours, too. Tomorrow it happens. At noon. Right here at Luxuria."

"I'm still invited?" The cold wind whipped through the alley, and a crumpled up piece of newspaper blew between them.

It felt a little bit like a tumbleweed in an Old West town.

"Yes." Theo narrowed his eyes. "Bring Eden."

"At noon I won't have much of a choice."

"Asmo will be ready for a meal when he's finished."

Darrak tensed. "That's not going to happen."

Theo smiled thinly. "At least you're honest. That's another thing. Since when are you so honest?"

Darrak cringed at the reminder. "It's a fairly recent problem I'm dealing with."

"This Eden." Theo walked around him, checking out the stolen body. "More trouble than any woman is worth. And you were telling me you can't even sleep with her to make it all worthwhile?"

"If I sleep with her again, it could destroy her further."

"But you want to."

"Duh. Of course. I'm not a monk."

"And she wants you?"

"I'd like to think so. But we have a hands-off agreement."

"Isn't that special?"

Theo's eyes glittered. He might be acting very polite, but he wasn't in a stellar mood at the moment. Darrak knew he had to tread softly. He had to protect Eden. Being that Theo hated her, her body was currently at risk.

Maybe he should have killed the cop after all.

Oh well. Hindsight was 20/20.

Theo shook his head. "My, my, Darrak. This is a side of you I never thought I'd see. You were even more brutal than I was back in the day. The things you're responsible for. Even I was disgusted by a few of them."

Darrak shrugged. "I appreciate the compliment, but times change."

He tensed as Theo clamped his hand down on his shoulder. "I want you to admit it to me."

"What?"

Theo smiled. "If she was full-on evil, this would all be easier wouldn't it? You wouldn't have to be so preoccupied with saving her soul."

Darrak couldn't help but snort. "You might be right about that."

Theo swallowed and took a step back. He braced his hands on his knees. "Not feeling well seeing you so broken like this. So pathetic. Makes me want to cry. Just a single tear. It'll be very dramatic."

Darrak glared at him. "You're hilarious."

Theo straightened up and flashed him a grin. "You're lucky I like you, Darrak, or I might have to destroy you."

"The feeling's mutual."

That earned a laugh. "You go back and tuck your Girl Scout in for the night. Make sure she's snug as a bug in a rug. Then drag her ass back here at noon so after Asmo does his thing, he can help you out of this vastly unfortunate situation you've gotten yourself into. Darrak the Good. Darrak the Self-Sacrificing. I only wish I had a camera to record this for posterity. Maybe upload it to YouTube. We'll laugh about this one day when we're eating the souls of virgins for breakfast."

"Promise?" Darrak grumbled.

"Cross my heart. If I had one." Then Theo took a step back and vanished behind a column of flame.

Show-off, Darrak thought. He really did miss the ability to phase.

He felt ill by what had happened. Or rather, what *hadn't* happened. He should have killed Ben without a second thought. But he'd had a second. And a third. And then a fourth. Even after Darrak let him go, the cop still threatened to end him. He was no further ahead.

But he hadn't done it to gain brownie points. That was the problem. He'd spared Ben's life because it was the . . . the . . .

. . . the *right thing to do.*

Okay, he thought, *so this is what nausea feels like, is it*?

The other revelation of the evening swirled around his thoughts.

Eden was a nephilim. How long had she known this, and why hadn't she ever told him? What other secrets was his beautiful host keeping from him?

Seriously. Where was the trust?

⇒ TWENTY-ONE ⇐

There was a moment in the middle of Eden's otherwise dreamless sleep that she'd seen a brief, fuzzy glimpse of a nightclub—possibly Luxuria. And then—*poof!*—it was gone.

Weird.

She snuggled back down into the warm comfort of unconsciousness. Still, no dreams.

Later, when she woke, she pried open her eyelids fully, expecting to be lying in bed wearing her warm flannel jammies.

But, no. She wasn't.

Instead, she realized that she was staring at her brightly lit reflection in her . . . bathroom mirror? Why was she in her bathroom? Standing up?

And—she looked down at herself—fully dressed, too?

Her eyes widened. "What the hell?"

"Good morning," Darrak said from inside her.

"Morning?"

"Almost morning. Still night. Still dark. We have a few minutes till sunrise."

"What's going on, Darrak? Why am I dressed?"

"Feel free to get naked any time you like. Don't mind me."

She gritted her teeth, finally pulling herself out of her groggy just-woken-up state. "Don't even tell me you borrowed my body again."

"Then I won't tell you that."

Eden glared at her reflection, the anger rising up like a thermometer ready to pop. A strangled scream pushed past her vocal cords, and she actually hit the mirror. It didn't break, but it hurt her hand.

"Do you want me to hate you?" she demanded.

"Sure. Feel free."

"Fine. I hate you!"

How was she supposed to deal with this? How could she control someone who had so much control over her life? It was beyond unfair, and it made her feel completely powerless.

Eden turned from her reflection, but not before noting that her cheeks had grown redder, her eyes glossy, but she refused to shed even one tear about this. The digital clock on her nightstand told her it was 7:40 a.m. Almost sunrise.

She stormed out of the bathroom and went to the kitchen to pour herself a big glass of orange juice that she quickly drained. Her morning "Florida sunshine" ritual didn't make her feel the least bit better. She poured another one.

Great. She was thirsty as hell. What had Darrak been doing all night?

"Let me guess. Out visiting your BFF again?" she snapped, slamming the glass down on the kitchen counter.

"I was."

"Any reason you didn't tell me last night what your plans were?"

"Because I knew you'd make a big deal out of it. And look, I was right."

He sounded sullen and oddly annoyed with her. And why was that? She was the one who should be pissed at him right now, not the other way around.

She rubbed her temples. "What did Theo want that was so damn important that it couldn't wait until morning?"

"He wanted to give me a gift."

"Wonderful. Flowers? Chocolates? Are you two the latest Netherworld power couple?" Sarcasm dripped.

"No," Darrak said. "Actually he gave me your friend Ben Hanson and allowed me the chance to carve him up and watch him bleed to death."

Eden froze, a breath caught in her throat. "And did you?"

There was a short pause. "What do *you* think I did?"

She'd begun to tremble, imagining Ben coming to a very unpleasant end. Darrak hated him. "I don't know, so you better tell me right now."

Darrak laughed humorlessly. "I gutted him, of course. You should have heard him scream. Like a little girl."

She clutched her throat. It felt difficult to breathe all of a sudden. "Darrak—oh, my God—"

"He deserved it. Now that he's with the Malleus, he's only going to cause harm to others. I did everyone a favor, don't you think? Besides, one less set of dimples won't make the world stop turning on its axis."

Eden squeezed her eyes shut and tried not to freak out. Darrak killed Ben? Just like that? With no conscience or guilt? She'd never known the real Darrak at all. It had all been a lie. He was horrible and sadistic and cruel and . . .

Her eyes snapped open. "Wait a minute. You're . . . you're lying to me, aren't you? *Aren't you*?"

"You're going to have to be a bit more specific," he said.

"About everything you just said to me. It's a lie." She felt the edge of the counter behind her. Currently it was the only thing helping to keep her on her feet.

"Well . . . Theo *did* give Ben to me as a present. He gave me the knife and everything."

A shiver went down her spine. "But you didn't kill him. I know you. You wouldn't do it."

"You know me, do you?" he said tightly. "You really think so?"

"Yes. I do. Despite our differences, despite everything that has happened up until now, I know you wouldn't kill him."

There was silence then, and it was enough to tell her she was right. The relief was so overwhelming she nearly collapsed to the floor.

Darrak didn't kill Ben. Even when he'd been given the opportunity.

"Say it," she said. She had to hear it out loud just to prove it to herself.

"What?"

"Say that you didn't kill him."

There was a sound of displeasure, like a grunt. "Fine. I didn't kill him."

"And you let him go."

"Yes. I let him go," he grumbled.

Relief continued to course through her. "I knew it."

"It's time," he said.

"Time for wh—?"

Then she felt like someone had just punched her in the stomach, and she huffed out a long breath of thick black smoke. It had taken her by shock so much that she stood there, holding her hand over her stomach, and watched as Darrak began to take form right in front of her.

First there was a glimpse of pale, muscled limbs before they were covered by dark clothing that appeared as if by magic. It was magic. In less than a minute he'd taken solid form and stood there a few feet away staring at her.

He raked a hand through his dark hair. "You're not usually conscious for that."

No, she wasn't. She'd only been awake one other time he'd taken form like that, and it was the first time she realized she was possessed. She'd managed to summon enough energy to force him out of her body.

"Where's Ben now?" she asked.

"I have no idea."

"Is he okay?"

"He'll live." He said it bitterly.

Eden couldn't help herself. She threw her arms around him and hugged him tightly. "Thank you."

"For what?"

"For not killing him."

"There was a time I wouldn't have hesitated."

"But you did and that's a good thing."

"Debatable." Darrak wasn't hugging her back. In fact, he felt tense. "Isn't Pussy Galore supposed to jump in right about now? Leena! Eden is actually touching me. You might want to stop her before things get out of control."

Eden *was* touching him, wasn't she? Her rage had quickly subsided and shifted into something else. Something strange and warm. Something that had her holding on to this hug of relief and gratitude for much longer than was polite.

She didn't want to let go of him.

Her heart picked up its pace.

Darrak hadn't killed Ben. This normally wouldn't sound like a reason to get all soft and mushy toward someone—the fact that he'd decided against committing murder—but this morning it had affected her in a decidedly soft and mushy way.

She'd doubted him, but it had only been for a moment. Despite their problems, she did trust him down deep. And he'd come through for her.

Eden flattened her hands against the hard planes of his

chest. Darrak smelled good this morning. He always smelled good to her—clean and warm and delicious. It wasn't a cologne, it was just him. She leaned closer and inhaled, moving her nose greedily up toward his throat.

"Uh . . . everything okay?" he asked.

She cleared her throat. "Yeah. Of course. Everything's fine."

"You're acting kind of strange. Especially considering that not five minutes ago you said you hated me."

She fought against this strange pull toward him. He was right. She was mad at him. Furious, in fact.

Oddly, though, furious was the last thing she felt at the moment.

Nevertheless, she forced herself to step back from Darrak and crossed her arms over her chest.

"I do hate you," she confirmed.

Darrak studied her carefully as if he didn't know what to expect next from her. "Okay."

She craned her neck, trying to bring her jumbled thoughts into some sort of order. "Where is Leena, anyhow?"

"She must be asleep." Darrak went to the refrigerator and opened it up. "This must be my lucky day. Who bought these?"

Eden glanced around as he pulled out a bag labeled Hot Stuff. He pulled a couple of chocolate donuts out from inside.

"No idea."

"A gift from the donut fairies. They must have known it was a rough night." He bit into one, and his eyes flicked to her. "Delicious. Want one? Or do you hate me too much to share in my bounty?"

"I don't want one." She couldn't believe that all she could think about at the moment was how good he looked eating that donut. What a stupid thought.

But he did look good. His lips . . . his tongue . . . his hands. A crumb fell to the black T-shirt that stretched over his muscular chest and abs. She bit her bottom lip as her gaze leisurely traveled over him. Damn, he was so attractive.

She really wanted his body right now.

Eden blinked rapidly at the thought.

Uh, hello? What the hell was wrong with her? This was not the way her brain normally worked. Especially at this time of the morning.

No more lustful thoughts about Darrak.

She hated him. It didn't matter if he'd spared Ben's life, she shouldn't be feeling this way. Not here. Not now. And not toward him.

Hang on to the anger, she told herself. *It makes things much easier.*

She felt flushed so she fanned herself with a piece of junk mail.

Something caught her attention on the counter. An envelope addressed to her. She sliced it open to find a handwritten note and a small key inside.

Eden,

I'm sorry I've been such a bother. You made it clear last night that I'm not wanted here. If there's one thing I can do it's take a hint. I've been taking the hint all my life, and this is no different. I've gone to fix my problems instead of hiding from them. Enclosed is a key to a locker at the bus station at Dundas and Bay. Inside is that little item I told you about last night. Hold on to the key for me. If I'm not back in two weeks to get it, you're welcome to the contents.

—Leena

P.S. Just because Darrak's in love with you doesn't mean he's not going to get you killed. Take it from me: men, demonic or otherwise, are scum.

There was a lot to digest in that note.

Eden looked at Darrak, who was quickly polishing off the second donut.

"What did you say to Leena last night?" she asked, trying to remain calm. "When she thought you were me?"

He stopped chewing for a moment. "Nothing."

"Enough lies, Darrak. Just tell me."

"Why?" He looked at the note. "What does she say I said?"

"You gave her the impression she's a bother."

"She is."

"You mean, she *was*. She's gone."

He raised dark eyebrows. "Really?"

"Yes."

"That's fantastic." He opened the fridge again. "Do you keep champagne around here anywhere so we can celebrate?"

Eden glared at him. "No, it's not fantastic. You made her feel unwelcome."

"I didn't mean to."

"Stop lying. Honestly, Darrak. You lie to me too much."

"I lie to you, huh?" He threw the empty crumpled-up pastry bag on the counter. "I lie to *you*?"

"That's what I said."

"I don't think I'm the only liar in the general vicinity." Darrak closed the distance between them and looked down at her. "Were you planning on telling me any time soon about your father?"

She froze. "What?"

"Your pops. Your daddy." He braced a hand on either side of her, effectively trapping her in place with her back against the edge of the counter. She couldn't move without touching him, and the heat of his body sank into her. "You know. The *angel*?"

Panic rose in her chest. "Who told you that?"

"Ben did. Part of his strange method of begging for his

life seemed to be shooting out lots of interesting factoids. That was one of them. You're a nephilim."

Her eyes widened. "I don't know if it's true or not."

Darrak took her face between his hands and stared deeply into her eyes as if searching for something there. "I don't sense anything like that. At least I . . . I didn't think I did. How long have you known? Since the beginning?"

She wrapped her hands around his wrists but didn't try to pull him away. Even now, his touch was distracting and oddly tempting. "No. I only found out the other night. And like I said, I have no idea if it's true."

"What does your gut tell you?" he asked.

"My gut?"

"Yeah. You have good intuition."

"Just what every girl likes to hear."

"Really gorgeous, hard to resist intuition," he clarified, with a twitch of his lips, but then the glimmer of a smile vanished and he frowned. "My head feels cloudy."

"My gut tells me that . . . that I don't really know. I don't feel any different."

He stroked the back of his hand across her cheek. "You feel the same to me." Then he shook his head as if trying to clear it. "Were you going to tell me?"

"I was. I . . . I just hadn't yet." Her eyes narrowed. He was the one keeping things from *her*. The nephilim thing shouldn't even count. "Were you going to tell me about the black diamond, the *angelheart*?"

"I didn't know about the angelheart."

"But you knew Theo was looking for a weapon. How long have you known that?"

"About four hundred years. Give or take."

Holy crap. He'd wanted to kill Lucifer for four centuries? That was a very long time to preplan. It had to be a record for premeditated murder.

"What's the weapon for?" she pressed. She wanted him to tell her.

"To help end somebody," he said.

Getting closer. "Who?"

"It's best you don't know, Eden. It's safer that way." Then he rolled his eyes. "There I go again."

"There you go again what?"

"All annoyingly concerned about your safety."

"I'm okay with that, really. My safety is also very important to me."

"Yeah, but . . ." He blinked, before his blue-eyed gaze hardened. "Maybe I don't want to be this way. This humanized version of a demon. Maybe it's making me feel like a lesser being, nonpowerful and in danger of losing any sort of hold I have on my past."

She tried to understand how he felt. Darrak didn't act like she ever would have expected a demon to act. It was the reason why she felt safe with him. "Do you want to be the way you used to be?"

"Why wouldn't I?" he said.

"Don't you feel guilty for the things you did in the past?"

"No," he said without missing a beat. "But I feel guilty for the things I do now. There's a difference—it's like I'm a totally different entity. Back then, I was in control, I was all powerful, and other beings feared me. I didn't second-guess myself ever. And I got what I wanted when I wanted it."

"Sounds horrible to me."

"And I wouldn't have cared if you thought I was horrible."

"Darrak—"

He glared at her. "Back when I was really me, you wouldn't have mattered to me at all."

She inhaled shakily. "So you're saying I do matter to you."

He got closer to her again, so close she could feel the warmth of his breath against her skin.

"The old me wouldn't have stopped you the other night

when you wanted me." His gaze traveled over her face to her mouth. He pressed closer to her, and her hands went to his sides, unsure whether to push him away or not. "The old me would tear off your clothes and take you up against the wall any time it suited me."

An excited shiver went through her at that blunt statement. "You made Leena leave."

"Don't try to change the subject," he said. "Leena has nothing to do with this."

"About you wanting to be as demonic as you used to be thanks to good old Theo's influence?"

"I'm a demon. I should damn well act like one."

"You didn't kill Ben," she reminded him. "You let him go."

"Exactly."

She tried to figure him out. It was difficult. "So is it mind over matter? Have you really changed, or is this all just a façade? In the beginning, you were desperate to show me you weren't evil, that I could trust you."

"And look what happened," he said. "You trusted me, and I steal your body whenever it suits me."

"I'm learning."

"Not fast enough." He traced a slow line down her suddenly sensitive arm. "Maybe it's good that Leena's not here right now. She'd never let me touch you like this, would she?"

"No, I don't suppose she would."

"Theo seemed surprised we weren't wearing out mattresses together. When I told him we'd only been together once, he was confused."

She felt breathless. "Glad you're announcing these things to the world at large. Really fabulous."

Darrak's touch moved up her arm and over her shoulder, then slowly down to the base of her spine. "I told him that we have to be careful that things don't get out of control between us. It's too dangerous."

"My mattress thanks you."

He grinned a bit wickedly. "I do have needs, though. Even though they're not currently being met."

"Oh, really?" Heat rose to her cheeks at that statement. "From the looks you get from half of the female population in the city, I'm sure you could find some willing non-magically inclined woman to help you with your needs. Even that doctor from the other day. I'm sure she has a mattress ready to be worn out."

"Yeah, I'm sure she does," he said.

Cocky, thy name was Darrak the demon.

She glared at him, even though her body continued to respond to his touch. Her skin tingled everywhere he touched her. Currently, he was drawing slow circles on her back. "Then why don't you find somebody and go knock some boots or whatever? I can stay a hundred feet away and put in earplugs. If you're really *that* desperate to get laid."

He was way too close to her at the moment. Why wasn't she moving? Putting space between them would be a very good thing. It was difficult to think when he was this close.

"I would," he said. "I could pursue other women. I don't think I'd have much of a problem finding someone. Or a lot of someones."

"So why don't you, then?" She was breathing rapidly. It was like she had no control over this desire she had for him. Her body felt like it was on fire.

"It's just that . . ."

"What?"

"There's just one little problem," he said.

"And what's that?"

His gaze closed on hers. "I don't want anyone but you."

Eden's eyes widened, and she looked up at him to see if he was kidding. But there was no humor in his expression right now. He looked as intense as she'd ever seen him before. And there was an edge of surprise there, too, as if he hadn't expected to make that admission out loud.

He didn't want anyone but her?

"I . . ." she began. "Darrak . . . I . . ."

"I'm really glad Leena's not here right now," he said.

"Uh . . . why?"

He kissed her.

Oh, that's why, she thought.

⇾ TWENTY-TWO ⇽

Darrak stroked her long hair back from her face as the kiss grew more intense and her mouth opened to his as though she had zero control over her current actions.

She'd dreamed of kissing Darrak many times—and doing a lot more than kissing, too. But reality trumped dreaming anytime.

Eden slid her hands down his back, pulling him closer, and noticed, not for the first time, that he wasn't joking about wanting her. She slid her hand down between them, and Darrak broke the kiss off with a ragged gasp.

"Leena would not approve of that kind of behavior," he whispered hoarsely.

"You're right."

"And yet you're not stopping."

"No, I'm not, am I?"

"She'd be angry with you right now," he rasped.

"Good thing you scared her away then, isn't it? Which, by the way, I'm furious with you about."

"Okay, if this is furious . . ." He swallowed hard. "I need to get you furious more often."

"Shut up." She found his mouth again and kissed him, a slow, deep press of her lips against his.

At the back of her mind she did wonder why she was being like this with him—how she'd felt this level of desire for him so quickly this morning. It had come out of nowhere, really. There was no black magic usage to blame it on. And the fact that she should still be angry with him made it not make sense for her to be molesting his lips to this extent.

It was dangerous territory she was treading on. And, well, *fondling* very brazenly.

They weren't supposed to do this. *She* wasn't supposed to do this.

But as Darrak's mouth moved down to her throat, she couldn't think about anything else. All she wanted was him. Despite the lies, despite the deceit, she wanted him so badly she could barely remain standing.

He pulled the straps of her camisole over her shoulders, pulling the thin material down and baring her breasts.

She looked down. So that meant when Darrak had borrowed her body, he'd neglected to wear a bra? How did she not notice this before? Out on the town without a bra. She was so embarrassed.

At least she was for the moment before he leaned over and circled his tongue around her right nipple. That cleared her brain of any embarrassment. Or, really, any other coherent thought, especially when he repeated the motion on the other side. She was sure her eyes literally rolled to the back of her skull.

She did manage to gather herself together enough to pull off his T-shirt and then run her hands over his chiseled torso. The kitchen counter bit painfully into her as he pressed her back farther, but she honestly didn't care.

He moved his warm hands up her bare thighs and under

her black skirt, raising it as he went. Hooking a finger in either side of her panties he pulled them down her legs.

"Darrak," she managed.

"Leena would be so pissed at me right now," he breathed.

"Very pissed. Uh, Darrak?"

"Yeah?"

"What are we doing?"

"What does it look like?"

"Oh, okay." She nodded, kissing him quickly as his hands moved over her bared skin. "Never mind, then."

Something about a spell, she thought. *I'm forgetting something. What am I forgetting? Oh, who the hell cares?*

Darrak picked her up in his arms, and she wrapped her legs around his waist as they kissed, tongues tangling together. She wanted him. More of him. All of him.

The sofa pressed against her back as he lay her down on it, his mouth not leaving hers for an instant.

"Oh, Eden," he said softly when he finally came up for air. "You're so beautiful."

She looked up at him and traced her finger over his lips. "I want you, Darrak."

Eden didn't resist. Not for an instant. She had no idea how much she wanted this, wanted *him*. Then suddenly his clothes were gone and he was against her in the most intimate way possible, and for a moment she thought he'd stop like he had the other night.

She'd wanted him then, too, so badly, but it had been different. More of a driving need that had been doused by a glass of water in her face. This was . . . this was more of an aching want. And there were no glasses of water within arm's reach.

"Shit," he murmured. "I think I need to stop, but I forget why."

"No . . . don't stop."

"Well, if you insist."

"This is me insisting."

He didn't stop. He slowly, very slowly, pushed himself inside of her.

Damn. Had she really thought being possessed was as good as this? This was so, so much better. His mouth on her mouth. His skin against her skin.

So perfect.

Oh, yes. *This* is what she'd been missing. The feel of him. Only him. Her demon. The one who spent half his days without a body, and the other half trying to resist their attraction to each other.

"I don't want anyone but you."

Eden held on to him as they made love. She captured his face between her hands and looked deeply into his eyes.

"Eden," he said, a frown creasing between his eyes, "what are we doing?"

She almost laughed. "As a former incubus, I think you're fully . . . versed in . . . oh . . . Wait. No conversation. I can't . . . talk . . ." She gasped as a shudder of pleasure rippled through her.

Darrak swore, then pressed his lips to her collarbone. "You feel so . . . so good. *Too* good."

"Don't stop," she commanded.

"I couldn't even if I wanted to," he said, then a breath caught in his throat. "I can't stop."

"Good."

"No . . . I—I mean I really *can't.*" He swore again. "Eden, this is wrong."

"But it feels so right."

Darrak tried to move away from her, but she put her arms around his neck and held on. Suddenly he was seated on the sofa and she was astride him.

"Damn," he breathed. "This isn't much better, is it?"

Eden really had to disagree. It felt even better now. She cried out as another orgasm crashed over her. He groaned low in his throat.

"You feel so good," she breathed into his ear.

"Eden . . ."

She kissed him, exploring his mouth and chin and jaw-line. He gasped against her lips then swore gutturally as he climaxed, his fingers digging almost painfully into her sensitive skin.

Suddenly a wave of golden light enveloped them for a couple of seconds before it disappeared completely. It reminded Eden of what had happened the first and only other time they'd been together like this. A literal afterglow.

It was the spell that the witch had cast, making Darrak a source to increase a witch's black magic whenever they had sex. It was the very thing they'd been trying to avoid by not being together again so Eden's soul wouldn't be at more risk than it already was.

But she didn't care about any stupid spell.

Or did she?

Eden stroked the dark messy hair off his forehead, not ready to move yet. They stared into each others' eyes without speaking for what felt like a very long time. His arms remained locked around her waist, holding her tightly in place against him.

Leena really would be pissed to find them like this. So much for being their chaperone.

Eden brushed her mouth against Darrak's, and he kissed her back softly.

"So . . ." she whispered, trying to hold on to this feeling of bliss for a little while longer.

"So," he replied.

"Lust elixir," she said.

"That's what I'm thinking."

"The donuts?"

He nodded. "I'm thinking your orange juice, too."

She was confused. "But why would Stanley do this to us? How would he even know where to put it?"

"Stanley's working for Theo now. In fact, Stanley told me last night that Theo had developed an interest in his elixirs. Didn't really make me suspicious at the time."

"And now?"

"Very suspicious. Stanley hooked up with Nancy at Luxuria last night, so that's likely how he got the info about the donuts. I told Theo about your orange juice addiction. The rest is history."

Eden swallowed. "He did say that for the elixir to work it has to be a mutually lustful situation."

He blinked. "And lo and behold, here we are."

"Yes." She squirmed a little in place.

"Okay," Darrak gasped. "I really wouldn't do that if I were you."

"Sorry." She bit her bottom lip. "So now what?"

"Well, I would suggest you remove yourself from my lap before I get excited again, but it's a bit too late for that."

"I noticed."

"I thought you might."

She'd definitely noticed. And the fact it didn't scare her that they'd done something they'd promised each other they wouldn't do again wasn't enough to make her budge an inch. Well . . . maybe an inch.

She'd had two large glasses of the tainted orange juice. And by the way she felt, her dose of the elixir hadn't come close to wearing off yet.

"You'd better get off of me or you're going to be sorry," he warned.

"I thought you wanted to be bad," she breathed, brushing her lips against his again. "You're a demon, aren't you?"

"Trust me, I've met my daily quota of evil today."

"Well, maybe I haven't," she whispered suggestively into his ear.

He groaned deep in his throat. It sounded like encouragement to her.

The phone rang. Eden ignored it as she kissed Darrak

again, swept away by this mindless need she felt for him. She couldn't resist it. She wanted to make love to him all day long and make up for lost time.

Suddenly, though, she found herself on her back. On the floor. Alone.

"Oof," she exclaimed as the wind was knocked out of her from the fall from Darrak's lap.

Darrak scrambled up off the sofa, looking down at her. "Sorry."

His gaze swept slowly over her, but then he seemed to force himself to look away. A moment later he was clothed, the black garments appearing as though a magic brush had painted them on.

He grabbed the phone.

Don't look at her, Darrak told himself sternly. *Because if you do, you'll pick her up and take her into the bedroom and you won't emerge for the rest of the day.*

"What?" he snapped into the phone.

"Good morning," Theo's voice greeted him.

His grip on the receiver was nearly tight enough to shatter the plastic. "You."

"You don't sound all that cheery. Everything okay there?"

Darrak willed himself to stay calm. "We found your little gift in the fridge."

"Oh, good. Wow, that was faster than I thought. She must be addicted to that OJ even more than you said she was." He snickered.

"Why did you do it, Theo?" Darrak tried to keep his voice even and conversational. It was a struggle.

"Just helping out a friend in need. I know you're in a bad place. This kills two birds with one stone, forgive the saying. Gets your rocks off *and* helps push our Girl Scout to the dark side so you don't have to worry about her so much."

Darrak almost laughed. Theo'd done this to help him, not to hurt him?

What a pal.

"There are wards up around the building. How'd you even get in here?"

"I phased. Didn't have a problem at all. Guess those wards don't work on me. Or maybe Red secretly wanted me to get through so I could help you two to a morning of pleasure."

He'd phased. Fury simmered just at the surface of Darrak's mind. He didn't want to scream at Theo over the phone. What was done was done. Theo had wanted to help—a demon's version of a kind gesture.

It didn't make it any better.

He and Eden had been compelled to have sex, and it had triggered the spell. Whether or not that spell was triggered every night when he possessed her was still unknown.

In any case, triggering had occurred.

And, by the look of Eden—who'd drawn the crocheted afghan around herself, the remnants of lust for his very accommodating body burning in her eyes—that compulsion hadn't yet worn off.

If Darrak concentrated, he could see it, the power lying just under the surface of her skin. Eden was turning into a five-foot-six nuclear power plant in serious danger of having a reaction if she wasn't very careful.

Theo's proverbial heart might have been in the right place, but he must have known this would enrage Darrak, hadn't he? The other demon had always been a trickster, playing practical jokes and finding humor in the most unlikely places.

Darrak wasn't laughing. And if he kept speaking to his old friend, he was sure to say something he'd regret.

After all, Darrak still needed his help.

"Tell Theo as soon as this elixir wears off I'm going to take that angelheart of his and shove it up his ass," Eden said sweetly.

Darrak chose not to relate the message.

"Is everything still on for noon?" he asked instead.

"It is. So, anyhow, about the—"

"See you then." Darrak hung up the phone. If Theo knew what was good for him, he wouldn't call back. Not until Darrak had had a chance to calm down.

He turned to Eden. "Are you feeling okay?" he asked cautiously.

"I'm feeling a bit too good, actually."

He clasped his hands in front of him. "Is it safe to approach you or, uh, should I stay over here?"

She gripped the afghan closer to her otherwise bare skin. "Don't make it sound like this is all my fault. It was a two-way street in the red light district a minute ago."

"You're right." Darrak moved closer and sat down on the sofa, then he looked at her. "You will never use your black magic again."

"But what if—"

"No, Eden," he said sharply. "Never. Ever, ever. Promise me."

Her jaw clenched. "The only times I've used it was only to protect myself. And you. And . . . uh, Andy, too. I had no choice."

"You do have a choice. You need to swear to me that you won't use it again."

She bristled. "Just like you swore you wouldn't borrow my body when I'm asleep?"

The woman was argumentative even when she was filled with lust. "Fresh slate. I promise not to steal your body, and you promise not to use your black magic." He held out his hand.

She looked at it for a moment before she took it. The touch of her warm skin was not helping him keep his mind on the current problem.

"Fine," she said. "I promise."

He nodded. "Good. I promise, too."

Eden brought her hand to his face. Sliding her index finger down his cheekbone, her thumb over his bottom lip. "So if I promise not to use my black magic, then I don't suppose it really matters if we—"

"It matters," he said hoarsely as she drew closer. Her mouth was only a couple of inches away from his own.

"You're sure about that?" she asked before brushing her lips against his.

He groaned deep in his throat. "This isn't helping, Eden."

"I know."

"How much damned orange juice did you have?"

"A lot. I was like a sponge. A thirstier than normal sponge."

Darrak stood up and paced to the other side of the room. "I need to tell you something."

"What?"

"It's about the singles' club, Luxuria, and why you got a strange vibe while there. It's because it's possessed by a demon."

Eden stared at him blankly. "The *nightclub* is possessed by a demon?"

"Yes." He proceeded to tell her about Asmodeus. He tried to keep it as family-friendly as possible but had to include the part about the semi-drained and addicted patrons. After all, Eden wasn't dumb enough to believe this was a Disney movie.

Her eyes moved back and forth as she attempted to piece it together. "Graham's murder. It was Asmodeus who killed him, wasn't it? Graham got too close, learned too much."

"No," Darrak forced out. "I still don't know what happened to him. Or the other missing women."

The last thing he wanted was for Eden to be tempted to dip into her growing pool of black magic to gain some vengeance today.

Darrak lied to protect her. That made it okay, right?

"Asmodeus wants to help us," he said.

Her eyes widened. "The demon who's possessing a nightclub wants to help us. With what? Buying us a free round of margaritas and an appetizer platter?"

"He's going to channel his energy into breaking my curse after he has his, uh, *awakening* today. And Theo thinks he can do it, too."

"Let me get this straight. This demon lord is going to use the power he's stolen from siphoning energy from hundreds of people, thereby turning them into mindless lust-filled zombies, to help us out."

"You make it sound like a bad thing."

"It *is* a bad thing." Eden got up from the sofa, drawing the afghan full around her body, and paced back and forth around her small living room.

"It's the only chance we've got," he said simply.

"What about the wizard master . . . Maksim? I thought he could help us?"

Darrak sighed. "That was a shot in the dark—I wasn't sure if that would work. Wizards are so unpredictable. But this is a sure thing."

"This Asmodeus—" Eden's eyebrows drew together in concentration. "He's very dangerous, isn't he?"

"Well, of course he is. He's one of the seven Lords of Hell."

"Would the black diamond Theo has be enough to destroy him with? That is, if he tries anything funny today?"

"Possibly," Darrak replied. "But until he has form it's no good. Besides, if he's going to help us break my curse, I don't really want to destroy him. Not yet, anyhow. If that makes me a shameless user, then so be it."

Eden shook her head with confusion. "Theo said the angelheart can only be used once. So if you use it on Asmodeus, you couldn't use it on Lucifer, too. Right?"

"Probably not. Besides, Lucifer's more powerful, so he'll need that diamond at full strength to even have a

chance of . . ." Darrak blinked. "Hold on. How do you know
the diamond is meant for Lucifer?"

Realization of what she'd said slid behind her green
eyes. "Uh . . . you must have told me."

"No, I didn't."

Color rushed into her cheeks. "You *must* have."

"I know for an absolute fact that I said nothing."

Eden tried to move past him. "I need to have a shower."

He blocked her way to the bathroom. "How do you
know about Lucifer?"

She bit her bottom lip. "Everyone knows about Lucifer,
don't they? He's the original fallen angel. All prideful."

Darrak grabbed hold of her bare shoulders. "I'm asking
you again. How do you know about Lucifer?"

"Be careful or I'm going to lose this afghan," she
warned.

He eyed her slipping cover. He really didn't need any
other distractions at the moment.

"I want to have a shower," she said firmly, then slid her
right hand down his chest. "You're welcome to join me,
though." She frowned. "Damn lust elixir. It's really not
helping right now."

Tempting. Very tempting. But he was too distracted by
what she'd said before. Why would she mention Lucifer?

"Fine." He stepped aside, and she went into the bathroom and closed the door without another word. He heard
the shower turn on. He waited, not moving from his spot.

Ten minutes later she emerged wearing a towel. She
flicked a glance at him.

"Just forget it," she said.

"No."

She glared at him and disappeared into her bedroom.
Another ten minutes went by, and she emerged fully dressed
in jeans and a black sweater. Her grayish amulet lay against
her chest and his eyes moved to it.

It was still the same color as yesterday. It didn't gauge

her level of black magic, only the darkness of her soul. She could be filled to the brim with black magic, but if she didn't use it, it wouldn't do any damage to her.

If she never used it again, the color—and her soul—would stay as it was right now.

Gray *was* better than black.

Theo had been trying to help. It was true, though. If Eden's soul went jet-black, it would be a one-way ticket to Hell when she died—just being immortal didn't mean she couldn't be killed. If he went back to Hell, they could be together.

They might even be able to set up house in the pit with a black picket fence and a family hellhound.

But Darrak had known black-souled humans before. They were . . . different. Eden wouldn't be the same as she was now. She'd be something else.

If Eden's soul went to Hell, Darrak would be there to protect it. Protect her. Till the end of time.

But it wouldn't really be Eden anymore.

Darrak had seen her soul when they first met. He'd touched it when he possessed her. It had been a shimmering, glowing pure thing unlike anything he'd ever experienced before. Despite the damage that had occurred since, it still filled him with such energy and life. A soul like Eden's deserved to go to Heaven.

And if she really was a nephilim, she deserved to go to Heaven even more.

One problem at a time.

"Tell me about Lucifer," he said firmly.

She paled. "I can't do that."

He was trying very hard to stay calm. It wasn't working very well. "Pretty please with sugar on top?"

"Being polite isn't going to change my answer."

He racked his mind. Where had she gone? Who had she seen and spoken to?

"Does this have to do with Ben?" he asked.

"No."

"The Malleus leader you talked to? The witch who dampened me?"

"No and no."

Who else had she come in contact with lately? It wasn't Andy, who'd been clueless about anything supernatural until just the other day. It wasn't Leena, so self-serving she wouldn't have offered any insight on anything, let alone his and Theo's plans toward the Prince of Hell.

Then who?

"Darrak, just forget—"

Then something just clicked.

"Lucas," he said.

She gasped. "Darrak, please . . ."

That was the reaction he'd been looking for. He'd hit the target.

But . . . *Lucas*? That bland, uninteresting teacher who wanted to borrow Leena's metaphorical sugar?

Darrak frowned deeply. "Is he . . . a servant of Lucifer's? Was he sent here to keep an eye on me? Is that it?"

"Please, no. Just forget it," she said, now panicky. "And don't mention him again. Ever."

Darrak studied her face, trying to glean the truth there and wishing again that he could read her mind. Why was she keeping this from him? And why did she look so afraid?

More clickage occurred for him. This time it came with a side helping of shock.

"Wait, I'm wrong," he said. "Lucas isn't Lucifer's servant, is he? Lucas *is* Lucifer."

Eden looked as if she was ready to hyperventilate. Her face had paled so much it was as white as the wall she braced herself against.

She didn't reply. That was confirmation enough for him.

Darrak pulled her to him, cupping her face in his hands, feeling a wave of protectiveness toward her at her look of fear. "It's okay. You can tell me anything."

Did she still trust him? Or had he managed to completely destroy that between them?

Tears shone in her eyes. "He has my mother's soul."

He tensed. "So he can blackmail you?"

"Yes."

"What does he want?"

She brought her voice down to a barely audible whisper. "He *knows*, Darrak. About the weapon. About Theo's plans. And he knows you're in on it." Her expression suddenly turned to annoyance. "Why would you be in on something stupid like that?"

He cringed. Terrific. Everybody knew. "I have my reasons. I just don't understand why I didn't sense it before. I talked to Lucas twice."

"Does he look different?"

"Yeah. But, of course, he has different forms, just like me. This is one I'd never seen before." He swallowed. "I didn't even know he could enter the human world. Thought it was part of his punishment that he had to stay in Hell."

"He has to take mortal form when he's here," Eden said quietly.

Okay, that was news. "He told you that? When?"

She twisted her fingers through her dark red hair. "We've spoken a few times. The marble he gave me yesterday—he called it a summoning crystal. You didn't even know I was gone."

She was right. He'd been completely and utterly oblivious, too consumed by his own problems to even notice anything like that.

So this is why she'd been so preoccupied and secretive lately. Lucifer had been summoning her for secret meetings.

"Wait a minute. You said he has to take *mortal* form." Darrak considered the word. "Do you mean that while in the human world, Lucifer is human?"

Eden nodded. "He's vulnerable while he's here. And it's

probably one of the reasons he insisted I didn't say anything to you about this."

Lucifer was here. Right next door as their friendly,
teacherly neighbor with glasses and an off-the-rack suit.
And he had been for days.

There was a moment of fear for Darrak—for himself and
for Eden—but it was quickly replaced by a wave of fury
that turned his vision dark red.

"I'm going to kill him," Darrak said softly.

Without another word, he turned toward the door and
stormed out of the apartment, headed to the one next door.

⇾ TWENTY-THREE ⇽

Oh, this was not good. There were no words to describe how completely not good this was.

"Darrak, stop! Don't do this." Eden hurried behind him as he stormed out of the apartment.

But he wasn't listening.

He knocked on the door to Lucas's apartment. Eden grabbed his arm, but she couldn't budge him an inch no matter how hard she tried.

"You don't know what you're doing," she said, trying to fight against the panic rising in her chest. How could she stop him from making a horrible mistake like this?

"I know exactly what I'm doing," he replied stonily.

The door opened. Lucas stood there holding a mug of coffee and looking very, totally, utterly human. Just a teacher getting ready for a regular school day.

"Good morning," he said.

"No, not good," Darrak replied. "Not for you."

Darrak's hand shot out, and he grabbed Lucas by his throat, pushing him back into the apartment. The coffee mug crashed to the ground, the hot black liquid splashing on the clean ceramic tiles. Lucas sputtered and his face began to turn purple.

"Stop it, Darrak!" Eden grabbed hold of his arm again. "Don't hurt him!"

Darrak's arm was like an iron bar. He didn't show the true extent of his power very often and claimed to be weakened by his curse, but he sure didn't seem all that weak at the moment. Compared to a regular archdemon, then maybe. But matched up against an average, everyday human male there was no comparison.

Lucas—or rather *Lucifer*—could be killed while in the human world. But it wouldn't change anything. He'd be returned to Hell fully sentient, and Darrak would be in huge trouble. Darrak was in enough trouble to begin with.

Darrak glared at Lucas. "Spying on me, are you?"

"I . . . don't know what . . . you're . . . talking . . . about," Lucas gasped. He fought against Darrak's grip but didn't come close to breaking it.

"Yeah, right. By the way, still looking forward to that housewarming party of yours. I already told Eden I want to be in charge of the four-layer fiesta dip. Is that cool with you?"

Darrak threw Lucas across the kitchen counter—identical to Eden's—sweeping off a few plates. Lucas crashed to the ground on the other side.

Was Lucas really living here? Eating here? Did he have to stay in the human world until his work here was done?

These and other questions Eden had—including where Darrak got that delicious-sounding recipe—could wait until this was over.

Darrak was in front of Lucas again in a heartbeat, grabbing hold of him long enough to toss him farther into the room, shattering the screen of the television set and knocking it off its stand. Blood now dripped from Lucas's fore-head and the corner of his mouth.

With one hand clamped around his throat, Darrak raised Lucas up so he was no longer touching the floor.

"Do you know that I blame you for everything?" Darrak said darkly. "Might be passing the buck a bit from my own personal responsibility, but that's just how I roll. And now to find you here, completely defenseless. Must be my lucky day. Do you believe in paying a heavy price for your sins, Lucifer? Out of everyone in the Netherworld I'm thinking you just might."

"Just let him go," Eden said again as firmly as she could.

"Stay out of this," he snapped. "You should leave. Go back to the apartment where it's safe."

Sure. Like that was going to happen.

Fear coursed through Eden, freezing her in place. Darrak was going to kill Lucas. This wasn't fun and games any-more. She had to stop the bullheaded demon or he'd only wind up hurting himself. Why couldn't he see that?

She remembered what Lucas had told her about demons like Darrak and Theo: *"Demons forged from hellfire can be pretty but are ultimately kind of stupid."*

She'd normally debate that statement, but at the moment—it seemed to fit the bill.

Eden had to stop this on behalf of the pretty, stupid demon on the verge of making a huge mistake. And she knew how to stop him.

"*Darrakayiis*," Eden said firmly, enunciating every single syllable. "Let him go. I command you to."

Lucas fell to the ground as Darrak released him, clutch-ing at his throat, coughing and sputtering and gasping for breath. Darrak went rigid, his arms held to his sides like a soldier awaiting an order from his drill sergeant. His eyes moved to Eden, and they burned with amber flames before returning to cool blue. He wasn't happy.

"Why did you stop me?" he bit out through clenched teeth.

"I couldn't let you kill him."

"Why would you protect the Prince of Hell?"

She glared at him. "You think I'm protecting *him*? Honestly, you are so annoying sometimes."

Lucas laughed, and it was a painful sound. "Lesser demons are like a dog with a bone when they get an idea into their heads."

"I'm not a lesser demon," Darrak growled. "I'm an *arch*-demon."

"Right. So sorry. I forgot how important titles are to lesser demons." Lucas rolled his eyes. "Since you're acting like such a spoiled brat, your official designation slipped my mind. It's been a long time, hasn't it?"

"Not long enough."

Eden watched the both of them tensely, not sure what to do or say next.

She'd just saved Lucifer's mortal life. It had seemed like a good idea at the time, but now she wasn't so sure what would happen next.

Lucas stood up, but it took him a moment. Blood trickled down his forehead. He brushed his shirt off, then crossed his arms and walked a slow circle around the prone demon.

"*Darrakayiis*," he said. Darrak's shoulders grew even more tense, and his attention flicked to Lucas now instead of Eden as the balance of power shifted between them. "Is that how you present yourself to me? I don't want to see your worthless human form. Have some pride instead of vanity. Show me your demon form."

Flames rippled forth on Darrak's body, and he grew taller and broader and more muscular. Long thick curved horns emerged from either side of his head. Razor-sharp talons extended from his fingertips. His body was now covered with shallow, translucent golden fire that made him one of the scariest—no, scratch that—*the* scariest thing Eden had ever seen in her life. The only thing that remained the same were his eyes—ice blue and filled with human intelligence as he scanned the room.

Otherwise, he was a monster.

"See? That's much better." Lucas's voice sounded raspy as if Darrak had done some damage to his larynx by throwing him around like a rag doll. He turned to Eden. "Why did this happen?"

Her mouth felt too dry to form words, but she tried anyhow. "I—I didn't say anything to him. I swear I didn't."

"And yet we are here right now, and I've just avoided being killed by a disgruntled employee."

"I stopped him," she pointed out, hoping that would help matters.

"Yes, you did. If you hadn't stopped him, it wouldn't have ended well for any of us. I can do a great deal more damage from Hell than I can live and in person."

Eden tried not to look away from Lucas's intense gaze. She tried not to feel any fear toward him. He looked so broken and beaten and incredibly human that, despite his angry words, it was difficult to remember who and what he really was.

Lucas looked at Darrak. "You know you're compelled to tell me the truth right now, don't you?"

"Yes," he hissed.

"Did she tell you who I am?"

"No." The demon's voice was deeper now and filled with darkness like something out of a nightmare. The sound of it raised goose bumps on Eden's arms.

"Then how did you know?"

"I guessed. And I was right."

Lucas studied him for a moment. "Interesting."

"Do I win a prize?" Darrak's tone was insolent.

Lucas turned to Eden and gave her a thin smile. "Our deal was that you don't directly tell him about me. It doesn't seem as if you did, so I can't fault you. You're very lucky that I always hold true to the exact wording of my bargains."

Funny. She wasn't feeling all that lucky at the moment.

Lucas touched his throat gingerly as if testing for deeper injuries.

"Are you okay?" she asked.

He frowned. "What?"

"It's just . . . that cut on your forehead is kind of nasty. You might need stitches." Eden dug into her pocket and pulled out a tissue, which she pressed against the wound.

Lucas flinched. "It's nothing."

"If you want to have a mortal form like this, you're going to have to look after it properly."

"This is only temporary." He took the tissue away from her, and her arm dropped back to her side. As she stepped away from him, he eyed her curiously.

"Excuse me," Darrak said. "If Eden's all finished kissing your boo-boos, can we move this along? I have a full schedule today."

Even in his demon form, Darrak was still sarcastic at inappropriate moments.

"You tried to kill me," Lucas said.

"Gee, you figured it out. I wish I was as smart as you, Lucifer. You're my hero."

Shut up, Darrak, she thought, hoping the glare sent in the direction of the scary-looking, fiery demon might be enough to quiet him, but she doubted it.

"I created you," Lucas said.

"Sorry I forgot the Happy Father's Day card this year. I made a really nice one with crayons." An unpleasant smile creased the demon's fearsome expression beneath the flames. "They melted a bit, though. Made it difficult to draw the bunnies and smiley faces."

"You aren't going to beg my forgiveness?" Lucas asked.

"Nope."

"And will you attempt to end my existence again?"

"More than likely."

"Darrak," Eden snapped. "What is wrong with you?"

He turned his horned head toward her. "You used my true name. *Again*. Thanks for that, by the way. Right now I'm compelled to tell the truth, remember? So sue me."

"No, I don't think I'll sue you," Lucas said. "Frankly, I'm not sure what to do with you."

"Bullshit," Darrak replied.

"What did you say?"

"I said *bullshit*. It's a common English expletive used to reply to insincere, nonsensical talk. You know what to do with me. The only penalty for a treasonous act like the attempted murder of someone like you would be immediate decimation."

Icy fear coursed through Eden's body.

"It is, isn't it?" Lucas agreed. "But I'm not quite ready for that yet."

"Oh, no?" Darrak still didn't move an inch. However, his eyes showed the strain of his attempts. "Why not?"

"Because I need you," Lucas said evenly.

A low, scary chuckle sounded in the demon's throat. "You're kidding. You need *me*?"

"Yes."

"This is the warm and fuzzy, sentimental moment I've been waiting the better part of a millennium for. I'm kidding now, of course. I don't do warm and fuzzy."

It's a mask, Eden thought suddenly. This whole sarcastic, kill-me-now thing Darrak was doing. It was masking how worried he must have been feeling at Lucifer's mercy like this.

"I'm going to give you a choice, Darrak," Lucas said. "I'm fairly well versed in what has happened to you all these years. Why you disappeared—"

"You mean, after you fired me and sent me out on my

own, an act that allowed a witch to summon my archdemon ass straight out of Hell? Besides, what you accused me of wasn't even true."

Lucas just shook his head. "That you were a conspirator? Perhaps not directly with Asmodeus, but you were not innocent of my accusations. I don't regret what I did. I need demons I can rely on to protect me and do what I tell them to do, not ones that gossip and plan uprisings behind my back." He sighed. "Maybe you simply were never right for the job and worthless as an employee and an archdemon."

"Don't be a hater."

"Theo was much better at following orders than you ever were."

Darrak smiled, showing the sharp teeth behind his coating of translucent fire. "Theo would be thrilled you think so."

"Speaking of Theo, I want the angelheart he plans to destroy me with," Lucas said.

Darrak's smile faded and he looked at Eden. "Is there anything you *didn't* tell him?"

"Uh . . . nothing actually comes to mind," she admitted. "But he already knew about the murder plot."

"It's strange," Darrak said. "You're allegedly mortal here and without any power. And yet you easily have me frozen in place like this."

"I allowed what happened earlier as I was curious to see what you'd do next," Lucas said. "I could have stopped you at any time, but instead Eden did that for me. My form or level of mortality is meaningless when it comes to those I created. Even here, I can send you to the Void if I choose to, but not before causing you more pain that you've felt in your entire existence."

"I don't believe you."

"No?" Lucas approached Darrak. "How about I give you just a little taste, and you can see how lenient I've been so far."

Lucas didn't move. His expression didn't change.

But Darrak's face convulsed and his body quaked. A

roar sounded out from deep in his throat as if he was experiencing sheer, unadulterated agony.

A cry rose in Eden's chest at seeing him in pain like this. "Stop. Please."

Lucas glanced at her, then back at Darrak. The demon went silent, closing his eyes, his chest hitching.

"The fact you still exist is because I am allowing it," Lucas said to him. "Look into my eyes and tell me if I'm lying."

Darrak slowly opened his eyes and looked closely at Lucas. "Did . . . anyone ever tell you . . . that you have lovely eyes?" His voice was slightly weakened from his short torture session. "For a lousy, self-pitying, ex-angel boss, that is."

Eden shook her head with frustration. She really couldn't help him if he didn't at least try to help himself.

"I will allow you to leave here this morning with your existence intact," Lucas said to him. "And in return, you will get me that black diamond."

"And if I can't?"

"There are several interested parties in the Netherworld who have heard rumors of your situation here in the human world." Lucas shook his head. "I can't help but sense that you've changed, Darrak."

"The humanity is temporary."

"You believe that?"

"Yes."

Lucas tilted his head to the side, studying Darrak as if trying to assess his true worth. "You'd never pass their tests. They would hunt you down and destroy you and anything you value."

"I don't have any possessions," Darrak said.

"Are you sure about that?" Lucas flicked a glance at Eden. "I believe there is something here you wouldn't want destroyed alongside you."

The moment Eden felt personally threatened, black

magic rose to the surface of her skin for her to use at will. It was like another sense. She supposed she was working on her seventh now.

Darrak's gaze moved to her as well. "Leave Eden alone."

"It's much too late for that." Lucas approached her, almost tentatively. "You know the truth about me. You're one of the very few who does."

She nodded.

"And you believe what I told you?"

"Yes." Eden didn't hesitate to answer. She knew deep in her gut that what he'd told her was true. That he wanted to destroy his own inner demon—Satan—so he'd have a chance to be redeemed in Heaven's eyes.

"Thank you for saving me from your demon," Lucas said.

"You said you didn't need my help."

"It's still appreciated. I won't forget. And I won't forget about our deal." He leaned forward and brushed his lips against hers. She froze in place at the unexpected kiss.

When he pulled back, his eyes flicked to her necklace and his brow furrowed. "I must remember that black witches are dangerous for me to be around."

Eden looked down at her amulet. With shock she realized it had suddenly become a shade lighter. "How is that possible?"

Lucas's expression shadowed. "It's part of my punishment. I'm a natural magnet for darkness. I attract it and it feeds my inner beast."

She touched her lips. One kiss from Lucifer had helped restore her soul? It was just a smidgeon, but it was more than she ever could have hoped for.

"Bring me that black diamond," he said softly. "And I will make good on our deal. I promise you I will."

Lucas turned and left the apartment.

Darrak flickered hellishly in her peripheral vision. "Did he try to slip you the tongue?"

She shot him a look. "Don't be ridiculous."

"Is that a yes or a no?"

"Did you see what he did to my amulet?"

He narrowed his eyes. "Maybe you should seek him out for an afternoon of tonsil hockey."

She thought about that. Could Lucas take *all* of her darkness away?

"I was kidding," he said firmly, still using that dark ominous tone of his that didn't match the words he spoke. "Forget tonsil hockey. It's a dangerous sport. Especially with him."

"Seems to be a dangerous sport with everyone lately."

"Touché. So are you going to release me or let me stand here all day like a tiki torch?"

Eden walked toward him until she stood right in front of him, then forced herself to look up at his intimidating visage.

He blinked. "I don't like it when you look at me that way. Like you're afraid of me."

"I *am* afraid of you."

"This form really isn't all that difficult to warm up to, is it? No pun intended."

She crossed her arms. "Darrakayiis, I release you."

Darrak's body immediately relaxed, the flames extinguished, and he returned to his human form in less than ten seconds. He grabbed both of Eden's wrists in his grip so she couldn't pull away from him.

"Do I really scare you that much?" he asked, his gaze searching hers.

"There's nothing to fear but fear itself."

"Do you think I'd ever purposely hurt you?"

She swallowed. "No."

"I wasn't thinking straight earlier. I may have some anger issues I need to sort through."

Eden exhaled shakily. "Okay. So now we just need to figure out how to get that angelheart away from Theo today."

Darrak crossed his arms and paced over to the glass

doors leading to the balcony. "So we can hand it over to your new buddy, Lucifer?"

"That's right. And he's not my buddy. This is a business transaction only. We give him something he wants, he gives us something we want."

"That's not going to happen."

"What?"

"There's no damn way I'm doing what he wants me to do. I hate him."

Eden hissed out a breath. "And there's nothing I can say to make you change your mind?"

"Can't think of a single thing."

"So I'm on my own."

"You attempt to get that angelheart today, and I'll have to stop you." Darrak's expression softened at her look of outrage. "I know you don't get it, but I'm doing this *for* you, Eden. Lucifer can't help us."

"He said he'd fix things between us."

"Then he's a big fat liar. He won't fix things. He will decimate me before he ever helps me. And whether or not you're open to playing kissy-face with him won't change his mind. I do believe I've told you about his well-stocked harem, haven't I? Does that sound like somebody who is keeping a list of people he owes favors to?"

"And if I refuse to go today to Luxuria to take part in this demonic awakening of Asmo-whatever-his-name-is? Will you force me to go?"

His lips pressed together. "Again, I say I'm doing this *for* you. Why can't you understand that? We're kind of a team. Team Darrak and Eden. Team Deden. Or Team Edrak. We'll get T-shirts."

"Sure we will." She felt utterly exasperated by this entire situation. "You really think this nightclub-possessing demon will help us?"

"I do. Theo swears he will."

Darrak seemed so certain he could trust Theo. She personally couldn't stand the demon, but she couldn't argue the fact he and Darrak were friends and had been for centuries. Friends helped friends. Theo wouldn't betray Darrak.

Lust elixir notwithstanding.

Besides, if she resisted going, she wouldn't be able to get close to that diamond again. She needed it. Her mother's soul needed it. And she was convinced that Darrak's entire existence rested on not crossing Lucifer this time.

"Fine," she said. "We'll go."

His eyebrows rose. "Really? I thought you were going to give me a hard time."

"I already did. Hard time is over. But . . . but you really, totally, completely trust Theo?"

"I trust Theo with my very existence," he said without hesitation.

"Fine. If you trust him, then I'll try to, too. Besides"— she looked at him—"we're in this together, aren't we?"

"Despite the fact you're afraid of me."

"It comes and it goes."

"For the record, I'm afraid of you, too."

Eden touched her amulet. "The black witch thing?"

He shook his head. "I wish it was that simple."

She did, too.

⇉ TWENTY-FOUR ⇇

"And the demon let you go?" Oliver asked.

Ben had answered these questions several times already. He was far past the point of being annoyed by them. "Yes."

"Just like that."

"Yes."

"And the demon was in full possession of Eden Riley's body at the time."

"Correct."

"Did you tell him anything about our organization in return for your freedom?"

"No."

As a Malleus elder, Oliver had an ability that helped him gauge when an underling was lying to him. Since Ben wasn't lying, he didn't have anything to fear. Still, the whole situation had a "trip to the principal's office" feel to it.

"It's just as I thought," Oliver said after a moment.

"What is?"

"The fact the demon released you. He should have murdered you without conscience. He's developing humanlike morals thanks to absorbing the nephilim's celestial energy."

"If you say so."

Ben still couldn't believe he'd gotten away—that Darrak hadn't used that knife to slice right through him. Then he'd stopped the other demon from finishing the job.

He was still breathing only because Darrak had saved his life.

No. He wouldn't feel grateful to that thing that lived inside Eden's body like a cancerous tumor. Ben had learned a great deal in his short time as a member of the Malleus, and he hadn't liked everything he'd learned, but he knew right from wrong. The most evil criminal was capable of doing a good deed if it served his ultimate plan. Ben was no chump.

"What about Eden's father?" Ben asked. "The angel. You told me he would be disturbed to hear what had happened to his daughter and he'd help us."

"I assume he will. We don't know exactly when. Until then we must be vigilant. Eden Riley is more dangerous than I ever could have predicted."

"I don't know about—"

Oliver cut him off. "She's a black witch and received her magic because of the demon. We'll keep an eye on her and wait for the right time to strike next."

"But what if—"

"No, Ben. You will follow orders. Until then you will wait and not initiate contact with her again."

He hated being interrupted. "I'm not afraid."

"And we appreciate your bravery. We will apply it to cases other than Eden's."

"But—"

"Ben"—Oliver smiled at him coolly—"arguing will not win you any friends here. You will do what you're told, when you're told. If you're unable to follow our rules and guidelines, I'm afraid we're going to have a serious problem. Now, go home and await further instruction. You're dismissed."

It was on the tip of Ben's tongue to tell Oliver to shove his rules and guidelines up his ass. But he said nothing. Instead he stood, nodded his head like an obedient child, and left the room.

His fleur-de-lis brand itched as he stalked through the halls of the underground Malleus headquarters. He'd been taken for a tour there and shown the cells where they kept various evil creatures locked away awaiting punishment or for experimental purposes.

Ben's face ached from where the other demon had used him as a punching bag. He'd been unable to move, held in place by magic. Hardly a fair fight. His eye socket and jaw had felt better, that was for sure.

He passed a cell just as a guard exited holding a tray. The tray held . . . feathers?

A deep, muted voice could be heard from inside the metal cell warded by magic. Ben couldn't make out the words. On the door was a tiny opening at eye level.

"Don't you want to help us?" the Malleus guard asked. "You came here to help, and now all you do is whine. You would be smart to keep your mouth shut."

He closed the door completely and it locked with a click, then he walked off down the hall. A white feather fell off the tray and drifted to the ground in front of Ben. He leaned over and picked it up, twisting it between his fingers.

"That's mine," a voice said.

Ben looked to his right. A face peered at him through the opening on the door to the darkened cell. A man. His face gaunt, his eyes sunken. A lock of bright red hair fell across his forehead.

Ben pushed the feather through the opening and the man took it.

"Thank you." The man's voice was weary and barely audible.

"No problem. Feather pillow?" he asked.

"No. My wings. Or, rather, what's left of them."

"Your wings?"

"Ben!" Oliver shouted down the hall. "I thought I told you to leave?"

"How long have you been here?" Ben asked the man.

"A while."

"Who are you?"

Distrust flickered in the man's green eyes. "What do you care?"

Ben glanced at the opening again but the man's face was gone. Talking to prisoners without permission was breaking the rules. The Malleus had a lot of rules.

He left the building without speaking to another soul and went back to his house. He picked up the phone and dialed Eden's number. It went through to her voicemail. He hung up without leaving a message. The next person he phoned, however, did pick up.

Twenty minutes later she arrived. Her face fell when she saw how beaten up he looked.

"Ben!" Sandy exclaimed. "What the hell happened to you?"

"Don't you mean, *who* from Hell happened to me?" He explained the events of the previous night to her, glossing over the worst of it.

He'd been given some healing ointments by the Malleus. He wouldn't scar, but it hadn't taken care of his wounds overnight.

She touched his face, worry filling her expression. "Honestly. You're a magnet for trouble, you know that?"

He snorted. "I know."

"At least you're okay."

"For now."

That earned him a stern glare. "So now what do we do?"

"We wait. At least that's what I've been told." He

frowned. "Do you know of any prisoner at the Malleus who has wings?"

"Wings?"

"With white feathers. And he has red hair and green eyes."

She seemed distracted by inspecting his wounds. "Sounds like an angel to me."

His eyes widened. "An angel?"

She nodded. "I've never seen one before—not one with wings, anyhow. They're usually up in Heaven. The earthbound angels who watch the Netherworld gateways temporarily get rid of their wings while they're here to ensure they're not damaged."

Then that was impossible. "Why would the Malleus be holding an angel in a prison cell?"

"They wouldn't, of course," Sandy said firmly. "The Malleus fights on the side of light—on the side of angels— against the darkness."

"You're right, of course. I guess I was just seeing things."

"Listen . . . Ben, I wanted to talk to you. About . . . about what happened yesterday. When you and I . . ." She chewed her bottom lip and averted her gaze.

"The kiss?"

"That would be the topic at hand."

"I think you already established how you felt about that. How it was a mistake and against the rules." He raised an eyebrow. It hurt a little.

"Yeah, I did say that already, didn't I?"

"And also how you know how much I care about Eden and my current obsession to save her from demons and other nasty creatures of darkness."

"So we discussed this already?"

"We did."

She forced a smile. "Then, well, that's good. Forget it. Why don't I just grab some bandages and I can patch you up a bit?"

Ben stood up from the couch. "Sandy, can I ask you something?"

"Sure."

"Do you like working for the Malleus?"

"Of course. It makes me feel like I'm doing something worthwhile."

He nodded. "Me, too."

"And even though they have a lot of rules, it still makes sense."

"Most of the rules I agree with."

"Most of them?"

"Yeah. There's just one I'm finding I'm not too fond of."

"And which one is—"

She tensed with surprise when he kissed her but didn't resist. He wondered if he'd forget about everything if he kissed her long enough. If breaking this one rule with Sandy would be enough to make the rest of it make sense.

It was definitely worth a try.

⇒ TWENTY-FIVE ⇐

Eden wondered exactly what would be involved in a demon lord awakening.

It didn't sound like a chance for balloons and streamers, but maybe she was wrong.

She needed that black diamond. The angelheart.

No matter what else happened here today, she had to get her hands on it.

The front door to Luxuria was unlocked when she and Darrak arrived at almost noon. She had to force herself to take each step farther along the hallway leading to the main club. She felt like Dorothy getting ready to approach the Wizard of Oz and ask him for a ticket back to Kansas.

"You okay?" Darrak asked. She was walking so slowly some might consider it standing still.

"Not especially."

And, as if she needed anything more to deal with at the moment, a wave of pain hit her without warning, almost bringing her to her knees. She cried out. Darrak grabbed hold of her before she fell.

It was gone as quickly as it had arrived. Just a drive-by.

Darrak's eyes were filled with concern as he helped her steady herself. "We can leave."

She laughed weakly. "You don't mean that."

"I do." His jaw set. "We'll wait for Maksim to get back from wherever he is. We don't have to do this if you don't want to."

"No, I'm okay now. This is your chance to get your curse removed. And I don't get the pain very often. That, hopefully, was my only dose today."

He didn't look convinced. "Fine. But when the curse is broken, I want you to leave immediately and don't look back."

"Why?"

"When I change . . . I can't guarantee how I'll act then. Toward you. I don't know."

Right. He felt that when the curse was broken, he'd revert back to his old demonic self—no humanity need apply, right?

"So you'll become dark, dangerous, and not a fabulous conversationalist?" she asked.

"The first two. I could always hold my own at a cocktail party."

"You really think that'll happen? Losing the humanity you've gained after all these years?"

He nodded solemnly, then stroked a strand of dark red hair off her face and tucked it behind her ear. "I do. I just wish . . ."

"What?"

He kissed her then. Just a quick brush of his lips against hers before he pulled away.

"Come on," he said. "Theo will be waiting for us."

Eden pressed her lips together and tried to ignore the lump in her throat.

Was it true? Would he change the moment the curse was broken? He believed it completely, so why wouldn't she? Probably because it made her sad that this Darrak she'd grown very fond of was only a façade. He seemed to embrace this chance to return to his former self, not doubting it for a moment. Not wanting to be anything else.

This unfortunate experience was just a blip in the video game of his existence.

And it was true, he didn't feel remorse for anything he'd done in the past—not even being the cause of death for all of his former hosts. He was a demon who did demonic things. Period. After all, a lion didn't apologize for eating a gazelle, did it?

Depended on the lion, she thought. *And the gazelle.*

They had no choice but to go forward with this. The last thing she wanted was for Darrak to continue to possess her. This really was their only answer.

However, it relied on a great deal of trust. For Theo and for this Asmo demon.

Eden would let Darrak handle the trust. She'd focus on getting the angelheart.

As they rounded the next corner toward the inner entrance, Theo stood there with his arms crossed as if waiting for them.

"Darrak," he greeted his friend. His black-eyed gaze moved toward her. "Lovely to see you again, Eden."

Her face felt tense. She bit her tongue so she wouldn't immediately tell him to go to hell. A demon would probably take that more as a suggestion than an insult, anyhow.

She couldn't help but sense something different in the club today. The lust and desperation that always hung in the air there had risen to palpable levels. There was an audible hum in the building, and electricity seemed to lightly charge the room. It felt like the air outside just before a thunderstorm—a restrained energy about to be unleashed.

A demon lord was preparing to take form.

That didn't help relax her very much.

"Is Asmo ready?" Darrak asked.

Theo nodded. "More than ready. He's been waiting for this for centuries."

Eden stayed silent, trying her best to look at ease. She watched Theo very carefully and wondered if he had the angelheart on him right now.

"You can talk to him?" Darrak asked.

"He's been able to communicate with me despite his incorporeal state. However, until today it's taken a great deal of concentration."

Darrak moved away from Eden's side. "Lucifer knows about our plan."

Theo waited, as if for a punch line, but when one didn't come, his eyes narrowed and he shot a fierce look at Eden. "Is that so?"

"It's not Eden's fault. He already knew. However, he's been sniffing around and trying to find more about that weapon of yours."

"That's so not fair." Theo stomped his foot. A frustrated, pissed-off demon was not a pretty sight. But it was a bit amusing.

"Better we know now, than later," Darrak pointed out.

"You're right, of course." He swore under his breath, and then patted his pocket. "I'll have to put this somewhere safe until there's a better time to use it. Honestly. How annoying is that?"

"The best laid plans," Darrak said.

"Yeah." Theo's sullen expression brightened a little. "Speaking of getting laid, how'd you enjoy your orange juice this morning, Eden?"

She wondered if she had enough black magic in her to decimate an archdemon where he stood, leaving only a black smudge behind. It would jeopardize more of her soul, but it might be worth it to wipe that smug, amused look off his stupid pretty face.

"It was refreshing, thanks."

His smug look grew. "Did it quench that little thirst you've got? I bet it did. Lip-smacking good."

She'd like to smack his lips. And then grind them into a paste.

"Theo." Darrak's voice held an edge of warning. "Enough."

Theo mock pouted. "Oh, you're no fun anymore."

She wouldn't destroy him, but she couldn't let this go completely unaddressed, though. "Darrak tells me you fell for a human woman a long time ago."

Smug look officially decimated. "I did."

"Were you in love with her?"

This earned her a smile, but it looked forced. "Oh, Eden, I knew you were a romantic. You'd like me to admit that I was, wouldn't you? Do you think that would help you find my weakness?"

"Just making conversation."

"There was a woman once. And yes, I allowed myself to feel emotion for her. But I was always the one in control. And when the time came for me to choose whether I wanted to save myself or save her, I made the only decision I could."

"You killed her."

That earned a flicker of something in his eyes as he looked down at the floor. It was either fire or pain, she wasn't sure. "No. But the result was the same. She died. Her soul perished. And it didn't really matter to me. It's not as if I pined for her for years, doubting the decisions that led to her demise. Demons can't fall in love the same way humans do. We don't do the unselfish thing." Whatever had been in his expression disappeared as if it had never been there in the first place, and he raised his gaze to hers again. "But we're great in bed."

"Do you still pine for her?" Eden asked.

His expression shuttered to one that was completely blank. Darrak wasn't the only one who could wear masks.

"I told you I didn't. The affair was so short it made no difference in my existence other than teaching me a valuable lesson."

"Which was?"

"Humans are forgettable. Now, why don't we get this show on the road so Darrak can be on his way to forgetting you as well?"

She glared at him. No romantic tale of lost love—whether or not he'd admit it was true—would ever help her get past the disdain she had for the demon.

Weird, though. She'd felt just a bit of pity for him. He was fooling himself if he thought that lost love *hadn't* gotten to him.

But it didn't matter anymore.

"This is so great," Darrak said dryly. "I thought you two would get along famously with each other. Glad to see I was completely and utterly wrong about that."

"Your girlfriend asks too many questions," Theo growled.

"She's naturally curious. It's one of her many charms."

"Follow me." He turned and walked away from them. Eden had to hurry to keep up.

They entered the main club, with the bar along one side and the dance floor in the middle. Without the flickering lights or the loud music it seemed a bit tired and drab.

They weren't alone.

"Who are they?" Eden asked. A dozen men and women were seated in the lounge area with their backs to them. All stared forward at the wall and didn't move.

"Human sacrifices," Theo said conversationally. "Asmo has a great deal of power at the moment, but he might need to recharge. Plus, he'll be very hungry when he takes form. But don't get upset. They're practically drained to start with. They'll just disappear. No mess to worry about."

Eden's eyes widened. Human sacrifices?

"The women who disappeared. It *was* Asmodeus who did it, wasn't it?" She looked at Darrak. "You lied to me."

"Ooh, point for Darrak." Theo grinned. "Maybe you're not as whipped as I thought. If he didn't tell you that, I guess he didn't tell you about the dude I strangled out back, either."

Eden felt like the wind had been knocked out of her. Theo killed Graham. She *knew* it.

She looked at Darrak. Why didn't he tell her? Why would he keep this from her?

"Don't make a big deal about this," Darrak told her. "Not now. Please."

Don't make a big deal about murder? About a demon who sucked the life energy out of anyone he wanted and who was about to do the same to a dozen more? About Theo snuffing out Graham's life like he meant nothing?

If she made a big deal, if she freaked out right now and ruined this, they wouldn't get the chance to break Darrak's curse. It pained her to bite her tongue, to restrain her power, even though she was shaking inside with anger and disgust, but that's exactly what she did.

For now.

"Later, then," she said quietly, her throat tight with trying to keep herself under control. "But these people have to leave here so they can have a chance to recover."

Darrak glanced at the backs of the zombies' heads. "Is there another way for Asmo to feed today, Theo?"

"Sure." Theo sat down on a leather armchair near the dance floor and put his feet up on a glass table. "One fully energized human—or *almost* human—will be better than twelve nearly drained ones any day."

Darrak's eyes narrowed. "Eden is not on the menu."

Theo sighed wearily. "Well, I guess that will be up to him, won't it?" He looked up at the ceiling. "Asmodeus? We're ready. Let's do this."

If Theo thought he could serve her up on a platter, then he had another think coming to him. Theo knew she was a black witch. She'd sworn not to use her power again—and she really didn't want to if she could help it. But she would if she had no other choice.

The air began to crackle with more electricity—but it wasn't because of her. It raised the fine hair on Eden's arms.

"It's over," she said. "I'm leaving. And I'm taking those people with me. This needs to stop right now."

Theo looked at her. "Oh, Red, it's way too late for that."

The lights in the club flickered. The ground trembled. The buzz that had been low frequency before grew louder and louder.

Darrak and Eden exchanged a glance before she forced herself to look away.

He'd lied to her again. He'd brought her here where a demon lay in wait ready to drain anyone who came into his path.

"I don't care what you say," she snapped. "I'll stop this. I'll—"

She suddenly realized she couldn't speak or move. She was frozen in place.

And a demon lord with a big appetite was about to arrive.

"This is perfect," Theo said. "I was concerned about Lucifer figuring things out, but it doesn't really matter. Asmo will protect us until we can figure out a new plan."

Darrak couldn't stop looking at Eden. It was Asmo who had frozen her in place. A glance at the other humans showed that they were unmoving as well. The best way to deal with potential prey was to paralyze them and ensure they couldn't fight back.

"He's coming," Theo said.

He was right. Darrak could feel it. The building felt alive, throbbing with energy, and . . . kind of lusty, too.

Suddenly, the club grew darker, the walls literally turning black. But it wasn't really the walls—it was smoke.

Black smoke coated every inch of the club and bled down to the floor. It looked like ankle deep, thick black mist that rippled and undulated.

Eden's gaze widened nearly imperceptibly, and Darrak could tell she was afraid.

It bothered him.

But he couldn't go to her. Not now. There was no time.

Asmodeus was about to have his awakening. Now Darrak wished he'd brought some of that fiesta dip. It seemed like an event worth celebrating. The beginning of the rest of Darrak's existence would begin after this short break.

Please stand by.

"Welcome, my lord," Theo said with reverence. He stood up from his seat.

"GREETINGS, ALL," a deep and booming voice sounded. It echoed through the club. "I'M GLAD YOU COULD JOIN ME TODAY. THIS IS GOING TO BE SO AWESOME!"

Asmo had always been one of the more enthusiastic demon lords.

"Welcome, Asmodeus," Darrak said as well.

"DARRAK! IT'S BEEN A LONG TIME. HOW'VE YOU BEEN, PAL?"

His eyes flicked toward Eden, standing so still and silent. "I've been better, actually."

"RIGHT? TRUST ME, I KNOW. I FEEL YOUR PAIN, MAN. I MEAN, LOOK AT ME RIGHT NOW. IT SUCKS TO BE BODILESS."

"Not for long," Theo said. "It's your time, what we've been building to. Take form now, Asmodeus, and show us your magnificence once again."

Theo had always been a bit of a brownnoser.

"YEAH, ABOUT THAT. THERE'S A TEENY BIT OF A PROBLEM."

"What?"

"I CAN'T TAKE FORM. JUST TRIED. NO LUCK."

Theo frowned. "Then what should we do now?"

"PLAN B. I'LL TAKE A PERMANENT BODY. NOW THAT I SEE I HAVE NO OTHER CHOICE, I'M COOL WITH IT."

"Oh . . . uh." Theo wrung his hands. "Great. Well, whatever works, right? As you can see I've assembled a nice assortment of humans here for you. Please, feel free to take your pick."

Darrak had moved to stand between Theo and Eden so he had a better view of the lounging zombielike humans. He realized for the first time that one of them was Nancy.

Why was she still here? Wasn't she with Stanley last night?

But Stanley worked for Theo. It all came back to Theo, didn't it?

Darrak pushed away the sinking feeling he felt at seeing the familiar face.

"I'VE TASTED ALL OF THESE ONES BEFORE." The smoke gathered and moved toward the group like an anchored storm cloud. "AH, THIS ONE I'VE ONLY NIBBLED ON."

Darkness covered the body of the man sitting next to Nancy like a shroud. There was a slight, strangled cry, and then the darkness moved away. Nothing of the man remained.

"OOPSIE. GOT A LITTLE CARRIED AWAY. I'M SO HUNGRY!"

"It's not a problem," Theo said tensely. "There are plenty more where he came from."

The same thing would have happened to the women who disappeared. It bothered Darrak more than he'd like to admit. Asmo took the lives of humans as if he was Forrest Gump sampling from a box of chocolates.

"HMM . . . WHAT ABOUT THIS ONE? SHE'S NEW, ISN'T SHE?"

Darrak thought he was referring to Nancy, but the smoke had shifted direction. It approached Eden instead.

"No," Darrak said, but it was too quiet, so he said it again, louder. "No. Theo, I told you. He doesn't get to touch Eden."

Theo shrugged. "What Asmo wants, Asmo gets. Just accept it, Darrak."

"Stop him."

"You think I have that kind of control?"

"If he harms Eden, there's going to be a problem."

Theo smiled and placed a hand on Darrak's shoulder. "Come on, just chill."

Darrak pushed his friend back from him. Hard. Theo staggered back, surprised, but then fire appeared in his narrowing gaze.

"Don't do that," he warned.

"Stop Asmodeus now."

"No." Theo shoved Darrak.

Darrak held his hand out to his side and summoned his fire. He turned to the smoke gathering at Eden's feet. Her expression hadn't changed. She looked almost serene, but there was a slight tension to her forehead and her eyes moved back and forth.

So not as serene as she looked at first glance. Terrified. And Darrak would be willing to bet that she had no access to her black magic at the moment, if she was tempted to use it. And he wouldn't blame her at all this time if she did.

Well, maybe a little.

"Asmodeus," Darrak snapped. "She's not for you."

"OH, YEAH? WHY THE HECK NOT?"

"Because she's *mine*."

"SHE'S FILLED WITH MAGIC LIKE AN OVER-FLOWING TEAKETTLE. I LIKE HER."

Theo grabbed Darrak's arm and held him in place. "Let her go. You'll forget her. Just like I forgot Kristina."

Darrak glared at him. "You never forgot Kristina."

He waited for the other demon's response. What he hadn't expected was feeling a blast of energy come off his friend, launching him across the nightclub like a bomb had gone off. Darrak got back to his feet in a flash.

Archdemon power. He missed having that much of it.

But he still had some.

He allowed fire to course down into both of his hands this time and moved toward Theo.

"What are you going to do?" Theo asked. "Fight me?"

"Looks like."

"Just like that. After everything I've done for you? Would you really want to mess this up? This is your answer. Asmo's going to take her. She won't be your ball and chain anymore. You'd throw that chance away? Are you that much of an idiot?"

There really was no way to answer that question. "Yes, I'm that much of an idiot," didn't really sound too good.

Maybe Theo was right.

Free from Eden. Free from the necessity of possessing her body at night. Free from his ties to her during the day. He could be restored to his former self, a demon who didn't care about anyone or anything and only cared about achieving more power and more pleasure.

It was for the best. When the curse was removed and Eden was gone, this would all be a distant memory.

"What will happen to her?" he asked quietly.

"I WILL POSSESS HER, USE HER SHELL, AND THROW AWAY THE YOLK. I WILL BURN AWAY ALL THAT REMAINS OF HER SO THERE'S PLENTY OF ROOM FOR ME TO PARTY. SHOULDN'T TAKE MORE THAN A FEW SECONDS."

"But . . . but she's a *woman*," Darrak said, trying to remain calm. It might be a little late for that.

"I'M VERY OPEN-MINDED. WHAT IS SHE, A SIZE

SIX? ARE THOSE BREASTS NATURAL OR SILICONE? FORGET IT, I DON'T REALLY MIND EITHER WAY."

The thick smoke began to crawl up Eden's body like a black boa constrictor. Her eyes closed.

Darrak surged forward, mindless to anything but saving Eden from this fate. Theo's hand clamped down on his shoulder again.

"Don't do this," Theo growled.

Darrak spun around and hit Theo hard, knocking him right to the other side of the club thirty feet away. Before the demon hit the ground he disappeared in a haze of fire and reappeared right in front of Darrak's face.

Phasing. He still missed that ability more than he could say.

Darrak grabbed hold of his friend and shifted to his demon form. Theo did the same. It was funny how similar they looked this way, then again, they'd been made at the same time. That made them almost like twins—the same.

But they weren't the same. Not anymore.

"I said I'd destroy you if you got in my way." Theo clenched his razor-sharp teeth.

"Right back at you."

"Over a woman?" Theo shook his head. The flames that coated his body were blue while Darrak's were amber. "How sad."

"*You're* sad."

"Not your wittiest comeback, I'm afraid. Besides, it's too late. No matter what you do, you can't stop this."

Darrak craned his neck to see that Eden was completely surrounded by the smoke now. It covered her like the man Asmo had already devoured.

He was too late.

"OH, SHIT."

Theo pushed Darrak away from him. "What's wrong, my lord?"

"PARDON THE SAYING, BUT THERE'S NO ROOM AT THE INN. SHE'S ALREADY DARRAK'S HOST SO SHE'S BLOCKED TO ANYONE ELSE. IF I HAD FORM, I WOULD BE SOBBING RIGHT NOW WITH DISAPPOINTMENT."

Theo shifted back to human form.

"You can still have her," Theo said. "But you have to break Darrak's curse first so he stops acting like a smitten schoolboy. Stanley!" He raised his voice so it reverberated through the entire club. "Could you come in here right now?"

Theo still believed Darrak was dealing with a temporary curse-driven shift in personality. Which was the truth, of course.

Eden was still in one piece. Still frozen, though, with her eyes closed. He hoped she was unconscious and not experiencing any of this firsthand.

He changed back to human form and looked at Theo warily.

"Somebody need a hug?" Theo asked, with a big shit-eating grin on his face.

Darrak forced a smile. "You are such an asshole, you know that?"

"I aim to please."

So all was forgiven? The shoving match? The threats of destruction?

Sure. Two could play at that game.

"Seriously"—Darrak slapped him on the back, as close to a real hug as he was comfortable with, and tried to laugh—"I'm going to kick your ass."

Theo shook his head. "You're just lucky I like you. Not too many others would have put up with all of your bullshit."

He was right. Why had Theo put up with him? Was he really and truly Darrak's friend? Selflessly and at the threat of his own existence? Well, that would go against demon nature, wouldn't it?

But so did falling in love. Theo hadn't been cursed when

he fell for Kristina. And he had been a mess after she'd died—at least until he'd pulled himself together and put on his public face. It had been a long time ago, but Darrak remembered it clearly.

"It'll be okay," Theo assured him.

"Fingers crossed." Darrak turned away so he could slide the black diamond he'd just stolen from Theo into his own pocket.

Theo was a true friend, despite many problems Darrak had with him.

But having a backup plan was always a good thing.

Stanley entered the club and looked at them warily. "So, I'm here. How goes it?"

"OH, GOODY. HE'LL DO FOR NOW."

The black smoke shot toward Stanley, surrounding him in an instant. Stanley shrieked, flailed his arms as if fighting off a swarm of bees, before the smoke disappeared and he stilled.

Then he inhaled a great gulp of air and opened his eyes, looking down at his hands and smiling.

"Not bad," he said.

"Asmodeus?" Theo asked tentatively.

Asmo, currently in the form of Stanley, approached them. "That's my name, don't wear it out."

"Uh, how do you feel?"

"Fabulous! And look at me." He pointed at his head. "I'm balding!"

"Congrats."

"Although," Asmo moved toward Eden again, "this one is more esthetically pleasing to me."

He slid a hand down to her butt and squeezed.

Without even thinking about it, Darrak found he was beside the demon lord and prying his hand away from Eden's body.

"Don't touch her, please," he said firmly.

"I can touch whatever I want."

Darrak squeezed Asmo's wrist tighter. "No. You can't."

Asmo smiled. "You've always been a funny one, haven't you?"

"I do enjoy making others laugh. Or scream in pain. Either or."

Asmo looked down at Darrak's grip. "Go ahead. Break the wrist if it makes you feel better. It won't be mine for much longer."

Darrak released him before he did any irreparable damage to Stanley. It had been very close.

Asmo cocked his head to the side, studying Darrak. "There's something strange about you. I didn't really notice it before, but now . . ." He leaned toward Darrak and sniffed, before a look of displeasure spread across his borrowed face.

"Do I smell bad?" Darrak asked. Not to be vain, but he did find that hard to believe.

"No. You smell kind of . . . uh . . ." Asmo's lips turned downward for the first time. "Good?"

"Thank you."

He scrunched his nose. "I mean *good* in the worst way possible. What have you been eating?"

Darrak glanced over at Theo, who watched their conversation carefully. "Donuts mostly. Chocolate ones."

"Not food. I mean from your power source." He sniffed Eden then. Darrak knew for a fact she smelled like lavender. It was from her body wash. She only wore perfume on special occasions. "I sense black witch, but there's something else there, too. Can't quite put my finger on it."

"Uh . . . she's actually a nephilim," Theo offered. "Didn't I mention that before? I could have sworn I did."

Asmo's eyebrows went up, and he took a big step back from her frozen form. "Ewww. Really? A nephilim? And she's your host? Darrak, how do you stand it?"

Did this mean he'd leave Eden alone now? "I manage."

Asmo literally gagged. It took him a few seconds to pull

himself together. "Oh, gross." He shuddered. "That's what I sensed in you. Celestial energy."

"In me?" He pointed to his chest.

"Uh, *yeah*."

Theo drew closer. "What does that mean?"

"What it means is the deal's off. All of it." Asmo held his arms as if he was hugging himself. "Yuck. Celestial energy. I've never been this close to it before."

"But, Asmo—" Darrak began.

"No. It's over, you disgusting hybrid. I've never seen such a thing before in my entire existence. It sickens me."

It took a lot to sicken the Lord of Lust. Darrak would have been honored if he thought it was a compliment. But, it wasn't.

"What do you mean by *hybrid*?" he asked.

"You've changed," Asmo said.

Darrak shook his head. "As soon as my curse is removed, I'll go back to the way I was before. Sure, it hasn't all gone smoothly, but there's no reason for me to believe otherwise. Theo convinced me that I'm the same underneath. Hell is my only home. It's where someone like me belongs. It's the only place I belong."

Asmo's lips curled with disgust. "Nope. No longer. You're not welcome there. Not like this. You'll contaminate the atmosphere."

What in the hell was he talking about?

Theo looked as confused as Darrak did.

But then realization came into both of their gazes at the exact same time.

Celestial energy. He'd been absorbing it from Eden. That's what had been powerful enough to give him form after all these years when no other human had been able to do that for him. Why her soul had been the brightest and shiniest thing he'd ever seen and he'd gone to it like a moth to a flame.

He'd taken it into himself. It had helped heal and help him.

It had become a part of him.

Removing the curse wouldn't change him, wouldn't take away this humanity and emotion he felt.

It was just the way he was now.

"Oh, shit." Darrak felt like he'd just been punched in the gut by the hand of God. Clarity was a bitch sometimes. When he composed himself enough, he looked at Theo. "Release Eden. I know you can do it."

Theo looked at him with shock. "Uh . . . I don't know if that's such a good idea."

"Just do it," he growled.

"Fine." Theo flicked a wrist at Eden and she stumbled forward. Darrak caught her.

She gasped for breath and then threw her arms around him tightly. "I heard everything."

He leaned back and looked down at her face. He wanted to hate her for doing this to him, for infecting him with this celestial energy. He'd known she was powerful, but she'd managed to destroy him without lifting a finger.

But Darrak couldn't hate her. All he could do is feel relief that she was still all right.

It was all kinds of annoying.

Darrak looked at Asmo. "Will you break my curse?"

Asmo made a face. "Why would I ever want to do that, you weirdo?"

"To help us out."

Asmo laughed so loud some would consider it a cackle. "Help you? Wow. That sounds like angel talk, loser. My advice to you, Darrak, is to kill this nephilim and find a new host. She's going to drag you down. And I don't mean to Hell." He shuddered again. "I'm just really grossed out right now. I touched her ass and everything."

"I'm sorry," Theo said. "If I thought it would make a difference . . . uh . . ."

"Shut it." Asmo paced back and forth, looking at each of them in turn. "I don't want this body. I refuse to be in this one, and it's not just because of the baldness, although, I must admit, that is a contributing factor to my decision. I need a perfect specimen and obviously that's not going to be a human. I'm going to have to go demon for this. It'll take a little more energy to burn out his insides, but I'm willing to make the effort." He sighed. "I mean, I'm the Lord of Lust. How can anyone worship me if I don't look the part?"

Darrak drew Eden closer to his side. He had a really bad feeling about this.

"We'll find the perfect demon for you," Theo said. "I promise."

Asmo cocked his head, looking at Theo as if for the first time. "You know, you're very pretty."

"Pretty?" Theo's expression soured. "I'm usually called 'handsome' or 'extremely hot.' But, okay. Thanks."

"Pretty demon." Asmo patted his face. "I want you."

"I've, uh . . . always preferred women, but . . . I suppose I might be open to—" Theo gasped as a stream of black smoke exited Stanley's mouth and entered his.

⇒ TWENTY-SIX ⇐

Stanley collapsed to the floor, unconscious.

The demon wheezed and braced himself on his thighs for a moment before straightening up. Then he slid his hands over his now-muscular chest and firm stomach. He reached behind his head and pulled the piece of leather out of his hair and shook it out.

"Way better!" Asmo said. "How absolutely yummy am I now?"

Darrak had a hard time talking at the moment. He kept his arm around Eden. Her fingernails dug into his arm to indicate her current level of stress.

"How can you possess another demon?" he managed. "I never knew that was even possible."

"He's on my staff. I might not have created him, but I can control him. Therefore his form is mine to do with as I please. Fun, right?"

"You need to let him go." Darrak had his problems with Theo, but he couldn't just turn his back on him now. Theo had tried to help break his curse. He'd stood by Darrak even when confused and dismayed by his behavior lately. As demons went, he was a true friend.

But Asmo didn't let him go. Instead, he squeezed his eyes shut and held his hands out to his sides. There suddenly was a sound similar to a furnace—a roaring blaze which finished after ten seconds with a sizzling sound.

Asmo opened up his eyes, which were filled with flames for a moment before they darkened to normal. Smoke wafted off his skin in wispy tendrils.

He grinned. "Too late. He's gone."

Darrak gaped at him. "What?"

"Remember what I said before about the shell and the yolk? It didn't take as much energy as I thought it would to fry him up over easy and send him on his way."

Theo was gone? Just like that?

That was impossible. He couldn't be gone.

What was this emotion Darrak felt? It didn't seem all that familiar to him.

It must have been . . . grief.

"Darrak . . ." Eden said quietly. "We need to get out of here. And we need to get all these people out of here, too."

Asmo had decimated Theo like he was nothing but a body with no past and no future. A nobody to be discarded to make way for someone more important.

But Darrak still existed. He still had a future. And so did Eden.

Asmo placed a hand over his stomach. "I'm so hungry."

Eden's grip tightened on Darrak. "There's a Greek place next door," she suggested tightly.

"Oh, ha ha. Shut up, nephilim girl." He shook his head. "Hey, you're funny, too, Darrak."

"I try."

"If you weren't tainted with celestial energy, I'd take you back to Hell to entertain me as my jester. I could make you wear funny clothes like an organ grinder's monkey."

Darrak summoned up enough strength to push his grief away and deal with the problem at hand. Theo might be gone, but he and Eden weren't clear of this mess yet. "I don't come cheap. And I don't wear little hats."

Asmo studied him for a long moment. "While I'm in this body, I feel a strange bond toward you. Like we're bosom buddies."

"Super," Darrak said dryly.

"I have an idea and I think it's a good one. After I finish my meal"—Asmo nodded toward the lounge area filled with waiting human snacks—"I'll kill your witch. You can possess this bald guy here," he nudged the unconscious Stanley with his foot. "Then I'll see if I can burn that celestial energy right out of you."

"Darrak . . ." Eden whispered. "I'm open to suggestions on how you propose to get us out of here. My magic is strong, but—"

"You're not using your magic," he said. "There's no guarantee you could defeat Asmo with it, anyhow."

"But—"

Darrak shrugged away from her. "You'd do that for me, Asmo? You think it's the only way I can be restored to my former self?"

Asmo shrugged his broad shoulders. "Dunno. Worth a try though, don't you think?"

"Don't listen to him," Eden said sharply.

Darrak glared at her over his shoulder. "Would you stop nagging me for one minute? It's really getting old."

She gasped and her eyes widened with confusion.

"Uh-oh." Asmo chuckled. "Looks like the angelic honeymoon is over. Always the way with relationships based entirely on lust. They start off with a bang and end with a whimper."

"We definitely started off with a bang," Darrak said.

Asmo smiled approvingly. "Now shall we make her whimper?"

Darrak looked at Eden, who gaped at him. He shook his head. "You had to have seen this coming, didn't you? How can I possibly exist with celestial energy inside of me like this, changing me into this disgusting guilt-feeling, emotional drip?"

"You can't, that's how," Asmo agreed.

"No, I can't. I want to be who I was. I want to be a demon, fully and completely. And I want to rid myself of everything human that has weighed me down for all of this time." Darrak's eyes narrowed on Eden. "And that, I'm afraid, includes you."

Eden shook her head, but it was barely noticeable. "Don't do this. You're better than this."

"But that's the problem," Darrak said. "I don't want to be better."

There were tears in her eyes now, and she looked away.

"Going to use your black magic on me now?" he asked. "Maybe my true name so you can boss me around even more than normal?"

"Do you want me to?"

"You know what I want."

Darrak noticed her hands were clenched into fists at her sides, but he didn't feel any of her magic in the air yet. She was holding back.

She nodded. "You're right. I know what you want. After all, you've drummed it into my head enough lately, haven't you? You don't want to feel this way; you hate it. You want to be a demon, evil to the core and able to go skinny dipping in the lake of fire every morning."

He almost laughed. "Sounds like fun, doesn't it?"

"I know you hate it here. You try to pretend that you don't, but it's obvious to me." She rubbed a hand under her nose. "Fine. Then do it. Agree with Asmo. Let him kill me and go off and be a demon if that's what you want so damned much."

Was she testing him? Pushing him to see if he'd break now that he'd come so far?

She would be sorely disappointed, if that was the case.

"Okay, then. I agree," he said firmly. Eden visibly paled as he said it.

"Hooray!" Asmo exclaimed. "So happy to hear it!"

Darrak realized the demon lord had dragged Nancy up off the lounge by her hair. She'd been released from whatever spell held her in place so she fought against him now.

"Oh, my God," Nancy gasped. "What's going on?"

"Yum." Asmo sniffed up her neck. "No angel here, that's for sure. I smell cinnamon and powdered sugar. This won't take long, Darrak. I just need to reenergize a little bit first."

He opened his mouth and began to inhale deeper. Nancy let out a frightened scream.

Darrak felt the air begin to energize. This time it was from Eden's magic, not from Asmo's. His gaze shot to her.

"We had a deal," he said. "We shook on it and everything, remember?"

"I guess you're not the only one who's a liar in this relationship," she snapped. Tears streaked down her cheeks. Looked like he'd managed to hurt his little nephilim-slash-blackwitch's feelings.

"Hold that thought for a sec, will you?" he said, and turned toward the body of his former friend. "Sorry, Asmo, looks like this really can't wait any longer."

Asmo stopped inhaling Nancy's energy for a moment. "What can't wait?"

"This."

Darrak grabbed him by his long black hair and yanked him forcibly away from Nancy. He grasped the angelheart from his pocket and crammed it into the demon lord's mouth, as far to the back of Asmo's throat as he could. Then he held Asmo's mouth shut, using every last ounce of his strength until he heard the demon gulp.

That was the sound he'd been hoping for.

It didn't last long. Asmo broke his hold, and Darrak went flying backward and crashed onto a glass cocktail table, breaking it on impact.

Asmo touched his stomach. "What the heck did you just make me swallow?"

Darrak stayed where he was on the floor for a moment, amongst the shattered glass. "Diamonds are a demon's best friend."

Asmo gasped. "A—a diamond? That's not even funny. What was the point?" After a second, he touched his chest. "Oh . . . okay, wait. That burns a little bit. It almost feels like . . . like . . ."

"Like angel juice, straight up?" Darrak slowly got to his feet. "Yeah, there's a really good reason for that. You'll find that having a body does have its downside. When you're incorporeal, you can't easily be hurt. But in a body—even a demonic one—well, that's a whole other story."

"Angels? I *hate* angels." Asmo looked incredibly confused.

A fine white line appeared on his forehead, slowly snaking its way across his stolen skin. He touched it gingerly. Then another on his cheek and chin. The lines traveled down his throat and down his arms under the black shirt to his hands.

"What is this?" Asmo asked, looking down at himself. "What did you do to me? I thought you agreed to my plan?"

"Yeah, about that," Darrak said. "I guess it's not the first time I lied today. Sorry about that."

"Do you want to be this way? You're tainted. You'll never be able to step foot in Hell again without drawing attention to yourself. You'll be destroyed if you ever try."

Darrak nodded. "One problem at a time."

Everywhere the lines had appeared on Asmo's skin, light began to pour through like cracks on the surface of a volcano. His eyes widened and light poured out from there as well. It didn't take long before his entire body, stolen from Theo, was bathed in bright white light like a star about to go supernova.

"Get down," Darrak yelled at Eden.

She didn't hesitate. She scrambled to get behind the nearest leather armchair.

Darrak shielded his eyes. Even he was bothered by light this bright and pure.

There was a loud crackling sound, like a thunderbolt, and the next moment the light extinguished completely.

Something solid and heavy hit the floor with a thump. It was the black diamond. It lay exactly where Asmo had stood a moment before.

The demon lord had left the building. And the universe as well.

Stanley blinked, stretched, and pushed himself up off the floor. He peered around cautiously. "Did something major just go down here?"

"You could say that," Darrak said. "Do me a favor and help get these people out of here, okay?"

The zombies were no longer zombielike. They shifted and stretched as if they were coming out of a deep sleep. Otherwise, they all looked healthy enough, if a bit confused.

"Where's Theo?" Stanley asked, turning around in a circle to check the rest of the club.

"Gone," Darrak said simply.

"Oh." Stanley nodded, as if he understood that *gone* truly meant gone for good. Then he ran over to Nancy and helped her up to her feet. They embraced.

Together they helped usher the trance-free regulars from Luxuria out of the club.

Darrak finally looked at Eden. She was staring at him with shock.

"What?" He shrugged. "You honestly thought I was going to let him kill you?"

"I didn't think so." She pushed her long hair back from her face and tucked it behind her ears. "But I . . . I didn't know for sure."

He nodded. He wasn't surprised by that. What did he expect? That she'd give him the benefit of the doubt after how he'd been acting lately? All "when the curse is broken I'll be evil again! Yippy!"?

Trust had to be earned. And he sure as hell hadn't earned any from her.

Eden stared at him for a moment longer, then walked toward him. He wasn't sure if he should expect a kiss or a slap. He got neither.

She leaned over and picked up the diamond and then turned to her left.

"You," she said. She didn't sound surprised.

Someone else was there. Darrak hadn't even noticed him enter the club.

Lucas stood at the far end of the bar. "Hope you don't mind that I followed you here. Missed most of the drama, but then again, the day is still young."

His gaze moved to Darrak, and he saw it clearly in the Prince of Hell's very human eyes.

He was going to be destroyed.

And there was nothing he could do to stop it.

Eden hadn't even gotten a chance to catch her breath and process everything that had happened. She'd been on the verge of using her magic to try to stop Asmodeus. She would have tried to stop Darrak as well, feeling he was lost to her.

But he'd been playing a game.

Eden did wish she hadn't doubted him, but she had. And that was just the way it was.

It hadn't been a fabulous week, to say the least.

"Is that it?" Lucas asked, nodding at the diamond.

She held it out to him. "Here you go, one black diamond delivered as per our agreement."

He took it from her and held it in his palm as if weighing it.

"There's a problem," he said.

Yeah, she already knew that.

"Oh?" She feigned surprise anyhow.

"It's already been used to destroy Asmodeus. I did manage to catch the last-minute fireworks to prove that the angelheart does indeed work as advertised. Certainly not a huge loss to the Netherworld. Never liked the guy. However, now it won't work again. The power is gone. It's only a pretty paperweight now, isn't it?"

Eden glanced at Darrak. He stood watching their discussion, and he didn't look as panicked as she felt, or fearful, or anything. No, he looked oddly calm.

Thanks for the support, she thought, wracking her mind to figure out what to do or say next.

Something Lucifer said came back to her then.

"You're very lucky that I always hold true to the exact wording of my bargains."

"Our deal was for the black diamond," Eden said then, firmly. "You didn't say the angelheart specifically. I've delivered the black diamond."

Lucas looked at her without speaking for a while. It was uncomfortable. Eden willed herself to remain calm.

"Did I say the black diamond, not the angelheart?" he asked.

"I have a feeling you remember exactly what you said."

"You're right. I do."

"And you said you always stick to the exact wording of your bargains."

"I said that, too, didn't I?"

"You did."

Lucas's lips curved. "Tricky, aren't you?"

Eden didn't feel very tricky. She was just doing what had to be done. "You will release my mother's soul, right?"

He curled his fingers around the diamond and slipped it into the inner chest pocket of his jacket. "A deal's a deal."

"Thank you." Eden finally allowed herself a measure of relief and braved another look at Darrak, before returning her attention to Lucas.

Lucas touched under her chin and brought her gaze up to meet his own. "I haven't forgotten about the second part of our deal, either."

"There's a second part?" Darrak asked warily.

Lucas smiled. "Why, yes, there is."

Hope sparked inside her chest. "That's right. You're going to help me and Darrak."

"Well, I believe the exact words were that I would fix things and make it so Darrak no longer has to possess you. That is what you agreed to, remember?"

"Of course. But, I . . ." Eden felt a strange sinking sensation. "But, of course I meant that I wanted his curse to be broken so he could have his body back all the time and everyone would live happily ever after."

"Right. Well, you should have been a bit more specific, then. But it's your lucky day, Eden. I *can* make it so he no longer possesses you. I'd be happy to destroy him for you."

Destroy him?

Lucas had called her tricky. She thought she'd gotten away with something—only giving him the black diamond, but making him stick to his deal to release her mother's soul, but . . .

He was tricky, too. Although, that really shouldn't have come as a surprise to her.

"It's okay, Eden," Darrak said quietly. "This couldn't have ended any other way."

She could barely breathe. She moved as if in slow motion toward the spot where Darrak stood, but it was too late.

The next moment, Darrak convulsed and dropped to his knees. His face was strained, and when he looked up at her, his eyes were filled with agony before flames filled them. He was burning from the inside out.

"Don't . . . come . . . near me," he bit out. His entire body shuddered.

"You're hurting him!" Eden yelled.

"That's sort of the point," Lucas said. He hadn't even broken a sweat yet. "I'm returning him to his base parts. A bit of hellfire and some magic. Shouldn't take too long."

"You have to stop!"

"But this is what you wanted."

"No, it's not!"

"Then you really should have been more specific."

Eden collapsed next to Darrak as he suffered this torture in near silence. She reached to touch his face but pulled her hand back the moment she made contact. His skin burned like fire.

"I'm sorry," Darrak managed, before a tremor went through him. "I should have told you that Asmo killed the women. I should have told you about Graham. But I didn't want you to try to get revenge. It was too dangerous."

"Darrak—"

"Just don't hate me."

"Hate you? But, Darrak—"

The next moment he fell to his side. He wasn't moving anymore. Amber flames burst through his skin to coat his entire body, and she scrambled back so she wouldn't get burned.

"Almost done," Lucas said. He sounded remarkably blasé about it.

She'd asked for this. She'd even made a deal with the devil to make this possible. In moments Darrak would be gone, and she wouldn't have to put up with his lies and deceit and body stealing and energy draining. It would be over. Forever.

Be careful what you wish for.

"No," she said softly.

"Pardon me?" Lucas asked.

"Stop this."

"But you asked for it. I'm only doing what you wanted me to."

She raised her gaze from Darrak's body to Lucas's deceptively warm brown eyes. "Don't be a sore loser."

He raised his eyebrows. "Excuse me?"

"Sorry you can't use the angelheart to destroy your inner demon today. But hell if I'm going to let you destroy mine."

Eden clenched her fists and felt black magic roll down her arms and into her hands. It was an ocean of power deep enough to drown someone in.

Lucas observed her carefully. "And what do you think you're doing?"

"I'm going to destroy you," she said matter-of-factly. "I might not have been able to destroy Asmodeus, but I have a feeling your current form is a little more breakable than his was. You didn't create me like you did Darrak. You have no power over me."

His lips thinned. "Killing a defenseless mortal with black magic will turn your soul jet-black," he warned. "Even if that mortal happens to be me. Besides, it won't even matter. I'll just return to Hell."

"Then I'll follow you there and kill you again. Stop what you're doing to Darrak right now or I swear I will. I don't care what I have to do, I will hunt you down and send you to the Void once and for all. I have a feeling that would make everyone very happy."

She meant every single word like she'd never meant anything before.

Lucas shook his head. "You'd do that? For him?" He nodded at the Darrak-shaped inferno ten feet away. "He's a lesser demon. A nobody. And you'd give your soul to save something like that?"

Did Lucas really, truly feel that way about one of his creations? Was that all Darrak was? Sentient, soulless hell-fire. A formerly evil monster now infected with a little bit of heaven. A demon who had no home or anyone who cared if he was destroyed forever.

"Yes," she said. "I would. Now release him or I'll prove it."

She allowed the black magic to fill the rest of her body. It felt cool and brought with it the focus she needed. Still, a tear coursed down her right cheek. She didn't bother to push it away.

With a thought, she made the long bar top next to her splinter down the middle, stopping right before the spot where Lucas stood. It didn't go unnoticed.

He smiled, but it was tight. "That's so adorable. I had no idea you cared so deeply for him. Sad, but adorable."

Eden moved toward him. Her hands were glowing—sparks of energy circled them waiting to be unleashed. Waiting to destroy.

The unfortunate thing was, none of this made Lucas flinch in the slightest. In fact, he looked vaguely bored with her display.

He sighed. "Fine, if he manages to survive this, you're welcome to him. What's left of him, anyhow. But don't ever say I tried to go back on our deal, because I didn't."

Eden looked to see the flames surrounding Darrak extinguish as if a switch had been flicked. He didn't move.

"Thank you," she said.

"Don't thank me. Not after what I'm about to tell you." Lucas drew closer to her, unconcerned with the danger that might pose to his mortal body. "What I did? Or what I *nearly* did? That is the only way this will end for you."

Her throat felt tight. "What do you mean?"

"The only way for this unfortunate situation to end is for you to die or Darrak to be exorcised. And anyone who tells you differently is lying."

She shook her head. "There has to be another way."

"There isn't. However, I do have good news."

She looked up at him, ready to grasp onto any possible flicker of hope. "What?"

"As a nephilim, you have endless celestial energy for him to draw on. It's what sets you apart from his previous hosts. Darrak won't kill you by possessing you. Only . . . I do wonder . . ."

Eden reeled from this piece of info. They'd been certain Darrak would drain her completely in no more than a year. "You wonder what?"

"How much of that heavenly drink he can lap up before my lesser demon turns into something else . . . something a bit more angelic." Lucas laughed at Eden's shock. "He'll never be welcome home then."

"He has a home," Eden said firmly. "With me."

He grasped her chin between his fingers. "I could have finished him, but I didn't. This means you owe me one. You work for me now."

"Great. Another shitty job with lousy pay. Just what I need."

Lucas stroked his hand down the side of her face and something slid behind his gaze—a strange longing. "I haven't touched an angel for a very long time."

She pushed his hand away. "I'm not an angel."

"Close enough."

She didn't wait a moment longer. She went to Darrak's side. He was unconscious, but whole. The flames had all disappeared without leaving any marks. This time when she touched him, his skin was still hot—too hot—but it didn't burn her.

"Darrak." Eden smoothed the hair off his forehead. "Wake up. Please."

"If he manages to survive this, you're welcome to him."

He might not survive. She might have been too slow to get Lucas to stop.

If what Lucas told her was true, their curse couldn't be broken. Darrak would have to keep possessing Eden just as it had been between them up until now, but with no end in sight.

At one time, she would have resisted that idea. She liked to be alone. She didn't want anyone to butt into her private business or her personal time. Trusting people was hard for her, it always had been. She didn't ask for this situation with Darrak. It had been a mistake—a textbook example of being at the wrong place at the wrong time.

Being possessed by a demon was the stuff of horror movies.

Yes, it was all of that.

She still didn't want to lose him. She'd only known Darrak a short time, but he'd come to mean everything to her. Absolutely everything.

His body began to shift to black smoke before solidifying again. That wasn't a good sign. It meant that he'd lost so much energy that he was about to lose himself completely. He wouldn't possess her again then; he would go directly to the Void—a place of nothingness. Death for demons.

Darrak took energy from her when he was nearly drained. He didn't like to do it because he'd said her energy tasted too good and he was tempted not to stop. He didn't want to drain her.

But if Lucas was right, he *couldn't* drain her.

More celestial energy coming right up.

She leaned over and kissed him.

Take it, she thought. *Please.*

Prince Charming and Sleeping Beauty came to mind. But only for a moment. After all, this wasn't much of a fairy tale.

It took way too long, but she finally felt it. A slight draining sensation and the press of his lips as he began to kiss her back.

Darrak really needed her energy to survive what Lucas

had done to him. And after using a bit of black magic in her showy display with the bar top, she really needed to kiss a demon.

Finally, his dark lashes flickered, and he slowly opened his eyes and looked up at her leaning over him like Pamela Anderson on *Baywatch*. Relief and happiness flooded her senses.

"Eden . . ." he rasped. "Don't tell me you . . . you used your black magic again."

That was the first thing he had to say to her?

"A little," she admitted. "But not much."

"Bad girl." His Adam's apple shifted as he swallowed. "I feel like a marshmallow that's been roasted over a campfire."

"I'm not surprised."

"Where's Lucifer?" he asked.

She looked over at the bar. Lucas was gone.

"Not here," she said.

"Too bad. Because I am so ready to kick his ass."

She snorted softly. "Yeah, I'm sure."

"Why did you stop him?" He wasn't smiling.

"From destroying you?" Her chest felt tight. "That's a stupid question."

"Still . . . why? I've destroyed your life, lied to you, stolen your body, uh, et cetera, et cetera. Why didn't you take this as the chance to finally get away from me once and for all?"

She stared down at him. "You really are pretty, but all kinds of stupid, aren't you?"

"Eden—"

"Because . . ." She wiped a tear away and then touched his face. "Because . . . I love you, Darrak."

His eyes widened and he struggled to sit up. He failed, but trying did count for something. "You love me?"

"Don't get cocky."

"Me? Well . . . I just—"

Eden bit her bottom lip. "You just need to be quiet and take more of my energy so you can get up off this nightclub floor. There are plenty of things to still deal with in my crazy new supernatural life, and I need your help with most of them. Obviously this is a partnership that I can't just break at the first, or second, sign of trouble."

Darrak looked up at her incredulously. "You love me."

She touched his hotter-than-normal chest. "Yes."

He placed his hand on top of hers. "If I didn't feel like a roasted marshmallow right now, I might be very happy to hear that."

"Oh, yeah?"

"Because you already know how I feel . . ."

She covered his mouth before he said anything else. "Demons aren't supposed to *feel* anything, remember?"

"Oh, right. Forgot about that for a moment. Guess it's the streak of angel juice running through me now. Makes me say crazy things."

Angel juice. She wondered if that celestial energy he'd been absorbing from her really would truly change him like Lucas had predicted. It already had changed him. The humanity he'd gained from his previous human hosts had stuck whether he wanted it or not. There was no going back now.

"Yeah," she agreed. "Pretty crazy. Now shut up and suck out some more of my energy, demon, and then let's get the hell out of here."

Darrak shook his head and grinned at her. "You are such a sweet talker."

She was. She really was.

⇒ TWENTY-SEVEN ⇐

Feeling drained after helping Darrak recover from their standoff with Theo, Asmodeus, and Lucifer, Eden slept through most of the afternoon. Thankfully, it was a dreamless sleep. She'd banked up enough nightmares to last her for many years to come.

She had no official confirmation, but if Lucas held true to their deal, her mother's soul had been released from Hell. It was a great relief.

You're welcome, Mom, she thought. *Now try your best to get into Heaven, okay? You're on your own now.*

Eden had woken at sunset only long enough for Darrak to possess her before she fell asleep again. It was beginning to feel like a natural part of her day—an oddly comfortable habit, despite its horror-movie trappings.

At the moment, she wasn't complaining. She was just relieved that he was still around. More relieved than she ever would have guessed.

Then again, she did tell him she loved him.

She hadn't been lying.

But love or not, having her privacy back one day was a goal she wasn't ready to give up on yet. However, if it came at the risk of Darrak being exorcised and destroyed—

Well, she could probably get used to this living arrangement.

If she *had* to.

Triple-A was closed for business that day as Andy recovered from the werewolf attack. But Friday morning, it was back to business as usual.

Andy smiled brightly as they entered the office. "Good morning, my favorite employees."

Eden eyed him cautiously. "You're looking good, Andy."

"Thank you! I feel good!"

"But we're not your employees, remember?"

He waved a dismissive hand. "Oh, you know what I mean."

"I'm your partner, and Darrak is, uh . . . he's our consultant on all things supernatural."

"Unpaid consultant," Darrak added. "I work for donuts. Preferably untainted ones."

Apart from what had happened with the lust elixir, Darrak had finally shared his theory with her about how the act of possession might trigger Selina's black magic spell, but it wasn't as much of an issue for her as it was for him. Eden felt that she was filled to the brim with black magic already and had a strong feeling that Selina's spell would have no affect on her anymore. The damage was already done.

So did that mean she and Darrak could be together and not worry about the ramifications?

It was a definite possibility.

She glanced at him—this handsome, protective, celestial-energy-infused demon from Hell she'd admitted to being in love with. Not exactly the boy next door, was he?

He watched her curiously.

"What?" he asked.

"Nothing." Eden cleared her throat and decided to focus

on something else. Something a bit safer. "Andy, you seem rather chipper today."

"I am chipper," he confirmed.

"So . . . you're okay with all of this? Everything that happened to you?"

He blinked. "You mean being bitten and mauled by a werewolf, infected with lycanthropy, and at risk of becoming a werewolf, myself?"

"That would pretty much cover it, yes."

Andy pressed his palms against the edge of his desk and stood up from his chair. "I've decided it's not going to happen to me."

Eden frowned. "Not going to happen?"

"That's right. It's all about mind over matter. I don't want to be a werewolf. Therefore, I won't be one. Easy."

Eden and Darrak exchanged a glance.

"Not sure it works that way, Andy," Darrak said. "But if you just—"

Andy held up a hand. "Anyway, like you noticed, I'm feeling terrific today. Better than ever, actually. Nothing like a brush with death to make you really start to appreciate life."

Terrific, Eden thought with a sinking feeling. *He's in complete denial.*

It didn't help that all of his wounds had healed, leaving no scars or marks behind. Denial would be much trickier with stitches, broken bones, and bite marks.

No, Andy had healed up perfectly. In fact, he looked younger than he had before. He could easily pass for forty now, instead of nearly fifty. His blond hair looked healthier. His skin was less lined—even when he smiled the wrinkles that used to fan out around his eyes had lessened significantly. His body looked fit and lean.

"You look good," she admitted.

"I've never felt so good in my life. You know what this means, right?"

"That you've been infected with lycanthropy and you're due to turn into a werewolf in two weeks?" Darrak asked, then glanced at a desk calendar. "Actually, make that twelve days."

Andy's expression tightened. "No. It means that we should go out and celebrate."

"Celebrate?" Eden asked.

"The fact we're all alive and well. The fact we're together. Friends you can trust are few and far between."

Eden glanced at Darrak. He hadn't spoken about Theo, but she knew his friend's death had hit him hard. Theo had killed Graham, so she wasn't sorry he was gone, but she did empathize with Darrak's pain.

"You're right," she said. "Friends are something to celebrate."

"How about breakfast? I'll treat. There's that buffet around the corner I've been meaning to try. I've never been so hungry in my life, and Nancy's coffee and donuts aren't going to cut it this morning. Besides, she called in sick today so the coffee probably won't even be as good as it normally is."

Yeah, Eden thought. *She's recovering from nearly becoming a snack for a demon lord. That's definitely worth using a sick day for.*

"Sounds fantastic," Darrak said. "Buffets are all you can eat?"

"They are."

"Do they have chocolate donuts?"

"They might have some chocolate croissants, which, trust me, are even better." Andy grabbed his coat from the rack and put it on. "Then we can discuss our case load. We've all been slacking this week so things are building up. A couple of fairy clients have been calling nonstop. Fairy folk are very persistent. Anyway, I'll meet you outside."

The bell on the door jingled as he left the office without giving them a chance to say anything in reply.

"Denial," Darrak said.

"Big-time denial."

"Twelve days till the next full moon."

Eden nodded. "I have it circled on my calendar. And until then?"

"He should be okay. But you might want to invest in a leash and muzzle. Possibly some doggy treats."

Eden smiled despite herself. "Great."

As she turned toward the door to follow Andy, Darrak grabbed her wrist.

"Eden . . ." he began.

She looked up at him. "That's my name."

"When the wizard master gets back from his tropical vacation, we'll talk to him. And we could also try summoning another demon to help—"

She shuddered. "No more demons."

"Maybe you're right."

"Lucas said there's no way to break the curse. We're stuck like this."

"He's been known to lie," he said. "Demons tend to do that a lot."

"Oh, I'm well aware of that."

The Malleus couldn't help them, she'd already seen what they considered "help." She hoped she'd never hear from Ben or Oliver or Sandy ever again, but she wasn't holding her breath. She'd continue to be aware of anyone approaching her carrying a syringe full of tranquilizers.

She'd told Darrak what Lucas said about her not having a death sentence from his possession anymore. While he knew what he was drawing on was celestial energy, he was unaware that it was turning him more angelic with every passing day.

He wouldn't like that very much.

All she knew for sure was that they'd keep looking for a way to break Darrak's curse. Even if it took forever. After all, being immortal, she did have time on her side now.

Darrak drew closer to her until she could feel the warmth from his body. He was still extra-hot after his fire-filled brush with destruction yesterday.

He was pretty hot to begin with.

"Okay," he said. "No more demons. Besides, they'd never understand what we have between us."

She raised her eyebrows and looked up at him. "Oh? And what's that?"

Darrak slid his arm around her, his hand coming to rest at the small of her back. His lips twitched into a wry smile. "Something that scares the hell right out of me."

Eden couldn't help but grin back at him—her personal demon, who was now just a little bit angel as well.

"That makes two of us," she said.

Turn the page for a special preview
of the next Living in Eden novel

THAT OLD BLACK MAGIC

Coming soon from Berkley Sensation!

⇉ ONE ⇇

Eden was in big trouble.

From the moment she woke, she'd felt the unrequested tingle of magic moving down her arms and sparking off her fingertips. This was a problem. She didn't allow herself to tap into her powers despite it being a constant itch for her. Magic—at least, *her* magic—came with dire consequences.

A cold trickle of perspiration slid down her spine as she hid her hands behind her back so Darrak wouldn't notice. But it was only a matter of time. The demon was very observant.

"Okay," Darrak said, sitting shirtless at the tiny dinette table in her tiny apartment, the daily newspaper spread out in front of him in a scatter of pages. "Here's your horoscope for today. Ready to hear your ultimate fate?"

Eden cleared her throat. "Uh, sure."

"Pisces. Sexy little fish girl." He grinned at her as he absently raked his messy dark hair back from his forehead.

Nice to see that one of them was in a stellar mood this morning. She grudgingly smiled back at him. "That's me."

"Be prepared for a blast from the past as an old acquaintance wants to reconnect. Do what you can to accommodate them because your destinies are irreversibly intertwined. Also, buy more peanut butter since you're completely out and it's an important nutritional staple in your favorite demon's diet."

She nodded. "Let me take a wild guess here. You added the last part yourself."

"Doesn't make it any less true."

"I'll put it on my grocery list."

"Life is good." He studied her for a moment before his grin began to fade. "What's wrong?"

"Wrong? Nothing's wrong. Nothing at all. Everything's wonderful. Fabulous, in fact."

"Overcompensating in your reply only leads me to believe that something is seriously wrong." He stood up from the table, and the horoscope page fluttered to the carpeted floor. His brows drew together. "What's bothering you?"

She was surprised how quickly he could switch from amusement over some silly human thing like a horoscope or a craving for peanut butter to deep concern for her well-being.

"It's nothing. Really." She forced another smile, and her gaze moved over his bare chest. "You need to get dressed. We have to leave for the office."

Without any movement or visible concentration, black jersey material suddenly flowed over Darrak's skin. Since he'd come into her life a month ago, she'd wanted to take him shopping at the mall, but other than the coat he occasionally wore—short sleeves here in Toronto in chilly November might be a tip-off that he was less than human—he magically conjured his own clothing, which solely consisted of black jeans and black T-shirts.

"I need to brush my teeth and then we can go." She slid

her hands into the pockets of her navy blue pants and turned away from him.

He caught her arm. "It's your magic, isn't it?"

She tensed. "My magic?"

"I can feel it, you know. Right now. It's coming off you in waves."

He was even more observant than she thought. "We need to get going."

She shrugged away from him, then grabbed her purse hanging off the back of one of the dinette chairs so she could fish into it for her new BlackBerry. She didn't want or need the fancy cell phone, but Andy McCoy, her partner at the investigation agency they co-owned, insisted they become more technically savvy now that their case load had increased. Triple-A had been on the brink of bankruptcy a month ago, but now it was busy enough for them to consider hiring extra help.

The sudden surge in business was directly related to Darrak coming into Eden's life. While working as a psychic consultant for the police, she'd been possessed by the cursed demon after being present at the death of his previous host, a serial killer gunned down by a police detective right in front of her. It had been a fifty-fifty chance that he'd choose Eden as his new host.

Thanks to her psychic energy he was able to take solid human form during daylight hours. But when the sun set, he became incorporeal and had to possess her body. It wasn't an ideal situation, to say the least, but Eden had made what peace she could with it. She'd recently had the chance to end his need to possess her, but it would have destroyed him completely. She didn't want to hurt him. Her privacy was a great motivator to find a solution to their problem, but not if it came with such an expensive price tag.

Unfortunately, all roads in their search for mutually beneficial separation had led to dead ends. Some deader than others.

When Darrak first took solid form, he'd created a supernatural hot spot on the location of Triple-A, which meant Others, those who were not human, were drawn there automatically as the go-to agency for paranormal investigation. Although the current cases included standard investigations such as cheating spouses, the clients were very nonstandard werewolves, fairies, and witches—beings who lived side by side with unsuspecting humans.

"What?" Eden said, feeling the burn of Darrak's close scrutiny. She finally tore her gaze away from the small screen of the phone to look at him. Her tight grip on the device increased at seeing the searching look in his ice blue eyes. "Darrak, I said nothing's wrong."

"Your phone is on fire."

She looked down to see that a spark from her magic had ignited her BlackBerry. She shrieked and threw it away from her. It skittered across the breakfast bar and landed with a *thunk* in the kitchen sink. "Damn."

She didn't have a chance to move before Darrak was right in front of her. He pulled out the chain she wore around her neck so her amulet lay flat against her white shirt.

"It's darker than it was yesterday." It sounded like an accusation.

She clamped her hand over the visible state of her soul. It was quite simple, really. The more she used her magic, the more damage it did. A black witch started with a pure white soul, but it grew darker and darker every time she accessed her very accessible black magic. Eden's amulet was currently pale gray, but it had darker veins moving through it, making it look like a piece of marble.

She shook her head. "I haven't done anything."

"Then what are these?" He brushed her hand aside and slid his index finger over the veins.

"A glitch."

"A glitch," he repeated skeptically. "Not sure it works like that."

"Then I don't know what to tell you."

"Eden"—all amusement was gone from his voice—"I'm worried about you."

She might normally laugh, but she didn't. A demon from Hell worried about the state of her immortal soul. It sounded like a joke. But Darrak wasn't any normal demon. And she wasn't any normal black witch.

Once upon a time, Darrak had been just as bad as any demon who ever existed—as immoral as he was immortal, sadistic, selfish, manipulative, and deadly. He'd even conspired with a demonic pal to overthrow Lucifer in an attempt to take his power. They hadn't succeeded.

Darrak was summoned to the human world by a witch over three hundred years ago and cursed, forcing him to possess humans ever since. A side effect of this was that he'd absorbed humanity, and it had infused his being. The demon had slowly developed a conscience. Morals. A sense of right and wrong.

In addition to being a black witch, Eden had recently learned she was a nephilim—human mother, angel father. By possessing her, Darrak had absorbed the celestial energy she hadn't even realized she had. A lot of it. And slowly—very slowly—if he continued to soak up that heavenly essence that she naturally had inside of her . . . well . . .

The once evil and unrepentant demon would find himself a bit more . . . *angelic*. Whether or not he wanted to be.

Eden hadn't shared this recent revelation with him. While Darrak had acknowledged that he'd changed permanently from his dark past and was a bit more open-minded about his infusion of humanity, he had no idea about the celestial side effects of living in Eden. Frankly, Eden didn't think it was such a bad thing. But she knew Darrak. It would shake his confidence, not to mention his identity, and both were already shaky enough as it was.

She was waiting for the right time to break the news to him.

This was not the right time.

"Eden," Darrak prompted sharply. "Are you going to talk to me or what?"

"Oh, you mean I have a choice here?"

"No. No choices. This is not a choose-your-own-adventure novel. Your amulet is darkening, and you say you're doing nothing to cause this. Is that right?"

Her eyes burned. She didn't want to deal with this, but sometimes fate didn't give you a chance to catch your breath before it threw another bucket of water in your face.

She pulled her hands out of her pockets and looked at them. "I can feel it this morning. Even stronger than before. It's right here waiting to be used. I—I don't know if I can control it."

"But you *want* to control it."

"Of course I do."

He took her hands in his and stared down at her palms for so long she thought he was going to tell her fortune. "I knew it wasn't going to be long before this became an issue."

She looked up at him with surprise. "You did?"

"Black magic is tricky stuff. It's like it has a mind of its own. I'm not used to helping black witches, of course. You're the exception to the rule. But I've been thinking long and hard about what to do when this became more of a problem for you. I've come up with a plan. I think."

"That sounds rather . . . *vague*." She shook her head. "I mean, maybe I should just give into it now and then. The itch is so hard to ignore. It's like a drug I'm addicted to. And if I make a conscious effort not to do anything evil with it, then maybe I can—"

"Eden," he said. "Don't be naughty."

She laughed despite herself. "Advice from a demon not to be naughty?"

"I know. It's fairly ridiculous. But I can't help how I feel."

"And how's that?"

He stroked a long piece of auburn hair off her forehead, tucked it behind her ear, then cupped her face gently between his hands. "Troubled."

She touched his hand but didn't pull away from him. "I'll be fine."

"You think you can handle this because you've had to handle everything else that's been thrown at you all of your life. But this is different. This is bigger and stronger and full of venom, and it's trapped inside of you so I can't protect you from it." He swore under his breath. "I wish I could think of a better way to deal with this, but I can't, so that's just the way it's going to have to be."

"What way is that?"

He looked directly into her eyes. "It's time to get some outside help."

"Outside of what?"

"Outside of *us*." He walked over to the kitchen counter and grabbed the cordless phone.

"Who are you calling?"

He held a finger up to her. She sighed and flopped down on a chair at the table, already exhausted by talking about something she would have preferred to just ignore, magically charred BlackBerrys or not.

"Stanley?" he said after a moment. "Do you know who this is?" A pause. "No, it's okay. Don't be scared. I'm not going to kill you." Another pause. "Seriously, I'm not. Stop crying. Be a man."

Eden cringed. This didn't fill her with confidence. Stanley worked for just about any supernatural creature who paid or threatened him. He also created lust potions so desperate, lonely women would find him more attractive and have sex with him. All in all, he wasn't Eden's favorite guy in the city.

"Is he back?" Darrak asked. "He is? Why didn't you let me know this? Stop crying."

Eden's hands were still tingling. She honestly wished the black magic felt bad, but it didn't. It was so tempting to throw out a spell right here, right now. Witches came in a few varieties—the good and beneficial white witches, who worked with nature and animals and read spells from books. Gray witches, who blended both nature magic and destructive magic, and had the control to do this successfully. And, of course, black witches who could effortlessly use their magic—usually to destroy or cause harm—with a mere thought. So easy. *Too* easy.

"We need to see him immediately." Darrak paced back and forth between her kitchenette and where she sat at the dinette table, her feet curled up under her as she watched him. "Okay. That sounds fine." He sighed. "Why are you still crying? We'll see you soon, Stanley."

He hung up.

"You made Stanley cry," Eden said. "I actually don't have a problem with that."

Darrak shrugged. "He's still intimidated by my fearsome reputation. Nice to know somebody is."

"Are you going to share?"

"We're seeing Maksim. Today."

She stared at him blankly for a moment. "The wizard master."

"The one and only. He's back from his vacation."

Maksim the wizard master had gone on vacation after surviving a torture session by a demon—a friend of Darrak's—a couple of weeks ago.

"You think Maksim can help me?" She didn't want to hope for too much from a simple phone call. Disappointment was a heartless bitch.

"I think so. Wizards and witches go hand in hand. Didn't you read *Harry Potter*?"

She just stared at him.

"I'm kidding, of course," he continued. "I didn't read the

books. But I did see the movies. A previous host was a fan. He even wore dress robes and pretended he'd been sorted into a house. Hufflepuff, if you can believe it. Who liked Hufflepuff best? I mean, seriously."

She didn't speak for a moment. "I don't think a knowledge of children's literature is going to be much help here."

"A wizard, especially one at Maksim's level, will know about all kinds of magic and the practitioners of it. At the very least, he'll be able to point us in the right direction to get help for you."

She did see his point and that it was at least worth a shot. "Okay, so when are we seeing him?"

"Right now."

"Now?" She glanced at the clock that read eight thirty. "But Andy's going to want us in the office. He has a new case he wants to talk to us about and—"

"And it can wait a couple of hours. It can wait a whole day if necessary. This is more important, Eden."

She took a deep breath. "Maybe you're right."

"Of course I'm right. Besides, the full moon isn't until tomorrow night. Andy will be just fine on his own until then."

They exchanged a knowing glance. Andy had been bitten by a werewolf recently and was in total denial about what that meant.

The denial would only last another day before the fur started to flow. That was, unless there was some sort of random miracle between now and then. Eden believed in a lot of things these days, but random miracles weren't one of them.

"Fine." She nodded with a firm shake of her head and clenched her tingling hands into fists at her sides. "Then we're off to see the wizard."

"Good. And, hey, maybe he's somehow related to your horoscope this morning. That person from your past whose destiny is intertwined with yours."

"I think I'd remember meeting a wizard master."

Darrak glanced down at the paper now laying crumpled on the floor. "Then who do you think it was talking about?"

"Don't know. Don't care."

Out of all the drama in Eden's life at the moment, an entertaining, but silly horoscope was the least of her worries.

Caroline Riley watched from the shadows as her daughter left her apartment building and headed toward her rusty Toyota. She was about to run up to Eden and give her a big hug, but held back when the demon came into view.

He was tall with unruly dark hair that fell almost to his broad shoulders. He casually pulled on a black jacket as he trailed closely after Eden. He was handsome, of course. Most demons had a highly attractive human visage they wore when not using their demonic form. It made it that much easier for them to prey upon humans.

He was going to be a problem.

She wondered why Eden would choose to spend time with this creature and allow him into her home. Maybe he was threatening her. Blackmailing her.

Or . . . *sleeping* with her.

Was her daughter having an affair with a demon?

Caroline ran the scenario through her mind, but it didn't sound right to her. Eden had always been a rule follower, a perfect student, a hard worker, although one who lacked career direction. Someone like that wasn't one who'd have her head easily turned by one of Lucifer's minions.

Despite her natural beauty—that she'd inherited from her mother, of course—Eden had never had very much confidence in herself, poor thing. That must have been what the demon had seized upon.

Caroline had arrived just in time. Sure, she had other pressing matters to attend to, but rescuing her only child from the clutches of a demon had now been added to her lengthy to-do list.

It would be nice to talk to Eden again. It had been much too long since they'd last spoken.

Then again, Caroline *had* been dead for the last three months.